THE STONE WHISPERER CHRONICLES 1-3

URBAN FANTASY MYSTERIES

PARKER BLUE

PARKER
HAYDEN
MEDIA

SAPPHIRES &
SOULS

Acknowledgments

With many thanks and much appreciation to:

My critique group who keeps me sane and on track: Laura Hayden, Angel Smits, Jodi Anderson, Karen Fox, Torie Fox-Phillips, Sharon Silva, and Jude Willhoff.

My beta readers who read this in a short amount of time. You rock!

My fans/readers who have waited so patiently for another story from me. Hope it's worth the wait!

CHAPTER
ONE

BEING able to talk to stones wasn't exactly an in-demand skill, but since the Demon Underground was nice enough to include me as one of their own, I attended their monthly socials. I enjoyed meeting with my friends—both part-demon and vampire—but I felt like a fifth wheel at times. Val had Austin, Alejandro had finally admitted his feelings for Rosa, Micah and Gwen were dating, and even the adult hellhounds had paired up.

Sure, at twenty-six, I still had plenty of time to find someone special, but when would it be my turn? I'd even settle for having some more important role in the underground that was doing so much for the part-demons it served.

I found a parking spot for my bumblebee-painted Mini Cooper outside Club Purgatory, and stepped out into the humid August night. Yeah, this was another thing I didn't care for—it was so hot in San Antonio compared to Sedona where I came from, so much so that even my silk hoodies were a bit too much sometimes. But wearing them was not optional—it was necessary to stop hearing the constant chatter of any gemstones in the area.

I chuckled at myself as I got out of the car. *Do you want a little cheese with that whine?*

I entered the jazz portion of the club and spotted the demon seer, Tessa, along with vampire Gwen in the opposite corner. I started to make my way toward my friends, but was stopped by an older woman who leaned out from the bar and eyed my many piercings.

"Isn't it bad enough you're part demon?" she said with a sneer. "Do you have to look like a freakin' pincushion as well?"

Fang bounced over and glared at the woman. *You have no room to talk, Greta,* the hellhound-terrier mix scoffed. *Maybe you should try using a brush instead of a weed-whacker on your hair.*

He had a point—besides her messy graying hair, the dumpy woman wore cargo pants with a shapeless T-shirt that had grease spots on it. To a party, no less. I couldn't tell what kind of demon she was, but there was such a thing as basic hygiene.

Fang added, *Ivy has good reasons for* her *appearance.*

"Yeah, sure," Greta said skeptically, taking me in.

Sniping back wouldn't get me anywhere. Education was the answer. *It's okay*, I told Fang. *Thanks for the assist, but I got this.*

As he rolled his eyes and moved on, I noticed Greta was wearing a garish garnet pendant, so I lowered my hoodie. Not only did it reveal my spiky blond hair, but it allowed me to hear my stones.

What a moron, my agate said.

The topaz was equally disapproving. *Stone deaf. Can't even hear what the garnet is saying.*

But I could, and the garnet was whining. *I'm hot. I'm dry. Need air. Need moisture. Take me home.*

Beneath its grousing was misery, and I couldn't help but feel sorry for it. The garnet needed me. I tuned out the voices as best I could and gave Greta a brief smile. "I'm Ivy Weiss, a rock demon." Well, part demon anyhow. All of us were—full demons were also full nasty, not the kind of creatures you'd invite to a party. "They call me the stone whisperer."

Greta snorted. "That's your ability? You talk to rocks?"

Too bad you're so stupid no one will talk to you, my aquamarine said, knowing Greta couldn't hear them.

Accustomed to their annoyance, I told the stones, *I appreciate the support, but if you'll all be quiet now, I can find a way to help the garnet.*

The stones grumbled, but subsided.

I sighed, hating having to explain myself to anyone. The multiple piercings in my ears, eyebrows, and belly button along with the numerous bracelets and rings on every finger weren't the in-your-face fashion statement she assumed—it was the best way to wear the gemstones I needed in my work. "Yes," I said calmly, accustomed to this reaction from the oblivious. "And they talk back. For example, now that I've removed the silk covering my head, I can hear that garnet you're wearing doing a lot of complaining."

She glanced down at it. "I just inherited it from my aunt. What's it got to complain about?"

"Gemstones absorb the emotions of people around them," I explained. "When they're in the company of one person for a long period of time, they take on the personality of the owner."

Fix me, the stone insisted. *I hate this.*

7

"And," I continued, "according to what I'm getting from your garnet, the previous owner was..." How could I say the truth without offense?

"Whiny and bitchy?" the woman said with an arched eyebrow.

Oh, good. She said it so I didn't have to. "Uh, yeah. Sometimes, if you're sensitive, you might pick up on those emotions." And, as was evidently the case here, it could affect the wearer as well. "The best thing to do is cleanse the stone. It will get rid of any emotions it's accumulated so you can start fresh."

Yes. Clean me, the stone whined.

She looked doubtful, so I added, "You might be interested to know that garnets are good for enhancing strength. Once this one is cleansed, if you keep it close and believe in its powers, the garnet will help protect your health and keep up your stamina."

She raised an eyebrow. "And I suppose you just happen to have a way to fix it for a low, low price."

Bitch, the topaz muttered.

I sighed. The cynicism had no end. "You could pay me to do that for you, or you can do it yourself." I pulled one of my special cleansing packets out of my bag and held it out to her. "These are herbs I use to cleanse stones. Instructions are printed on the outside."

She eyed my packet like it was a snake about to bite her.

Use it, you moron, the garnet practically bellowed.

The hellpuppy called Delta glanced up at me. *She was just a total meanie to you. Why would you help her?*

"Hey," Greta protested, glaring down Delta.

"I do it for the stones," I said. "I hate to hear them hurting."

That seemed to convince her, because she finally took the herbs with a grudging, "Thanks."

"Really, it's best for both of you," I assured her. But if she didn't change her attitude, the garnet wasn't going to get any better.

Sighing, I put my hood back up so I needn't hear any more rocky comments and headed for my friends. After I greeted Tessa and Gwen and gave the hellpuppies at their feet an ear rub, I looked around for our friendly neighborhood succubus. "Where's Val?"

"She's heading for the stage," Tessa said.

The hellpuppies visibly perked up.

We're not puppies anymore, one of them told me.

Sorry, I said. *You're right.* I corrected my own thoughts. The young *hellhounds* perked up.

Everyone is here. Can we do this now? another one asked excitedly, broadcasting to everyone. Luckily, my silk hoodie didn't block *their* voices.

Yes, it's time, Fang said. *Kids, to the stage, please.*

"Time for what?" I asked.

Charlie bounced in excitement. *Time to come on down! You are the next contestants in The Hellhounds' Choice Ceremony!*

The demons laughed or rolled their eyes as Tessa translated for the non-demons and scratched Charlie's ears affectionately. "Ya think maybe he's watched a tad too much TV?"

Naw, Fang said. *He's just clowning around, like usual.*

Everyone else gathered in front of the stage as Fang and his four kids bounced up on it, the young hellhounds vibrating with excitement.

I knew how they felt—I was doing a bit of trembling myself. They were finally making their companion choices.

Please, please, please let me be chosen, I prayed to whatever deities were listening.

Val glanced down at her hellhound. "Fang wants you to know that he and the other hellhounds are only going to talk to me now. I'll translate so everyone can hear this at the same time. Are you ready?" That was smart—keep the human and vampire allies informed at the same time since they couldn't hear the hellhounds.

There was an enthusiastic murmur of approval, and someone called out, "Did you have any influence on the puppies' decisions?"

"Absolutely not. I have no idea what's going to happen tonight. Not even their parents know. So, don't blame Fang if you're disappointed," Val said with a grin, the message obviously passed on from Fang. "Each one will announce their choice of companion in the order in which they were born, then tell their new companion the name they have chosen." She stepped back and waved one of them forward. "First up is the one we've been calling Alpha."

Of the four, Alpha looked most like Princess with the markings of a Cavalier King Charles Spaniel but a rougher coat. She stepped forward and sat regally, as if she were a queen, much like her dam.

Val looked down at the hellhound and shook her head. "I just want you all to know that this is not me saying this —I am merely a mouthpiece for the hellhounds."

I chuckled as Alpha glanced up at Val with a dirty look, obviously telling her to get on with it.

Shaking her head, Val said, "Since she was the first born and obviously the most important..." everyone laughed, and the three other puppies looked disgusted, "...she has chosen to pair with a leader in the demon underground—Micah!"

Micah smiled and approached the stage where his new hellhound graciously allowed him to embrace her. Yep, she was Princess's offspring all right.

Micah scratched her ears. "I am honored," he said, beaming. "And she wants you to know that she wanted her new name to be a reflection of me and my incubus abilities, so henceforth, she will be known as Amoré."

Everyone applauded, obviously content with this choice. I'd guessed one of the hellhounds would choose Micah—he was an obvious selection. As the two of them left the stage, everyone, including me, seemed to have their fingers crossed, hoping they'd be just as lucky.

"Next up is Bravo," Val announced. Fang's lookalike trotted forward and took his spot confidently. "Bravo is the best fighter amongst the four, so he wanted to choose a warrior he would be proud to spend his life with. His choice is...Pia!"

Looking surprised, but very pleased, the diminutive Paladin from the Austin Demon Underground stepped forward and touched her nose to her new hellhound. She paused for a moment, then turned and signed to David, the Austin leader.

To my surprise, David grinned. "They want you to know that he has also chosen a name to complement his new companion and her choice of weapons. Since he plans on *being* one of those weapons, his name is Blade."

People seemed surprised that he had chosen someone outside the San Antonio DU, but I had to admit they fit together very well. Since the siren had been brutally silenced by her father and couldn't speak, and since most of the others didn't understand sign language, Blade would be able to communicate with other demons for her. His name was especially apt since she kept small knives secreted cleverly in her messy-looking hairdo.

Okay, don't worry, I told myself. There were still two more hellhounds who hadn't chosen yet. Though if they were all looking for leaders and warriors, I certainly wouldn't make the cut.

I closed off the negative thought. *Think positive.*

Charlie was next, and he bounded forward with enthusiasm, plopping down with a goofy doggy version of a grin, his tongue hanging out the side. He looked a lot like Princess and Amoré...without the attitude.

"Charlie makes no claims to be the best at anything..." Val said drily, and the crowd chuckled. "But he feels one of our members has gotten an especially raw deal and deserves someone to love and to love him back. Someone who is full of hope and plans for the future. And to help make sure his companion is never controlled by anyone again, his choice is...Andrew?"

Val sounded surprised, and there was complete silence as shock filled the other attendees as well. Andrew, really? Then again, I remembered Val telling me about her discussion with the fire demon when they were in the other dimension. He wanted to be important, to be special. And it wouldn't hurt to have the level-headed hellhound keep him in line. Maybe it wasn't such a bad decision after all.

Looking totally dumbfounded but ecstatic, Andrew ran forward to greet the hellhound, pressing their foreheads together. Grinning, he said, "In honor of my abilities as a fire demon, he has chosen to be called Sparky!"

As Andrew retreated back into the crowd with Sparky, a lot of the demons present clapped him on the back and congratulated him. Apparently, choosing someone who wasn't in a position of power was popular with the audience.

One hellhound left. Andrew wasn't a leader or much of a warrior, so maybe I had a chance? My nerves strung taut, I crossed my fingers again and prayed with all my heart. *Please, please, pick me.*

"Last, but definitely not least, is Delta." Delta, a small female replica of Fang, though with her mother's smoother coat and a funky, cute mohawk that wouldn't stay tamed, strolled forward. "The most particular of the group, she has interacted with many of the demons in this room to make sure she made exactly the right decision. She chose the person she felt is the most worthy. And her choice is..." Val paused dramatically.

The audience groaned in frustration as several people shouted, "Who is it?"

I could easily wring Val's neck for making this play out so long.

"Ivy!" Val exclaimed.

Wait. That's my name. Did she really call my name?

The hellhound's voice sounded in my head. *Yes, she did. Come get your prize—me!*

Laughing and flushed with happiness, I rushed forward to hug the pup and kiss her on the nose. *What name have you chosen?*

I felt my eyes fill with tears as I relayed her choice to the crowd. "Because she can hear the stones in my head, she has chosen to name herself after what she considers the most magnificent gemstone—Ruby!"

Rubies were also protective stones, guarding against psychic and psychological attack, and removed negative energies while instilling confidence. A perfect choice.

I know, Ruby agreed smugly. *We will be good together.*

Wiping the tears from my eyes, I nodded and cuddled the adorable little dog. "We will," I confirmed.

Fang spoke in my head, to me alone. *Val wants me to warn you that your hellhound is the snarkiest of the four. For some reason, Val thinks she takes after me.*

Gee, I wonder why. Her small size evidently made her feel she had something to compensate for. But that was not a problem—at all.

I headed back into the crowd, knowing I was getting lots of congratulatory remarks, but unable to comprehend any of it as I made my way toward Gwen and Tessa.

Over the roar of the crowd, Val made herself heard. "But remember, even if you weren't chosen today, you may get one of Fang and Princess's *future* puppies." Val raced down the steps and over to where I had just reached Gwen and Tessa.

Surprisingly, no one seemed upset about the puppies' decisions. Probably because Val and Fang had made it very clear that it was their choice, not anyone else's.

My three best friends—no, make that four now— crowded around me with squeals, laughter, and congratulations.

Until Tessa hugged me. As soon as she touched my skin, she gripped me tight, and her eyes went vacant as she went into a trance. "To avoid widespread bloodshed, you must unshackle Selene's troubled son where Zebulon Pike made his fateful discovery."

What the heck?

CHAPTER
TWO

I FELT the blood leave my face and gasped. "Is she talking to me?"

Val rolled her eyes. "Do you see her clutching anyone else? Of course she is—the prophecy is about you."

"But I'm not important. I don't matter," I protested. Why would the soothsayer single me out?

Micah, the owner of Club Purgatory and leader of the San Antonio Demon Underground, approached us. "Was that a trance? Did you just prophesy again?" he asked Tessa.

Tessa blinked in astonishment and removed her hand from my arm. "I guess so. Feels like it, anyway."

"She did," Gwen confirmed. "For Ivy. And it's a doozy."

Micah glanced at me in bewilderment, which didn't surprise me at all. Who was I to get one of the seer's famed cryptic prophecies? "Let me gather the council in my office," he said, "so Ivy and Tessa can tell us what happened."

I nodded, and Val went to get Alejandro, the city's vampire leader and his second, Austin, as well as Lt. Ramirez, who oversaw the Special Crimes Unit. I followed

Tessa to Micah's simple and elegant, yet comfy office, and we all convened there—with the companion hellhounds present, too, of course. Everyone took seats around the comfortable room.

Noting Tessa's presence, Austin asked, "Did Tessa do her fortune-cookie thing?"

Tessa shrugged, not annoyed by Austin's comment since that's what *she* called her enigmatic prophecies. "Apparently. But you know I never remember what I say at times like these."

"Oh?" Alejandro asked. "Who was the prophecy for?"

Everyone looked at Val, who shook her head with a grin. I raised my hand tentatively. "Uh...me?"

You go, girl, Fang said approvingly.

"But there must be some mistake," I protested.

"No," Micah said. "Tessa is never mistaken. Sometimes the message's meaning is a bit obscure, though..."

"Try always," Tessa said with a roll of her eyes.

Ignoring her aside, Micah continued. "But it always comes true, even if you don't understand what it means at first."

"What was the prophecy?" Lt. Ramirez asked.

I was too discombobulated to remember exactly, but Val said it for me: "To avoid widespread bloodshed, you must unshackle Selene's troubled son where Zebulon Pike made his fateful discovery."

"Well, that's pretty clear for a change," Tessa said.

"It is?" I shook my head. "Who is Zebulon Pike?"

Lt. Ramirez said, "He was an explorer, the first American to survey Pikes Peak in Colorado Springs."

"Oh, that's right. I just didn't make the connection," I said.

16

But how will freeing some random dude avoid a bloodbath? Ruby asked.

Good question. Everyone looked at each other to see if anyone else had a clue. Apparently not, for Alejandro said, "We don't know yet."

No, this can't be about me. I was no fighter, no hero like Val. All I did was talk to rocks, for heaven's sake. Plus, driving to Colorado Springs? I'd promised myself two years ago when I got here that I would stay in one place for awhile. "Sorry, but no. I don't want to go."

They all looked at me as though I'd suddenly sprouted horns or something. "But you have to," Micah said. "Tessa's prophecies always prove to be important to the entire supernatural community. They are not about random people, and widespread bloodshed sounds very serious. You have no choice."

Afraid so, kiddo, Fang said. *You're just going to have to suck it up and go be a hero.*

Fang has a point, Ruby added.

You don't call him Dad? I asked her privately. *Naw,* Ruby said. *That's a human thing. We call each other by the names we chose. And you don't have to worry about going—I'll be with you.*

They all looked at me expectantly. Too bad—it didn't change my mind. But they'd been so nice and welcoming, I hated to disappoint them by giving them a harsh no. "I— I'll think about it," I hedged.

Ruby interjected, *Ivy hates driving across long stretches of the country, and refuses to fly.*

Gee, thanks, buddy, I griped at the mind-reading hellhound. Looks like we'd have to have a talk about boundaries.

As Val explained Ruby's comments to the non-demons

in the group, Micah asked, "Is what Delta—uh, Ruby, said about your aversion to travel true?"

"Yes," I admitted. "I'm not afraid of flying. It's just that, as a rock demon, I'm grounded firmly in the earth, and flying makes me feel unnatural and disconnected. But driving long distances is a pain."

The dawning realization in their expressions showed they all understood the weirdness with my powers.

"No problem," Micah said, "We'll have someone go with you so you won't have to drive alone."

Val spoke up. "What if Fang and I go with her?"

"Absolutely not," Micah said. "We need you here."

Val looked like she wanted to argue, but Austin spoke quietly to her and she subsided.

"I don't need help," I explained. "I don't like to drive, though I can do it just fine."

Micah added, "Okay. I'll also ask for help from the underground there, but I don't know them, so I don't know how well that will work."

"I have a contact in Colorado Springs," Alejandro said. "One of my progeny, so I'm sure he'll help ensure you're protected while you're there."

"And I may be able to find a counterpart there as well," Lt. Ramirez said.

"Hey, I haven't said I'll go yet," I reminded them.

"You'll go," everyone said in unison.

I frowned. Maybe if I didn't agree, they'd forget about it.

Ruby snorted. *Fat chance. Looks like we got ourselves a mission!*

But—

Besides, weren't you wanting to find a way to be of more help to the underground? This is something only you can do.

Dang it, she had a point. "Okay," I said. "I'll do it."

"Good," Micah said. "But before we do anything, we need to do our homework. Find out what we can before we send Ivy into a hornets' nest. We don't want to go off half-cocked."

No problem, Fang said. *I'm fully cocked at all times.*

Ignoring Fang's aside through long practice, Micah said, "Let's do that tomorrow when we're fresh. I'll set up a video conference call with our counterparts in Colorado Springs. For now, let's return to the social."

I swore to myself. How on earth was I going to be able to do this?

Ruby bumped me with her nose. *With my help, of course.*

THE NEXT AFTERNOON, a bunch of us crammed into Micah's office. With the water demon Ludwig added along with Shade, the shadow demon techie, there were now five demons plus Lt. Ramirez and four hellhounds. A bit crowded. "Looks like you need a bigger office," Val said to Micah.

At least Alejandro wasn't here in person. To avoid the sun, he was calling in from his home office on the huge monitor.

Micah's mouth twisted in a wry grin. "I'm beginning to see that. But we need to get ready for our call to Sybil Warburton at the Colorado Springs underground. Ivy, come sit by me in camera range so she can see you." Ludwig, the very large water demon Val called a man-mountain, crossed his beefy arms, and stood sentry behind me. Micah glanced at Shade, Val, and Lt. Ramirez. "I don't think it's necessary for you three to be in the shot, but you can listen in."

19

That made sense, especially since seeing the dark ribbons swirling through Shade's shadow demon's face had a tendency to make others uncomfortable.

Micah double-checked to make sure we were all in place, then said, "She should be coming on at any moment. I'll unmute now, so she'll hear everything. Watch what you say. And don't forget your physical reactions." This last remark was directed mostly at the hellhounds, but I'm sure their telepathic thoughts didn't travel over the internet. Our reactions to their comments, however, would be visible, so Micah had a good point.

Fang, Princess, Amoré, and Ruby grumbled a bit, but all headed toward their besties. It was still very new for Amoré and Ruby. Would they behave?

I'll make sure they do, Fang said.

Good—he was excellent at keeping his kids in line.

About five minutes later, the meeting connected at the other end, and a tall, thin woman with a long blond braid over her shoulder appeared on screen, her face set in disapproving lines. Yikes. Such a contrast to Micah's friendliness and pleasant expression.

"Thank you for talking to us on such short notice," Micah said. "With me are two of my members, Ivy and Ludwig, plus our ally, Alejandro, on screen."

I waved at the camera, looking a bit goofy, no doubt.

"I don't usually get calls from out-of-state branches," Sybil said curtly. "What is it you want?"

Oooookay, so there were to be no niceties then.

Micah faltered for a moment, then recovered with a smile. Too bad his incubus abilities wouldn't work on her over the internet. In great contrast to her tone, he said genially, "We would like to come visit your organization sometime in the next few days to follow up on a prophecy."

She scowled. "What prophecy and who made it?"

Micah repeated Tessa's prognostication, and added, "The person who gave it to us is a seer in my organization, and she gave it to Ivy, our stone whisperer."

"Well, it obviously refers to Colorado Springs, so I see why you called, but we have no one in the organization named Selene."

"Are you sure?" Micah asked. Good question—if her organization was like the one here, she couldn't possibly remember everyone's names.

"Positive," she said abruptly.

"Well, perhaps it refers to a vampire or human in the area," Micah conceded. "We really need to check it out."

Her mouth twisted in distaste. "Perhaps. How many people would be coming and what are their designations?"

Micah gestured toward Ivy. "Ivy, who received the prophecy, is a rock demon, or stone whisperer. She will be accompanied by Ludwig, a water demon, and Ruby, her hellhound."

Sybil's eyebrows raised. "I thought the famous San Antonio hellhound was named Fang."

Fang perked up. *I'm famous? Did you hear that? I'm famous.*

"Ruby is his daughter, er, child, er, pup," Micah explained.

And someday I'm going to be just as famous, Ruby muttered to me alone.

"I see. Well, I'm sorry, but we won't be able to accommodate you," Sybil said with a haughty look.

Yeah, right, Ruby grouched. *I bet they wouldn't be able to accommodate us no matter when we said we were coming. I'm surprised she even said she was sorry.*

Evidently hoping to sweeten the pot, Micah added, "We

21

also hope to share knowledge between our two organizations, and you might be interested to know that Ivy is also the keeper of the *Encyclopedia Magicka*."

Sybil's eyes narrowed and she said, "That's interesting...I've heard of it." She thought for a moment or two, then shook her head, saying, "We still won't be able to help you."

"That's fine," Micah assured her. "We weren't expecting to impose on you to put us up. We'll find our own lodging. We are simply informing you so you will be aware of our presence." He paused, then added, "We have to come. You know that soothsayers are extremely reliable—one probably selected you for the leader position there."

What kind of seer would choose her?

A better question is, what kind of organization would want her? Ruby said.

Sybil sighed, obviously hoping that her refusal would have been the end of the discussion. "Noted. Please have them call me to let me know when they arrive in town. I don't want my people to be surprised."

"They'll do that," Micah promised.

She gave a curt nod. "Is that all?"

"Yes. I appreciate—"

But she didn't even wait to hear his pleasantries as she disconnected without warning.

"Wow," I said. "What great interpersonal skills she has." Then, suddenly remembering she was one of us, I asked, "Do you know what kind of demon she is?"

Micah shook his head, but Val said, "One who has powers that make her cranky, obviously."

I hesitated. "Is this really a good idea? She doesn't sound very welcoming."

"We don't need her welcome," Micah said, "just her

tolerance and awareness of the situation. You still need to go. We'll find you a place to stay." He glanced around. "Did anyone else get the impression she was holding something back, something important we should know?"

"Absolutely," I said, and the others agreed as well. "I wonder if there really is a Selene, and she's not telling us for some reason."

Shade spoke up from where he was working on a laptop in the corner, Princess now touching him so he was grounded in reality and we could see his face. "According to what I can find, she really doesn't have a Selene in her organization."

"How about a human or vampire in Colorado Springs with that name?" Micah asked.

Shade shook his head. "That will take time to find out. There could be hundreds, if not thousands in the area. I'll narrow the search down to women old enough to have given birth, then see if any have a son."

"Excellent," Micah said. "When do you think you can have this ready?"

Shade shrugged. "Tomorrow, maybe? I can email Ivy the list when I have it, with addresses."

"Will that be enough time for you, Ivy?" Micah asked.

"Uh, sure. I just need to arrange for someone to watch my stock at Astral Reflections." Val's mother and stepfather had set aside a small space in their new-age store for me to sell the stones and crystals in jewelry that I designed.

Val nodded. "You know Jen will be glad to help." Her half-sister—who was bummed she *didn't* have the demon father and was therefore fully human—was fascinated with gemstones and since she had graduated from high school, she was able to spend more time in the store.

"Yeah, she probably would," I agreed. "How long do you think we'll be gone? I need to know how much to pack."

Micah shrugged. "There's no knowing, so I'd plan on a couple of weeks at least. If you stay longer, you can always use a laundromat or purchase new. Don't worry—we'll cover any of your out-of-pocket costs." He paused, then added, "I'll set up a conference call for later today so we can talk and discuss any progress we've made. Sundown?"

We all nodded, and Alejandro added, "Just ensure you watch your back at all times. It doesn't sound as though Sybil plans on making your mission easy."

Yeah. I just hoped my trip didn't turn into a battle instead.

I don't know, Ruby said with a little bounce. *It would certainly be exciting.*

Just what I didn't need.

THREE

THE NEXT MORNING, I ran by Astral Reflections. Since dogs were allowed inside, I called Ruby to come with me. When we went in, we were immediately accosted by several customers who wanted to pet the hellhound. Ruby accepted the petting patiently, then asked, *Why can't I talk to them?*

Because they're human. You're part demon, so you can only talk to others like you.

Huh. How lonely they must be.

She wasn't wrong. They were just like me, pre-Ruby.

When the customers wandered away, Jen looked down at Ruby. "Is she..." she glanced around, looking furtive, "...special?"

Ruby snorted. *Of course I am.*

I grinned. "She's one of Fang and Princess's litter, if that's what you're asking."

"Cool!"

"I'm glad you're here. I was hoping to talk to you."

"About what?"

"You've been doing a great job of handling my part of

the store when I'm not here, so I was hoping you would be kind enough to watch it for me full-time for a while."

Wow, great job of sucking up, Ruby said, and I stifled my laughter. Looks like I'd have to learn to do more laughter suppression in the future.

"Sure," Jen said. "I like your jewelry better than most of the stuff in here anyway. How long will you be gone?"

"I'm not sure yet. Maybe a week or two, could be longer. And, of course, you'd get a commission on each piece you sell."

"Sounds good. Oh, that reminds me—you received a package here."

Awesome! Ruby declared when Jen handed me the small package. *Open it!*

I checked the wrapping—it was from Australia where my parents were off mining opals. Rockhounds to the core, they'd been quietly elated when I was old enough to move out on my own so they could take off on their own adventures.

I opened the package and gasped. A large opal pendant lay inside on a silver chain. The elegant filigree around the oval setting had to be my mother's work. Bright blue and green with subtle flashes of other colors against a black background, the black opal was absolutely gorgeous. What a thoughtful gift.

I opened the note that came with it. *You will probably need this,* it said. *And if you meet its standards, the opal will be a big help.*

Its standards? What the heck? I pulled down my hood as I slipped the opal over my head.

You need me, the opal confirmed.

Who was I to argue? Especially since Mom's hunches about stones were often accurate.

What do you need an opal for? the amethyst asked. *You have me.* When the others protested, it added hastily, *Us. I mean us.*

There was a chorus of annoyed agreement from the other stones, so I said, "An opal, especially one this size, can enhance and amplify the abilities of other stones."

There was silence, then the amethyst said, *Okay, it can stay.*

I grinned, wondering why I hadn't thought to wear one before.

You honor us all, the opal said.

Adding a new gemstone to my daily wardrobe was always a trial, convincing the ones I wore to accept another one, dealing with jealousy, and waiting until they established their own pecking order. But I had a feeling this time might not be so bad.

"It's gorgeous," Jen said.

"Isn't it? It's from my parents." I heard my phone ding and found a reminder text from Micah. "Well, I'd better go. I have a conference call this afternoon and need to pack."

As we went back out to the car, I asked Ruby, *Do you need to pack as well? I mean, do I need to stop and get you any kind of special food, a dog bed...a collar?*

Ruby snorted. *I'm a hellhound. I eat what you eat and sleep where you sleep. As for collars...just no,* she said in disdain.

I chuckled and headed back to the townhouse where I'd taken over Gwen's old room. Val used to be my roommate, but now that she was living with Austin, it felt a little lonely.

Not anymore. Now you have me.

"I just thought it would be nice to have someone pay part of the expenses."

I can't help with that, but I can help in other ways, you know. Why are you so worried about this trip? I'll be with you.

I shrugged. "I don't have the super reflexes, speed, strength, and healing abilities Val and Austin do. I'm afraid I'll just be a liability." Or a failure.

But you're the reason for the trip.

I headed toward my laptop to sign in for the meeting. "No, 'Selene's son' is the reason."

But you have an advantage they don't.

"Let me guess...you?"

Of course, but I meant because you're the stone whisperer and the keeper of the Encyclopedia Magicka. *Doesn't it have a lot of spells and stuff?*

True, but I'd been able to avoid using it so far. "I don't know how to use it, and I'm too nervous to try it. After all, remember what the books did to Andrew?"

Ha, Ruby scoffed. *Shade said it was the mage demon inside the books that got to him, not the books themselves. But the mage demon is gone now.*

I quirked an eyebrow at her. "You talk to Shade a lot?"

I grew up mostly at his place, remember?

Oh, that's right. With Princess as her mother, where else would she be? *Duh.*

And he put together a...thing that lists a lot of the spells.

"You mean a database?"

Yeah, that thing. He talked with the books a lot.

"How?"

I dunno. Ask him.

"I will," I agreed.

I packed and when it was time for the conference call, I connected with the others—Shade, Micah, Alejandro, Ludwig, and Val. There were a few pleasantries, then Micah said, "First, Shade, can you tell us what you found?"

"Sure." He looked like a normal person, so Princess must be snuggled up to him. "Luckily, Selene is not a very common name. There were only eight I could find, and two of them are too young to be a mother, so that leaves six. I'll text the names and addresses to Ivy."

"Thank you, Shade. Alejandro, do you have anything?"

"I have a contact and a place where Ivy and Ludwig can stay."

Micah nodded. "Excellent. I called the Denver Demon Underground, but he doesn't know much about Sybil because he's new there. He's heard she's rather prickly, though."

Confused, I asked, "So what am I supposed to do? Are we supposed to find out why she's like that?" How the heck would I do that?

"No. Stick to your mission of finding and assisting 'Selene's son.' But, keep it in mind while you're dealing with them." Micah frowned, then added, "And, one of you should check in at least once a day or so, so we know how you two are doing."

Ludwig nodded, and I said, "Will do." It would make me feel better as well.

"Does anyone have anything else?" Micah asked.

I raised my hand, then felt silly for doing so. "Uh, I know you were thinking of sending Ludwig with me, but I don't think he'd be very comfortable in my Mini Cooper."

Micah chuckled. "No problem. You shouldn't be in any danger until after you start your investigation, so we've already scheduled a flight for him."

"Oh, good," I said in relief. "I also need to talk to Shade separately...about the books. Can you do that, Shade?"

"Yes, but not over this line. I'll stop by later this evening so we can talk."

That made sense. "Thank you."

Without any other agenda items, Micah closed the call.

A few hours later, Shade showed up, Princess in tow. She and Ruby took off to the bedroom, to gossip no doubt, and I put up my hood to block the stones' chattering while Shade sat on the couch, all swirly.

"I emailed you the database I put together," he said. "I catalogued the dictionary part of the entries and some of the spells, but not all. Once they chose you as keeper, they became less clear to me. That's why I gave the books to you to hold onto."

I nodded, and tried to look him in the eyes, but didn't know where to look. He must have seen my eyes darting about, because he said, "Come sit next to me. I'll take off my sandals, and if you take off yours..."

"We'll play footsie?" I asked with a grin.

He laughed. "No, so you can touch my foot with yours, and see the human me."

"Good idea." And after I did, it was a whole bunch easier to talk to him when I could actually see his face.

He smiled. "I've been wondering when you'd finally ask about the books."

I shrugged. "I haven't really seen a need before now."

"What did you want to know?"

"Well, someone suggested I take them with me, since we don't know what we're going to run into."

"Not a bad idea."

"But...I don't know how to use them, and I might need to."

He glanced around. "Where are they?"

"In a safe in my room," I said sheepishly. "I'll go get them."

When I brought them out into the living room, Shade

set them out individually on the coffee table and said, "The books can communicate very effectively with anyone. All you have to do is ask."

"Ask what?"

"Ask for the spell you want to use."

"But what if I don't know which one I want to use?"

"First, use the communication spell. Just ask the books for the spell."

"Okay. Books, can you show me the communication spell so I can talk to you?"

One of the three tomes vibrated, opened, flipped quickly through pages, then stopped on a page that glowed. Freaky, but I'd seen the book in action before, so I wasn't too weirded out. "That's the spell," Shade said. "Go ahead and try it."

"But...how much of my own power do I lose if I use the spell?" I knew each one had a cost, which was why I hadn't tried any so far.

"See, at the bottom, it tells you how much power you'll use and how long it lasts. For this spell, the power loss is negligible, and the spell won't fade. I guess they want to be able to talk to us."

I read through the spell silently, but nothing happened.

"To activate the spell, you have to say or think the invocation, and focus your intent squarely on what you hope to achieve."

"Okay." I said the spell again, this time aloud with intention, and words seemed to burn in fire across the page.

What do you want to know, Ivy?

Whoa. That was seriously cool. I felt silly for talking to a book and expecting it to talk back, but that's exactly what had happened. "What spells do I need to know for this trip tomorrow?"

The words disappeared, and another sentence burned across the page.

I don't know. What are you lacking? they asked.

"Uh, I don't know yet. I know Val used one for super strength when she lost her powers for a while. Can you show me that one?"

The pages flipped until they stopped at the glowing page with the spell on it. I skimmed it quickly. "The cost in magic is rather high."

"Not if you really need it to save your life or someone else's," Shade said. "Just memorize any spells you might want to use later. You can say the spells out loud, but they won't work—or take any of your power—until you say the invocation." He cocked his head, "And you do know that the drain in your power will fade along with the spell, right?"

"It does? Thank heavens." I didn't want to lose my abilities forever. They were the only thing that made me special.

"What else do you want to ask?"

"I...don't know. Let me think about what I might need and ask them later."

"Okay. If you plan to take them with you, you might want to take precautions."

"Like what?" I asked, not sure if I really wanted to hear this or not.

"They emanate magic most demons can feel. If you wrap them in silk, it will deaden the effect."

"Oh, good. I do the same thing with my stones." I gestured at the silk hoodie covering my head then stood and held out my hand. "Thank you so much for taking the time to explain this to me."

"No problem," Shade said. "Feel free to ask anything you like. You might want to skim through the database to see your options. Or, ask the books. That's what I did."

"Now that I have the communication spell, I will."

"Time to go," Shade shouted to Princess, who entered at a leisurely, sedate pace, with Ruby trotting behind her.

As I closed the door behind me, I wondered, *What* do *I need to know?*

What don't *you need to know?* Ruby asked wryly.

I sighed. Unfortunately, she was right.

CHAPTER

FOUR

I TOOK one long day to drive from Texas to Colorado since I knew I needed to reach our destination after the sun went down. When I hit the Colorado Springs city limits a little before sundown, I pulled over to read the instructions Alejandro had sent via Shade.

I rolled down the window and sighed in relief. The air was a bit cool here, even in August, especially compared to the oppressive heat and humidity in San Antonio. It seemed the weather here was much like where I grew up in Sedona.

"Shade says the place we're looking for is in the...Kissing Camels area near the Garden of the Gods on the west side of the city."

Very odd place names, Ruby said.

"Yeah, I guess." I yawned and stretched. "He sent the address, so I'll just put it in the GPS."

"Is it a hotel?"

"No, it's a house. It belongs to one of the people Alejandro sired who moved to this area. He—Maurice—has agreed to let us stay in his home and provide protection for us."

As I followed the GPS directions, I gazed around at what I could see of the red rock formations in the Garden of the Gods in the fading light. Wow, it reminded me even more of Sedona, and nostalgia for the Arizona mountain town filled me. But I couldn't see as much as I'd like. I'd bet it'd looked even more gorgeous during full daylight.

The directions led me to an exclusive gated community where I gave my name and our host's to the guard who let us in. I drove to the house, gazing around in wonder. The ample streetlights showed this entire neighborhood was high-end, with immaculate lawns and huge houses that had humongous windows to take in the mountain view. It was probably magnificent in daylight.

I stopped in front of a house that had fewer windows than most, but it was still stunning from what I could see.

A tall, thin man with dark brown skin and a wide smile greeted us inside the door. Dark-framed glasses accentuated his cheekbones, and, with his purple suit, lavender shirt, and sockless loafers, he totally rocked his trendy look. He was even prettier than Alejandro, though his wavy hair was much shorter.

He clasped his hands together. "How lovely! You must be Ivy, the stone whisperer. I'm Maurice."

He gathered me in an embrace that lingered a bit too long. Not that it felt at all skeevy—more like he was just a real touchy-feely kind of guy. And he smelled wonderful—citrusy with a hint of spice.

"Well, don't just stand there. Come in, come in." He waved us into the foyer of the house which had a gorgeous open floor plan with beautiful marble floors and an understated elegance. "Welcome to Maison Maurice. Now, I understand you need lodging for an unspecified period of time for you and your hellhound." He glanced down at

Ruby. "Surely this can't be a hellhound. Much too cute for such an unpleasant-sounding label."

I like this guy, Ruby said.

I grinned to myself. *Remind me to tell you later about a practice known as brown-nosing.* Aloud, I said, "Yes, that's true and she is. Her name is Ruby. Thank you for hosting us. We really appreciate it."

"Oh, no problem," Maurice said, waving his hand as if to swat away the idea. "Alejandro saved my life—well, my undead life—and I would do anything to help him. Now, follow me and I'll show you to your rooms."

We followed Maurice up the grand staircase. "You have a lovely home," I said.

"Thank you, I try. When you have an unnaturally long life, you can accumulate an equally unnatural fortune with the right investments."

With this impressive display of wealth, Alejandro must have turned him a long time ago. I would have inquired exactly how long ago, but I got the impression it was impolite to ask, and I didn't want to insult or annoy our host.

He led us to something like a mother-in-law suite with a small living area, tiny kitchen, and a sumptuous bathroom I couldn't wait to use. Unlike the understated elegance of the downstairs, these rooms had vibrant jewel tones everywhere.

Ruby glanced around. *Wow, we really leveled up.*

Maurice gestured at one of the bedrooms. "Ludwig has already arrived, and is staying in another part of the house, so this is all yours. He's out at the moment, but will return shortly, I'm sure."

He clasped his hands together. "Now, is there anything else I can help you with?"

"Yes," I said. "Can you tell us what you know about the Demon Underground here?"

"Very little," Maurice said, looking regretful. "I don't really deal with them." He paused for a moment, then added, "But Alejandro assured me that you are a perfectly delightful representative." He glanced down. "And that hellhounds are, uh, house-trained?"

Ruby growled a little at the rude question.

I grinned. "Yes, she is probably less trouble than I am. And she understands what you're saying. But she can't speak with you—only with other demons."

Maurice looked embarrassed. "Oh, I'm so sorry. I didn't realize. I know so little about hellhounds. Please forgive my *faux pas*."

Ruby looked up at Ivy. *A foe paw? An...enemy paw?*

I answered her out loud, glancing down at the hell-hound so Maurice would know I was responding to her. "No, *faux pas* is a French phrase that means false step—he was apologizing for his mistake."

Oh, that's nice.

"She forgives you," I said with a grin.

"Fabulous. Now, can I get you something to eat or drink? Perhaps a cocktail?"

"Something to drink would be good. Something non-alcoholic." Anything boozy would probably put me right to sleep. "Water is fine."

"Wonderful." He waved toward the couch. "Please, have a seat while I get that for you."

After he left and I sat down, Ruby flopped down next to me. *Why does he wear glasses? I thought vampires were cured of human afflictions and didn't need them.*

I shrugged. "He shouldn't need them. It must be a fashion choice." Everything about him and his home seemed meticulously chosen to convey the impression he wanted—understated, classy elegance.

Maurice returned with the water, accompanied by another man who was tall and broad, with short blond hair. As Maurice handed the glass to me, he said, "This is Billy. He takes care of the household during the daylight hours. Let him know what you'll need to eat and he'll stock it for you. In fact, if you need anything at all, ask him."

Sheesh. With his chiseled physique shown off by his tight clothing and his killer smile, Billy could easily work as one of the Chippendales.

What's a Chippendale?

Embarrassed, I said silently, *I'll tell you later.*

Ruby cocked her head. *He's not a vamp or a demon.*

"He's human?" I said aloud, then blushed. "I'm so sorry —Ruby just told me he's not a vampire or a demon."

"She can tell?" Billy asked.

"It's one of her abilities as a hellhound," I explained.

Billy just grinned. "Well, she's right. I'm definitely human. For now, anyway." He exchanged a private, heated look with Maurice that indicated he hoped to become one of the undead at some point in the future.

Ludwig came in then, and Maurice gestured for him to join us. After they all sat, Maurice said, "Alejandro told me who you're looking for. I'll see what I can learn from my people here, and I'll be happy to provide protection for you after sundown, if needed. I'm sure Ludwig is very capable, but Billy can also help out during the day. He's a former Marine."

"That sounds good. Uh, Micah promised Sybil I'd let her know when we arrived. She wanted us to call, but I think showing up at her headquarters and surprising her might be a better idea." I glanced at Ludwig, but he just nodded, as if content to let me take the lead. "I figure we might get a better idea of her organization and if there is anything odd going on if we can get a look at it. But it's a little late to be showing up right now...unless the underground is housed in a club like Micah's?"

"No," Maurice said. "They provide security guard and private bodyguard protective services, so it's in an old, converted warehouse, under the name of Relentless Protection Services."

"Sounds like a good way to fund the organization," I conceded. Especially using their members' capabilities. "What are their hours?"

"They have someone available twenty-four hours a day, but I assume the offices are open mostly during the daytime." Maurice glanced at Billy. "You can go with them tomorrow, right?"

"Sure. No problem."

I nodded. "Great. I also have six people to talk to with the name Selene, and I thought we'd check them out tomorrow morning, then go to the underground in the afternoon."

Ludwig leaned forward and joined the conversation for the first time. "What's the plan? How are we going to determine if we've found the right Selene?"

Good question. What would we ask them? Baffled, I said, "I'm not sure. It's not as if we can tell them about the prophecy, especially if they're human."

Billy nodded toward Ruby. "Your hellhound just proved she can tell if they're human or not. And maybe we could tell them we're thinking of moving to the neighborhood and want to know what they think about the area."

Ludwig frowned. "How would that let us find out if we have the right Selene?"

Billy shrugged. "Okay, strike that. How about we say we're looking for someone to claim an inheritance from a distant relative, one whose name is Selene and who has a son?"

"That might work," Ludwig conceded.

"But what will we do if we find someone who fits the description?" I asked. "We don't even know what help their son needs from me."

"Alejandro says you work with gemstones," Maurice said. "Could one of them help?"

"Maybe. I do have a stone that can assess truthfulness, my emerald." I gestured at my hoodie. "When I don't have silk covering my head. But we have to know what to ask them first." I explained how my abilities worked. "Let me think about it."

"Okay," Billy said. "Let me know when you two are ready in the morning, and we can head out." We exchanged numbers, and he said, "Do you need any help carrying things in?"

"That would be great, thanks."

Billy and Ludwig helped carry in our belongings, and Billy said, "I'll make an early evening of it so I'll be available when you need me tomorrow. There's food in the main kitchen—yell if you need anything."

"Thank you so much—you've already been a big help by letting us stay here."

As Billy left, Ruby said teasingly, *Kinda easy on the eyes, huh?*

Don't get any ideas, I warned her. *I get the impression he and Maurice are...together.*

Really? How would that work?

Sheesh—with the questions she asked, it was like dealing with an inquisitive toddler. *I don't know,* I said

40

hastily, then changed the subject, addressing Ludwig. "Have you learned anything useful?"

He shook his head. "No, I just got the lay of the land a bit. The conservative nature of much of the city makes it not so good for supernaturals, but it seems to be a nice place to live. Good climate, beautiful scenery, not so big and congested as Denver, with a good size demon and vampire population. I didn't learn much about them, though. They're rather secretive."

"Good to know."

He rubbed his hands together. "So, have you researched the books at all? Find anything useful?"

"Maybe..." I pulled up the database Shade had sent, then searched through the spells. "Okay, here's something. It makes someone want to tell us everything about them without wondering why we're asking." I tapped the entry thoughtfully. "It doesn't call for much of a trade-off in power, but I should probably use it only when we need to —only if I'm unsure about someone. The more my power is reduced, the less I'll be able to use it to help 'Selene's son'."

I continued searching, and Ludwig asked, "Why don't you just ask the book for what you need?"

I sighed. "I'm not sure that will help, but I'll try." I pulled the books out of my luggage and turned to the communication spell. "Do you know our mission?" I asked the books.

I have heard you speak of it.

"Can you add anything that might help us find this Selene?"

I don't have enough information to know what would be useful and what would not.

I chuckled. "That does not compute, apparently."

Trying again, I asked, "Can you find the Selene the seer spoke of?"

No, the mysteries of seers are beyond my ken.

I groaned. "So it looks like we have to be specific about our needs to find a spell that might work...but we don't have time for that." I closed the book with a thud. "Okay, let's go with the original plan." If everything worked out the way we hoped, we would find Selene's son tomorrow, fix his problem, then be back on the road home to San Antonio.

Yeah, I know. Wishful thinking. When was anything ever that easy?

CHAPTER
FIVE

THE NEXT DAY, we had absolutely no luck. Billy drove one of Maurice's cars so we didn't have to find a way to fit all of us in the Mini, and we interviewed the six candidates. Ludwig, who people often found intimidating, hovered in the background. Billy's charm helped open people up, and Ruby didn't detect any supernaturals in the households. I didn't even have to use the spell to make them more forthcoming, so we headed off to see what we could find out about the local underground.

When we arrived at Relentless Protection Services where the Colorado Springs Demon Underground kept its headquarters, it was more than just one converted warehouse—it was a whole compound on the west side of town, backing up to the national forest. Apparently, they took security very seriously. It made sense, given how they made their money, but the tall fence, concertina wire, and the number of guards and large dogs patrolling the area seemed a bit overdone.

Ya think? Ruby snarked.

Billy drove up to the gate and the armed guard there leaned down to look at us through the driver's side window. "Afternoon. What's your business here?"

Ruby laughed in my head. *Looks like Billy is going to have to use his charm again.*

I don't think that will work on this guy. I leaned over Billy to answer the man. "We're visiting from San Antonio, and Sybil told us to check in when we arrived in town. So, we've arrived," I said, making a *ta-da!* gesture with my hands.

Billy raised his eyebrow at me, and I felt my cheeks heat.

The guard's stern expression didn't waver. "If you'll give me your names, I'll let Ms. Warburton know you're here. You can stay here."

"Oh, no, that won't work. We really want to get to know other organizations like ours, learn best practices, that sort of thing. It would be very helpful if we could come inside."

"I don't think—"

"Unless you have something to hide. You don't have anything shameful here, do you?" I pushed.

He jolted back in surprise.

That got a reaction, Ruby said in approval. *And, in case you needed to know, he's not part demon.*

That didn't mean he wasn't aware of exactly what he was guarding.

The guard scowled. "No, ma'am, but this is a security company, and as such, we need to keep our clients' information private."

"Oh, I'm not interested in your clients—just in the organization. The *super* organization, *naturally,*" I clarified. If he wasn't in the know, he'd just think I was being weird. Billy's raised eyebrows showed me someone already did.

The guard frowned, then said, "Just a moment." He

went inside the guardhouse to make a phone call, then came back out. "Ms. Warburton will see you, but you can't bring the dog inside."

"She's not a dog, she's a hellhound." Okay, she was part dog, but he probably didn't know that. "She's one of us too."

"I don't care what it is, it has to stay outside the gate. You can park over there." He gestured toward a gravel parking lot on the side.

It? Ruby grumped. *It?*

"Ignore him," I told her. I parked where I was told and raised my hands in exasperation. "Why would they object to dogs?"

"Maybe because of *their* dogs?" Ludwig suggested.

Okay, he had a point.

But how will I be able to help you if you're in there and I'm out here? Ruby asked petulantly.

"Don't worry," I assured her. "We'll leave the windows down, and you can take a nap. If we run into trouble, I'll mentally yell for help, and you can...charge to the rescue."

That seemed to mollify Ruby, who settled back with a sigh. Though how she'd get over the fence and the concertina wire was anyone's guess.

I'd find a way, my hellhound assured me.

At Billy's questioning look, I explained my conversation with Ruby.

He shook his head. "Do you ever get used to having her in your thoughts all the time?"

I grinned. "Not yet. It's better than the stones though— she's far more intelligent." Luckily, I had my hood up so I didn't have to hear the stones' response to that.

We found a shady spot at the far end under some trees and opened all the windows for Ruby, then the three of us approached the gate again on foot. The guard let us in, pointing to the closest building. "Go to that door on the far right, and nowhere else, okay?"

Sheesh, was all this security really necessary? "You got it," I said. I would've been a little snarkier, but we'd gotten what we wanted, after all. We headed across the expanse, and I saw a few men strolling around with weapons and large dogs who seemingly patrolled on their own. They seemed so well-trained, I wondered if they were part hellhound. None of them let on if they were.

Sybil stood at the door, her arms crossed and her face set in a frown. "She seems really ticked off to see us," I murmured so she couldn't hear.

"You want to come back some other time?" Billy asked.

"Nope. She's hiding something and I want to find out what it is."

"Is that part of the mission?" Ludwig asked disapprovingly.

"Not necessarily," I conceded. "But Micah did wonder what she was up to—maybe I can find out for him."

"You're the boss," Billy murmured. Ludwig just shrugged.

When we reached her, Sybil didn't bother with polite preliminaries. "You could have checked in by phone. I don't see how touring the facility will help you find someone named Selene."

"But I wanted to see your operation as well," I said. "It's ingenious how you have a security company to keep your members employed." Maybe a little buttering up would help?

Apparently not. Her mouth tightened. "It's not really a good time, as I told you before."

I shrugged. "We'd do the same for you, but if we can't

tour the facility, I was hoping we could talk to your people and see if any of them know someone named Selene. We interviewed the ones we found locally, and none of them were our target."

"Why are you looking for this person?"

"We told you," I said patiently. "Prophecies are always about supernatural occurrences. A friend is checking with the vampires, and since you have the other source of supernaturals in the area, I thought you could help." I tried to sound as reasonable as possible so she'd feel like a churl if she turned us down. "We can just wander around, if that's all right with you."

"It's not." She fiddled with her large citrine ring as she thought.

Maybe the citrine would have more information. Casually, I took down my hood, but the citrine's mood was mellow, and it didn't seem inclined to talk. Weird.

Sybil nodded decisively. "I'll ask them for you—no need for you to meet all three shifts."

That was definitely a dismissal. Really? She'd ask everyone? Somehow, I doubted it. "Thank you so much for your help."

Sybil just sniffed and closed the door.

"Help?" Billy muttered. "What help?"

I just shook my head as we passed by the guard, who was still keeping a close eye on us.

When we were a few feet from the car, I said, "Did you see her citrine ring?"

"Yeeees?" Billy said, obviously wondering why I'd asked. "Oh, that's right—stone whisperer. Did it tell you something?"

"Yes, but not what I expected. I expected the stone to be in agony due to Sybil's irritability and negative emotions.

Instead, the stone seemed perfectly calm and happy, though a little worried about something." Didn't sound like a reflection of Sybil to me.

"Maybe it belongs to someone else."

"Maybe, but I should still get more negativity if she's been wearing it all day."

I shrugged, and when we got to the car, Ruby bounced up and down. *I talked to a dog! He wants to talk to you.*

Not likely—she couldn't talk to animals, only other demons. "We don't have time if we're going to meet Maurice right after sundown. We'll try to come back another time to talk to him," I said soothingly. At Ludwig's disbelieving look, I muttered, "It's nothing, I'm sure. You try being newly paired with an immature hellhound."

Hey, Ruby protested. *I'm plenty mature. And it* is *something.*

A desire to find some way to make herself look better than Fang, no doubt.

Billy shook his head. "Well, I hope Maurice will have more success, because we sure didn't."

We returned to Maison Maurice, and since it was now after sundown, Maurice was up and greeted me as though I was a long-lost family member.

"How did your talk go?" I asked.

"I haven't actually had it yet," Maurice said apologetically. "Maybe I should explain how we are structured here. My people are governed by the Colorado Springs Protective Board which consists of four people, one for each cardinal direction of the city. Bartholomew is Protector of the West, Iona in the north, Nicolai in the south, and Janus in the east. Each one holds periodic meetings with those of us who want to live in harmony with the humans. They pass the information to the rest of us. I'm waiting for their next meeting."

I ignored the implication that there were some who *didn't* want to live in harmony with humans. "This is the west side, so your...boss..?"

"Chairman," Maurice replied with a smile.

"...is Bartholomew?"

"That's correct, "Maurice said. "You see, we're sort of loosely structured under these four chairmen, but our primary goal is to keep the humans from finding out about us. We keep the rogues under control so we don't have angry villagers showing up on our doorstep with torches and pitchforks."

Well, Alejandro won't be happy with that—he definitely wants to come out to the world. "Were you unable to get hold of your...chairman?"

Maurice looked apologetic. "He talked to the rest of the board. Since their relationship with the Demon Underground here is rather fractious, they are reluctant to meet with you. I told them all three of you are perfectly lovely, but they don't want to take my word for it. Plus, they are dealing with a rather heavy problem of their own."

"Like what?" Billy asked in surprise. "Something that will affect you?"

"I don't think so. Janus went berserk at one of the last meetings and had to be subdued." Maurice shuddered. "It was like he totally reverted to a savage state of being, and we have no idea why." He glanced guiltily at Ludwig and me. "Oops. You didn't hear that."

"Of course not," I assured him. It wasn't like I could do anything with the information anyway. Ludwig grunted agreement.

Now what? Ruby asked.

Good question. This whole thing was a bust so far. Maurice didn't get to ask the board much, I hadn't made any progress with the underground, and we had absolutely no leads whatsoever in the search for Selene's son. I sighed as I placed my call to Micah to report our lack of progress.

THE NEXT DAY, at Ludwig's suggestion, we parked outside the security company, out of sight of the main gate, to see if we could talk to people who came out at shift change.

"Let me check things out first," Billy said. "I can let you know if it's safe, and find the best position to catch people leaving."

"Good idea," Ludwig said. "I'll go with you."

"Yeah, we'll stay here," I said. "I'd just be in the way."

Billy raised an eyebrow at me again. He could say more with that eyebrow than most men did with a mouthful of words.

"Okay, the truth is, I feel safer here," I said.

Well, I'm going with them, Ruby declared.

"You'd really leave me unprotected?" I poured on the guilt trip.

Ruby looked at me, then at the guys, and thankfully seemed to understand the difference between a ripped ex-marine, a man-mountain-sized demon, and a wimpy girl who just talked to rocks.

Okay, I'll stay. Ruby flopped down in the seat and pouted. *When do I get my chance to do something?*

"Soon," I promised her as the guys took off. "After you have more experience."

But how can I get experience if you won't let me do

anything? And I am *experienced. Fang has taken me on lots of real missions already.*

"Really? How many?"

Three, she muttered, knowing I could verify the number with Fang later. *But we took down some really mean bloodsuckers.*

I shuddered. If she thought that was the sort of thing she'd learn with me, I hoped she was sadly mistaken. "Normally, I might agree, but these demons aren't nice like the ones back home. I really need you here to protect me."

Ruby looked at me in suspicion. *You're just saying that 'cause you think I'll be hurt.*

That was only one reason. "No, really. I honestly want your protection." Though I wasn't sure how much help such a diminutive hellhound could be, I wouldn't dismiss any of Fang's progeny.

Ruby looked longingly out the window, then turned to me with a doggie smirk. *But sitting in the car doesn't make it safer—it just makes it easier for them to find us, a better target.*

"What do you have in mind?" I asked suspiciously.

Let's explore the woods. Please. Ruby looked up at me with pleading puppy-dog eyes.

Dang, she was good at that. I considered it. We'd still be within hearing distance of the guys, so it was probably all right. "Okay, for a little while, but if they call, we have to go."

Okay, she agreed, a little too readily. *Look, there's a path. Let's see where it goes.*

Ruby bounded out the open window, and I followed her. "If you hear any strange demons, let me know right away. Privately," I added. I didn't want the entire Colorado Springs Demon Underground to be alerted to our presence.

Sure, Ruby said, but I wasn't even sure she heard me. She was too busy following her nose.

Fairly quickly, she ran out of sight, and I followed her with a sigh. Sure, she was well able to take care of herself, but, to err on the cautious side, I pulled my hoodie down so the stones could talk to me. They didn't have much to say since there was no one else around to gossip about. I took that to mean there was no danger as well.

Fairly soon, Ruby came running back to me, her tail going wild with excitement. *Remember that dog I talked to yesterday? He's here, and he wants to meet you.*

I hesitated. "It's not one of those vicious guard dogs, is it?"

He, Ruby corrected me, *and he's not mean—he's super nice. His name is Mateo.*

"Did you just make that up?" I asked as I slogged through dead leaves and fallen logs.

No, I told you—he talks to me. Come on, he's not far. You promised.

"Okay, okay." With a sigh, I followed Ruby deeper into the wood, knowing she wouldn't lead me astray. Well, hoping anyway.

All of a sudden, a huge black dog walked out of the shadows. Wow—there really was a dog. Was this Mateo? "Wait a minute. I thought you said he wasn't mean. He looks like he could easily tear me limb from limb." And it looked like he'd been living rough as well.

The dog halted abruptly, as if sensing my unease.

Yeah, he can smell that you're scared, but he just wants to talk to you.

Well, he looked docile enough. "I don't think that's possible," I said gently." I can't hear him like I hear you."

Ruby stared at the dog, acting like she really was talking

to him. I decided to humor her and let this play out. "Does he have some way I don't know about that we can have a conversation?"

He says when you talk to me, he hears it as a kind of echo in his mind. Maybe it will work the other way too. Let me try. She closed her eyes and concentrated really hard, her brow wrinkled adorably and her mohawk quivering.

After a couple of minutes, Ruby said, *I think I have it. Say something, Mateo.*

Hello, Ivy. I am glad to meet you.

Stunned, I stumbled back. His mental voice was a lovely whiskey-roughened baritone that reverberated in my mind. Must be that echo effect Ruby was talking about.

Wow, you really can talk, I said through our Ruby connection.

I told you! Ruby said in elation.

But what did you say to a talking dog? And how was this even possible?

Yes, I can talk, he said. *But only to you two at the moment.*

I decided to speak aloud to keep from overloading Ruby's mental capacity. "Why can't you talk to anyone else?"

He regarded me with a serious expression. *Because my human side is missing.*

"Human side?"

He's like that guy in the werewolf movie we saw last week, Ruby exclaimed, projecting images of rabid, slavering beasts.

No, Mateo said bluntly. *We're friendly. Shifters, not werewolves.*

They really existed? I checked in with my emerald. *Truth or a lie?*

The emerald assured me he was telling the truth. I

sighed and sat down on a fallen log near the dog...wolf...shifter, and eyed him warily.

You mean you don't go all scary when you shift? Ruby asked in disappointment.

Do I look scary to you? He sounded offended.

Kinda, Ruby said. *You're a lot bigger than we are. And, you know, a wolf.*

I am a wolf shifter. Like mundane wolves, we do not attack unless necessary.

He sounded very matter-of-fact, as though he wasn't accustomed to speaking in human terms. It must be uncomfortable for him.

Oh, Ruby exclaimed. *Are all those guard dogs we saw yesterday like you, too?*

Yes, but we are not dogs. We are shifters. He sighed. *Though I, alone, cannot shift.*

That explained the autonomy of all the...canines I'd witnessed yesterday. I vaguely wondered what Mateo looked like in human form. Once he was cleaned up, he would be an absolutely gorgeous dog...er, wolf. Shifter?

"Okay, I believe you," I said. My emerald had assured me he was telling the truth—at least, he believed he was telling the truth. "But why can't the other shifters help you?"

I have been banished from the pack. Because I cannot shift, they believe I must have done something bad to deserve it.

"Did you?"

No. That was vehement.

The emerald told me he was telling the truth. I nodded. "I believe you."

I do too, Ruby said.

"But what do they think you did?"

54

I don't know, but they're certain I'm guilty of something. It is likely they think I killed someone.

That sucks, Ruby said in commiseration.

"Why would they banish you—convict you—without evidence?"

Because they think my inability to shift is the sign of our goddess pulling her favor from me.

"Why can't you shift?"

I don't know, he said, sounding frustrated. *But I was hoping you would plead my case for me.*

Baffled, I said, "I'm not a lawyer."

Not in human court. Will you speak to my alpha for me, so I can undo this injustice? I am lost without my human half.

Is that why it sounded as if he'd never even heard of a sense of humor?

Oh, please, let's help him, Ruby begged.

Yes, the stones chorused, all in agreement that we should help the shifter.

But where could I possibly start? "No one believes you're innocent?"

My friends and sister might, but they might not dare go against the alpha's will. And they may have been turned against me.

"Don't you know?"

Removing me from the pack also removed me from the pack bonds, so I cannot communicate with anyone in the pack.

Wow—he really *was* isolated.

Ruby declared, *We'll help you, won't we, Ivy?*

I cocked my head at him. "Your mother's name wouldn't happen to be Selene, would it?"

No, it's Alice.

Of course not. That would be too easy.

Selene is the name of our goddess. She is the mother of us all.

A slow smile spread across my face. Oh, wow, this had to be it—I'd finally found Selene's son. I ignored the fact that any demon with a hellhound companion could help him, not just me as the prophecy seemed to imply. No, this was my task, and I was determined to complete it.

Now that I'd found him, I had to help him. "I'll do it," I said decisively, and Ruby cheered. "Ruby, can you call Ludwig and ask him to join us? Just don't tell him about Mateo yet."

A few minutes later, Ludwig and Billy made it through the forest with a lot less noise than I had. "Sorry, we didn't have any luck," Billy said. "No one came close enough to talk to."

I grinned. "Well, maybe you didn't have any luck, but I did." I pointed at Mateo. "Meet Selene's son...and he just so happens to have a problem I can help him with."

I explained how he was related to Selene, and Ludwig stared at Mateo. "What's his problem?"

"He's a wolf shifter who can't shift."

Billy nodded. "That explains it."

Ludwig and I gaped at him. "You're not surprised he's a werewolf?" I asked.

Wolf shifter, both Ruby and Mateo corrected me.

Billy did the eyebrow thing again. "I knew about vampires and demons, so why are you surprised I know about shifters?"

"Uh, because I didn't know. None of us in my underground know...that I'm aware of."

Ludwig shook his head, telling me he hadn't known either.

Vampires and demons in Colorado Springs are aware of us, Mateo explained. *They help keep our existence secret as we do theirs.*

"I need to help him," I told Billy. "Do you think Maurice would be okay if we brought him back to your house?"

"I'm sure it's fine," Billy said. "We've had shifter visitors before, and he seems to be the one you're looking for."

Excellent. "Want to come with us, Mateo? Be around some people you can actually converse with, get a soft bed and good food?"

He sighed heavily. *Yes, very much.*

Yay! Ruby declared as she ran to the car. *Let's go!*

CHAPTER
SIX

Mateo settled into Maison Maurice just fine. Since he had been living rough, I helped him bathe, with Ruby's "helpful" advice. He was very patient through the whole thing, and grateful to be clean.

That evening, Maurice told us, "Bartholomew says they haven't scheduled a new meeting yet, and they are baffled by Janus's continued madness. They have found someone to substitute for him until he regains his...sense."

Billy nodded. "Does Mateo want us to try to contact his pack tonight? If we meet at night, Maurice will be able to join us."

Me, too, Ruby exclaimed. *You need me to relay messages.*

I assured her she could come, especially with Maurice, Billy, and Ludwig along to help.

"Where is your pack located?" I asked Mateo.

He hesitated, then said, *It is not a good idea to just show up without notice. They might think it's an invasion.*

"Okay, do you have a friend we could call or something?"

He hesitated. *I wouldn't want to get them in trouble.*

If he still *had* friends. I tried a different tack. "How is the pack's relationship with the Demon Underground?"

It is good—that is why we work with them in the security company.

"Then how about I call your alpha and ask to meet with him as a representative of another Demon Underground?"

That should work, Mateo conceded. *Maurice should be able to reach him.*

I glanced at Maurice. "You knew there were shifters here, and you didn't tell us?"

"I'm so sorry. I thought you already knew. Everyone here in the supernatural community knows about the Pikes Peak Pack...and others."

I wondered if there were any other kind of supernaturals the books hadn't mentioned. Maybe they didn't consider the shifters a threat, which is why they'd left them out. Or maybe they didn't know about them either.

Or maybe it's because you didn't ask, Ruby said.

"Don't you have shifters in San Antonio?" Maurice asked in surprise.

"I don't know." I turned to Mateo. "Do you know if San Antonio has a shifter population?"

I have no idea, Mateo admitted. *The alpha might know.*

"Another reason to talk to him," I said. "What's his name?"

Endymion.

Ruby let out what sounded like a giggle. *What a weird name.*

Mateo explained, *In Selene's story, she fell in love with Endymion, so it is a common shifter name to curry the goddess's favor.*

Maurice had Endymion's phone number, so I dialed the number he gave me and turned on the speakerphone so everyone else could hear.

After I introduced myself and where I was from, not letting him know the others were listening in, Endymion asked, "What can I help you with?"

"Would it be possible to set up a meeting with you?"

"That depends. What did you want to talk about?" Endymion asked.

"I understand you have a disgraced member..."

"Yes." Endymion's tone turned flat and hard. "Did he hurt someone? Rex said I should have put him down."

I raised my eyebrows at that, but Mateo didn't seem surprised by the vitriol. "No, I have information you need to know. It would be better to do in person."

He hesitated for a moment, then said, "Okay. Do you know Ute Pass?"

At Billy's nod, I said, "I can find it."

Endymion gave me instructions on how to find a pullout area in the pass, then gave me GPS coordinates so we could find their meeting point off the road in a secluded location. "Can you meet tomorrow night at seven?" he asked.

"Absolutely," I agreed. "Thank you for agreeing to meet with us."

"Us?"

"Yes. I'm not familiar with the area and I don't want to come alone."

"All right," Endymion said. "Tomorrow night, then." He hung up.

"How many wolves will he bring?" Ludwig asked Mateo.

It depends on how big a threat he thinks you are. Since you're visiting members of the underground, I'd guess between three and six. Some in wolf form, some in human.

I passed the information on to Billy and Maurice. "Okay," Billy said, obviously confident we could deal with that. "Tomorrow night, then."

He and Maurice left the four of us alone in our little suite, and Ludwig turned to me. "What's the plan?"

Plan? I had to come up with a plan? "Uh, I'm not sure." Maybe we should learn more about the shifters' capabilities. I glanced up at the three-quarters moon and asked Mateo, "Is it true that you have to change to wolf when the moon is full?"

No, but we are stronger during the full moon, because of Selene's influence.

"What *are* your strengths and weaknesses?" Any knowledge would be an advantage.

We are strong and fast, and able to smell a wider range of scents than humans. And we heal quickly. But...I cannot give you our weaknesses. That would be a betrayal of my pack.

I understood where Mateo was coming from, but Ludwig asked, "What if they attack us?"

I doubt they will. You may defend yourselves, but please do not hurt anyone seriously.

"They may have kicked him out," I explained, "but his sister and friends are still a part of the pack, and we wouldn't want to hurt his chances for reconciliation."

Ludwig nodded, then regarded me thoughtfully. "What about your stones? What can you do with them?"

I sighed. "Short of throwing them, not much. Not that will help with this, anyway." It wasn't like I was The Rock—I just *talked* to stones, for heaven's sake.

Ask them! Ruby insisted. *They might know of something that could help. Or maybe the books have a spell you can use.*

"I'm reluctant to use the books' spells because they diminish what demon powers I do have," I explained to the others. Then, to pacify Ruby, I lowered my hoodie to talk to my gemstones. "Do any of you have any abilities that might help with meeting shifters tomorrow?" I asked, not expecting anything.

So much chatter broke out that I couldn't distinguish one voice from another.

One broke through the rest—the opal. *Silence please,* the opal said sternly. *When you all talk at once, Ivy cannot understand any of you.*

They quieted immediately. The depth and weight of the opal's voice definitely made it sound like an old, wise man, so I was going with a male pronoun from now on. I asked him, *Can you control them so I don't have to wear this hoodie all the time?*

I don't believe they realized how their chatter distracted you, the opal said repressively. *I believe they will at least attempt to be more courteous from now on. Especially if they wish me to enhance their capabilities.*

The feeling I got from the other stones was meek chagrin. Excellent.

The opal added, *In answer to your hellhound's question, I believe we might be able to assist, if your intent is honorable.*

"Honorable?"

Yes, I would be happy to help you if your intentions are for the greater good. If they are not, I am afraid you will have to do without my help.

I guess this is what my parents meant by "if I met its standards."

With Ruby's help, Mateo and Ludwig were able to follow along with the conversation. "What can you help with?" Ludwig asked.

Some of your stones have some meager ability, but with my amplification, we might be able to do something significant.

While the stones muttered about being categorized as "meager," I said, "Really? Like what?" Was it possible that my abilities might actually be worth something?

Cinnabar has persuasive abilities. I am uncertain how well it will work on others, though. Combine that with clear quartz, another amplification stone, and it will enhance your communications...with other stones, at least. I am uncertain how it will affect humans, shifters, vampires, and demons.

"We could test it on those here," Ludwig said, "see if it would help."

I nodded. "Good idea. What else might help?"

The opal threw out a few more ideas, but right now, testing the cinnabar and clear quartz seemed like our best option. I dug the stones out of my luggage.

"Try it on me, first," Ludwig said.

"Okay, if that is okay with you, Mr. Opal...?" Sheesh, that felt silly.

With the water demon's agreement, it is perfectly acceptable, the opal said.

What if I wanted to use it on someone else who wasn't so agreeable? I shook my head. No matter—we had to see if it would work, first. "How do I do this?"

Concentrate on what you want to accomplish, and push your intent through the stones.

The first time I tried it, the rush of energy surprised me, and I forgot to express my intent. With the opal's coaching, I concentrated on focusing the energy into the cinnabar and quartz in combination to persuade Ludwig to take a step toward me.

When he didn't move a muscle, I sighed in frustration. "Anything?" I asked.

Ludwig shook his head. "I felt a slight compulsion, but was easily able to ignore it."

I had the same results with Mateo. Later, when I tried with Maurice and Billy, I wasn't able to reach the vampire at all, but Billy actually took an involuntary step forward when I compelled him to.

"That worked?" I asked in excitement. "Let's try it again."

It turned out that if I concentrated really hard, I could convince him it was his idea, and he would go along with it. It took a lot of energy, though, and gave me a headache.

"Thanks, Billy," I said finally. "But I think we need to take a break for a bit. I'm not sure how that will help me since it only seems to work on humans."

"And rocks," Ludwig said, nodding down at my feet.

Interesting—the loose stones in my luggage had rolled their way to me as well.

Though it did not work on me, Mateo said, *I do not have access to my human side. It is possible it will work on other shifters, especially when in human form.*

I repeated what he said to Billy and Maurice.

"That may be so," Maurice said. "But we cannot count on it."

I must have looked as dejected as I felt, because Billy added, "But we don't know that for sure, and if we got larger versions of the stones, it might help?"

It would, the opal concurred.

"The opal says it will. Do you know of somewhere I can buy gemstones?"

"I'll find out," Billy promised, "and we can go shopping tomorrow."

"Okay, it's a plan," I said. It might not do any good, but it was certainly worth trying. And maybe it would help me be good for something other than just talking to pretty rocks.

CHAPTER
SEVEN

WITH BILLY'S HELP, I found some larger specimens of cinnabar and clear quartz the next day, and was able to combine them together in a silver cuff bracelet. I tried them briefly on Billy, and he acknowledged that the compulsion was stronger. Whether it would help at all tonight remained to be seen, however.

And now it was time to head out. Billy drove up Highway 24 at the bottom of Pikes Peak through Ute Pass. The beautiful pass was carved through the steep, red mountain rocks that were covered with trees and scrub brush. We arrived a little early at the pullout near Green Mountain Falls, and got out to survey the area. The rocks above the pullout didn't look very stable, so I took my hoodie down to see if the opal knew anything about them.

The rocks are somewhat unstable, the opal said, *but nothing to worry about. We will inform you of any danger.*

You will be fine, Mateo confirmed. *I'll try to stay undetected so the pack won't have any reason to be antagonistic.*

Maurice took charge. "Billy, stay here with the car in

case we need a quick getaway. Ivy, do you have the GPS coordinates of where we're going?"

No need, Mateo said. *I know the place.*

"Mateo knows the way," I explained as he took off up a narrow trail. I followed him, picking my way gingerly up the rocks. Sheesh—this was hard work. I might talk to rocks, but I certainly wasn't experienced in climbing them. The others didn't seem to have any difficulty though, and it irritated me that I was holding them back.

You are not. We need you to talk for me, Mateo reminded me.

"Now that we're here, I'm not sure what to say to the shifters," I admitted.

Don't worry—I'll help you, Mateo assured me.

That reminded me. *Ruby, don't include any of the shifters in the conversation unless we ask you to,* I told her silently.

You got it.

We only had to wait a few minutes before the shifters showed up. Four of them—two in human form, with two wolves flanking them.

The alpha is not here. That is the beta, Mateo told us.

Is that a bad thing?

He does not like me, and I prefer to speak to the man at the top.

I smiled to myself at the notion of wolf bureaucracy.

"Are you Ivy?" one of the humans asked.

"Endymion?" I asked, though I knew he wasn't.

"No," the strong-looking guy on the right said. "I am Rex, the pack beta. Endymion couldn't make it, but I can represent the pack with no problem."

Ruby cracked up.

Why are you laughing? Mateo asked.

Because so many humans name their dogs Rex. It seems odd that a shifter would use it.

Not if that's the name his parents gave him, I said sternly.

Ruby didn't reply, and Rex didn't bother introducing the others. I, however, introduced myself, Maurice, and Ludwig. I didn't introduce Ruby, hoping they'd think she was merely a dog. And Mateo, of course, stayed hidden downwind, though close enough to talk to me through Ruby.

"You have questions about our ostracized pack member?" Rex asked.

"Yes," I said, stepping forward. "We fear a great injustice has been done. We talked with your pack mate, Mateo, and he has convinced us he was unfairly banished."

Rex made a slicing motion with his hand. "Mateo Duran is no longer a member of our pack, and even if he was, he cannot talk."

"He can," I said patiently. "Otherwise, how would I know about this?"

He still looked skeptical. "Prove it."

Ruby, open a link between me and the shifters, please.

Okay.

Is this proof enough? I asked through her.

The two wolves looked startled, but the humans didn't. The wolves looked up at their human companions and apparently had a quick conversation through their pack bonds.

They think you're an animal communicator, which is proven by the fact that your "dog" is very well-behaved, Ruby said in amusement.

"You really can communicate with animals?" Rex asked.

Mateo and I decided to let him think that's what was

going on. "Yes. But I normally speak out loud so everyone can hear me."

Rex folded his arms across his chest belligerently. "Well, even if you did talk to Mateo, that doesn't mean he was telling the truth."

I hesitated. I couldn't tell him about the truth-telling nature of my emerald because he thought I was an animal communicator. "We believe he is. He doesn't know how or why he is stuck in one form, but he did nothing to bring this on. He'd like an audience with your alpha to discuss it." I paused with a raised eyebrow. "Or is it guilty until proven innocent in your pack?"

Rex snarled. "He can't be innocent. He lost the goddess's favor."

One of the wolves lifted his nose and sniffed the air, then focused intently on Rex as if speaking to him.

Uh-oh, Ruby said. *They know he's here.*

Rex looked even more steamed. "How dare you bring that felon onto pack lands." He grabbed my arm, but got my bracelet instead.

Let go, I screamed mentally at him.

He let go *real* quick. I guess the stones did work on the human side of shifters, at least when he was touching them. Good to know.

Mateo took off running. Maurice and Ludwig readied themselves, and I passed on Mateo's shouted warning. "Don't hurt anyone!"

The two wolves dashed past us and charged after their main target, Mateo, obviously not considering Ruby or me a threat, thank goodness. Ludwig shot a fountain of water at the two shifters in human form, bowling them over. Before they could regain their balance, Maurice darted forward and he and Ludwig each grabbed one.

They want to hurt Mateo? Ruby said incredulously. *We can't let them do that!*

This way, Mateo urged and darted faster up through the rocks and scrub brush.

"Follow them," I yelled at her.

Upward? Why the heck was he going up? When we reached him, I realized he was following a narrow track.

This is no way to lose them! I yelled at him.

Trust me, Mateo said in determination.

Trust him? I didn't even know him, but since he knew the area and I didn't, I followed. I glanced back, wondering what Maurice and Ludwig were doing.

Maurice is using his vampy mojo to make the human shifters stay put, Ruby explained. *Ludwig is helping hold one still.*

Thank heavens I didn't have to try my limited skills on them.

Why are we going up? I called mentally. *Going down is much quicker.* I wasn't very nimble, especially in unfamiliar territory in the dark, with shifting rocks underneath. It was a bit humbling.

Mateo has a plan, Ruby assured me.

What is it?

It would take too long to explain, she called back. *Just keep moving.*

Was he trying to tire them out? Well, it was sure working on me.

Mateo was headed for a narrow space between two rocks. What the heck? Since when did a choke point sound like a good idea? I continued to run up after them, though I was afraid I was losing ground fast.

Crap. Even if they got away, they would be in trouble if

they had to stop and wait for me. *Don't wait for me,* I yelled. I'd find a way to get away...somehow.

Yeah, right, Ruby said. *Incoming!*

Bewildered, I wondered what exactly was coming in. It turned out to be Maurice, moving faster than I'd ever seen him do before. He swept Ruby then me up in his arms and ran as though he were the roadrunner, and the wolves were the coyote. Unfortunately, I didn't think an anvil was going to magically fall out of the sky to squish them.

He zoomed past the wolves who had almost caught up to Mateo, dropped us on the other side of the choke point, then ran back, pushing one wolf into the other as he did so. They tumbled down the slope, giving Mateo some breathing room.

As the two wolves tried to regain their equilibrium, Mateo yelled, *Talk to the rocks.* He dashed through the choke point behind us. *Make them fall.*

What?

Yes, the opal concurred. *This is a good use of our abilities, to save your companions.*

Oh, crap. Could this really work?

Yes, Ruby said. *Remember how the small rocks all responded to your call at the house?*

Okay, I'd try. I stood watching the narrow gap, concentrating as I clutched my large opal stone.

As Maurice came racing back clutching Ludwig and panting hard, Maurice yelled, "Now, Ivy!"

I screwed my face up in concentration, calling upon the cinnabar and clear quartz, willing the red rocks to listen to me. The opal's amplification energy surged through me as I urged them to fall into the gap. It took a moment, but the rocks responded to my urging.

Craaack. The sound of boulders breaking apart filled the night air as rocks crashed down into the narrow crevice, right in front of the wolves' noses. With the high walls of the small box canyon, it effectively trapped the wolves on the other side.

"You did it!" Maurice exclaimed.

Whew! I relaxed for the first time in what felt like eons.

They aren't happy, Ruby said, *and they are thinking some very bad words.*

"Wow," Ludwig said. "That was a close one. I didn't know you could do that."

"Neither did I," I confessed. "But Mateo and Maurice were certain I could."

Yes, Mateo agreed. *She just needed someone to believe in her.*

Really? I needed to think about this later. "But how are we supposed to make it back to our car before they do?"

I know a shortcut down to the pullout, Mateo said. *Follow me.*

We scrambled back down over the rocks. Exhilarated by my success in convincing the rocks to come down for me, I didn't even mind when Maurice carried me down like I was a child. I had to admit it was the fastest way, and I didn't want to slow them down any more than I already had.

You were awesome! Ruby exclaimed as she bounded down the rocks.

Yes, you were, Mateo agreed. *I knew you could do it.*

But how, when I didn't even know myself?

All you needed was the confidence to try.

Stunned, I realized this shifter, who I'd only known for a day, had so much insight into me. *But if you were wrong, you could have been hurt or killed.* How could he be so reckless?

The goddess would not have sent you to help me unless you actually could.

Hmm. I wasn't sure I believed in goddesses, but fate? Maybe fate had something to do with it. And the opal, of course. I'd thought I could only talk to stones who had been cut and polished, but it turned out I was wrong. The influence of the opal probably helped with the others.

When we were back to Maison Maurice and all seated around the dining table, I said, "Well, that was a bust."

Not totally, Mateo said. *As I mentioned before, Rex has never liked me, so the meeting was bound to fail with him present. But the other shifter in human form, Kai, is a friend of mine...and he didn't look at all happy with what was going on. Rex overstepped—he must have done so without Endymion's authority.*

I told Maurice what he said, then said, "But I spoke to Endymion on the phone, so he must have sent Rex in the first place."

Endymion often sends his beta in his place. He didn't know Rex would take this kind of initiative.

"But how are you going to meet your alpha alone if he always sends his second in his place?"

Mateo sighed. *I'll just have to talk to Kai. If you can relay my thoughts to him, I can probably convince him to bypass Rex and go straight to the alpha for me.*

"But if he's on pack land, how do we reach Kai?" It didn't look like that was doable, since Mateo was banished.

By catching him after one of his shifts at Relentless Protection Services at the compound. They all have to check in and out through there, no matter where they work.

Ruby giggled. *Shifters work in shifts? That's funny.*

I smiled at her, but said, "I don't suppose you know his number?"

No—it is in my cell phone, Mateo said.

Yeah, and with no clothes and giant paws, he couldn't

use one anyway. I wondered idly where his phone was, then figured it didn't matter. "When would be the best time to catch him?"

Kai works first shift, so right after that.

"Good," I exclaimed. "We have a plan."

THE NEXT DAY, after shift change, we decided Kai wasn't much of a risk, so Ludwig and Billy stayed home.

Mateo reminded us that Kai would be in human form, so Ruby wouldn't be able to talk to him.

Then how are we going to convince him you are innocent? Ruby asked.

Ivy will have to do it.

"Me? I don't even know what to say."

You will be fine, Mateo said. *I will help.*

"Okay, but it's probably a good idea to keep my true nature a secret so we have an ace in the hole...just in case."

Mateo agreed, so we watched as men started coming out. Mateo pointed out his friend, and I waited until Kai was somewhat separated from the others to approach him.

"Kai?" I asked.

"Yes?" He looked puzzled.

"Hello," I said, proud the uncertainty didn't show in my voice. "We kind of met last night."

His expression brightened. "Oh, right, you're the animal communicator."

"That's right," I said, relieved he didn't seem upset about it. "And sorry about the...you know." I gestured vaguely, to mimic Ludwig's blast of water and Maurice's beguilement.

Kai folded his arms and nodded. "No problem. In fact, I

appreciate how all of you refrained from violently engaging with us." He uncrossed his arms as a thought occurred to him. "Hey, is it true that you can actually speak to Mateo?"

"Yes, I can." Through Ruby, of course, but he didn't need to know that.

"He's not...insane?"

"No, why would he be?"

"Rex told us he was incapable of communicating even with you."

"Rex doesn't know what he's talking about, and I can prove it...if you're Mateo's friend."

"Yeah," Kai said, scratching his stubble. "I didn't quite buy the story they're telling about him."

I believe him, Mateo said. *Can you ask him to shift so we can talk?*

"Well, if you'd like to hear his side of the story..." I told Kai.

"I would."

"Then, if you can shift, I can put you mentally in contact with him."

Kai nodded. "Let's go somewhere a little more private."

I followed him into the woods, and Kai shifted. It was nothing like I expected—one moment, he was a human, the next there was a swirl of light, then he was a big brown wolf. Thank goodness there was no nudity—I didn't want to know him quite *that* well.

Mateo, can you come over? I said it in both their minds through Ruby so Kai would understand I really could talk to him

Kai took a step forward and sniffed. Apparently convinced it was Mateo, he asked, *How do I know I'm really talking to you and the demon here isn't spoofing your voice somehow?*

Ask me something she wouldn't know the answer to.

Okay, what happened on my sixteenth birthday?

You convinced your older brother to buy you some alcohol, then you drank way too much, tried to drive into a lake and...became ill.

I vomited up my guts, you mean. Okay, I believe it's you. He glanced at me. *Is it okay to talk in front of her?*

"You kind of have to, if you want to communicate," I reminded him.

He took that in stride and said, *All right, tell me what happened.*

I am not sure, Mateo admitted. *It was the middle of the night, and Rex told me Endymion wanted to see me in the ritual space.*

When I arrived, it was just the three of us—

Kai interrupted. *You were in human form? The elders weren't there?*

Yes, I was human, and there were no elders present.

That's not right, Kai said.

I didn't even think about it, Mateo confessed, *especially when Rex accused me of violating pack law. When I asked how, Endymion gave me a goblet to drink from, saying it would ensure I would tell the truth while he questioned me.*

"Is this normal?" I asked.

No, Mateo explained. *But he said it had been spelled to make me tell the truth.*

We sometimes use artifacts the pack has acquired from allies, Kai explained. *But I haven't heard of this one being used before.*

Artifacts? "What happened next?"

I drank from it, Mateo said. *And I said I was innocent of any wrongdoing. Immediately, I was forced to shift into wolf form, and felt as though I had been ripped apart—my human side was gone.*

His description tore at my heartstrings.

Mateo continued, *Kai, you know I would never do anything against the goddess's wishes, but since I couldn't talk or change back when Endymion asked me to, Rex told him I must have done something horrible and had the pack bonds ripped away and me banished.* He paused for a moment. *Did he really tell everyone I was crazy?*

Kai snorted. *More like rabid.*

You believed him?

Well, you weren't there to defend yourself, so I didn't know what to think, though some of us tried to check out his story.

I gathered the beta wasn't the most popular member of the pack.

Mateo accepted his explanation. *But now that the goddess has sent me Ivy so I can defend myself, I can talk to Endymion and tell him my side of the story, and get reinstated to the pack.*

Oh, Mateo, you don't understand, Kai said in a sorrowful tone. *Rex was just carrying out our alpha's orders. Endymion is the one who wants you gone.*

Why? Mateo asked in shock.

I have no idea.

CHAPTER
EIGHT

AFTER WE RETURNED HOME and Maurice left for his meeting with the vamps, Mateo laid down on his bed with his head between his paws. Hoping to cheer him up, I said, "Maybe Kai can talk to the elders for you?"

No, Mateo said with a sigh. *They won't interfere with the alpha's decisions unless we can prove what he did.*

"Well, Kai said he would try to find a way to help you."

Yes, but I don't know how he can. We don't have any clue how I got this way, so how could he help me get back to normal?

"Well, since your human half disappeared after you drank from the goblet, maybe there was something in the drink that did it?"

I don't know. I have no knowledge of anything that could do that. And I don't know why they would use it. It would be very dangerous in the wrong hands.

Yeah, like theirs. "What we really need to know is why your alpha would do this to you. Do you have any idea?"

Not really. I've been trying to make sense of it.

Ruby piped up. *On TV, they say the reason is usually about money, sex, revenge, or power.*

"That's a good point," I mused. "What does Endymion gain by trapping you in wolf form? Is there some monetary reason? Does he get all of your worldly goods or something now that you're banished?"

Well, the pack does, through my family, but I don't have much he would want, so I doubt it.

"Revenge?"

I've done nothing to him, so no.

Though I found it embarrassing to ask, I had to. "Er, how about sex then?"

Surprisingly, he turned thoughtful. *Well, his sister, Luana, has been sort of pursuing me.* Mateo seemed reluctant to talk about it, as if he didn't want to brag. *I never encouraged her, though.*

"Do you think it could be her spurring this on—as revenge for you rejecting her?"

No, I haven't really rejected her—I didn't want to hurt her feelings, and she's never given up.

"Maybe he doesn't find you good enough for his sister?"

That can't be it. I'm one of the strongest wolves in the pack, and bring—brought—in substantial earnings to the pack with my security work.

Ruby interjected, *He's being too modest. I can see in his mind that he's one of the most in-demand security specialists, and he's very strong. He might even win if he challenged the alpha.* She thought for a moment. *He probably would.*

Now we were getting somewhere. "Power is always a good motive."

He must know that I have no desire to be in charge and I wouldn't challenge him.

I thought for a moment. "Have you told him that, or are you just assuming he knows?"

Well, I never actually said it out loud, but it stands to reason that if I was going to, I would have done it by now.

But reason didn't always operate in these sorts of situations. "So, it's possible he considers you a threat, especially with Luana enamored of you. I don't know your pack dynamics, but maybe he thinks by courting his sister—"

I am not.

"Yes, I know, but he may not know that. He might think you are doing so to slowly usurp his place. Gaining or retaining power can be a strong motive."

Wait, Ruby said. *Mateo—that thought right there. What was it?*

Rex might think that, Mateo said reluctantly. *He's been upset with me, thinking I was trying to steal Luana's affections from him.*

"He wants her, and she wants you?" Holy love triangle!

I guess you could say that, he said sheepishly. *And Rex and I both know I'm stronger than him.*

"So, between the two of them—Endymion and Rex— they have reason to want you out of the pack. Not just power, but jealousy."

Maybe. They have been suggesting I should find a different pack that would appreciate me more. He sounded so sad. Mateo obviously didn't want to think bad of his former alpha.

"And you refused, I take it?

Yes. My family and friends are here, plus I'd just been promoted at work... He paused. *I can see why he might have felt threatened.* He sighed in exasperation. *What does it matter? Knowing why won't help me reverse it. And I can't join another pack like this, either.*

"Well, it helps to know where the threat is coming from. But we still don't know what caused your inability to shift.

Your alpha probably got help from someone else. Your pack has good relationships with the local Demon Underground. Do you think one of the demons has this ability?"

Not that I know of. But I don't know everyone's abilities.

Or it could it be a spell, Ruby said. *Ask the books. Maybe they'll know.*

"Good idea, Ruby," I said. I retrieved the books and used the communication spell. To make sure the books understood, I explained the whole situation, though they probably already knew. I suspected they were privy to a lot of our private conversations and plans.

Addressing the books, I asked them, "Is a spell responsible for his plight?"

Once again, fiery words scrolled across the pages. *There is no spell within me that would do that.*

"Can you reverse it?"

I don't know. Certainly not without knowing how he got this way in the first place.

Well, neither of those answers were a flat "no." But since the encyclopedia had failed me, I did the only thing left that she could think of. "Let me call Micah—our leader in San Antonio." I put it on speaker so Mateo and Ruby could hear what was going on.

Luckily, he was in his office and not too busy. "How goes the mission?" he asked. "Everyone doing okay?"

"Everyone is fine," I assured him. "At least I've found 'Selene's son,' a wolf shifter who can't shift."

When Micah didn't react to the existence of shifters, I asked, "You knew about them already?"

"Yes, my father told me."

"But why have you kept it a secret? Don't we deserve to know all of the supernaturals living in our area?" Why would he do this?

Micah sighed. "My father made an agreement years ago with the local alpha. They want to stay hidden from even the members of the underground, and they agreed not to encroach on the city, or bother the humans. But that's not important," he said in exasperation, "and I would appreciate it if you and the others could keep it to yourselves. Only a few of us know."

"Ruby and I will, of course." I gave the hellhound a stern glance. "But I can't speak for Ludwig."

"Let me worry about him," Micah said. "The important thing is, have you figured out yet what the bloodshed part of the prophecy is?"

"No, we haven't."

Micah made an agreeing noise. "You may be right, but how do you know you have the right 'son'? You do realize anyone with a hellhound could speak with him as you have done."

"Yes, and that's bothered me from the start." But my gut, and the fact that I was able to talk to him through Ruby, was a good indicator. "There must be some connection to my stone whisperer abilities. And my stones insist I help him, regardless of what the prophecy is about."

"Then he probably is the right person. Is that why you called?"

"No, I was wondering if you knew of any spells, demon abilities, or whatever that could have done this to him. The books might be able to reverse it if they know what caused it."

"I don't know of anything that will do that, but I'll ask Shade to research it."

"Okay, thanks."

"What's going on with the vampire coalition? Something we should be worried about?"

"I don't really know. Maurice is working on that independently. Though I do know one of their leaders has gone feral, and they are trying to figure out why. The underground hasn't turned any friendlier either."

Micah gave a heavy sigh. "I appreciate you keeping me posted."

"No problem."

We both hung up and I turned to Mateo. "I'm sorry. It doesn't look like I'll be much help."

That's not true, he declared. *You've already been a big help just letting me communicate. But what was that bit about preventing bloodshed?*

"The entire prophecy was: 'To avoid widespread bloodshed, you must unshackle Selene's troubled son where Zebulon Pike made his fateful discovery.'" Since you're at the foot of Pikes Peak, you're troubled, and one of Selene's children, I hoped you would know what it means."

I'm sorry, no. I cannot imagine how my situation could lead to widespread bloodshed.

"Me neither."

He flopped down on the floor, looking dejected. *It looks like we're back where we started.*

"Not totally—at least we know who is responsible for your condition." I gave in to my impulse and hugged him. "Don't worry. We'll figure it out." We had no other choice.

I called Ludwig in and explained the situation to him. "The only thing we've figured out is that his problem seems to be caused by Endymion and Rex, so we probably won't get any help from them. Beyond that, we figure it either has to be a spell or a demon ability—we're not sure which." We hadn't heard back from Shade yet, and the books were no help. "I don't know what to do next to help him."

"Surely someone else knows more."

I threw up my hands in exasperation. "How could we possibly find that out? I kind of have to know what I'm looking for before I can find it."

I can help, Ruby said eagerly. *I can listen in on the shifters when they are in wolf form, see if I get any info.*

I nodded. "Not a bad idea—especially if you can get close to the alpha or beta. You didn't get anything from them when we met?

No, sorry, Ruby said, hanging her head. *I was concentrating too much on doing what you needed.*

You did the right thing, I assured her. I turned to Mateo. "Do you think your friend might know or have access to someone who does know something?"

I have no idea.

"Well," I said, "Kai gave us his number, so we can ask him."

I called Kai, putting the call on speakerphone so they could all hear. "Hello, Kai, this is Ivy. Do you remember me?"

"Oh, yeah. Mateo's friend," he said cautiously.

"We just wondered if you know anything beyond what you already told us."

There was silence for a long moment. "Maybe. I can't talk now. Can we meet later tonight? I'll bring some friends with me—they need to talk to...our friend for themselves."

"How many?" I asked, worrying my bottom lip with my teeth.

"About five."

"Where should we meet?" I looked around as though I'd find my answer somewhere nearby.

Ludwig said, "Maurice wouldn't have a problem with you meeting here."

"Is Maison Maurice okay with you?" I asked Kai.

"Sure, just give me the address."

"What time can you be here?"

"Maybe an hour after shift change."

Sure enough, six shifters showed up, an hour after shift change. The five we didn't know introduced themselves. Though a couple were big and buff, like I expected security guards to look, the others weren't. I guess shifters didn't actually have to *look* the part when their strength was innate.

They all glanced at Mateo. "That's him all right, but how do we know this is on the level?" one said.

Ruby, can you relay for me? "I'll show you how I can communicate with Mateo and let you know what he says." Mateo fed me some information, and I sat back and grinned. Interrupting them before they could start grilling me, I asked, "Stan, do you still have that stupid rabbit's foot?"

"Uh, how did you know about it?" one guy, apparently the Stan in question, asked.

"Mateo told me. And Devon, remember the incident with your underwear on the flagpole, or Terry, how you were caught—"

One guy held up his hands as if he could stop me spilling secrets. "Okay, okay, we believe you." I assumed that was Terry, interrupting to keep Mateo and me from spilling the beans on his secret.

"The rest of you believe as well?" I asked, trying not to look smug.

I got six nods, rather quickly.

Gee, Ruby said, *ya think they were trying to keep some secrets?*

"How do we know you didn't get that information from someone else?" Terry asked.

"Well, I can prove it to you if you're in animal form. It doesn't work with your human one."

Yeah, Ruby said eagerly. *That way I can tell you what they're thinking.*

Kai nodded. "She's right. Why don't some of you shift and hear for yourselves then share through pack bonds? Uh, Richard and Owen?"

The two who hadn't said anything obediently shifted. How awesome—once again, one moment they were human, the next, a bright light enveloped them, and when it dissipated, they were in wolf form.

"Mateo, could you please speak to them through me?" We'd already decided to keep the real animal communicator secret.

Hello. It is nice to be able to talk to you again, Mateo said through Ruby.

The two in wolf form reared back as if startled.

It sounds like Mateo, one of them said hesitantly, *though a little more stilted. Not as cheerful as he normally is.*

Cheerful? Mateo? "That's because his human half is missing," I explained.

It is me, Ricky, Mateo said. *You should know my voice even if it doesn't come through pack bonds.*

I've told you a hundred times, don't call me Ricky, Richard snapped. He paused, then grumbled, *Okay. Only Mateo is stupid enough to call me Ricky.*

Just one more thing to make sure, Owen said. *What did you do with my little brother's teddy bear at Christmas last year, Mateo?*

Well, you think I am the one who dressed it like an elf and put it in your bed, but you were never able to prove it.

Okay, Owen said. *It's him. And don't think I didn't notice you didn't deny it.*

Kai and the others in human form looked down at the two in wolf form. They must be communicating through the pack bond.

They are, Ruby said. *Want to know what they're saying?*

Since the shifters didn't look annoyed, they obviously didn't hear that. *No*, I told her. *Let them think I can't hear them.*

They weren't saying anything interesting anyway, Ruby grumbled.

Kai, obviously the spokesman, asked, "What do you want to know?"

"What do you know about Mateo's situation?" I asked them.

"Well, the six of us have never been comfortable with Endymion's leadership, and we questioned what he had to say about Mateo. There was something wrong with his story, but we didn't have any proof until I talked to Mateo." He looked at Owen. "Tell them what you heard."

Owen shifted back into his human form, and Richard followed suit. "I only came in on the tail end of a conversation," Owen said, "but I overheard Endymion and Rex talking about how effective the witch's method was."

"Witches exist?" I asked in disbelief. How many supernaturals were there, anyway?

I looked at Ludwig and he shrugged. "Well, you just met a bunch of shifters you didn't know existed."

True.

"I don't know if witches exist or not—I just know he called her one," Owen said. "It could have been a slur." He looked around at the other shifters, raising an eyebrow. "Anyone know any differently?"

They all shook their heads.

Owen continued, "They called her to see if there was

any way to reverse it, and I heard her say it's impossible to reverse, and they should be happy she did it for them. For free, even."

Impossible to reverse? Mateo said in dismay.

"Don't worry about that too much," I reassured him. "She could have been lying, and the seer wouldn't have sent me to you if I couldn't help you." When he made no response, I asked Kai, "Is it possible for you to find out more?"

They did that silent communication thing again, and Kai said, "We'll see what we can find out for you, but it might be better if you ask your own people in the underground. None of us have that kind of power."

I scoffed. "You mean ask Sybil, the iceberg who has frozen us out?"

Kai looked surprised. "She's actually quite nice."

"Really?" I said in disbelief.

They exchanged messages silently again.

"I'm afraid that's our fault," Kai said. "We have an agreement with them, and she must have been trying to protect the secret of our existence a little too enthusiastically." He shrugged ruefully. "We'll let her know you are aware of our existence and don't plan to exploit or expose us—that you just want to help Mateo. She's sympathetic to his plight. Especially since you took care not to hurt anyone in the pack because Mateo asked you to."

She knew that already? She must really be an ally. But... "I'll believe it when I see it."

Kai smiled. "In that case, I'll ask her to call you." He glanced at Mateo. "Do you want to come with us?"

I passed on his answer. "No," I said. "He says it's not safe for him there, and not safe for you either if he's there.

I'll give you our numbers so you can call if you learn anything."

"Good. I'll have Sybil call you as soon as possible," Kai said.

I showed the shifters to the door, then sat down to wait.

It didn't take long for a call to come in. I raised my eyebrows when I saw it really was from the security company, then put the phone on speaker.

"Hello, Ivy. I apologize for the cold shoulder."

"Wait," I said in disbelief. "Is this really Sybil?" If so, she was far more polite than before.

She laughed. "Yes, it is. Kai told you the reason why I was trying to keep you away from my employees?"

"Yes, he said you have a lot of his...people on your rolls." I didn't think I should I say pack over an open line.

"We do indeed. And now that you've been vetted by them, I am interested in hearing more about your organization and your abilities. Would you like to come back to the compound? I promise you'll receive a better reception this time, and I can give you that tour you requested."

"Sure." We set up a time to meet and I stared at Ludwig.

"What's the matter?" he asked.

"I never thought she'd actually react as a feeling human being. I'm in a bit of shock at the moment."

Progress, Ruby reminded me bracingly. *It's a good thing.*

I hoped so. I certainly hoped so.

CHAPTER
NINE

THE NEXT DAY, Ludwig and I approached the compound with Ruby. I didn't think we'd need Billy for this.

"Do you think they'll let us through without being a pain this time?" I asked.

"I have no confidence in that idea," Ludwig said.

But Sybil was true to her word. The guard at the gate—a different one this time—let the three of us in promptly. Sybil was even there to greet us at the same door. "Please, come in and be welcome," she said with a smile.

I smiled back, even more so when Ruby muttered privately, *Was that woman we met before her evil twin?*

No, she's wearing the same citrine ring.

Oh, I got it now. The reason I didn't get any distress from her ring earlier was because she really was normally mellow.

"I apologize for your reception before," Sybil said, "but we have pledged our support to the pack, and to keeping any knowledge about the shifters quiet. Others elsewhere have wanted to exploit them or hunt them, and we help keep them under the radar."

Yep, Ruby said. *She's telling the truth. If you'd let me come inside with you last time, we would have known then.*

She didn't allow it, remember?

Excuses, excuses...

Sybil escorted us to her office, which would have been kind of drab without all the plants filling it, covering every surface and even hanging from the ceiling. They were everywhere. She must really be into plants.

After we sat down across from her, she said, "I did check on the name Selene, and no one knows a person by that name, though the shifters reminded me that's the name of their goddess, if that's helpful."

I gave a rueful grin. "Yes, we figured that out, and it led us to the one I believe I am intended to help—Mateo. I believe he worked for you?"

"Yes, he's always been an excellent employee, but the pack banished him. I can't believe he'd do something as bad as they're saying. I think Endymion and Rex have it out for him for some reason."

"Yes, we talked to Mateo—"

"You talked to him?" Sybil repeated in astonishment. "I thought he was trapped in a permanent wolf shape, with the pack bonds cut off." She hesitated, then said, "Oh, that's right. Kai mentioned one of you is an animal communicator." She knew I was a rock demon, so she glanced at Ludwig.

I shared a glance with the water demon, wondering how much I should tell Sybil.

Ruby interjected, *Go ahead, tell Sybil. From what I hear from her and the other demons, she's actually trustworthy.*

"Well, that's what we let the wolves believe," I told Sybil.

"So how were you able to communicate with them?"

How much did I need to explain? "Are you familiar with hellhounds?"

Her eyebrows went up. "Just what I've heard about Fang."

"Well, they are part demon, like us, only they've mated with dogs."

Sybil's gaze shot down to my feet, to Ruby. "Is that the hellhound Micah mentioned?"

"Yes. Hellhounds can bond with a demon of their choice and help them. They can also sniff out vampires, fight them off, and speak to other demons." I pointed to Ruby. "This is Ruby, Fang's daughter. She's chosen me." When Sybil looked skeptical, I added, "Ruby, can you demonstrate for us?"

Nice to meetcha. And I'm going to be even more famous than Fang, you'll see!

Sybil looked surprised...and covetous. "Does every demon in San Antonio have their own dog, er, hellhound?"

No, Ruby said. *Last year there were only two, Princess and Fang, but they had a litter together and now there are four more, including me. We've all already chosen our demon partners.*

Sybil grimaced in disappointment. "Well, if you ever have one who might like to live in Colorado Springs, let us know."

I didn't bother to tell her how unlikely that was.

"But wait," Sybil said. "You said they can talk to demons, right?"

"Yes."

"But Mateo is a shifter, not a demon. Isn't he?"

"So far as we know," I assured her. "We learned we can also talk to shifters, but only while they are in their wolf form."

"Fascinating. What did Mateo—"

She was interrupted by a uniformed employee who threw open her office door and said urgently, "We have a problem."

Sybil rose, obviously ready to take off and address things. "What is it?"

"It's Phineas. He's lost his marbles, and he's been blasting flame everywhere with no regard for anyone's safety."

"Where?"

"The cafeteria."

Sybil rushed to follow him, and we followed her.

Oh, good, Ruby said. *A fire demon on the rampage. Can't wait!*

"Do not engage unless Ludwig or I tell you to," I said sternly as we ran down the hallway after Sybil. Though why I did so, I didn't know. I doubt I could be of any help. Ludwig, on the other hand...

When we reached the cafeteria, the guard leading them said, "We have him locked up in there, to contain the damage."

"What about Eddie?"

Sandman, Ruby confided.

"Eddie keeps putting out his fires, but Phineas seems ten times as strong as he usually is, and won't listen to reason."

Sybil charged into the cafeteria, with us right behind her. Inside, a tall skinny redhead was rapidly throwing fire-balls at random, yelling, "Let me out of here!" Another guy, presumably Eddie, was smothering them just as fast with gobbets of sand.

Sybil, to her credit, strode toward the fire demon. "Phineas, please calm down."

"Don't tell me what to do," he screamed and threw a

fireball at us. We ducked, but Sybil stood fast as the guy who'd come to get her threw up a shield to protect us. She threw her hands out to the potted plants around the room, and the plants struck out, lightning-quick, one reaching out to grab Phineas by the ankle.

"No, you don't." He incinerated the plant runner with his fire.

Just as fast as she threw plants at him, he threw fireballs to burn them to cinders.

Ludwig said, "That's weird. He's not acting like he's part-demon, more like a full demon."

How was that possible? Did some idiot open a portal to the demon dimension? How else could a full-blooded demon be here?

"I can help," Ludwig told Sybil.

"Can you do it without hurting him?"

"Absolutely," Ludwig said.

"Then please do."

Sybil stepped out of the way and Ludwig took her place. He thrust his hands toward the fire demon and yelled, "Stop!" Water gushed toward Phineas and inundated him.

"Ah, water demon," Sybil said.

"Yes. You're an eco demon, right?" I shot back. When she nodded, I asked, "Why don't you have green hair?" The only other eco demon I'd heard of had naturally green hair.

"Luckily, that gene skipped me," Sybil said with a smirk.

Ludwig didn't keep him down for long. "I need to freeze him," he gritted out. "Can you help?"

Without prompting, the opal said, *We can enhance the water demon's abilities temporarily with the quartz to help him restrain the trouble-maker.*

Excellent! I concentrated and, under the opal's direction, I sent a burst of power to Ludwig, who turned the water encasing Phineas into ice. Soon, the fire demon was trapped fast, like Han Solo in carbonite.

Sybil gave a sharp nod as she snapped out orders to several people around them who grabbed the fire demon. "Where do you want him?" one of her guards asked. "The holding area?"

"How long will he be frozen?" Sybil asked.

"I'm not sure," Ludwig admitted. "Especially since he's a full demon."

"But he's not. He's only part demon like the rest of us."

Ludwig is right, Ruby said. *Nothing human in his mind at all.*

Looking startled, Sybil said, "Hold onto that thought."

You got a freezer big enough to stick him in? Ruby asked.

We all looked at her in surprise. Out of the mouths of hellhounds...

"There's the walk-in freezer in the cafeteria kitchen," Sybil said.

One of the guys holding the frozen fire demon snorted. "Yeah, that'll really tick off chef."

Sybil frowned at him. "He'll get over it—Phineas won't contaminate the food, for heaven's sake. And it's for the good of the entire organization, until we can find a way to deal with him long-term." She turned to Ludwig. "He won't suffocate or anything, will he?"

"He shouldn't. It's as if he's been cryogenically frozen—in suspended animation."

"Okay, good. Let's do that." Sybil gestured toward Phineas. "Take him to the freezer and turn it down to the lowest temperature. If chef balks, have him talk to me. And ensure there's a twenty-four-hour watch on the freezer."

The guys carried him off, then, when we were all back

in Sybil's office and she'd closed the door, she said, "Why do you think he's fully demon?"

"Ruby can read demons' minds," I reminded her.

"But...Phineas wasn't like this yesterday. What could have happened?"

"I don't know, but there have been a lot of strange things going on around here."

"Oh? Do you think this is related to what happened to Mateo? What exactly did happen to him?"

"Rex and Endymion happened to him."

"I'm not surprised. They've been hassling Mateo for a while, as if they hoped he would crack under the pressure. How did they lock him into his wolf shape?"

I shrugged. "One of the shifters heard them talking about someone they called a witch."

"Really? I've never heard of one before."

"It's possible it's a derogatory term and not a species designation—we aren't sure. But Kai seems to think the only one who could have done something like this is someone from your organization."

Sybil gazed at the ceiling for a moment. " I can't think who would. No one here has that kind of ability."

"Maybe not your organization, but it could still be a demon," Ludwig said. "A rogue."

Now you're thinking, Ruby said in approval.

"Possibly. I've heard rumors...let me check them out and get back to you. And see if I can figure out what happened with Phineas." She gave us an apologetic glance. "I'm sorry, but I don't think this is the best time for a tour."

"No problem," I agreed. "Don't worry. We can see ourselves out."

As we headed back out through the gate, I realized that I'd even been able to help this time.

96

Yeah, you rock! Ruby said, holding her paw high. *High paw!*

High paw?

Yeah, I don't have fingers, so I can't do a high five. High paw! she repeated.

I laughed and Ludwig and I both met her high paw with a high five of our own.

"It will be good to tell Micah we finally have some progress," Ludwig said.

Yes, it would. Maybe we were finally getting somewhere.

CHAPTER
TEN

THE NEXT DAY, we visited the security compound and Sybil confirmed that none of the demons registered in her organization had the ability to remove Mateo's humanity, but she had found three demons in the area who were unaffiliated with the local underground. She didn't know their abilities, and therefore, they might be involved.

"Do you have addresses?" I asked.

"Yes. The leader before me left a few notes. Are you going to track them down?"

I glanced at Ludwig. "I think we have to," I said. "We have to see if one of them is the 'witch.' It's the only lead we have."

"What kind of cover story should we use?" Sybil asked.

Ludwig shrugged. "Maybe we say we're from your demon underground and want to invite them to join."

I nodded. "Sybil, do you know of any reason why that's a bad idea?"

"No, though I would like to go with you, in case they take you up on the offer."

Good point. "Sure. We'll bring Mateo and Ruby as well." At her puzzled look, I added, "Ruby and my emerald can suss out the truth from a part-demon, and Mateo may be able to identify one if he's seen them around." And since my stones had been behaving, I might not even need the hoodie anymore.

"Shall we go now?" Sybil asked.

"Sure."

Since my Mini was so small, Maurice had loaned us one of his big black cars that seemed *de rigeur* for vampires, I asked, "Okay, where do we go first?"

"Well, they're spread out all over the place, so let's try the one in Widefield first. It's a suburb south of the Springs," she added when I gave her a questioning glance.

Ludwig followed the directions she gave us, and we pulled up to a small house that looked old but well cared for. "What do you know about this one?" I asked.

"It's a man by the name of Horace Fielding, demon type unknown, reason for leaving unknown."

"We can't just show up at his door with a 'dog' and a wolf," Ludwig protested. "He'd be dumb to let us in."

"Or with someone who looks like a WWE wrestler," I said wryly, with an apologetic glance at Ludwig. When he shrugged, unoffended, I added, "But hopefully he won't find two women a threat." Even if we were. "Is he even here?"

Ruby responded. *He's in there.*

"Can you tell what kind of demon he is?" Sybil asked Ruby.

Yeah, that might be good to know before we went in.

I can't tell unless he uses his abilities or he thinks about it. But, since I can *read his mind, he definitely is part demon.*

"Just ask him," Ludwig said. "If he won't tell you, he'll

at least think about his abilities, and Ruby can read his mind to learn what they are."

Yeah, Ruby said. *I can make sure he doesn't hear when I'm talking to you guys.*

"Good idea," I said. "And if we can draw him to the door, Mateo can get a look at him, see if he recognizes him."

"Let's do it," Sybil said.

Ludwig and Mateo stayed in the car as we knocked on the door. A wizened old man opened it, looking disgruntled. "I'm not gonna buy anything, so you're just wasting your time."

He started to shut the door, but Sybil said, "We're not selling anything, Mr. Fielding. I'm Sybil Warburton, and we're members of the Demon Underground."

"Yeah, so?" he said belligerently.

"Sir, we're here to update our records and invite you to rejoin."

Ask what kind of demon he is, Ruby reminded her.

Sybil nodded, and added, "May I ask what your ability is?"

"No," he snapped and tried to close the door on us, but Sybil wedged her foot in the opening.

He's a necromancer, Ruby supplied, proud that she was able to glean that.

Sybil continued, "Our records say you are a necromancer. Is that right?"

"Yeah, what of it?"

What an off-putting ability. "Are you really able to bring people back from the dead?" I blurted out.

He shrugged. "My ancestors could, but my power is diluted and weak."

He's telling the truth, Ruby confirmed. *He's embarrassed because all he can do is wake them for about five minutes.*

He got a little more testy. "Why? You people never wanted anything to do with me before. Everyone looked down on me, thought I was disgusting, and were afraid of what I can do. Now you need me to raise the dead? Forget it. I don't do that anymore."

Oh, Ruby said in a sad tone. *He's always felt unwelcome, unwanted. He's very lonely.*

"No, sir," Sybil assured him. "That's not why we're here. You left us about twenty years ago, right?"

"I guess so."

"Well, since then, the former leader—the one you knew—has passed on, and I was selected as the new one."

He peered up at her. "What's your name again?"

"Sybil Warburton. I'm an eco demon."

He nodded sagely. "Plant growers." He seemed to relax a little more.

"I assure you things have changed since his leadership, and we would be most happy to have you back." Sybil sounded like she meant it; otherwise, she wouldn't be pushing so hard.

She does, Ruby said to me privately. *In fact, she feels a little guilty for not reaching out sooner. Her predecessor's old-fashioned and narrow-minded ways alienated a lot of people.*

When Horace hesitated, Sybil added, "We are having our monthly celebration in a couple of weeks. We would love to have you come, get reacquainted with those you knew, and maybe make some new friends." She gave him a card with her information and the date, time, and place of the party. "I hope you can make it."

He glanced down at the card with trembling fingers. "I'll think about it." Obviously acting more gruff now than he actually felt, he went back in and closed the door.

When we got back in the car, I asked Mateo, "Did you recognize him?"

No. And I don't think a necromancer would be able to remove my human side.

I nodded. "I think we can cross him off the list. He didn't seem to have a motive either. Where's the next candidate?"

"North of Woodland Park—that's a mountain town west of the city—in what looks like an isolated place," Sybil said, biting her lip.

"That concerns you?"

"Just thinking about a possible prepper. They like this kind of place. And they're not always forthcoming."

"I think we can handle whatever he throws at us."

"*She*—the next one is a woman named Veronica Thompson. Again, abilities and reason for leaving unknown."

"Would a woman be a prepper?" I asked.

Sybil shrugged. "I've learned not to make assumptions about anyone."

When we pulled up to the isolated home an hour later, a woman in her thirties with warm brown skin and a thick dark braid down her back was working in a garden. She straightened when she saw us.

Definitely part demon, Ruby said. *And she's worried about something.*

"Just a moment, please," she said, then went into the house and came back wearing a strange sort of turban made of silver and silk. Weird.

Sybil, Ruby, and I had exited the car, leaving Ludwig and Mateo inside like before.

"Can I help you?" she asked.

"Veronica Thompson?" Sybil asked.

"Yes, that's me." She seemed polite but curious, unlike Horace.

Sybil held out her hand. "Hello, we're from the Demon Underground and wanted to invite you to our next party."

Veronica seemed wary of taking her hand, but did a quick shake and release. "Thank you, but I'll have to pass. I'm an empath demon, and being around a lot of people with strong emotions is very wearing on me. It's better to stay home."

That explained why she lived in the back of beyond.

"I see," Sybil said.

"Your headgear," I said, fingering my own hoodie. "Does that help keep the emotions at bay?"

"Somewhat, but it can get heavy and very tiring to wear, and not something I can sport out in public without getting strange looks."

"I understand that," I said, "I have to wear silk over my head as well, to keep out the voices of my stones. But I never thought of pairing it with silver."

"No, I can see why you wouldn't. It's a strange combination empaths use. I don't hear voices or words like you do —I just get slammed with everyone's emotions whether I want to share in them or not."

She's lonely, too, Ruby said. Apparently, neither silver nor silk would stop a hellhound from getting through. *Is there a way you can help her?*

"I see why you wouldn't be interested in a physical gathering of people," Sybil said. "But can you feel emotions over the phone or the internet?"

"No, people have to be within twenty feet or so before I feel them."

Sybil nodded decisively. "Well, we have some distant and disabled members who can't come every month, so they meet monthly in an online chatroom. Is that something you'd be interested in? There's no requirement or obligation to keep going if it doesn't work for you."

Veronica's face brightened. "My internet is spotty out here, but I'd like to try. What a wonderful idea. Thank you. I'll take you up on that."

After Sybil gave Veronica the information, we got back in the car. Mateo confirmed he hadn't seen her before, and since none of us could figure out how an empath could remove Mateo's abilities, I said, "Two down, one to go. Maybe the third one is the charm."

Sybil shook her head. "I should have done this before—reached out to them."

I patted her on the shoulder. "Don't beat yourself up—you had no way of knowing what was going on before you."

"I'm not so sure about that."

Before Sybil could spiral down into berating herself, I asked, "So, who is the third one?"

Sybil glanced down at her notes. "Another isolated person, not too far from here, on a ranch southwest of Woodland Park. Name is Dahlia Deveraux. But maybe we could eat something first?"

"Sure," I said.

After lunch, we drove to the next address. The ranch was isolated, all right, but the shabby-looking acreage had a nasty-looking barbed wire fence around it that screamed "keep out."

"There's a road," Ludwig pointed out, and I drove up to the gate.

Since the mailbox had Dahlia's name on it, we'd obviously found the right place, but the locked gate and intimidating fence was a hint to be polite. I rang the buzzer to ask for entry, and after a few moments, a woman's voice came over the speaker. "What do you want?" she clipped out.

Charming.

Sybil leaned over me to talk into the speaker and went into her spiel about the party again, but the woman cut her off abruptly. "I'm not interested in anything to do with the underground. You can tell everyone you tried, so goodbye."

"We want to bring our database up to date," Sybil pushed. "Can you tell me what kind of demon you are?"

A bark of laughter sounded through the speaker. "That's rich, coming from you."

Looking startled, Sybil said, "I beg your pardon?"

"You really don't know?"

"No, I really don't."

"Well, let's just say your people have never treated me with anything but scorn. And I feel the same about you. Now get lost before I come out there with my shotgun." I heard the ratcheting sound of what definitely sounded like a shotgun. "And don't come back. Ever."

Wow, she's mean, Ruby said.

I toggled the speaker off, and Sybil asked, "What now?"

Not wanting to storm the house without a good reason —especially in the face of a weapon—I said, "Let's go. This is getting us nowhere." I glanced toward the backseat. "Ruby, did you get any sense of her or what she is?

No, she's too far away, Ruby said. *If we could get closer...*

"Not a good idea today," I said as I turned the car around. "Think she's our 'witch'?"

"It's possible," Sybil said. "Let me see if I can find someone in the organization who knows why she's so hostile."

"Could her attitude be because of something the last leader did?" I asked drily.

Sybil's mouth quirked. "I have no doubt."

Yeah, me too. "Mateo, did you recognize her voice? Or have any dealings with her?"

Not that I know of, Mateo said, sounding down in the dumps. *I'm beginning to think this is impossible.*

"Don't worry, Mateo," I said. "We'll figure this out and get you back to normal."

Let's just hope I'm not lying.

ELEVEN

When we got back to Sybil's compound, she took a seat at the computer in her office and typed away. "I'm not finding any other information on Dahlia Deveraux, except for when she left the organization—ten and a half years ago."

"Is there any indication as to why?" I asked.

"No, and that's before my time. I haven't met her, that I know of," Sybil said, her expression showing she would remedy that as soon as possible.

I spoke up. "Do you have anyone who might have known her then, to give us some insight as to what kind of demon she is, and why she left?"

"Maybe," Sybil said. "Let me see who was around then." She did a search on the computer, then made three unfruitful phone calls until she finally reached someone who knew her. "Mavis, would you mind coming to my office? I need to ask you more about Dahlia."

When she hung up, Sybil said, "She works here in the cafeteria, so it shouldn't be long."

When Mavis showed up, she was a tiny bird-like woman who looked all bones and sinew, and about a hundred years old. Her expression was a mixture of rampant curiosity and trepidation. I guess getting called to the boss's office wasn't something to set your mind at ease.

Sybil asked her to take a seat, and introduced us. "You said you remember Dahlia?" Sybil asked.

Mavis squirmed a little. "I remember the scandal, if that's what you mean."

"What was the scandal?" Sybil asked.

"You don't remember it?" Mavis asked in surprise.

"No, I was in the Denver underground then, and didn't move here until eight years ago, after I met my husband. I elected to join him here rather than stay in Denver."

Mavis darted a glance at Ludwig and me. "It doesn't exactly show us in the best light...."

"It's okay," Sybil assured her. "You can talk in front of them. No one here will be offended. It was before I came here, and they don't know anyone here well enough to be scandalized."

"But..."

"They know about the shifters, too, if that's your issue."

Mavis nodded and stared down at her clasped hands. "Well, I have to go back to about twenty-eight or thirty years ago, when her mother first moved here." Mavis thought for a moment. "Her name was a flower too..." she closed her eyes for a moment as if searching her memory, "...Aster, that's it. She was looking for a husband to strengthen her demon power in her offspring, and thought she might find one here."

"What was her demon power?"

Mavis scrunched up her face. "I'm sorry, I can't remember. It was a long time ago."

"Did Aster find what she was looking for?"

"Sort of. She didn't find a demon with powers like hers,

so she gave up on that. But she wanted children very badly, so she married a human to have a child with. Sometime later, she had a daughter."

"Dahlia?" I asked.

Mavis nodded. "Everything was fine until the girl turned sixteen, and they learned she didn't just have the one power—she had another as well."

"That's not possible," Sybil said. "Two different kind of demons can't have children together."

"That's true, but she didn't have two demon powers. When she turned sixteen, signs began to show that she was half shifter, though she was never able to fully shift."

I turned to look at Mateo. "Did you know shifters and demons could have children together?"

Yes, but it's very rare. And I've never heard of a birth where the child actually lived.

Mavis shrugged. "Apparently, the human Aster married was infertile, though he wasn't aware of it, so she found another way to have a child."

"What happened when they found out the child was part shifter?" I asked.

"Her husband beat the name of her shifter lover out of Aster, then killed them both."

That didn't make sense. "But if he was human, how could he overpower a shifter and a demon?"

She shrugged. "Dynamite doesn't care what your strengths are. They died."

Yeah, that would do it, Ruby agreed.

Oh, Mateo exclaimed. *I remember...*

"Remember what?" I asked him.

When Mavis looked surprised, Sybil said, "Ruby, her hellhound, helps her communicate with shifters."

I relayed the information Mateo gave me. "He just realized that was the same time Endymion's father, the former alpha, mysteriously died in an explosion, though Mateo never heard the whole story." When Sybil started to ask a question, I held my hand up. "He also says we're asking the wrong question."

We glanced at each other, and Ludwig asked, "What happened to the daughter, Dahlia?"

Mavis laughed. "Ding, ding, ding. Give the man a cigar. Dahlia, being half shifter and half—or rather, part—demon, wasn't accepted by either side, so she was essentially kicked out to fend for herself."

"At sixteen?" Sybil asked in disbelief.

Mavis wouldn't meet her eyes. "I told you it didn't paint us in the best light."

"What did she do then?" I asked.

Mavis shrugged. "Her human 'father' had a working ranch somewhere around here, so she took it over when he went to jail. I don't know if she's still there or not. I rarely see her around."

"She is," I confirmed. "And she still seems pretty bitter about it, too."

Why would she stick around when she wasn't wanted? Ruby asked in puzzlement.

"Maybe she had nowhere else to go," Ludwig said gently.

Oh. I didn't think about that.

"So, Endymion is her half brother," I said. "Do you think she would help him do this sort of thing?" I nodded toward Mateo.

"Why would she, if she was so bitter she didn't want anything to do with either group?" Sybil asked.

"Maybe they reconciled," I suggested. "After all, they

did share a father, and neither were responsible for the scandal"

Mavis snapped her fingers. "I remember now—Dahlia was part mage demon, like her mother."

Yikes.

"And now that I think about it," Mavis added, "I'm pretty sure I saw Dahlia hanging around outside earlier."

"Really?" Sybil asked. "Did she make it inside the compound?"

"No, the guard turned her away." Mavis stood abruptly. "Well, if that's all you need, I have to get back to work."

"Yes, thank you," Sybil said.

I waited until Mavis had left before I exclaimed, "A mage demon! They can be very dangerous." Especially in conjunction with the encyclopedia. "That doesn't sound good. And why was she hanging around outside the compound?"

"Maybe she changed her mind about talking to us?" Sybil said.

I snorted. "I doubt it."

"It's possible she is the 'witch' we've been looking for," Ludwig added. "I wouldn't put anything past a mage demon."

"Maybe," Sybil said doubtfully. "But she is also half shifter, which makes her mage demon bloodline very diluted. She's probably not very powerful."

I nodded. "Mage demons can only pass on one spell to their family that is unique to them. So, if her mother taught her a spell, she might be able to use it... But what kind of spell could possibly take away Mateo's human side and freeze him in wolf form?" I asked.

"Like a soul-sucking spell?" Ludwig asked in disbelief. "Is there such a thing?"

We all exchanged glances. "I don't know," Sybil said. "We asked her about Dahlia's powers. If Mavis had remembered something like that, she would have told us."

"Dahlia might not need to be strong in her demon powers to just activate a spell..." I realized. Crap, she really might have done this.

But how does knowing this help me? Mateo sounded frustrated.

Sybil seemed at a loss, so I jumped in. "If she can cast a spell, she can probably reverse it too, no matter what she told Endymion."

"Maybe," Ludwig agreed. "Given the right incentive."

I chewed on my bottom lip for a moment. "How do we find out if she did it or not?"

I can read her mind, Ruby reminded us.

"Yeah," I said. "If we can even get near her. She wouldn't let us on the property, remember?"

Then we'll just have to be sneaky about it, Mateo said.

Oooh, I like that, Ruby said. *I can be sneaky.*

My stomach dropped. I had no doubt, but sneaky enough? That remained to be seen....

When we arrived back at Maison Maurice, Ludwig said, "We need to plan this carefully. You can't charge in, guns blazing, and hope to learn anything from Dahlia."

Why would we use guns? Ruby asked in confusion.

I smiled at the young hellhound. "That's a figure of speech. He meant we should make a plan that has the best chance of learning what we need to know."

Oh. That's easy, Ruby said. *Just get close enough to read her mind, make sure she's the one who cursed Mateo, and find out how to reverse it.*

Patiently, I said, "But what if she's not thinking about Mateo at the time? It's not as though you can rummage around in her brain—you only get the surface thoughts, right?"

I guess so, Ruby grumbled.

"We'll just have to make sure she's thinking about what we want her to," I said in an attempt to buck up my hellhound.

Ludwig frowned. "How do we do that? And how do we get close enough? Do we even know how her place is laid out?"

I thought for a moment. "Well, we can call Shade and ask him to use his computer skills to find out what he can about the property and see if he can get her phone number."

"For what?" Ludwig asked. "I don't think she'll be any more likely to talk on the phone."

"Yes, but if we ask Sybil to call and ask questions once we're close enough to read Dahlia, we might be able to learn something that way."

Ludwig raised his eyebrows. "Huh. Good idea."

Mateo turned out to be good at making plans, once we printed out the maps and put them on the floor where he could see them. *If we go up this road,* he nosed the spot on the map, *we can cut through the fence and we'll be right behind the barn. Is that close enough to read her thoughts?*

"How much space between it and the main house?" Ludwig asked. "We assume she'll be at the main house?"

"I would think so." I leaned down to look at the map legend. "Maybe fifty feet?"

That should work then, Ruby said. *If not, we might be able to slip in closer since it's dark.*

Billy and Maurice came in then, looking worried. "Can we talk to you?" Maurice asked.

"Of course," I said. "How can we help you?"

Maurice, looking distraught, said, "Eight newly turned vampires attacked some of our people just after sundown."

When Billy shared a wary glance with Maurice, I asked, "Is that unusual?"

Maurice took on a lecturing tone. "The accord we all agreed to says we will not turn anyone and increase our population without notifying the rest of the board, to ensure we stay under the radar. Exceptions can be made for extenuating circumstances like a life-or-death injury, but not *eight* of them."

"Especially since new vampires can be hard to control if they give in to the blood lust," Billy added.

"Could Janus be responsible?" I asked.

Maurice grimaced. "I doubt it. Janus is still insane, so he's been...incarcerated." Maurice sighed. "Whoever is responsible, the fact remains that these fledglings are at large. Bartholomew has gone to find them."

"Billy and I are headed out to help, but..." Maurice looked pleadingly at Ludwig. "Could you join us as well?"

Ludwig looked at me, the one they *didn't* want. Well, who could blame them? I would be of no use in this situation. "Go," I told him. "We can finish the plans up by ourselves."

Ludwig nodded decisively. "I'd be happy to help," he told Maurice.

Maurice's cell phone dinged, and he checked the text message, letting loose with a four-letter word I was surprised to hear coming from his mouth. Hurriedly, he said, "Janus escaped and has issued an ultimatum—turn the city over to him or he will release the fledgling vamps on the general *human* population. He's meeting with the board at the Chuckwagon Pavilion in the Garden of the Gods after the park closes."

"What time does it close?" I asked.

"At ten." Maurice checked his watch. "It's 8:35 now, so we need to leave and rally the troops to stop him."

I didn't see any way I could help him, and I still had to help Mateo, so I said, "Good luck," as the three rushed out the door.

CHAPTER
TWELVE

AFTER MAURICE, Billy, and Ludwig left, I went back to the map. "Okay, we're agreed that we'll sneak up behind the barn, and hope Ruby will be able to read Dahlia from there."

Right, Mateo confirmed.

Yes. Can we go now? Ruby asked eagerly.

"It would be better to wait for the guys to get back."

Do we really need them? Ruby whined. *Who knows how long they'll be gone while tracking down rogue vamps? Besides, Dahlia might be asleep by that time, and I'll only be able to read her dreams.*

I glanced at Mateo for reassurance, but he didn't say anything, meaning he tacitly agreed with Ruby. "Let me call Sybil," I hedged, hoping she would back me up.

When Sybil answered, I told her the plan, then said, "We'll have to delay a bit as we wait for the guys to return."

"Are you sure? I had my people stake out her ranch and they reported it's essentially empty of people at the moment. You'll never have a better time to go than now."

Well, crap. "I don't know...." Charging in without backup seemed like a bad idea.

Mateo looked up at me, those big brown eyes pleading. *It does sound as though we shouldn't wait.*

I dithered, then realized this was one of those moments I'd been waiting for, where I could step up and prove I wasn't a wimp...even if I was. I took a deep breath. "Okay, we'll go," I said, ignoring the way my stomach churned like a rock tumbler.

"Good," Sybil said. "Text me when you're in place and I'll make the call."

"Okay," I said and hung up.

Mateo pushed his head under my hand. *Don't worry. I can protect you.*

Me, too, Ruby added enthusiastically.

I rubbed Mateo's ears. "You two are much better at this type of thing than I am. Maybe you two can go on your own?"

Nope, Ruby said. *We can't drive or text. We need you for that. C'mon, let's go. We can take one of Maurice's cars so we'll be less conspicuous.*

I guess my bumblebee Mini did stand out. Still, I hesitated. "Shouldn't we leave a note or something?"

Naw, we'll be back before them, I'm sure. We're only checking things out, right? Ruby said.

Yes, Mateo agreed. *We'll sneak in, Ruby will tell you when she can read Dahlia, then you'll notify Sybil. Once Sybil gets Dahlia thinking about what we need to know, Ruby can nip in and get the information from her mind.*

"You make it sound so easy."

It should be. Once we have the info we need, we'll come back here and wait for backup before we do anything else. He nudged me with his nose. *We won't engage with Dahlia, I promise.*

I wasn't as confident as these two were, but I changed into some dark clothes that made me feel like a cat burglar. Once I grabbed some bolt cutters and other tools we might need from Maurice's garage, I programmed Dahlia's address into the GPS and drove there.

Mateo watched out the window as we neared her spread. *There,* he said, his nose pointing to the right. *Take that road, though you might want to turn off the headlights first.*

No light? Which was worse—driving on an unfamiliar dirt road in the dark, or risk signaling everyone within miles around that we were here? I sighed heavily. Definitely the latter.

I turned the lights off and drove carefully down the access road Mateo had pointed out.

Stop, he said. *We'll go in through here.*

I reluctantly got out of the car and went to look at the fence. Sure enough, it looked like the bolt cutters I'd borrowed from Maurice's garage would cut through that. I squatted down next to the fence and held the tool in place. This was the moment of no return. "Are you sure this is the right spot?"

Yes, Mateo said, rubbing his head up against me. *Please, Ivy, this is the closest I've come to finding out what happened to me and how to reverse it.*

I hugged him around the neck. I'd become fond of him, and really wanted to help him. I just hoped this wouldn't be a washout.

You have nothing to worry about, Ruby said. *Come on, do it.*

"All right." I used the cutters to make an opening big enough for us to get through, then stashed the tool back in the car, then silenced my phone. But when I crawled through the hole, my hoodie caught on the cut wire, pulling it off my head.

Don't do this, one stone urged. *You have no idea what's going to happen.*

That's right, another said. *We might be able to help you fight magic, but we can do nothing against brute force.*

Wait a minute, a third one said. *We've got her back, right?*

They continued to argue, and the opal made no effort to stop their chattering, so I guessed it didn't care for this plan. When the bickering became too much to deal with, I muttered, "I have to do this," then shut them up by pulling the dark hoodie back over my head. Besides, I needed to cover my blond hair which would shine like a beacon in the dark.

Stay low, Mateo urged. *It will be harder to see any movement from the house. And don't say anything else out loud. Think it, and Ruby will relay it to me.*

Feeling like an idiot, I squatted down behind Mateo with my hand on his back, and, using him as a brace and a shield, I sort of duck-walked with them. It seemed to take forever, or so my complaining quads insisted, but we eventually arrived at the dilapidated barn.

Once we were all hunkered down, Mateo asked, *Can you hear Dahlia from here, Ruby?*

Yes, but she's watching TV, so that's all she's thinking about.

Just as we'd feared. Quickly, I texted Sybil to let her know we were in place.

The phone is ringing, Ruby said. *And she's picking it up. Sybil is asking Dahlia what her abilities are...and Dahlia refuses to tell her. She's rude.*

Did you get anything from her? I asked

She's definitely part mage demon and half shifter, but I can't get anything more.

Do you—

Shh, Ruby said sharply. *I need to concentrate.*

I felt restless, then realized there was something I could do. I texted Sybil to let her know what Ruby had found out.

There was silence for a few moments, then Ruby said, *Sybil is telling Dahlia one of her employees is stuck as a wolf, and asking if she knows anything about that.* Ruby gasped. *Boy, is Dahlia ticked off. She hung up after using some rather naughty words.*

But did you get anything else? Mateo asked.

Just that she's glad her plan worked, and soon, she'll have her revenge.

Well, that was—

Heads up! Mateo shouted in my head. *Someone is here. We'd better—*

Before Mateo could finish his sentence, three men were in front of us, moving so fast they had to be vampires. "You don't belong here. What are you doing here?" one demanded.

I froze.

Ruby said, *Tell them we went for a walk and got lost.*

A fast thinker she was not. Then again, neither was I. When we remained standing in gaping silence, one grabbed for each of us, and Mateo shouted *Run,* but it was too late.

They had some kind of net they used to grab Mateo and Ruby, and it wasn't as if I could escape from a vampire. The third one grabbed my arm and tugged me along.

"What do we do with them?" the second one asked. "Janus said to pick up Dahlia, not deal with trespassers on her property."

The third one snarled. "Dump them in the bunker for now and let her figure it out later."

Swiftly, they dragged us to a wooden door set flat

120

against the dirt. One opened it while the other two threw us in. Not gently, either. We dropped about eight feet, and I had to protect my head, but my shoulder hit some kind of shelf. *Ow!* Then they shut and bolted the door above us.

Crap. This was not good. I helped Mateo and Ruby free of the nets, and they were both spitting mad, but neither was hurt.

Check the door to see how tight it is, Mateo said.

I didn't have to worry about speaking out loud now. "How? I can't see a thing."

I can. Wolf senses, remember? There's a pull chain on the ceiling above us, next to the door. You can reach it. I'll guide you.

With Mateo giving me instructions on how to find the chain, I located it quickly, but was reluctant to pull it. "What if it's not connected to a light?" I had visions of triggering open a chute that sluiced water in to drown us.

It is attached to a light bulb, Mateo said patiently. *Just pull it.*

I did, cringing, but all it did was light the space we'd been tossed into. Hewn out of the dirt and rock, the space looked like someplace to stash a cache of secret weapons or something.

Don't worry about that now—check the door, Mateo said.

Carefully, I pushed the metal shelves beneath the door then used them to climb up. I pushed on the door, but I couldn't budge it. With a sigh, I dropped down to do a little more exploration. I didn't find any weapons or tools, but I did find a couple of cots and some MREs on the shelves.

I pulled out my phone and thought about calling Maurice or Ludwig, but they might be busy fighting those bad fledgling vamps, so I texted Sybil instead. Or, at least, I tried to. Unfortunately, my phone couldn't get a signal through all the earth around us. And when I pulled my hoodie down, I didn't sense enough rocks that could actually help.

What now? Sheesh. We might not starve to death, but since I didn't see another way out, we were stuck here until they released us. Dejected, I slumped down on one of the cots.

What's wrong? Mateo asked.

"I thought I could step up, be less timid and afraid, and really help you. Instead, we're locked up."

You're not at all timid, Mateo protested, snuggling up against me to lay his head on my lap. *You're one of the bravest people I know.*

I buried my hands in his lush, soft fur, which was remarkably soothing. "Yeah, right." It was nice of him to try to cheer me up, but the fact was, I wasn't of any use at all.

Bravery is not about fighting. It's about doing what's right, even when you're afraid. You feared meeting my pack, but you did it anyway.

Ruby nudged me with her nose. *Yeah, you even saved the day when you brought down those rocks in the pass.*

"Talking to rocks—such a great talent," I said with a roll of my eyes.

Mateo shouldered me. *You don't just talk to them; you persuade them to help you solve problems. Besides, didn't the seer tell you that you were the only one who could help me?*

"I think she was wrong—how can talking to rocks possibly help you?"

I don't know, but—

I have some good news, Ruby interrupted, though her voice was tentative.

"What's that?" I could use some right now.

I'm still close enough to read Dahlia. Aaaand...the bloodsuckers told her about us.

"How is that good news?" I asked in disbelief.

She's thinking she can't deal with us now. She'll do that after she takes her goblet to the Garden of the God with the vamps.

The goblet that Mateo had drunk from? A reprieve could be good news, but... "Isn't that where the guys went?"

Yes, Mateo confirmed.

I chewed my lip. "Maybe they'll take care of her?"

Ruby jumped to her feet. *Oh, no. She's gone to help Janus, thinking she's gonna suck the humanity from every supernatural she can—including those three.*

I exchanged glances with Mateo. Looks like we really had found our "witch."

"How can she do that?" I asked in bemusement. "By forcing everyone to drink from the goblet? I don't think that's possible."

No, Ruby said in sudden understanding. *The goblet's contents don't activate the mage demon spell—the goblet is just a setting for the real artifact.*

What is it? Mateo demanded.

It's an inset stone—a sapphire. Ruby looked at me in horror. *There's a soul-sucker demon imprisoned inside the stone—and she can make it remove the humanity from anyone two-souled.*

THIRTEEN

I STARED AT MATEO. "You didn't mention the goblet had a stone in it!"

I didn't know—I wasn't paying attention to the outside of the cup when I drank from it.

All of a sudden, the pieces clicked into place. Two-souled... Vamps, demons, and shifters all had two souls. I turned to Mateo. "So, if she removed Janus's humanity as well as yours..."

He would be pure vampire—pure evil.

No wonder they thought Janus was insane.

"And that must be what happened to the fire demon, too—Ludwig said Phineas acted like a full demon," I remembered.

So that's why Dahlia was at the compound, Ruby exclaimed.

"Yeah, she probably tested it on different supernaturals, to make sure it worked."

Why would she strip humanity from the vamps? Mateo asked. *They've done nothing to her.*

"That we know of. Besides, she may just be using them

to help get her revenge, not caring what happens to anyone else." I glanced at Mateo. "But why didn't you go mad like the other two?"

He shrugged. *Full vampires and demons are evil beings, so when you remove their humanity, they revert to their base, malevolent nature. Remove the human part of a shifter, and you have a wolf, not an evil being.*

That made sense. I snapped my fingers in sudden realization. "So her revenge will remove the humanity from all the supernaturals and turn them on each other." Not to mention any humans who got in the way. I gasped, remembering the prophecy. "Widespread bloodshed…"

Mateo jumped off the cot to pace in the small space. *That's what's going down tonight. We have to stop her!*

Ruby whined. *But what if she takes away your humanity, Ivy? I don't want you to be a big meanie!*

"We'll just have to make sure that doesn't happen," I said, sounding braver than I felt. "Besides, Tessa said I was the one who could stop it." *Oh, crap. I'm an idiot.* "Maybe I can convince the sapphire to make her stop."

I reached out, but Ruby said, *Too late. She's gone, and taken the goblet with her.*

Sure enough, the sapphire was too far away.

Frantic, Mateo whirled to face me. *Can your stones get us out of here?*

Screwing my face up in frustration, I said, "I don't think so. It's mostly dirt and grass here—not many rocks. But let me see what I can do."

Holding onto the opal, I pled for assistance. "Mr. Opal, do you see any rocks we can shift to help us get out of here?"

We can try, the opal said doubtfully.

Wait! Ruby cried out. *I hear someone.* She listened for a moment. *Oh, it's Kai! Kai, we're over here! Under the wooden door in the ground.*

Elation filled me, then worry. Would he be captured too?

I don't think anyone is left on the ranch except animals, Ruby said.

Soon, I heard scratching at the door, then the sound of the bolt being thrown and dirt sifting down as the door was opened.

Stan stared down at us, Kai's wolfy face beside him. "Are you okay?" Stan asked. "When Sybil lost touch with you, she asked us to check on you." I noticed all six of Mateo's friends were there—some in wolf form, some human, wearing their security uniforms.

"We're good," I assured him. "We just need to get out of here and get to the Chuckwagon Pavilion at the Garden of the Gods immediately. It's a matter of life and death."

The shifters exchanged worried glances. *That's where Endymion told us to meet him after ten tonight,* Kai said.

Is the whole pack going? Mateo asked urgently.

Most of us were called there, Kai said. *We're meeting to help the vamps and demons with a problem that threatens the city and the secret of our existence.*

"You have to stop them," I told them. "Dahlia is planning on ripping the humanity out of everyone who shows up."

"So we'd all be like Mateo—unable to shift to human?" Stan asked in horror.

"Worse," I assured him. "She also turns vamps and demons into pure evil, and she plans on setting you all against each other. You'd be lucky to leave with your lives."

You're sure about this? Kai asked. *Endymion wouldn't do this to his pack.*

"I'm sure," I said, and Mateo echoed me. "Endymion probably doesn't know what Dahlia really has planned."

Quickly, the shifters in human form pulled out their cell phones—all of them texting madly, though it might be too late to reach anyone in time.

Help us out of here, Mateo demanded.

Stan jumped down into the hole with us and helped Mateo and Ruby up, then picked me up and tossed me to Devon. I'd forgotten how strong these guys were.

As soon as I was out, my cell phone went nuts with notifications. Most of the messages confirmed the supernaturals were converging on the Garden of the Gods, and warning us to stay away.

Crap. They had no idea Dahlia was coming and what she was capable of. I tried calling, but everyone's phones went to voicemail. Hoping they'd check text messages, I quickly texted the guys and Sybil with what I knew.

"We have to stop Dahlia," I said urgently. "Come on, let's go." I hurried toward where we'd left the car.

"It's too dangerous for you," Stan said with a frown as he ran beside me.

"But I'm the only one who can stop her."

They don't believe you, Ruby said. *They think you're an animal communicator, remember?*

Oh, right. Quickly, I explained about Ruby being a hellhound and me being a rock demon/stone whisperer.

It's true, Mateo sent through Ruby. *And a seer foresaw that she's the only one who can stop this.*

How I could do that, I wasn't sure, but it must have something to do with that sapphire.

Luckily, Maurice's car was where we left it, and the shifters had parked behind me. Kai shifted back to human form and grabbed the keys from me. "I know where we're going," he said. "It'll be faster this way."

He got no argument from me. I checked the time on my phone. "It's almost ten now. How long will it take to get there?"

"Twenty or thirty minutes," Kai said, speeding down the dirt road like a madman.

We managed to avoid any cops and arrived at the park in twenty minutes. There was a parking area nearby, and we jumped out of the car, hearing screams and the sound of fighting.

Everyone ran toward the sounds. I hesitated for a moment, then realized I had to follow them if I wanted to help. The area was mostly hidden by huge rock formations on the east and west sides, and when we neared, I didn't see a pavilion, but there was a large paving-stone circle between the formations, partially bounded by a short stone wall.

Most of the fighting was there. Demons, vamps, and shifters indiscriminately ripped into each other with teeth, claws, water, fire, and many other things I didn't care to identify.

No! I wasn't made for this. Cringing, my heart pounding, I stayed back, out of the way, looking for Dahlia, but I couldn't spot her in the pandemonium.

A vampire rushed me, and I screamed, but one of the wolves with me barreled into him, and another staked him through the heart.

Oh, my God. I'm going to be sick.

You can't be sick yet, Ruby yelped. *Dahlia is here and she's using the stone! Follow me!*

"We'll protect you," Kai said as I ran after Ruby.

Ruby yelled to everyone who could hear her, *Get out of here! Dahlia is stripping the humanity from everyone.*

Some of them paused at Ruby's yell and she continued, *She's up on that huge gray boulder across from the opening. Get her down from there—she can only use the spell through line of sight.*

Immediately, plants stretched up to snatch Dahlia's ankles, and water slammed her off her perch—Sybil and Ludwig in action, no doubt. Dahlia landed on the other side of the rock where I couldn't see her. Mateo took off running, and I darted after him.

You all stay here, Mateo told his friends grimly. *She can't do anything more to me.* He dashed around the rock.

I couldn't let him go alone! I rounded the rock and crouched down to avoid flying dirt, fire, water, and other missiles. Luckily, not many of the combatants had made it to this side of the boulder. Ruby stood beside me, and Mateo's shifter friends stood guard, keeping anyone on the other side of the rock from getting near me.

Dahlia was down, but not out. The fall may have knocked the wind out of her, but she was gasping for breath. Her gaze narrowed on me, and she reached for the goblet, words forming on her lips.

I froze.

Do something, Ruby yelled, *or she'll rip out your soul too!*

That galvanized me. I lowered my hoodie but immediately cringed. I couldn't even hear my stones—just the agony of the sapphire screaming and wailing. It was so overwhelming, I fell to the ground clutching my head. *This is too hard. I can't do this. She's going to take my soul!*

Mateo, stop her! Ruby screeched, her words cutting through my pain. A moment later, Ruby said, *Whoa! Mateo just ripped Dahlia's throat out.*

The shifters around me cheered, and Mateo rushed over to drop the bloody goblet next to me. *She's dead, but it didn't reverse the spell,* he said in desperation.

Ivy, do something, Ruby yelled.

Please, Ivy, Mateo begged. *We need you. I need you.*

Crap. I couldn't let him down. Grasping the opal for help, I fought, moment by moment, through the sapphire's pain and anguish in an attempt to reach it. "I can help you," I gasped out.

No one can help me, it sobbed.

Bracing against the onslaught of its fear and suffering, I said. "I *can*. What is causing your pain?"

So many souls...trapped inside.

I could feel the pulsing anguish of the stone—the souls had to be in agony as well. "How do I release them?"

Reverse the spell....

"How?" I asked urgently.

Fighting through its torment, the sapphire told me haltingly how to reverse the spell. *First, don't...touch me yourself. Ensure the...spellcaster's blood is...on my facets.*

I examined the goblet. "It is!" Mateo had made sure of that.

Stare into me and...say "I release you"...three times...in succession.

I gazed into the blood-covered stone and said quickly, "I release you. I release you. I release you!"

Immediately, I felt the relief of the stone as dozens of wispy souls rushed from it, blowing past me.

One of the wisps surged into Mateo. He erupted into a bright light, then abruptly turned into a man with dark, wild curly hair and a bushy beard.

"Mateo," Kai exclaimed, and embraced him.

Thank heavens—it worked!

Human Mateo looked very confused and disoriented. "What happened? Where am I?"

"Later, man. We have work to do." As I tried to calm the pounding in my head, Kai clambered up the rock to Dahlia's former perch and crouched to peer down at the battle. "Some people are confused like Mateo, but many are still fighting," he yelled down.

Guess I wasn't done yet. I couldn't compel everyone, but maybe I could reason with them. "Can you amplify my voice?" I asked the opal.

Consider it done.

I felt the opal's energy surging through me, seeking an outlet. "Stop," I boomed. "There is no more need to fight. Everyone's humanity has been restored. There are no more enemies here." Ruby reinforced the message with the demons and shifters in human form.

It took a few moments, but the leaders understood what was going on immediately, and got their people under control. But the sapphire still sobbed uncontrollably.

"What's wrong?" I asked it. "Aren't all the souls gone?"

It calmed itself down as much as it could, but misery still pulsed through it. *All but one...the soul-snatcher demon that the...mage demon locked inside me. There is no way to...separate us, and we no longer want to...exist. Please, end us.*

Horrified, I could do nothing but gape.

It is for their good and the greater good, the opal agreed. *End them.*

"How?"

Break the stone.

I picked the goblet up carefully by its stem and rose to my feet. Shutting my mind against the waste of it all, I smashed the stone into the large boulder. It took a few hits, but with the opal's help, I finally felt the stone break and expire with one last whispered, *Thank you.* The throbbing in my own head ratcheted way down, and I was grateful the stone and soul-snatcher demon were finally at peace.

Sybil and Ludwig stared at me. They were bruised and beaten, but seemed fine.

"It's done now," I explained, feeling a bit shaky. "The stone can never be used to pull someone's humanity again." I wiped a tear away. "I'm so glad you two are all right."

"I'm sorry we stayed out of sight," Ludwig said. "But we wouldn't have been any use to you if our souls were ripped out. You were very brave to face her."

"Stupid, more like," I muttered.

No, brave, Ruby insisted.

Sybil nodded and glanced at Ruby. "Thank you for pointing out where Dahlia was—that helped tremendously."

"Your help was very timely," I told them. "You really caught her off-guard." Shaking my head, I asked what I really wanted to know. "How is everyone else?"

Sybil frowned. "Some demons, shifters, and vamps alike died, and many are injured."

"Anyone I know?"

Ludwig nodded. "Rex is dead and Billy was mortally wounded."

No! My hand flew to my mouth. "Billy's dying?"

"Maurice is bringing him over now, to his second life," Ludwig explained. "The vampire board agreed, and Maurice thinks it's not too late."

God, I hoped so. I looked around. "Where's Mateo?"

He's not in wolf form, so I can't hear him anymore, Ruby lamented.

"The shifters took him," Ludwig said.

Without even saying goodbye? I wondered if I looked as stricken as I felt.

"He is very confused right now," Sybil explained gently, "and may not remember you."

For some reason, that horrified me more than anything. With my brain muddled and my head pounding, I asked Sybil, "What happens now?"

She sighed heavily. "Tonight, we will remove the bodies, take care of the wounded, alter the memories of any humans who observed us, and return the area to as close to normal as we can." She patted my hand. "It would have been worse, if not for you. Thank you."

Ludwig nodded. "If you hadn't restored their souls, they would have moved on to take out the human population. Widespread bloodshed averted."

Well, I did something right, after all.

You did everything right! Ruby said.

With a great deal of help—yours especially, I told her.

Yeah, I rock. Even more than Fang!

Sybil continued, "I will call a convocation tomorrow night with all interested parties to sort out what happened. We'll need you there to tell your part of the story. Are you up for that?"

"Of course." It would be easy, compared to everything else.

The danger was past, my mission complete. So why did it feel so...empty?

CHAPTER
FOURTEEN

WE ALL MET the next evening at the security compound since it was secure, the demons and shifters were familiar with it, and the vampires were guaranteed safe passage. That made for quite a large group: the vampire board, Sybil and her councilors, and the five shifter elders along with the witnesses. The only place big enough to hold everyone was the cafeteria. It didn't exactly have the look of a court, especially with the scorch marks Phineas had left in it, but it certainly felt like it.

Ruby and I sat with the underground members, and when the shifters came in, I looked for Mateo. But since I'd only caught a glimpse of his wild-man human form, it was hard to identify him.

That's him, Ruby said. *In the blue shirt.*

Oh. *Oh!* I saw now why Luana had pursued him. He was a handsome wolf, but in human form, he was even better-looking than I imagined. He looked to be a little older than me, and was tall and lean with broad shoulders. He'd cut his hair so it wasn't quite so wild, and shaved the scraggly beard off to reveal dimples and a generous smile.

He was very involved with his friends and the elders, and didn't even look my way. Did he know I was here? Did he even remember me?

I glanced at Ruby, but she shook her head. *I don't know —I can only talk to him when he's in wolf form.*

Okay, thanks. Please refrain from talking to anyone else during the convocation unless it's absolutely necessary. We'll need to concentrate.

Since Sybil hosted the meeting, she called it to order once everyone was there. She introduced Bartholomew as the representative of the vampires, and a white-haired gentleman named Silas who represented the shifter elders.

"We have called this convocation to learn the truth about the events that led up to the battle last night," Sybil announced.

Bartholomew asked, "How will we know what we hear is the truth?"

It might sound belligerent, but he had a point. If Endymion could spout his lies without fear of being called out, this would be of no use.

"I can tell truth from lies," I blurted out.

Everyone turned to stare at me.

"I mean, one of my stones can. The emerald." I held out my right hand to show them the square-cut emerald ring on my middle finger.

"And how does that work?" Bartholomew asked gravely.

Good question. "Uh... With my opal's amplification I can..." Quickly, I consulted the opal. "I can have the emerald pulse with light when it detects a lie."

One of Bartholomew's fellow board members leaned forward. "That is consistent with what I have learned about rock demons," she said.

My eyebrows raised. So she'd checked up on me, had she?

She continued, "But everyone will need to be able to see it. Will it work if you removed it from your hand?"

I nodded, and one of Sybil's demons rounded up a white cloth napkin which he placed on a small table in the center where everyone could see it.

I placed the ring there. "Please," I said, "make a statement and the emerald will respond...or not." I concentrated on sending energy from the opal to the emerald. It was rather pleased to be the center of attention.

Deadpan, Bartholomew said, "I am a shifter."

The emerald pulsed in the negative once, in a bright enough light everyone could see it.

"How do we know you are not controlling the light yourself?" the doubting vampire asked.

I shrugged. "Make a series of statements that I don't know the answer to and verify for yourself."

The vampire made a series of random statements.

The emerald said, *True, true, false, true, true, true, false, true.* A pulse of light accompanied each detected falsehood, luckily strong enough that everyone could see it.

"I am satisfied with that," Bartholomew said, and almost everyone else nodded as well.

After that, Sybil asked me to describe the prophecy I had received, and I explained how I came to my conclusion that Mateo was the one I needed to help. Mateo then took up his tale and explained what Rex and Endymion had done to him. Not once did the emerald flash.

Silas turned to Endymion. "Explain your part in this."

The alpha glared at the emerald, but apparently tried to brazen it out. "Mateo lies."

False! The emerald chuckled and flashed.

Scowling, Silas said, "Tell us your version of what happened."

"I—" Endymion started, then stopped and I could see the calculation in his eyes. "We judged Mateo to be a threat." No flash. "He was rising in the security company too quickly, and was interfering in Rex's courtship of my sister. We feared he was making a move to take over the pack."

Again, no flash. *He believes what he's saying,* the emerald confirmed.

Silas frowned and crossed his arms. "So, why did you take action yourself, instead of bringing your grievances before the elder council?"

"We judged the threat to be too...imminent," Endymion said. When the emerald didn't flash, he continued more confidently, "He posed an imminent threat to the entire pack."

Liar, liar, pants on fire. Whoa—big flash there.

The elder raised an eyebrow. "To the entire pack or to just you two?"

Endymion scowled. "Okay, to Rex and me, but we are what's best for the pack."

Apparently, he believed that as well.

Silas nodded. "So, according to Mateo's testimony, you decided to use your half-sister Dahlia's ability to remove the humanity from two-souled beings, and his was ripped away from him when he touched the sapphire."

The alpha winced but said, "Yes."

"And you then told everyone you didn't know why he couldn't shift and that he had lost the favor of our goddess. Is that right?"

"Yes," he said in a smaller voice. "But it was for the good of the pack."

His pants are burning.… The emerald didn't flare quite so brightly this time, but it did flash.

"Thank you," the elder said and nodded to Mateo's friends who now had the alpha surrounded. Endymion looked annoyed, but made no effort to escape. Maybe he hoped he would be free from retribution as the alpha.

Silas nodded to the vampires. "I understand the mage demon used the goblet against one of your people first?"

Bartholomew nodded. "Janus, can you explain what happened to you?"

With apparent relief, Janus recounted his story. Dahlia's ranch was running on a very thin margin and she was losing her employees to other, more successful ranches. Her business was about to fail, the banks wouldn't loan her any money, and she blamed the demons and shifters for putting her in that position, so she went to Janus for financial help. "When I refused," Janus continued, "she shrugged and offered me a drink."

"From the goblet?" Bartholomew clarified.

"Yes. I figured, why not? But when I took it, I felt this horrible sundering as it ripped out my human soul." He closed his eyes in what looked like pain. "I…I no longer had any humanity remaining, and I'm afraid I did things I wasn't proud of. I am deeply sorry for my actions while a full vampire." He seemed extremely remorseful, and the emerald confirmed he was telling the truth.

Phineas, who had been unfrozen after they realized he was no longer a full demon, explained he'd been stripped of his soul when he tried to stop Dahlia from entering the compound. It appeared she was testing her abilities to see how they worked on demons.

Sybil then asked me to recount what had happened

after we had learned exactly what Dahlia was. I did my best to tell it accurately and succinctly.

Kai, Owen, Mateo, Sybil, and Ludwig added what they knew, and Bartholomew nodded. "It appears Janus, Mateo, and Phineas were not responsible for their actions while under the influence of the loss of their humanity."

Hey, Ruby protested to me only. *Mateo didn't do anything wrong.*

I know. Shh.

"So," Bartholomew said, "I propose the three of them be exempt from retribution for their actions during that time."

"We concur," Sybil said immediately.

"As do we," Silas said. "And we will restore Mateo's standing in the pack and return him to the pack bonds."

Mateo grinned in relief, and his friends pounded him on the back in congratulations.

Silas looked around at the four other elders and they seemed to have some sort of silent conversation. "However, Endymion and Rex put us all in jeopardy with their selfish actions and lies. Rex has paid the ultimate price, but Endymion must be punished commensurate with his crimes. He will therefore be removed from the pack bonds and banished from the pack, never to return."

Endymion looked devastated, but the rest of the pack present—mostly Mateo's friends—seemed very pleased by this verdict.

"The pack will await the emergence of a new alpha. Until then, the elder council will be in control." Silas's face softened and he turned toward me. "In addition, in appreciation for all you have done, we now declare you, Ivy Weiss, and your companion Ruby to be friends of the pack."

Several gasps went up around the room and I glanced around in confusion.

Sybil says this is unprecedented, Ruby said quickly, *and a huge honor. Accept, accept!*

I bowed to him. "Thank you so much for this incredible privilege. We are honored to accept."

Bartholomew spoke again. "I agree. We have much to thank you for, young demon," he said to me. "You have our respect, and may call upon us in your time of need."

Whoa, Ruby said. *That flabbergasted Sybil too. We're dripping in honors. Take that, Fang!*

Sybil added, "The Demon Underground also appreciates your bravery and dedication. In return, we'd like to invite you stay with our organization and have a seat on our council."

Nope, too much. "But I don't want to be a councilor, and I'm not planning on staying," I protested.

Sybil looked surprised, but Bartholomew said, "We are sorry to hear that," before anyone could protest. "Does anyone have anything to add before we bring this convocation to an end?"

I'm afraid I do, Ruby said with a sigh.

Huh?

Sybil passed on Ruby's comment to the vampires and shifters. Silas nodded at Kai, who shifted immediately so he could hear Ruby's thoughts and pass them on to the rest of the pack.

"I'll let you know what she has to say," Sybil told Bartholomew.

Ruby sighed. *Well, you see, when you were all fighting, I was inside Dahlia's head, and I learned a few things.*

She paused, and I gave her an encouraging nod.

Aster, Dahlia's mother, was part mage demon and had the ability to capture a demon's soul and imprison it in a gemstone. Anyone who touched the stone—like Mateo and Janus—was affected, but Dahlia could also use a spell to activate it within her line of sight, which is probably what she did to Phineas.

When Sybil translated, Bartholomew said, "We knew this."

Yeah, but though Dahlia wasn't strong enough to capture demons in gemstones herself, she did think about all the other demons her mother had imprisoned in other stones.

A gasp went around the room, and more than one gaze darted to the emerald, which didn't flash. The questions came thick and fast.

"How many demons? How many stones?"

"Where are they?"

"What can they do?"

I don't know, Ruby said with a whine. *That's all I heard from her before she...died.*

"Ivy, we need you to locate these spelled stones and negate them," Sybil said urgently. "What will it take to convince you to stay?"

Torn, I didn't know what to say.

"Can I speak to her alone?" Mateo asked.

Sybil raised an eyebrow at me in question.

"Uh, sure," I said. But though I was very comfortable with the wolf part of Mateo, this very hunky human side of him made me a bit unsettled.

He pulled me aside into another room, and immediately drew me into a fierce hug. I tentatively returned it, and when he let go, I said, "What was that for?"

He cupped my face in his large hands. "I'm so sorry I was out of it after the battle and didn't know who you were." His human voice was the same lovely whiskey-roughened baritone as his mental voice. "Once my souls reintegrated, I was able to recall everything you did for me. I owe you so much."

"No, you don't—"

"I do," he said, interrupting me. "I owe you everything. We all do. And it appears we need you more than ever. Please, won't you stay?"

"I don't really have a job here, no place to live..."

He snorted. "We'll employ you to find those stones, and help you with whatever else you need—you know that. And you won't be wanting for friends. Everyone will want to get to know the famous stone whisperer who saved the day. We need you."

My face heated. Move again? "I don't know...."

Let's do it, Ruby said, eagerly eavesdropping from the other side of the door. *You wanted to be of more use to the underground. They really need us here. And they love us. They want us.*

Mateo chuckled, a deep rich sound I'd love to hear more of, and squeezed my shoulders. "Ruby wants to stay, doesn't she?"

"Yes, how did you know?"

"Just a guess, seeing your expression and knowing Ruby. Please stay?" he asked. "I'd love to get to know you better, and let you get to know the human side of Mateo."

I gulped. Tempting...

What would keep you in San Antonio? Ruby asked me.

Well, I had friends there, sure, but I'd made friends here too, and earned a lot of respect. I could probably move my jewelry business here easily, and they really did need someone here to track down those rogue gemstones.

Plus you like the climate here, and you reeeally want to get to know Mateo better, Ruby snarked.

Oh, crap. There went the hot face again. Thank goodness human Mateo couldn't hear that. And she wasn't wrong. That decided me. "Okay, I'll stay."

"I'm so glad." Mateo enveloped me in a hug again.

Ruby pushed open the door to bounce around the two of us. *Yay! That calls for a high paw.*

Laughing, I obliged her.

She must have passed on the news because more demons and shifters surged into the room to hug me, elated by my decision.

Those evil stones won't know what hit them, Ruby crowed. *We're gonna take this town by storm!*

Well, we'd try anyway.

Deleted Scene Offer

I originally had alternating points of view with Val and Ivy, so if you're interested in seeing the original first scene from Val's point of view, you can get it at
dl.bookfunnel.com/j1pmlhfysp!

DIAMONDS &
DECEIT

CHAPTER
ONE

LUANA STOOD, arms crossed and face scowling, in the doorway of Dahlia's bedroom. "So, Ivy, have you located any cursed stones yet?" the wolf shifter asked belligerently.

I sighed inwardly and looked up from where I was searching Dahlia's nightstand. I stifled the retort I really wanted to make, and forced myself to be polite. "No, no cursed stones yet," I said.

I wished I'd find something soon, but I'd had no luck so far. And, truth be told, it felt kind of skeevy going through Dahlia's things.

Why skeevy? Ruby, my hellhound companion, asked. *She's dead. It's not like she's going to care.*

Sure, though she certainly would have objected if she was still around. But since Dahlia had left all her worldly goods to her half-sister, Luana, she had reluctantly given us permission to search her ranch for cursed stones. I had a feeling the shifter elder council had insisted.

"Then what good are you?" Luana bit out. "Aren't you supposed to be the famous stone whisperer?"

I was, but I hadn't sensed any stones at all in Dahlia's ranch house, which seemed rather odd.

Sybil, the head of the Demon Underground—the DU—in Colorado Springs, swept in. "That's enough, Luana," she said. "Weren't you searching the kitchen?" Luana huffed and stalked off, and Sybil looked at me apologetically. "She's hurting and taking it out on you."

"I know." Luana blamed me for her brother Endymion's disgrace, though he'd brought it on himself by using the soul-stealing sapphire to try to get rid of Mateo. All I did was use my emerald's truth-telling ability to determine that Endymion was lying. His own actions had gotten him banished from the Pikes Peak Pack, not me.

Ruby snorted. *Luana's also jealous that Mateo likes you better than her.*

Stop that. Mateo and I are just friends. I hadn't seen much of him in the three weeks since Endymion had been sentenced and Mateo had been restored to the pack. It seemed he had a lot to catch up on after being stuck as a wolf for so long without the ability to shift. Not that he owed me anything, but I was hoping I'd found a friend here in Colorado Springs.

Besides, Luana had nothing to be jealous of—she was the personification of femininity, with her long dark hair and curvy body. She made me, with my short blond wispy hair and slender frame, look pretty ordinary.

My gemstones muttered insults about Luana to each other and to me, until Mr. Opal shushed them.

Another voice came from the doorway—my new friend Ren. "Hey, Sybil, you wanted me in here?" Part electro demon, Ren was short, with a mop of curly light brown hair, and a positive, upbeat attitude. Thanks to Sybil putting us together, she was also my new roommate, in an apartment downtown that allowed dogs.

"Yes. You take the closet," Sybil told Ren, "and I'll take the dresser."

"Okay," Ren said. "What are we looking for?"

Sybil opened a dresser drawer. "Stones. Dahlia's mother captured demons in gemstones, and we need to find the cursed stones before they can do any damage. Unfortunately, we don't know what gemstones she used or what demons are in them. So, let us know if you find any artifacts or clues to where they might be." She shot Ren a warning glance. "But if you find a stone, don't touch it. Let Ivy take a look first."

"Okay."

There was nothing in this nightstand, so I started searching the one on the other side of the bed.

About five minutes later, Ren turned from the closet, a large shoebox in her hand. "This was on the floor, hidden under some clothes at the back of the closet," she said breathlessly. "Like she was trying to hide it. Think it's important?"

Oh, yeah, Ruby said. *Open it.*

Ren laid the box down on the bed, and the rest of us crowded close as she lifted the lid, revealing a journal and a heart-shaped rose quartz pendant on a silver chain.

A stone? Why hadn't I sensed it?

Maybe it's not real? Ruby said.

Maybe. My abilities only worked on gemstones that had been cut and polished.

Yeah, Ruby said. *Unless the opal powers you up, and then you can convince big ol' rocks to make a landslide for you.*

Only once, I told her. *And I was pretty desperate at the time.* Who knew if I'd ever be able to do it again?

I touched the stone gingerly, but didn't feel anything, so I picked it up. It was a genuine rose quartz, so I should be able to read it. *Hmm.*

As Ren flipped through the journal, Sybil peered at the pendant in my hand. "Is it dangerous?"

"Uh, I don't know. This is very strange."

"How so?" Sybil asked.

"I should be able to get a sense of the stone, but there's nothing there." It felt like a void where the stone should be.

Yeah, it's like it's in hiding, one of my stones said.

"Nothing?" Sybil said.

"Well, there is sort of something, but it's hard to describe. It's like the essence of the stone is blocked—hidden or occluded by something else."

"Something like a demon?" Sybil asked with a raised eyebrow.

"Maybe," I said hesitantly. "But the cursed sapphire didn't feel like this at all."

"Why do you think that is?"

I shrugged. "I don't know."

"But if you had to guess?" Sybil insisted.

"Uh, maybe they have to be activated somehow, like by a spell or something?"

"No," Ren said in excitement. "Not a spell, but the person who touches the stone has to be in desperate circumstances before the demon will activate. Until then, it's inert."

"How—" Sybil began.

"It's in the journal," Ren said, holding the book out with a grin. "This whole thing is about what Dahlia learned about her mother's cursed stones."

Sybil all but snatched the book from Ren's hands. She skimmed the passage quickly. "You're right," she said, beaming. "The vampires and shifters will be glad to know we've made some progress. I'll call a meeting right away. This should help you immensely, Ivy."

It might—if we could actually find the cursed stones.

TWO NIGHTS LATER, I joined the representatives of the shifters, vampires, and demons at the security compound for the meeting Sybil had called. Luana was there with the shifters, clutching Mateo's arm. He gave her a tight smile, then removed her hands from around his bicep. Luana glared as he headed toward me.

Woo-hoo, Ruby caroled. *If looks could kill, you'd be dead, dead, dead.*

I shrugged. I wasn't responsible for Luana's misconceptions.

Mateo crossed the room and gave me a hug. "It's been too long," he said. "How have you been?"

Ooh, he huuuuugged you, Ruby said.

Stop that. He hugs everyone—it's the kind of guy he is.

Everyone but Luana, Ruby snarked.

That probably had something to do with the way Luana wouldn't stop fondling him. *Stop trying to 'ship us. We're friends—nothing more.*

To Mateo, I said, "I'm good. The DU in San Antonio shipped my stuff, and I've found an awesome roommate and an apartment." Maurice, the vampire we'd stayed with, would have let us continue to live with him, but with a newly turned vampire in residence, he didn't think it would be safe for either of us—Billy might not be able to control his blood lust yet, and drinking my demon blood would make him—or any vampire—insane. "I still need a place to consign my jewelry, but I haven't talked to anyone yet, though I have a few leads. How about you?"

"I've just about caught up with everything I missed." He grimaced. "It's been a bit busy with the new alpha."

That's right—I'd heard the shifters used something similar to the ritual demons used to get the pack's consensus on who the new leader should be. "Who is it? Is he here?"

Mateo nodded. "The pack chose Duncan Alexander. That's him—talking to Silas."

I glanced over. The stern-looking Native American looked to be in his mid-forties and was built like a tank. Seeing he was wearing turquoise stones, I lowered my hoodie to see what I could get from them. The impression they gave me was of someone with strength and integrity along with a no-nonsense attitude. "Seems like a good choice."

Mateo chuckled. "Yeah, luckily, the pack went with substance and experience over flash and youth this time. I think he'll be great for—"

"It's time," Sybil said, calling the meeting to order. Mateo gave me a small smile and mouthed "Later" before returning to the group of shifters. I noticed he stayed far away from Luana, which made me smile.

Sybil explained that we had found Dahlia's journal and learned that her mother and her mage demon ancestors had created quite a number of cursed "artifacts" over many decades, entrapping demons who had ticked them off or gotten in their way. Mostly, they kept their collection hidden, and each generation had added to it over the years.

"Collection?" Bartholomew, the vampire spokesman, said in distaste. "How many are there?"

"I'm getting to that," Sybil said. "Since Dahlia's mage

demon powers were very weak, she couldn't create any artifacts herself. And, perhaps because Dahlia was still so young when her mother was killed, she never learned how they were created...or even the true nature of the collection."

"Then how did Dahlia use the soul-stealing sapphire?" Duncan asked.

"At first, she had no idea that the stones were cursed or what they could do," Sybil explained. "The stones have to be activated by the desperation of the person holding them before the demon's powers will be functional. Dahlia learned that when she feared losing the ranch and accidentally activated the sapphire. Her mage demon powers, though weak, allowed her to communicate with the demon in the stone and learn how to use it. She put the rest together with bits and pieces of things she remembered her mother saying over the years."

"Did she say how many other stones she activated?" Bartholomew asked.

"She doesn't say she activated any others. Apparently, it only works if the captive demon's abilities would help alleviate the situation the person is desperate about."

Duncan relaxed. "Then we must simply ensure the rest of the collection is never activated."

Sybil winced, and here was the part I'd been dreading. "Unfortunately, we don't know where the rest of the collection is," Sybil began. She waited until the inevitable cursing and exclamations died down. "Or how many there are. Before she learned what they could really do, she had sold off most of the artifacts to fund her failing ranch, thinking only of the monetary value of the gemstones and their settings."

"Who'd she sell them to?" Duncan demanded.

"She didn't record that in her journal," Sybil said.

I grimaced. Obviously, she hadn't intended to reclaim them, so she hadn't kept any records.

Bartholomew's jaw tightened. "So, let me get this straight. You don't know how many cursed stores are out there in general circulation, you don't know what devastating abilities they might have in the wrong hands, you don't know who she sold them to, and you don't know how many have been activated. Is that correct?"

Well, Ruby said. *When you put it like that, it doesn't sound so good.*

Sybil squared her shoulders. "Yes, that's correct."

Bartholomew turned to me. "Do you even know how to destroy or deactivate them if they are put to use?"

I raised my chin. "Not yet."

Everyone frowned at that.

Hey, Ruby protested. *She's already helped your people, not only with getting rid of the cursed sapphire, but with helping you learn the truth about what that stupid alpha started. What do you want? Perfection?*

Of course, the shifters and vampires didn't hear that, and neither Sybil nor I repeated it.

Duncan regarded me steadily. "What *do* you know?"

I'd gained self-confidence from recent events, so I was able to answer with assurance. "We know Dahlia sold the stones locally, so I can start checking pawnshops, jewelers, and other places to see if we can recover what she sold. Plus, we did find one unactivated stone in her house." Apparently, she knew the rose quartz pendant wouldn't be worth much. "I can experiment to see what I need to do to remove the cursed demon from it. And we do know the stones aren't dangerous unless they're activated."

"Unfortunately, we don't know when a desperate

person will randomly activate one, now do we?" Bartholomew bit out.

"No, we don't," I conceded, remaining calm despite his attitude. "Since we would have to deal with the fallout if someone did activate one and you haven't seen that yet, I'm going under the assumption it can only be activated by a part demon, maybe a shifter or vampire. But I'll do my best to find the artifacts and make sure they can't harm anyone." Though, since she'd been selling them over the past five years or so, it wouldn't exactly be easy.

"Let us all hope your best is good enough," Duncan said with a sigh.

My sentiments exactly. I gave a curt nod as Mateo gave me a sympathetic look.

Bartholomew and his contingent stormed out of the meeting, and some of the shifters left as well.

I glanced at Sybil, unsure if I should stay or go.

The wolf shifter alpha stepped forward. "Ms. Weiss, may we speak with you privately?"

"Uh, sure. But please, call me Ivy."

He nodded then raised a questioning eyebrow at Sybil, who said, "Let's talk in my office."

I followed her, wondering what this was about.

Nothing to worry about, Ruby assured me. *Sybil's thinking about an assignment for you.*

Oh, excellent. Relentless Protection Services had contracted me as a consultant, and they hadn't used me for anything beyond searching the ranch for the cursed stones so far. I was eager to be of use.

Once we were seated in Sybil's office, she introduced me to Duncan, then said, "You know that Relentless Protection Services is a joint demon and shifter operation?"

I nodded. I'd learned in the past few weeks that Sybil

served as the RPS Office Security Manager. The pack alpha, now Duncan, was the Chief of Security, with both demon and shifter field security managers reporting to him.

"Well, one of our security guard jobs just went south." Sybil grimaced. "I'll let Duncan explain the rest."

Duncan turned to face me. "We have guards on duty at the Stratton Art Museum, and there has recently been a theft on our watch. Though the police are looking into it, they are baffled, and are looking at our people as suspects."

"So, you want me to use my emerald to see if they are telling the truth?" I ventured.

"Not exactly," Duncan said. "The stolen items came from a traveling exhibit of Edwardian jewelry."

Puzzled, I said, "I'm not sure I follow. If they were stolen, I won't be able to hear them unless they are within fifty feet or so. Do you think you know where the thief stashed them?"

"No, but there are other jewelry pieces remaining that might be able to...er, tell you what happened."

Ruby cackled. *Whining, self-centered gemstones as witnesses to a crime. This oughta be good.*

Hey, a couple of my gemstones protested, but were quickly brought in line by Mr. Opal.

I bit back a smile. "I can't promise anything, but I'd be happy to try."

He nodded. "Thank you. You'll be working with the field manager who supervised the guard who was on duty during the theft—Mateo Duran."

"Oh, good. I know Mateo."

Duncan regarded me thoughtfully. "I understand you and Mateo are...close?"

What was he implying? "We're friends," I said sharply. "After all, I proved his innocence and the guilt of your former alpha when no one else even tried to learn the truth."

Duncan's eyebrows raised, but he said only, "That is good. Inter-species relationships can be...problematic, as Dahlia and her mother learned."

True, they had been ostracized by both demons and shifters after Dahlia had been outed as part shifter, part demon. But I wasn't planning on having the man's baby, for heaven's sake. "We're friends," I repeated. "Nothing more."

Duncan sighed. "I'm glad to hear it. Mateo is well-liked and an excellent employee. I'd hate to see his reputation tarnished again."

Did he really just imply a relationship with me would tarnish Mateo's reputation? That was just insulting.

Before I could say anything, Ruby said, *Unfortunately, Sybil agrees. And he'd tarnish yours within the DU.*

Words spewed out before I could stop them. "Perhaps you two should look at overcoming prejudices within your organizations. Maybe Dahlia wouldn't have been so desperate if she'd had someone to ask for help."

Duncan frowned as Sybil winced. "You may be right," she said. "We'll talk about it."

Duncan stood, indicating the meeting was at an end. "Mateo will introduce you to our contact in the police department tomorrow, and you can take it from there."

"Of course," I said stiffly. And if I could do it without pissing off Mateo's alpha, even better.

CHAPTER
TWO

THE NEXT DAY, Ren gave Ruby and me a ride to the security compound where the guard at the gate directed us to Mateo's office. He was talking to a slender black man who looked to be a few years older than me.

Mateo gave me a big smile. "Come in, Ivy," he said warmly. "I was just telling Derek about you. He's our contact on the police force. Derek Thompson, meet Ivy Weiss and her hellhound Ruby." He turned to me. "You remember Veronica Thompson, the empath demon?"

I nodded. We'd met her in the search for Dahlia.

"Derek is her son."

I shook his hand and glanced at his baseball cap. "So your hat...?"

He smiled. "My abilities are only about half as strong as hers, so I don't have as much need for shielding, but the hat does have some silk and silver inside, just in case emotions get too strong."

"I see. So, does everyone in the police department know about supernaturals?"

"No, not at all. Just those of us in the Special Crimes

Unit. I understand there's a unit with the same name in San Antonio where you came from."

I nodded as Ruby said, *So you're like the Lt. Ramirez of Colorado Springs?*

Derek gaped at my hellhound. "Wow—you're right, Mateo. She really can talk." He shook his head and answered her. "Uh, no. My *boss* would be Lt. Ramirez's counterpart. We're called in whenever there appear to be supernaturals involved in a crime."

"His abilities come in handy in interviewing suspects, since he can sense emotion," Mateo told me, then turned to Derek. "And since Ivy can talk to gemstones, she should be able to get an idea of what happened by talking to the jewelry that wasn't taken."

I smiled. "Don't oversell my abilities, Mateo. I have no idea if I can help or not."

"It's worth a shot," Derek said. "I can get you in the exhibit where the jewels were stolen to see if you can learn anything."

Me too? Ruby asked eagerly.

Derek glanced at her skeptically. "I don't think dogs are allowed in the museum."

"How about as a K-9 sniffer?" Mateo suggested. "Or maybe as an assistance dog?"

"I don't know..."

I can provide lots of assistance, Ruby said eagerly. *I can spot vamps, demons, and shifters, and pass private messages between you and Ivy so no one else can hear. Not Mateo, though, unless he's in wolf form.*

Derek thought for a moment, then nodded. "Okay, then. You sold me. Let's go with making you a service dog. It would be easier than trying to pass you off as a certified K-9."

Yay! Ruby exclaimed, bouncing up to give me a lick on the hand. *I can go!*

I petted her head, smoothing down her ever-present feathery mohawk. "But you have to behave, or no one will believe you're a trained service dog," I warned her.

I can do that!

"I'll get her registered as an assistance dog," Mateo said, "and we have extra vests. I think we have one in your size." At my questioning look, he added, "Sometimes we shifters pose as service dogs, so we have the gear. She'll also need a leash and harness."

Oh, of course. Before Ruby could say anything. I gave her a stern look. "That won't be a problem."

Well, if I have to... Ruby whined.

You do.

Mateo got Ruby fitted out while Derek made arrangements to visit the museum, then the four of us headed there.

The Stratton Art Museum was an older two-story brick building that blended in nicely with the lovely old Victorian homes around it. Derek parked in their lot, saying, "They asked us to come in through the side entrance." He took off his hat as he entered the building. I wasn't sure if it was to be polite, or so he could read the woman and two men who met us inside.

A bit of both, Ruby said, sitting politely and doing her best to act like a trained service dog.

Derek introduced the white-haired woman as Mrs. Honeycutt, the museum director, and the middle-aged dark-haired man as curator Phillip Horvath. The blond man who appeared to be in his mid-thirties was assistant curator Chad Nowicki. "You know Mateo Duran. And this is Ivy Weiss, our consultant, and her assistance dog, Ruby."

"Consultant on what?" Horvath asked.

"Stolen gems," Derek said blithely, and no one even questioned that whopper.

Hey, you're an expert on gems, whether they're stolen or not, Ruby said.

Okay, I could see that. Since Ren had made me some simple business cards with my name, phone number, and "Gemstones Consultant" printed on them, I handed them each one.

Mrs. Honeycutt escorted us in. "We've temporarily closed the Edwardian jewelry exhibit as you requested. Have you learned anything about who might have done this?"

"Not yet," Derek said.

She nodded in resignation, but Horvath looked irritated. "Well, at least we're insured," he snapped. "You wanted to see the scene of the crime again?"

Derek nodded. "We do."

Horvath turned to the assistant curator. "Chad, can you show them to the area and answer any questions about the exhibit?"

"Of course," Chad said. "Follow me."

He didn't look happy about playing tour guide, probably because we were dumped on him as the lowest ranking person of the three. As Chad unlocked the door, I asked him, "What can you tell me about what happened?"

"I don't know much," Chad said. "Last night, someone broke in and stole about a dozen pieces from the Edwardian jewelry exhibit. No alarms went off, and there was nothing on the surveillance recordings. Seems like someone had inside knowledge." He cast a suspicious glance at Mateo. "Ask him," he said pointedly. "His people might know something."

Mateo raised his eyebrows but didn't respond to that blatant accusation.

"We're looking into everything and everyone," Derek assured him. "Though we have no reason to suspect the security company."

I glanced around. There were obviously some pieces missing in the exhibit, but I didn't see any damage that indicated a break-in. Not exactly a smash-and-grab.

Derek wants to know if you've learned anything yet, Ruby said privately.

Not yet with my hood still up. Can you ask him to get rid of Chad so we can talk freely?

Sure.

Derek glanced at Ruby then gave me a tip of the head. "Mr. Nowicki, while Ms. Weiss looks around, could you provide her with photos of the missing items?" When Chad took out his phone, Derek added, "She'll need hard copies, please."

Chad grimaced. "Okay, but it'll take some time to print them."

"No problem. We'll be here for a while yet."

When Chad left, I pulled my hood down and crossed to the bow-shaped brooch near the empty spots where the stolen jewelry had been displayed. It was made up of a couple dozen small diamonds in a pavé setting. Multiple gemstones set together in one piece like this tended to speak in unison, like an alien hive mind or a Greek chorus. Especially when they were all the same kind of stone, like these. When there was more than one kind of stone in a piece, like the sapphire and diamond swan brooch, there was often discordance and sometimes disagreement.

That's why solitaires are superior, my garnet said. *We speak our own minds.*

Yeah. Often to my annoyance. Luckily, the jewelry pieces were silent, mellow.

The garnet hurrumphed, but the stones fell silent when Mr. Opal reminded them I was working.

I addressed the stones in the bow, speaking aloud so both Derek and Mateo could hear. "There were several pieces of jewelry stolen from here the other night. Can you describe who took them?"

No, they chorused.

I shook my head at Derek. Then, facing the stones again, I asked, "Did you see or hear anything out of place during that period?"

Again, the response was negative. I asked the other pieces but got the same answers.

Derek frowned. "Ask if they heard anyone talking about stealing them."

I grinned. "They heard your question, and their answer is no—all they heard was everyone commenting how stunning and beautiful they were." Except one annoying man who made disparaging remarks—they all hated him.

Do any of you know anything else? Mr. Opal asked.

It was a little difficult to decipher when all the jewelry pieces spoke at once, but they all agreed. "They said one moment the jewelry pieces were there, the next they were gone, and they couldn't hear them anymore."

Mateo frowned. "That tracks with what I saw on the recording."

"Were they all gone at once, or one at a time?" I asked.

"One at a time. What could do that?" Mateo asked. "A shifter isn't fast enough, but a vamp might be."

Derek shook his head. "I doubt a vamp could move fast enough that they'd be almost invisible, which was what happened here."

"Some kind of invisible demon then?" Mateo suggested. "Or one who can teleport?"

"Maybe," Derek said. "I'll see what kind of info Sybil has on demon abilities. It does seem as though some kind of supe was responsible, which is why the SCU is investigating."

How can soup steal something? Ruby asked in bafflement.

Derek grinned. "Supe is short for supernatural. Were any of the people you met today supes, Ruby?"

Only you guys. The museum people are all human.

Chad came back then and gave me printouts of the stolen items. The ink was obviously running out on his printer, but I could still make out the pieces well enough.

"Could I take a look at the surveillance tapes?" I asked him. I wasn't sure what good it would do, but I hadn't been useful so far, so why not try?

"Of course," Chad said and escorted us to the security room. "But there aren't any tapes—it's all digital."

I looked through the photos of the missing pieces on the way.

"See anything interesting?" Mateo asked.

"Just that the stolen pieces all had larger stones in them. The ones they didn't take have smaller stones."

"That makes sense," Derek said. "The thief likely wants to break them apart and sell the stones, so they'd naturally want the larger ones. The pieces would be too recognizable to sell as is, unless they have a private buyer for them. But I don't really think there's a big demand for Edwardian jewelry among the art fanciers who purchase stolen goods. At least I don't think so. Is there, Chad?"

"I wouldn't know," Chad said stiffly.

Chad left us at the security room, muttering something

about having to get back to work. Mateo introduced us to Hank, the beefy security guard on duty.

Shifter, Ruby told me privately.

"Hank was on duty when the stones were stolen," Mateo told me.

Hank crossed his arms and glared at us. "I didn't do it."

I checked with my emerald. *Truth.*

"We didn't think you did," Mateo said soothingly. "Can you show Ivy the recording for the evening of the burglary?"

Hank relaxed and cued it up. The camera view was from a corner in the large room, so it didn't have a lot of detail, but just as Mateo said, the missing pieces each disappeared one by one, simply vanishing from the recording.

"Is there any time missing?" Derek asked.

"Not according to the time hacks," Hank said as we continued to watch.

Wait. What was that? "I think I saw something... Can you play it again?" I asked. "Slower?"

Hank did as I asked.

"Stop there."

"Did you see something?" Derek asked eagerly.

"Maybe a flicker, right before that emerald ring disappears."

Derek leaned closer. "Hank, back up and play that again, frame by frame."

When Hank did, I gasped when a figure appeared for one frame. "There—that's the thief," I exclaimed in excitement.

"Yeah," Mateo said, peering at it. "Too bad it's too far away and fuzzy to make out."

Derek sighed. "We have a copy back at the station. I'll see if we can clean up the image."

"Could a vampire move that fast?" I asked dubiously.

Derek shook his head. "I don't think so. Plus, don't forget they'd have to get past the alarms. Speed won't help with that."

Mateo nodded. "It might be an inside job, with help from someone on the staff. Did you get any vibes from the people we met?"

Derek shrugged. "I didn't get much from the three of them. Irritation, primarily, and worry, but that could be because of how the theft impacts the museum and their reputation."

And probably their jobs. I didn't need to be an empath to figure that out.

Derek glanced at Mateo. "Did any of your guards hear or see anything unusual over the past couple of weeks or so while you were on duty?"

"Not that I know of," Mateo said, then noticed Hank's grimace. "Did you?"

"Well," Hank said, scratching his head. "I saw something weird, but I don't think it has anything to do with the theft."

"What was it?" Derek asked.

"Last Tuesday, I was coming in to work when I smelled something...off, outside."

With his shifter nose, I imagined he smelled all sorts of funky things.

"I assume you investigated?" Mateo said.

Hank nodded. "There was a paper bag with three white mice in it—dead."

"Weird," I agreed. Especially since field mice were usually brown or gray. They must have been purchased at a pet store.

"Actually, that wasn't the weird part. Each one had a

puncture wound in the back of its head." He glanced at us, puzzled. "Do you know of any kind of mouse trap that would do that?"

I shuddered at the thought. *Ew, ick.*

"No, I don't," Derek said. "And you're right. It's strange, but it doesn't seem to relate to the case."

Mateo scowled. "Now what? It doesn't look like we're any farther along."

"Well, folks," Derek said. "It looks like we have a real mystery on our hands."

CHAPTER
THREE

DEREK DROVE us back to the compound, saying he was going to do some digging on all the employees at the museum to check their alibis, their backgrounds and possible motives, and whether or not they associated with any supes who had the ability to pull this off.

After Derek dropped us off, I followed Mateo. He texted someone then ushered me into his office.

I sank into the chair next to his desk. "I'm sorry I was no help."

"No help?" He tapped his chin. "Let me see...you gave me back my humanity, identified the guy who cursed me, then saved the entire city and beyond from widespread bloodshed. That's more than helpful. I'd say that makes you a hero."

My bestie is a hero! Ruby said proudly.

I felt my cheeks heat. "Well, I haven't done anything lately," I said lamely.

"You spotted that image on the video, remember? Plus we wouldn't have hired you if we didn't think you'd be useful." He snapped his fingers. "That reminds me—I'm also your field supervisor for anything to do with the cursed stones. Have you had any progress there?"

"Not really. I tried cleansing the rose quartz to see if that would separate the stone and the captured demon, but it did nothing." In fact, I'd tried as many things as I could think of with no luck. "My parents might have more ideas. They're hard to reach since they're constantly traveling, but I left a message on their cell phones. They're not fans of technology, but I'm hoping they'll check their messages soon and call me back so I can see if they have any advice."

Mateo nodded. "Luana mentioned you had a problem sensing the stones at Dahlia's house?" When I frowned, he added, "I know she can be...difficult at times, so I wasn't sure how truthful she was. Are you able to sense the cursed stones if they haven't been activated?"

"I couldn't at first, because something suppressed the stone's awareness—I assume it's the trapped demon. But I've been experimenting, and I know what an unactivated cursed stone feels like now—kind of like a void I can sense. There's a physical limit, though. I have to be within a hundred feet or so before I can sense it."

"Well, you're still the only one who can," he reminded me. "So we definitely need you. I also asked Ren to use her mojo on Dahlia's laptop to see if—"

A knock on the door interrupted him, and Ren stuck her head inside. "You wanted to see me?"

"Yes," Mateo said with a grin. "Perfect timing. Come on in."

Ren slid into a chair and grinned at me. "Hey, roomie."

"You two are roommates?" Mateo asked, looking between us.

Me too, Ruby piped up, pushing her nose into Mateo's knee.

Mateo said, "I mean, you three?" as he scratched Ruby's ears. He knew her well enough to know exactly what Ruby would say, even if he couldn't hear her in his human form.

"Yeah," Ren said. "Sybil introduced us, and it's worked out great."

"Glad to hear you're settling in," Mateo told me with a smile. "Ren, what did you find on Dahlia's laptop?"

Ren grimaced. "Not much. Apparently, she wasn't very computer savvy. I didn't find accounts on any sale sites, except for those she bought ranch equipment and supplies from. In fact, it appears that's all she used her laptop for—running the ranch." She shrugged. "I'll keep looking, but I pretty much scoured the thing, and found nothing so far."

"Thanks for trying," Mateo said. "Now, about our other case..." He detailed the facts of the museum heist. "Ivy noticed a brief flicker of the thief in the recording. Derek is having his people look at it, but can you see if you can get an image we can use?"

"Sure."

"Good. I'll email you a copy. And can you check Sybil's database for any part-demons with powers such as invisibility or teleportation—something that would allow the thief to remain virtually unseen?"

Ren shrugged. "I can, but remember, the database only lists those here in the Springs who have registered with us, and other organizations we have reciprocal agreements with, mostly in Colorado."

"Yeah, I know, but it's a start."

"Okay," Ren said. "I'll get started on that now."

After she left, I grinned at Mateo. "Do you have an assignment for me, too, boss?"

He chuckled. "Since Dahlia wasn't very tech-savvy, she probably used jewelry stores or pawnshops to sell the artifacts. We didn't find any pawn tickets, but we wouldn't have if she sold them outright. Can you visit some to see if you can sense any of the stones?"

"Sure, but the journal indicates she sold them over a period of several years. They might not be there anymore."

He sighed. "I know, but I don't know where else to start."

"Okay. what do I do if I find one? Buy it?"

"No—just notify me, and I'll take care of retrieving it. I'll have Ren send us a list of the stores in the area." He checked his watch. "While we wait, want to get lunch at the cafeteria?"

"Sounds like a plan."

Yay! Ruby enthused and bounced eagerly as we headed out.

"Ruby's excited about eating at the cafeteria?" Mateo asked quizzically as he texted Ren.

"I think it's because they have pizza—her favorite." Just like Fang.

"Is that good for her?"

I arched my eyebrow at him. "She's part demon hell-hound, so she can eat anything we do. Is it okay for shifters to eat pizza?"

He chuckled. "Point taken." He bowed toward Ruby with his hand over his heart. "I apologize. I wasn't thinking."

No biggie, Ruby said and jumped up to lick his hand.

Mateo scratched her head. "I take it I'm forgiven?"

"Yep."

We went through the line, where I got a sandwich for myself and pizza for Ruby, then cut up her meal and set it on the floor next to our table.

Mateo dug into his substantial meal, then said, "While

you're at the pawnshops, you could also ask about loose stones, in case the museum thief decided to pawn or sell them."

Me? "I'm not sure..."

"What's wrong?"

"I've never actually...interrogated anyone. I'm not sure how."

He laughed. "It's not an interrogation—more of a dialogue." Seeing my uncertainty, he added, "Tell you what. I'll come with you this afternoon and show you how it's done. Will that work?"

I sighed in relief. "Yes, thank you."

He put his hand over mine. "Don't worry. You'll do fine."

I felt my face flush. "I hope so."

He pulled his hand away and frowned at a shifter at another table.

"What's wrong?"

"Nothing," Mateo said shortly. "Just ignorance."

Oh. He must have heard something through the pack bonds. I glanced at the person he'd frowned at and saw the man glaring at me. *Ah, I see.* "Your alpha warned me that people might not like...seeing us together. There's prejudice against...inter-species relationships."

"He said something to you?" Mateo asked in disbelief.

"Yeah, more of a warning to stay with my own kind. It wasn't just him—Sybil thought so, too. Duncan mentioned how Dahlia and her mother were ostracized."

Mateo blew out a breath. "I can't believe this. First, it's none of their business. Second, this is the twenty-first century. Surely people are more open-minded these days."

I shrugged. Apparently not.

"Besides," Mateo said, "I've been told I flirt with everyone. They should know we're just friends."

"And that's what I told them."

"Good." He reached for my hand again, then pulled back as if he thought better of it. Scowling, he said, "Well, I'm not going to do anything differently just because they have their heads up their rearends." He grabbed my hand again and squeezed it firmly.

Good for you, Ruby exclaimed, while still wolfing down her pizza.

"Ruby approves, and so do I," I said with a grin.

We ignored the people around us and finished our meal. Ren had emailed both of us the list of pawnshops in the area, sorting them by distance from the ranch.

"I rode in with Ren today, so I don't have my car with me," I told Mateo.

"No problem—we'll take a company SUV and I'll take you home afterward."

We headed toward the black SUV, and when we got in, he programmed the first address in the GPS. "With any luck, Dahlia will have sold them all at the first place and we'll find them there."

"Do you really think we'll be that lucky?"

He chuckled. "No, it's more likely she had to go to more than one, to avoid nosy questions if nothing else."

Can I go in, too? Ruby asked. *I've never seen a pawnshop.*

Neither have I, but you'll have to wear your vest and leash, I told her. *And since you're supposed to be my assistance dog, no wandering off.*

She pouted, but conceded it was necessary.

When we reached the first pawnshop, Mateo shrugged off his uniform shirt and belt, and tossed a button-up shirt over his T-shirt. When he caught my curious gaze, he said, "Might make them more willing to talk."

I nodded and put the leash on Ruby, then made sure my hood was down. There were a couple of customers inside—a teenager looking at musical instruments and a skinny little guy who poked around the electronics. Mateo headed toward the person at the counter—a heavyset bald man—and chatted him up. The only stones I sensed were in the case at the glass counter, so I joined Mateo and gazed down at them. Some were whining and others were sulking or missing their owners, but none had that distinctive void feeling.

Mateo slid an arm around my waist. "See anything you like, hon?"

Understanding it was just part of the game, I didn't react to his unexpected affection. Good thing no other shifters were around. When I shook my head, Mateo spoke to the man at the counter. "We're looking for some items sold by Dahlia Deveraux. Do you recall if she sold you anything over the past few years? The items would have all had gemstones set in them."

The man's expression, which had been open and friendly, turned suspicious. "Why? Did she steal them?"

"No, nothing like that," Mateo reassured him with a smile. "She had the right to sell them, but she's passed on, so she can't tell us what she did with them. They were family heirlooms, and the family would like the opportunity to buy them back if possible. Do you keep records?"

The guy relaxed. "We record all transactions in the LeadsOnline database that the police can access, but that information is private."

"Would the records show who you sold them to?" I asked.

"Yes, but again, that's confidential. I'm sorry, I can't help you."

"We understand," Mateo said with a smile. He squeezed my waist and smiled at me. "My girlfriend here is also looking for loose stones that she can set into her own unique jewelry." He gestured at my multiple gemstone rings. "Like the ones she's wearing. Do you get many of those?"

"Not many," the man said. "Just the few you see here."

Playing my part, I shook my head. "I don't see what I want." I handed the man one of my cards. "I'm looking for all kinds of loose stones. If you get any more in, could you call me?"

The man took my card and smiled, but made no promises.

Mateo squeezed my waist. "Okay, sweetie, let's try somewhere else."

"Sure, pookie, let's do that," I said wryly.

Ruby snorted in amusement and Mateo couldn't hide his grin as we left, with his hand at the small of my back.

"Pookie?" Mateo said when we got outside.

I snorted. "Well, you called me hon and sweetie. I figured you deserved a pet name, too."

He laughed. "Fair enough."

When we got in the SUV, I belted myself in and asked, "Do you think Derek could search that database?"

Mateo programmed the next destination into the GPS. "I imagine he could, but I'm not sure he would. The cursed stones aren't connected to any cases he's actively working, and I imagine it's tedious work. But now that we know there's a database, maybe there's something Ren could do."

"True." My smart roomie was something of a hacker.

"But only you can search for the stones' presence. You ready for the next pawnshop?"

"Sure."

We visited four more, getting varying levels of helpfulness and suspicion, but none of them would provide seller or buyer information, and I didn't sense any telltale voids or stolen gems.

After the fifth one, Mateo checked his watch. "Shall we call it a day? It's past quitting time."

"Sure. Ren should be home by now, too, so we can tell her about the database." I gave him the address.

"Good idea." He drove us home and parked in front of our first-floor apartment.

Ruby ran to the door and pawed at it. *Hurry. Ren's upset.*

"Something's wrong," I told Mateo and unlocked the door.

Ren rushed toward us, obviously flustered. She held out a trembling hand and pointed to the dining room table. "I —I found that when I got home. It was stabbed in the door with your business card."

What the heck? I leaned over to read the note and gasped.

I know who you are and where you live. Back off before someone gets hurt.

CHAPTER
FOUR

MY GEMSTONES BURST INTO HYSTERICS, expressing outrage, fear for me, and panic about what would happen to them if something happened to me. I couldn't think with all that noise, so I tossed my hood over my head and reveled in blessed silence.

Strangely, I wasn't afraid—just pissed off.

You should be, Ruby said indignantly. *How dare they!*

His expression grim, Mateo pulled out his phone and punched in a number. "Derek? We have a situation. Ivy has received a threat, and it may be related to the museum burglary." He listened for a moment, then gave Derek our address and hung up. "He'll be here right away," he told us.

Even though Ren was upset, she'd had the presence of mind to wrap the handle of the cheap pocketknife in a plastic baggie before she removed it from the door. Smart.

"Would you mind moving it to the floor, Ren?" Mateo asked.

"No problem," Ren assured him.

Why...?

But my question was answered when a bright light suddenly filled the apartment and Mateo shifted into his wolf form, his clothes transforming with him.

Mateo! Ruby exclaimed. *Oh, good. Now we can talk. I've been wanting to—*

"Not now," I told her, and pulled her back so she didn't jump all over him. "He's working."

We can talk later, Mateo assured her. He put his nose down and sniffed the note, card, and knife thoroughly. Ruby mimicked him.

"Do you know who left it?" Ren asked.

I don't know the scent, Mateo said. *It's faint, but I think I'll be able to recognize it if I smell it again.*

Me, too! Ruby said.

Ren stared at him, her mouth open. "How did I hear his voice in my head? I'm not part of the pack."

"No, but you're part of Ruby's pack," I told her. "She's able to share Mateo's thoughts with us when he's in wolf form, and ours with him."

Ren grinned. "That's a great trick."

It's 'cause I'm special, Ruby said smugly. *Not even Fang knows how to do that.*

A knock came at the door, and Mateo poofed back into his human form.

It was Derek. "That was fast," Mateo said.

Derek shrugged. "I was close by. What happened?"

Ren answered him. "When I got home, shortly after five, I found that note stabbed into our door, along with the card. I removed it from the door so it wouldn't scare anyone, but I didn't touch anything, I swear."

"I sniffed it," Mateo added, "but it's no one I've scented before."

Me either, Ruby added.

Derek nodded. "Thank you. Do you have a paper bag?" Ren gave him one and he carefully put the items in it. "Show me where you found it?"

Ren opened the front door and pointed to a small split in the wood, right about the center of the door. "Right here."

Derek examined the location and took a photo, then mimed stabbing with an overhand grip. "Judging from the placement, the person who put it there was about my height, maybe a little shorter." He glanced at me. "Any idea who might have done it?"

"Not really." Who would want to hurt me?

"They used your business card. Do you remember who all you gave your cards to?"

"Oh, that's easy. Ren just gave me the cards this morning, and I only gave them to the pawnshop people we met today...and to the three people we met at the museum."

Derek eyed Mateo. "So, when you said you thought it was related to the museum, that's what you meant?"

Mateo shook his head. "Not necessarily. We visited five pawnshops looking for cursed stones, but we also asked about loose ones. So, it might be about the museum theft, but could be about Dahlia's artifacts."

Derek nodded, apparently having been read in on that situation as well. "Did either of you sense any animosity from anyone you met today?"

I shook my head. I was too busy paying attention to the stones.

"Not really," Mateo said. "But I can give you the names of the shops we visited if you want to check them out."

Derek sighed. "Yeah, I'll do that."

"What have you learned so far?" Mateo asked.

Derek paused, and I realized we were all still hovering in the doorway. "Oh, I'm an idiot," I said with a facepalm. "Please, come in, sit down." I waved them to seats in the living room and offered them drinks, but they declined.

Ren joined us and Derek glanced doubtfully at her.

Mateo said, "Ren is an RPS employee and familiar with the case. I asked her to look at the image Ivy found on the recording. Any luck, Ren?"

She shook her head. "The outline of a man showed up on a frame or two right before each piece was stolen, but though I enhanced the image, I couldn't find any defining features other than general height and body type."

"Neither did we," Derek confirmed. "I did check alibis on the museum personnel. Of the three Ivy gave cards to, Honeycutt was at a charity event and Nowicki's roommate confirms he was at home. Horvath says he was home alone, but we're unable to confirm that. Everyone else at the museum had alibis except for one of the janitors, and, given his advanced age, I doubt he had anything to do with it." He shook his head. "But this threat to Ivy doesn't seem like something any of those three would do."

Yeah, I couldn't imagine prim and proper Mrs. Honeycutt stabbing a cheap knife into a door. But since Horvath didn't have an alibi, he was still a suspect—for the theft, at least. He was taller than Derek, so the location of the stab didn't add up, though it didn't rule him out.

Mateo frowned. "Just in case, let's not visit any more pawnshops for a while, okay, Ivy?"

Yet another delay in finding the stones…. But I saw his point. I sighed heavily. "Yeah, okay. But why would they threaten me?"

Derek answered. "I'm not sure if this is about the cursed

stones or the museum theft, but either way, they obviously think you are getting close to something."

"That kind of makes sense," I acknowledged. "But isn't that exactly why we *should* check out more pawnshops?"

"The police, yes," Mateo said. "You, no. Not until we're sure it's safe." He turned back to Derek. "Are any of them acquainted with a supe who could have helped them?"

"That's difficult to discern without revealing ourselves, but we are checking into their known associates."

Yeah, I guessed asking humans straight out if they had demon, vamp, or shifter friends was out of the question.

Derek shrugged. "I haven't found anyone yet. But we'd like to review the recordings from the last few weeks before the theft to see if we recognize any supes checking out the exhibit."

"Do you have the resources for that?" Mateo asked.

Derek shook his head. "Not really, especially with people who are able to spot a supe."

I can do that, Ruby said eagerly.

"You can recognize a supe from a photo?" I asked her. I didn't think that was possible.

Oh. Ruby huffed in disappointment. *I can't do that.*

"I can, though," Ren said. "I can do facial recognition on everyone who passed through, and compare them to our demon and shifter personnel files. I don't have any for the vamps, but they'd only visit in the evening anyway."

Mateo appeared doubtful "Will you have time to do that?"

"Sure," Ren said, beaming. "Sybil said the museum theft and the cursed stones have priority over everything else, so I'm all yours."

"That would be great," Derek said with a smile. "I have permission to deputize you, Mateo, given our reduced staffing and the great working relationship with RPS, so I'll send you the recordings and you can pass them on to Ren." He paused, his hands on his knees. "If there's nothing else...?"

Mateo rose. "Not right now. Thank you for coming so quickly. We'll keep you posted on anything we find, and I hope you'll do the same for us."

Derek nodded and shook Mateo's hand, then Ren's and mine. "Be careful, Ivy, and let me know if you get any more threats."

"I will," I assured him.

Ruby cozied up to me and rubbed her chin on my leg. *I'll protect you.*

I know. It was surprisingly comforting.

After Derek left, Ren asked Mateo, "Are you staying for dinner?"

He glanced at his watch. "No, I guess I'd better be going. Ivy, can you come see me first thing tomorrow, and wear workout clothes?"

"Uh, sure. Why?"

He grinned. "If you're going to be in danger, you need to work on self-defense."

"But—"

"See you tomorrow," he said firmly, then gave Ren and I a hug and Ruby a pat on the head.

Annoying. As the door closed behind him, I asked, "Did *you* have to learn self-defense?" I asked Ren.

"Nope," she said. "I'm only in the office, not out in the field." She opened the refrigerator. "Leftover lasagna good for you?"

Yes! Ruby exclaimed.

Smiling, I said, "Sure. But why should I learn self-defense? I'm no Val Shapiro."

182

You don't need to be, Ruby assured me. *After all, you have me.*

"Who's Val Shapiro?" Ren asked as she put our meal in the microwave.

"She's the Paladin for the underground in San Antonio —part succubus demon with supercharged speed and strength. There's no way I can fight like her."

"No, but maybe Mateo can show you a few tricks."

"We'll see." But I really didn't want to do it at all.

Pout much? Ruby snarked.

Oh, hush.

I SHOWED up at work in yoga pants and a T-shirt as Mateo requested, along with my ever-present hoodie, but hoped I wouldn't have to go through with learning self-defense moves. In fact, I'd come up with a plan to avoid it entirely.

I knocked on his office doorjamb, noticing he was already dressed down in sweatpants and a T-shirt that stretched tightly across his broad shoulders. I could see why Luana had a thing for him.

He smiled at me. "Right on time. Come on, let's hit the gym. I've reserved a room."

The shifters and demons who worked security had to stay in shape, so the company had a gym onsite for them to work out in. He led me to a smallish room that was pretty much covered in soft, spongey mats. Well, crap. It looked like he intended for me to become up close and personal with the floor—definitely *not* in my plan.

Ruby lay down in a corner and Mateo placed his phone near her, jokingly telling her to guard it. When he closed the door, I said, "Look, I really don't want to do this. I don't think it's necessary."

He frowned and moved to the middle of the room, shaking his arms out. "But you've been threatened. Don't you want to be able to defend yourself?"

I didn't want to *have* to defend myself. Wasn't that what Ruby was for?

You got it, bestie, Ruby enthused.

I shrugged. "I'm a lover, not a fighter."

He grinned at that. "Well, I don't think an attacker is going to let you love them to death, so maybe learn to fight back a little to protect yourself?"

I sighed heavily. "Seriously, what could I do against a shifter or a vampire? Or even against a demon with an offensive power?"

"Not much," he admitted, "but the person targeting you is probably a garden-variety human. Let me show you a few moves."

He stepped forward, but I held out my hand to stop him. "I already have my own defenses against humans."

He glanced at Ruby. "Your hellhound may not always be around..."

"I didn't mean just her, though she is a heck of a weapon."

You betcha, Ruby said with satisfaction.

"I also have my stones."

He raised an eyebrow at me. "What? You'll throw them at your attacker?"

"No," I said in exasperation. "Remember this?" I twisted my quartz and cinnabar silver cuff bracelet.

"Yeah...?"

Apparently not. "I guess a demonstration is in order. Ruby, you ready for this?"

Yep.

Good. Do it like we practiced.

I clutched the bracelet tighter. I didn't really need to, but it made it easier to concentrate. "Okay, come toward me," I told Mateo. When he did, I shoved the opal's amplification energy through the stones in the cuff and yelled, "Freeze!"

His eyes widened as he went rigid, his muscles straining. Ruby leapt up, pushing her nose into the crease of his thigh.

Casually, I said, "Ruby just ripped off your gonads as I ran away."

Another minute later, and he burst out of the frozen position. He rubbed his hand over his face. "Okay, that might be effective. But how long does it last?"

"Judging by how it affected you, about two minutes right now, but I've been working on lengthening it."

"With who?" he asked incredulously.

"With Ren. It doesn't work as well on her since she's part demon, but, as you can see, it works much better on shifters in human form and probably even better on full humans." Before he could protest, I added, "I know it wouldn't work on other supes, but you can't teach me anything that would help with them, anyway, right?"

He didn't seem to want to agree with me, but he had no choice. He chewed his lip. "I'm worried about your safety," he admitted.

I stepped forward to squeeze his arm. "I know, but don't you think I'd be better off finding stones to help me rather than learning how to hit someone with my puny fists?"

"Maybe. Have you found other stones to help?"

"Well, I haven't looked yet, but I'm pretty familiar with

the natural abilities of most stones, so it's just a matter of figuring out which combinations of gemstones would help, then trying it with the help of Mr. Opal. He's pretty smart."

"Okay," Mateo said. "Let's do it now."

"Right now?"

"Why not?" He hesitated for a moment, then said, "I want to help. I need to make sure you're safe."

Suddenly, a light blinded me, and Mateo was a wolf.

This way I can hear what the opal says, too, he told me. At my surprised look, he added, *Sit down, get comfortable.*

I sank to a sitting position on the mat, and Mateo did the same, saying, *Okay, ask the opal.*

"I'm not sure what to ask."

But Mr. Opal didn't need me to say anything. *I have been thinking about the possibility of creating a protective shield,* he said.

"You have?" I didn't realize Mr. Opal did that kind of stuff on his own.

Yes. Amethysts and citrines are powerful protection stones. Of course, opals are mighty protectors ourselves, but combine my amplification ability and your vast untapped power along with that of a larger, stronger amethyst and citrine, and I believe you'd be able to construct a protective shield and repel negative forces.

I had vast power? Where the heck was it hiding?

Awesome! Ruby exclaimed.

How would it work? Mateo asked.

We won't know for sure unless we have the stones in place, the opal said.

The other stones muttered in protest, especially my current amethyst and citrine, until the opal reminded them it was for their protection as well. That shut them up.

So, you need to find larger stones? Mateo asked.

"Apparently. The opal can help me find the right ones. But I'm not supposed to go to pawnshops or jewelry stores, right?"

Right. Mateo thought for a moment. *Didn't Billy help you find your other stones in a rock shop or new age store?*

"Yes, that's right."

They should be okay to visit.

"Okay, we'll do that."

Weird how Mateo sounded the same now whether he was in human or wolf form. His wolf had sounded so different when his human side had gone missing.

Mateo's phone rang then, and he transformed back into his human form to answer it. "Duran here." He listened for a moment, then said, "Can't you tell me over the phone?" The answer must have been negative, because he said, "Okay. I'll meet you on your break."

He hung up and said, "That was Hank. He's learned something he thinks might help with the museum case and wants to talk in person about it."

"Okay, I'll just go—"

"Nope. Until you get better at using your stones for self-defense, you need a bodyguard."

"I don't think—"

"No argument. You've been threatened, and we can't have our assets compromised."

Well, when he put it that way… "Okay. Who will guard me?" I hoped it wasn't Luana.

"Me, for now. I need to change and get some work done before I meet Hank this afternoon. You have some research you can do here?"

"Yeah, I can check with Ren to see if she's made any progress. Maybe call around to see if anyone has an amethyst and citrine."

"Good. Then, when I go to see Hank, you can either stay here or come with me to the museum."

The museum, Ruby said eagerly.

I sighed. "Okay. Let me know when you're ready to go."

"Sounds good. Let's catch a thief."

CHAPTER
FIVE

I CHANGED out of the workout wear I thankfully hadn't needed and found Ren in her cubicle. "Hi, Ren." I slumped down in her guest chair.

"How'd the training go?" she asked.

"Luckily, I talked him out of it, but I need to find a couple of large stones to see if they can help shield me. Can you get me info on local rock shops and new age stores?"

"Sure—I'll email it to you. But what about the threat?"

We've been benched, Ruby told her. *Mateo thinks I can't protect her well enough.*

"I'm sure that's not the case," Ren protested.

"It's not," I assured them both. "He's just being overly cautious, so he wants to be my bodyguard until the threat is over."

Ren raised an eyebrow with a smirk. "Oh, he wants to guard your *body*."

Yeah, girl, Ruby enthused. *You know it.*

Embarrassed, I said, "Oh, hush. He just wants to protect an RPS asset." Though it was interesting that Ren didn't seem offended by the thought of us together. Before they could argue with me, I said, "Any progress on the museum case?"

"Not yet. Derek sent over the recordings of all the museum visitors for the last few weeks, and I'm running facial recognition against our database, but it'll take a while before I have results, if any."

"Okay, let me—"

My phone rang, and I said, "I need to take this. It's my Mom." I went out into the hallway to talk. "Mom, thank you for calling me back."

"Hello, darling. I have your father here, too, and we're on speaker. Our friend showed us how to do that."

"Can you hear me too?" Dad asked.

"Yes, I can. Where are you now?"

"We're in Antwerp, helping to identify blood diamonds," Mom said.

Yikes. I couldn't imagine the pain a blood diamond would emit. "That sounds horrible."

"We're coping," Dad said. "We got your message. How can we help?"

I explained about the soul-stealing demon I'd released from the sapphire. "The stone was in so much pain, it just wanted an end to its suffering, so I...I broke it." Guilt filled me—I still wished I'd been able to find another way.

"I'm sure you did what you had to do," Mom soothed. "You said in your message that there are more cursed stones?"

"Yes, but the method I used on the soul-stealer can't be used on other trapped demons. I only have one cursed stone at the moment, but it hasn't been activated yet, and nothing I've tried seems to work to separate the demon from the stone. Do you have any ideas?"

"Well," Dad said. "If you could find a way to exorcise the demon..."

"How would I do that?"

"I'm not sure," Dad admitted. "I don't know of any stones with that ability."

"Maybe not a stone," Mom said, "but I have heard of demons being exorcised from their human sides. Not a soul-stealer. Another demon with a similar ability, maybe?"

"Maybe," I said doubtfully.

Ren might know, Ruby said.

Yeah, I'd ask her to search the database for me.

"You might also ask the opal for help. I assume you've found it useful?" Dad said.

"Very much so. With Mr. Opal's help and amplification abilities, I was able to bring down a rockslide with stones that hadn't been polished and cut."

"Mr. Opal?" Mom repeated in amusement.

I felt my cheeks heat. "He's so wise, it seems impolite to call him anything else. And...he said I was able to bring them down because I have vast, untapped power. How is that possible?"

"You are the daughter of two one-eighth rock demons," Mom reminded me. "Instead of making you one-eighth as well, it's possible your powers are multiplied."

I knew it! Ruby exclaimed. *That's why you're so special.*

"As for the landslide," Dad added. "Were you in a highly emotional state at the time?"

"Yeah, I was kind of desperate to save my friends."

"That explains it," he confirmed. "Strong emotion, combined with your powers and the amplification of the opal made you more powerful."

"Oh." I wasn't quite sure how to take that.

"We're so proud of you, honey," Mom said. "We always

knew you'd be stronger than either of us. That's why we never worried about you."

"Really?"

"Really," she confirmed. "Remember, right after you got your learner's permit, when you were driving in Oak Creek Canyon and you almost hit a deer?"

I shuddered. That had been terrifying on that twisty, narrow road. "Yeah, I remember. A rock came out of nowhere and saved me." It had hit the deer's shoulder, diverting it in another direction so I was able to avoid hitting anything.

"Not out of nowhere—you did that."

Huh? "I thought you did."

"No, sweetie," Mom assured me. "That was all you. That's how we knew you'd be just fine—your abilities will always watch out for you."

I didn't know what to say.

Me, too! Ruby said. *I'll always watch out for you, too!*

I scratched her ears. *What would I do without you?*

You'll never have to find out, she said smugly.

Dad broke in. "Your mom's right. But we have to go soon. Did you need help with anything else?"

"No, that's all. Thank you so much. I love you."

"We love you too," they chorused and hung up.

Bemused, I went back to Ren's cubicle. *I wonder why they never told me?*

They probably hoped you wouldn't need to know, and would discover it for yourself when you did, Ruby said.

I glanced down at her. *When did you get so smart?*

I've always been this way, she said with a little wiggle.

You really are. I went back to Ren's desk.

"Check your email," Ren said. "I sent you the addresses and phone numbers of the places you asked for."

"Thanks. Say, could you do me a favor and see if there are any part-demons who are registered that can maybe exorcise a demon?"

"For the cursed stones?" she asked. At my nod, she added, "I think I'd remember someone like that, since it sounds really dangerous to other demons, but I'll check."

"Thanks. Since Mateo doesn't want me to go out without him, I guess I'll call around to those places you gave me." I glanced around. "Is there a desk I can use?"

"Sure—the one behind me is empty. No one will mind if you use it."

I nodded in thanks and began calling. A few hours later, I had a few leads on shops that might have what I needed, I'd eaten lunch with Ren, and was at loose ends. Luckily, that's when I got a text from Mateo to come to his office.

When I did, he gestured me to a seat. "Any progress?" I asked.

He grinned. "Derek's been busy. There were no fingerprints on the card, note, or knife in your door, but he tried to contact everyone you gave your cards to. Honeycutt and Nowicki still have your cards, as well as three of the pawnshops. The first two pawnshops said they threw the card away."

"What about Horvath?"

"Derek hasn't been able to locate him yet."

I nodded slowly. "So that leaves Horvath and the first two pawnshop personnel as suspects?"

"Yes." Mateo rose from his desk. "I'd like to go back to those shops and...sniff around."

He grinned and I realized he meant literally.

Ooh, good idea, Ruby said in excitement. *I'll help.*

"Ruby will help," I told him. "You think you might be able to find the guy who threatened me that way?"

"Yes, though I'd have to go as a wolf. That means you'll need to drive. You okay with that?"

"Of course. What's the plan?"

"Derek gave me the license plates of the two guys at the pawnshops. I'd rather we not get out of the SUV, so we'll roll the window down and scent their cars to see if we have a match. That means I'll need to wear my vest. I'll need your help getting into it once I've shifted."

"Okay, sure."

Yay, Ruby said. *Mateo can talk to me!*

Mateo handed me his K-9 assistance vest and the plate numbers, then poofed into his other form. I helped his wolf into the vest.

Let's take your car this time, he said.

"Really? My bumblebee Mini Cooper isn't exactly incon-spicuous."

I know, but just in case they're watching out for a black SUV...

That made sense. I helped Mateo into the backseat of my little car—a tight fit for the large wolf—and Ruby jumped into the front seat. As I drove toward the pawn-shop, Ruby chatted with Mateo, bragging about everything she'd done since she talked to him last. Mateo was a good sport and listened attentively, responding in the appro-priate spots.

When we arrived at the first pawnshop we'd visited, I spotted the license plate of the first suspect in the back, and pulled up next to it, then rolled the windows down. "Hush, Ruby. Time to go to work."

Ruby stopped talking, and she and Mateo stuck their noses out of the window, inhaling deeply.

That truck belongs to the guy we met at the counter, Ruby confirmed.

Agreed, Mateo said. *But it's not the scent from the note.*

I drove to the second one, but we had the same results.

"I guess that leaves Horvath as our main suspect for leaving the note," I said, though the height didn't seem to be right.

Do you remember what Horvath smelled like? Mateo asked Ruby.

Yeah, but the note didn't smell like him.

Okay, Mateo said. *I need to change back. Ivy, can you help with the fasteners on this vest?*

"Sure."

Pull over there, behind those stores, so no one sees my transformation.

I did as he asked, then leaned into the backseat and unfastened his vest. He shrugged out of it and asked, *You see anyone around?*

I glanced around. "No, all clear."

He poofed back into his human form, kneeling on his hands and knees in the confined backseat, his curls falling into his eyes. "I didn't think this through," he said wryly.

I chuckled and opened the door so he could ease out of the tight space. Ruby went into the back as he got into the front.

"This isn't much better," he said with a grin as he folded his long frame into the front seat of the Mini.

I laughed. "Hey, it was your choice. Scoot the seat back."

He did so. "That's better."

"Good." I started the car again. "To the museum?" I asked.

"Yes, please."

On the way there, his phone rang. "It's Ren," he said. "I'll put it on speaker." He held the phone between us. "Hello, Ren. You have something for us?"

"Maybe," she said, sounding smug. "Facial recognition identified someone who visited the museum a week before the theft—a part-demon teleporter who lives in Castle Rock and belongs to the Denver DU. Maybe she was casing the joint."

I stifled a giggle—she sounded like a gangster from an old movie.

"Her name?" Mateo asked.

"Bernadette Osmund. I'll text you her information."

"Good work. Send it to Derek, too."

"Will do. Hey, Ivy, I looked for a part-demon who could exorcise a demon, but didn't find anything."

Well, it was a long shot. "Okay, thanks for checking."

"I'll keep looking for more face matches, Mateo, in case there are others," Ren said.

"Thanks," Mateo said. "We'll check back with you before quitting time." He hung up.

Since we had arrived at the museum by now, Mateo climbed carefully out of the Mini and led us toward Hank's post.

Partway there, Ruby halted, then broke into a run. *I smell blood! It's coming from the guard room.*

"She smells blood in the guard room," I told Mateo urgently.

He bolted after her, with me not far behind. Mateo wrenched open the door, then froze, staring down at the floor.

I peeked around him, then wished I hadn't. Hank was lying on the floor in a pool of blood, a knife stuck in his neck.

Right in the carotid artery, Ruby confirmed. *He would have bled out quickly.*

Mateo squatted, leaned over him, and checked his pulse. "He's dead."

Oh, no! Poor Hank. One hand to my mouth, I pointed the other shakily at the piece of paper lying next to him. "What's that?"

Mateo peered at it, then sat back on his heels in apparent shock. "It's a suicide note. It says he did it—he robbed the museum."

CHAPTER
SIX

My STOMACH TWISTED and my heart raced as I stared at Hank's lifeless body. Completely stunned, I said, "Hank robbed the museum?"

Mateo shook his head. "That's what the note says, but there's no way he killed himself."

Appalled, I said, "If he didn't commit suicide, then..."

"Then someone murdered him," Mateo said grimly.

"Who? How could someone have done something so heinous?" I clutched my stomach with trembling hands to keep it from revolting all over the floor...and Hank. It all seemed so surreal, like some kind of nightmare I couldn't wake up from.

Mateo rose to his feet and took my hand in his, squeezing it gently. "Don't worry—we'll figure this out and find the truth. We'll get justice for Hank."

Damn skippy, Ruby said.

I'd never seen Mateo like this before—so fierce and determined. I was used to seeing him joking, teasing, and laid-back, but now he seemed totally pissed off and focused.

"Why don't you wait outside the door and keep everyone out while I call Derek," Mateo said. "I need to shift to see what I can scent."

I nodded numbly and slipped out the door with Ruby, trying to ignore the fact that there was a body in the room behind me. But it was difficult with the smell of blood seeping under the door, causing my hindbrain to jibber in panic. I wrapped my arms around myself and forced myself to be calm. Mateo was right—we would find the truth and make sure that whoever did this paid for their crime. Though how had a simple burglary escalated to murder?

After about five minutes, Mateo joined me outside the door. "Anything?" I asked.

"Not here," he muttered. "I'll have Ruby tell Derek when he gets here." He put an arm around my shoulders and held me close. I sighed in relief at the feeling of safety he gave me.

Soon, we heard sirens, and Derek arrived with several other people. We waited outside the room while they went inside. After a few minutes, Derek came back out and approached us, all business. "Did you touch anything?" he asked. When we shook our heads, he asked, "Did you see the note?"

Mateo grimaced. "Yes, but I don't believe it."

Derek raised an eyebrow. "Because..."

"For one thing, the note is typed and not signed. For another, he carried a gun and pepper spray, but not a knife. And if he had, it wouldn't have been a stiletto."

"But there doesn't seem to have been a struggle." Derek frowned. "Do you think someone could have sneaked up on him?"

That would be hard to do with a shifter.

Mateo shook his head. "He may have known the person, or was taken by surprise. I'm not sure."

"Okay," Derek said. "We'll see what forensics finds."

Mateo nodded. "Earlier, Hank called me and said he had information that might pertain to the theft. It's rather suspicious that we found him dead before he could tell me what he learned. Ren could check his phone and laptop for you, see if he recorded anything, left any clues. You don't want..." he lowered his voice, "...humans going through those."

"Good point," Derek said. "I'll get them to you later." He glanced around for a moment, then whispered, "Were you able to scent anyone in there recently?"

"Ruby can tell you what I found." He glanced down at Ruby and raised an eyebrow.

Good idea—no one but Derek and I would be able to hear her.

Yeah, Ruby piped up. *Some of the scents were older, but we did smell Horvath, the janitor, and the guards who took the other shifts. Chad and Mrs. Honeycutt, too, but those were fainter.*

Derek nodded, saying, "Museum personnel might have legitimate reasons for being in that room, but I'll question them anyway." On a sigh, he added, "This will take a while. Why don't you come back in a few hours to pick up the electronics?"

Mateo nodded. "Do you want me to call my alph— Uh, Duncan, so he can notify Hank's family, or will you do it?"

"Go ahead and call Duncan—my people will notify the next of kin."

"Okay." Mateo glanced at me. "We should go now."

Once we were in the SUV, Mateo called Duncan and had a tense conversation with him. Telling him about the murder of one of his shifters didn't go well. Mateo hung up on a sigh. "I hate this."

"Me, too. But...what do we do now?"

"We do what we have to do," Mateo said. "Hopefully, Ren will be able to find out why Hank called us, so we can learn who he was suspicious of. Until then, we can't do anything else about the murder."

Hank was dead. It seemed strange to just set aside our feelings on that, but the investigation had to go on if we were to find out who killed him. "We can check out some more places that might have the cursed stones," I suggested.

He sighed heavily. "Probably not a good idea. I need to talk to you."

Uh oh, Ruby said. *On TV, nothing good ever comes after that statement.*

Mateo continued, "With Hank's murder, the situation is even more dangerous—for you."

"We don't know if they're related," I protested.

"True, but I'm not taking any chances with your life. Both events involved knives—one a cheap warning, one lethal."

"So what are you saying?"

He better not be benching us, Ruby growled.

"Are you sure you won't reconsider learning some self-defense moves?"

"Why?" I asked, exasperated. "It didn't help Hank, did it?"

He grimaced, but didn't press the point. "Okay, but let's get those stones for you. The ones you said would help you build a shield."

"Good idea." I needed some kind of defense if the killer came after me the way they did Hank. Not to mention wanting something to distract me from thoughts of seeing Hank lying there, dead in a pool of his own blood. I shook my head to get rid of the image.

"Any idea where to look for the stones you need?" Mateo asked.

"Yeah—I called around earlier, and there're a couple of rock stores and a new age store that might have what I need."

"Okay, just give me the addresses."

He drove me around and accompanied me inside the stores. Unlike when we visited the pawnshops, this time Mateo was all business. He acted like a bodyguard, his eyes constantly moving as he let me do all the talking. It was strange to see him so serious again, but it just made me respect him even more.

I found an amethyst at the second shop, but Mateo insisted RPS cover the cost because it was for my protection. Since we hadn't found a citrine that would work yet, we went to the new age store in Old Colorado City on the west side of the Springs.

As soon as I walked into Crystal Mystique, I felt at home. Delicate chimes announced our entry, and we were greeted by the faint scent of patchouli. The store carried the normal new age paraphernalia like books, candles, tarot cards, and other aids to divination, but it was the large selection of different colored crystals in the glass cases that drew me.

These were happy stones, well cared for, and shining brightly. The proprietress, a lovely woman who appeared to be in her forties with dark spiral curls down to her shoulders and a serene expression, greeted us. "Hello, I'm Amber." Amber took in my multiple gemstone piercings and smiled. "I think you're in the right place."

"I think you're right," I confirmed. "I have an affinity for gemstones."

"Yes, I sensed that," Amber said in her calm voice.

Is she part demon? I asked Ruby.

No, just a really perceptive human, Ruby said in surprise.

I smiled. "I called earlier, looking for a large citrine. You said you have one?"

"Indeed I do." Amber moved to a display case and pointed to a collection of several of the yellow stones. "Will one of these work for you?"

I assessed them. Though one was larger than the others and therefore would potentially draw more power, I was drawn to a medium-sized oval stone. The size and shape matched the amethyst I had just purchased.

A good choice, Mr. Opal assured me. *Bigger is not always better. That stone is more suited for what you need, since it will mesh better with the amethyst.*

Excellent. I pointed to the one I had chosen. "This one, please."

Amber took it from the case and put it in a box. "May I ask what you plan to do with it?" she asked as she moved toward the register.

"Well, I make jewelry," I said, "and I plan to use it in a cuff bracelet, like this one." I showed her the cinnabar and clear quartz one I had made.

"What an interesting combination. To enhance communication?"

She certainly knew her gemstone properties. "Yes, who doesn't need that?" I paused, then said, "I just moved here, and I've been looking for a place to sell my jewelry. I don't suppose you take jewelry on consignment?"

She smiled. "I do, on occasion. If the pieces feel right." She glanced down at my rings. "And yours certainly feel right. Why don't you bring some by, and we'll see if we can come to an arrangement?"

I betcha she has some rock demon lurking way back in her family tree, Ruby said, *though it's not strong enough for me to sense it.*

I bet you're right.

"I'll do that," I said with satisfaction.

She rang up my total, and, as Mateo paid, she added, "I also get the occasional person asking for loose stones to be set in jewelry or for jewelry to be repaired. Do you do that as well?"

I grinned. "I do." The gemstones consultant business card didn't seem appropriate here, so I jotted down my contact information and gave it to her. "Here's how you— or they—can contact me. So, when would be a good time to bring some of my inventory by?"

"Weekdays during the day are the least busy."

"Good—I'll come back soon." I hesitated, then said, "You are aware that stones can be imbued with the aura of their owner?" At her serene nod, I added, "I have a cleansing formula that would help if they seem to have absorbed negative energy." I handed her a packet of herbs I kept for that purpose. "The instructions are on the side."

She weighed them in her hand thoughtfully. "Thank you." Smiling, she handed me my purchase. "I look forward to seeing you again."

As we left the store, Mateo said, "Well, that was a fruitful visit."

It sure was. Now, I not only had a consultant job, but I had somewhere to sell my jewelry on consignment as well. Looked like moving here was the right thing to do.

Ruby did a happy little wiggle. *I like it here, too.*

"Do you need anything else to put the shield together?" Mateo asked.

I considered for a moment. "Mr. Opal suggests I put them on the same cuff bracelet as the cinnabar and quartz —the amplification won't hurt and it's easy since I already have the tools and materials I need at home."

He frowned as we got in the SUV. "Since things have escalated, I'm not sure that's the best place to be."

I huffed. "What do you suggest? I don't have anywhere else to go."

"RPS has a safe house and I confirmed it was available while you were talking to Amber. I think you and Ren should stay there until this is over. We can pick up what you need from your apartment, then you can both work from the safe house. With a guard, of course. Me."

Sounds boring, Ruby sulked.

I had to agree with her. I sighed, knowing I wasn't going to be able to change his mind. And Sybil and Duncan would probably agree with him since they were all so security conscious. "When?"

"I got a text from Derek saying the electronics are ready for pick-up. I already notified Ren of the move, and she'll send you a list of what she needs so you can pack that up for her. I don't want you driving your own cars, so we'll pick her up at work after we get the electronics."

My eyebrows raised. "You've been busy."

He shrugged. "I texted everyone while you were talking to Amber."

Derek met us in the parking lot outside the museum. We stayed in the SUV and Mateo rolled down the window so Derek could hand him the bagged items. "Good idea taking Ivy and Ren to a safe house," Derek said. "Let me know if Ren finds anything."

"Will do," Mateo said. "What have you learned so far?"

Derek lowered his voice. "We questioned the ones you scented, and they all had legitimate reasons to be there, but we were unable to interview Horvath. He left early, but hasn't come back. He's not at home, either."

Gee, that's not suspicious at all, Ruby said.

Derek nodded. "Nowicki said he's in danger of losing his job."

"That sounds like a possible motive for the theft," I said. "You think he killed Hank?"

"It's possible." Derek shrugged. "Or he may have a legitimate reason he's not here. I'm not going to make any assumptions until we find him."

I just hoped it was soon. Very soon.

CHAPTER
SEVEN

THE SAFE HOUSE ended up being in the northern part of Colorado Springs, a lovely rancher in a family neighborhood. Though it was weird staying in the same house with human Mateo, we each had our own bedroom. Rather than try to make dinner at the unfamiliar place, we stopped for takeout on the way there.

I still felt unsettled with what had happened to Hank, so, after we ate, I immersed myself in the task of adding the new stones to my cuff bracelet, hoping that concentrating on the work would make the horrific flashbacks go away. Ren and Mateo both stayed glued to her laptop as they continued to search for more facial recognition matches.

Finally, when I was done with my bracelet and the two of them looked as if computer screens were permanently imprinted on their retinas, Mateo yawned and stretched. "I think that does it."

Ren copied him. "Yeah. I'm beat. I'm off to bed."

"Did you find any more matches?" I asked Mateo after she left.

Mateo shook his head. "No, just the one—Bernadette Osmund. Derek wants me to check her out tomorrow."

Can we go with you? Ruby asked eagerly.

When I repeated he question, Mateo said, "I don't think it's a good idea. I have a guard coming to relieve me here tomorrow morning. You'll be safer here."

I frowned, disliking that idea as much as Ruby did. "But we can't help you if we're stuck here. What can we do?"

Mateo raised an eyebrow. "You can practice putting that shield in place."

Wrong answer. "I can work on that while you're driving. Besides, you need us." At his skeptical look, I added, "This Bernadette is part demon, right?" At his nod, I said, "Then Ruby will be able to read her mind and let me know what she's thinking—and if she's telling the truth."

She's got you there, Ruby snarked.

He opened his mouth to argue, then obviously realized I was right.

Mateo sighed. "Okay, but you have to promise to work on the shield in the car."

I grinned. "Don't worry, I will."

THE NEXT MORNING, we headed north up I-25 toward where Mateo said the Castle Rock outlet stores were. As promised, I concentrated on following Mr. Opal's instructions to build a shield.

First, he said, *focus on creating a wall in your mind between you and that which would hurt you, then push that image to your stones.*

I focused on creating a hard, impenetrable barrier

around me and shoved energy through the opal into the protective stones.

Okay, I did it, but how do I know if it worked? I can't see any difference. I kind of expected a shimmer or distortion of the air around me, but there was nothing to show if it had worked or not.

Have Mateo or Ruby try to touch you. If they succeed, your shield failed.

Oooookay.

"Hey, Mateo, I need to test to see if the shield is working. Can you try to poke me with your finger, without taking your eyes off the road?"

"Sure," he said with a grin. "Will it hurt?"

"It won't hurt me. And I don't think it'll hurt you...."

"Okay, then." He jabbed me in the ribs with his finger. I jumped, and he chuckled. "I guess it didn't work."

"Yeah, well, I wasn't ready. Try again." I concentrated this time, but still felt his prodding. I kept trying, he kept poking, and Mr. Opal kept providing advice until finally, about half an hour later, I succeeded in blocking the jab.

Yay, you did it, Ruby exclaimed.

"I stopped it that time," I told Mateo. "Did you feel anything different?"

"Well, your ribs had some give, but the shield didn't give at all—it was like poking a brick wall. It didn't hurt, though."

"Good." I sighed. "I need to stop for a while. Building walls is hard work, even if they are only mental."

Mateo chuckled. "I can imagine. But don't forget to practice later. You need to be able to bring the shield up without thinking."

"I'm not sure I'll ever be able to do that."

You will, Mr. Opal promised me, *with practice.*

Soon, we arrived at the outlet stores and headed toward a designer handbag and accessory store. The woman at the counter had a blond bob haircut, dressed sharply, and wore almost as much jewelry as I did—without the multiple piercings.

"Bernadette Osmund?" Mateo asked.

"Yes," she said politely. "Can I help you?"

Mateo showed her his ID. "We're from RPS, associated with the Colorado Springs DU. Can we ask you some questions?"

Huh—I saw why he used the initials instead of the words—it made it easy in the human world to disguise what he was talking about. Bernadette would know, though.

Her eyes widened. "I'm working right now." She cast an apprehensive look at the annoyed-looking woman in the back. Her boss? "What is this about?"

Yep, Ruby confirmed. *And Bernadette is a little afraid of her.*

"We just want to ask you a few questions," Mateo said. "Can we talk to you on your break?"

"Yeah, I guess so. My lunch break is in ten minutes. I can meet you then."

"That sounds good," I said, letting Mateo know she wasn't planning to bolt. "Shall we meet you at the food court in fifteen?"

"Okay, sure," Bernadette agreed, and went to wait on a customer.

We headed toward the food court to wait for her. "She was nervous because of her boss," I let Mateo know. "And Ruby didn't detect any deceit."

Sure enough, she joined us as promised, and Mateo treated us all to lunch. We took it to an outside table where there was less chance of being overheard.

Bernadette took a bite, but looked apprehensive. After she swallowed, she asked, "Okay, what's this about?"

Mateo smiled reassuringly. "You visited Stratton Art Museum last week?"

"Yes, I love jewelry, as you can tell." She twisted her wrist so her bangles jangled. "They have a traveling exhibit of Edwardian jewelry, and I wanted to see the collection before it leaves Colorado."

"Were you aware some pieces were stolen a few days after you visited?" Mateo asked.

"No. I—" She broke off, her mouth dropping open. "You don't suspect me, do you?"

Naw, Ruby said. *She's clean as a whistle. She just wanted to see the pretty jewels.*

"We did," I said quickly, "but not anymore." I laid my hand on Ruby's head so Mateo knew where the information came from.

"But...why suspect me at all?"

"Your ability," I explained. I glanced around. No one seemed to be listening, but just in case, I lowered my voice. "The mysterious disappearance, teleportation...it seemed a match."

She relaxed, but her mouth twisted in a rueful expression. "I understand, but my ability doesn't work that way. I can only move myself, and not very far at that. I can't move objects at all, unless I'm carrying them." She took a sip, looking thoughtful. "Do you know what it looked like? The mysterious disappearance, I mean."

I glanced at Mateo, who said, "On the video, it shows a

person flickering into view for just a moment, then disappearing, along with the stolen jewelry. That happened separately for each piece that was taken."

"Huh," she said, and chewed on another bite of sandwich. Keeping her voice low, she said, "It could be a phase demon."

When Mateo looked at me in question, I shrugged. "Can you describe how a phase demon's abilities work?" he asked Bernadette.

"From what I've heard from my dad, they can phase in and out of solid objects. I don't know any phase demons, though, so I might be wrong. I'm sorry, but that's all I know."

"Well, we appreciate your help." Mateo picked up his burger.

"No problem," Bernadette said with a smile. "I'm just glad I'm no longer under suspicion."

We finished our lunch, then, after we got in the SUV to head back to Colorado Springs, I said, "Well, at least that wasn't a total bust."

"No, it wasn't," Mateo said. "And, thanks to you and Ruby, questioning was a lot easier than usual." He checked his phone and smiled with grim satisfaction. "I knew it. Derek says the evidence from the crime scene is inconsistent with suicide."

Well, Mateo might be happy about that, but that meant a murderer was still on the loose. And it probably had something to do with what Hank wanted to tell him. "Have you heard if Ren found anything on his laptop or phone?"

"Not yet. She'll call if she finds anything. I'll also text her and see if she can locate any phase demons in the area when she gets a chance." He shook his head, looking pensive.

"What's wrong?"

"I'm not sure which to tell her is the higher priority—learning about phase demons, or searching Hank's electronics."

Hey, Ruby said, poking me with her nose from the backseat. *You know someone who knows about all kinds of demons.*

Oh, that's right. "Ruby just reminded me we have a friend with a database on demons—Shade, in the San Antonio DU. He has even more info than the *Encyclopedia Magicka,* and may be able to tell us about phase demons while Ren continues to research Hank's electronics. Let me call him."

When Shade answered, I said, "Hi, Shade. This is Ivy. I'm here with Mateo Duran and Ruby, so I'll put you on speaker."

"How can I help you?"

"I'm looking for information on phase demons and how they work. Do you know anything about them?"

Shade chuckled. "You're in luck. I have a friend who's a phase demon—Josh. He can pass through most solid objects, but not anything living. Why do you ask?"

Mateo leaned closer to the phone and introduced himself. "We're trying to find a thief who stole some jewelry." He explained what we'd seen on the video. "Is that consistent with what a phase demon could do?"

"Absolutely," Shade said. "You wouldn't be able to see them when they are out of phase."

"But if they're out of phase, wouldn't their hands pass right through the jewelry?" I asked.

"Not if they phased back into existence, grabbed it, then phased out again," Shade informed me.

That made total sense, and matched what we'd seen on the video.

"So, if it was a phase demon, it wouldn't have to be an inside job at all." I exchanged a glance with Mateo who seemed to think the same. "Would Ruby be able to smell them when they're out of phase?" I asked Shade.

"Huh," Shade said. "I have no idea. Let me check and get back to you."

Mateo leaned closer to the phone. "Has your phase demon friend left San Antonio in the past week or so?"

"No," Shade said, sounding annoyed. "And Josh wouldn't steal jewelry either."

"Hey, I had to ask," Mateo said.

"It's probably someone who lives around here," I assured Shade. "We're looking into that."

"Good," Shade said shortly. "And I'll see if I can find any phase demons who live in or might've been in Colorado recently."

"Thanks," Mateo said. "That would be very helpful." Turning to me, he said, "I'll let Derek know what we learned right away."

Before Shade could hang up, I said, "I do have something else to ask you about. You know about the cursed stones I'm looking for?"

"Yeah, Micah mentioned it. Why?" Shade sounded more curious than annoyed now.

"Well, we found one that's not yet been activated, and I'm trying to figure out how to separate the demon from the stone. My parents mentioned it might be possible to exorcise it. Do you know of a part demon in your database who could do that?"

"No, but Val used a spell from the encyclopedia to do just that."

Duh. "The books! Why didn't I think of that?"

Mateo gave me a sidelong glance. "Maybe because you gave the books to Sybil for safekeeping?"

"Yeah—out of sight, out of mind, I guess." I grimaced. I should have thought of them before. "Thanks so much for all your help, Shade. And say hi to everyone there from Ruby and me."

"Will do. I'm sure Princess will be glad I heard from one of her pups."

We hung up, and I asked Mateo, "Can we go by RPS and get the books?"

He frowned. "It's rather out of the way, and, for security reasons, I'd rather ask Sybil to bring them to the safe house."

"Okay, great." I didn't care how I got them, so long as I got them in my hot little hands.

SYBIL BROUGHT the books by the safe house after dinner, and she and Mateo watched while I asked the books to show me the spell to exorcise demons. The pages flipped and stopped on a spell. Sybil read over my shoulder. "Is that it?"

"Yes." I read through the notes. "Hmm."

"What's wrong?" Mateo asked.

"Well, it looks like it will do what we want, but if I use it, my powers will be depleted significantly."

"Forever?" Mateo looked appalled.

"No, but I'm not sure for how long."

Mateo lifted the book from my hands. "Here, let me see that." He read through it silently, then said, "It says if you say the spell out loud, it won't trigger until you use the activating words. There's no time limit on how long you have to wait before you trigger it." He glanced up at me. "It wouldn't hurt to read it out loud now, so you'll have it ready to go when you need it."

Sybil nodded. "I agree."

"All right," I said reluctantly. This seemed to be the only way I'd found so far to do what I promised to do—without hurting the rose quartz. At least, I hoped it would be okay. Taking a deep breath, I read the spell aloud. "Demon thou art, demon thou shalt not be. Say it times three, I exorcise thee."

Whoa—goosebumps rose all over my body and I felt a swell of power rush past me as my hair blew in an invisible wind. Surprisingly, the words of the spell vanished from the page. Had they disappeared into me? Weird.

Mateo grinned. "That was insanely cool."

I shook out the last of the tingles. "If you say so. Now that spell is sitting like a burning lump in my gut, and I suspect it will do so until I use it." All I had to do was concentrate on the demon in the stone and say the activating words—*I exorcise thee*—three times.

"Try it on the rose quartz," Sybil urged.

"If I do, my powers will be reduced. I may not be able to find other stones for a while without them. Or practice the shield I've been working on."

Sybil frowned. "We can keep you safe, and finding the other stones is pointless if you don't know for sure that this works." When I hesitated, she added, "And we do need to show the shifters and the vamps that we're making progress on the cursed stones. You saw how they were at the last meeting."

Yeah, telling them I didn't have a clue what I was doing —not fun. I glanced at Mateo. "What do you think?"

He shrugged. "The decision is up to you. As Sybil said, we'll protect you until your powers come back."

Yeah, Ruby said. *Try it.*

"Okay..." I got the rose quartz from my room and stared down at it, taking a deep breath. *Here goes nothing.* Concentrating on the demon within the quartz, I said firmly, "I exorcise thee, I exorcise thee, I exorcise thee!"

A wisp of ethereal smoke escaped from the stone, and the void was gone. I could hear the rose quartz now, though very faintly. "It worked," I said on a breath of wonder.

Sybil clapped her hands. "Excellent. Now we have progress to report."

If you called losing a gutload of my power progress....

Tentatively, I asked my stones, *Can you hear me?*

I heard their voices, but barely, as if they were far away. *We can,* Mr. Opal said, sounding distant though stronger than the others. *But it will be a while before you can hear any but me.*

Well, I knew that was going to happen, but it was still disconcerting.

Sybil interrupted my musings. "What kind of demon was in the stone?"

"I couldn't tell, but the stone may be able to tell me later. Right now, I can't hear well enough to know how it's doing, but I don't hear any screaming. It appears groggy, as if it just woke from a sound sleep."

That is correct, Mr. Opal said, his voice a pale echo of what it normally was.

I carried the stone toward my room. "I'll just put it in my cleansing solution in case there's any negative residue from the demon."

Mateo followed me. "Are you okay?"

I stared at him, not knowing what to say. "Uh...not really. It feels wrong...like something's missing. I guess this may be how you felt when you lost your human side."

He gathered me into his arms and squeezed me tight. "I'm so sorry. I wouldn't wish that on anyone. But they will come back, right?"

I hugged him back, needing his warmth and reassurance. "I hope so. I certainly hope so."

CHAPTER
EIGHT

THE NEXT MORNING, my powers didn't seem to have gotten much stronger. Everything felt muted, wrong. I never thought I'd complain about not being able to hear my stones, but now I kinda wished I could hear them arguing again.

Unfortunately, the loss of power made working on my shield or finding cursed stones too difficult to even try. And, though Mateo and Ren found a lot to do online, I was left with nothing constructive to work on. Reading and watching TV was getting old. I guess I could create more jewelry, but I really wasn't in the mood.

I know what you could do, Ruby said. She sat up on her hind legs, her front legs dangling in front of her like a meerkat. She looked at me expectantly. *You've been holding out on me.*

"Uh, what?

Come on, this belly isn't going to rub itself.

I couldn't help but laugh. I rubbed her belly, asking, "Where did you learn this?"

On TV.

Of course. Where else? Before Ruby could insist on more belly-rubbing goodness, I got a text from Amber.

> Amber: A customer brought in a necklace. Would you be able to repair it?

She sent a picture of the damaged garnet choker along with the text.

> Ivy: Sure, no problem. If you have the customer leave it there, I can come pick it up.

> Amber: She wants to know if you can do it soon, and how much it would cost.

I got Mateo's attention and showed him the text conversation. "Would it be possible for someone to take me to Crystal Mystique to pick up the necklace?" When he hesitated, I added, "Come on. I'm bored out of my skull here, and need *something* I can do."

He gave me a crooked smile. "Okay, I'll take you."

"Great!"

Ruby jumped up and whirled around. *Thanks be to the Great Chiweenie!*

Ren and I cracked up and I told Mateo what she'd said.

He laughed. "Why wouldn't a hellhound's deity be a cross between a chihuahua and a dachshund? It makes as much sense as anything else."

It's just a saying, Ruby said in exasperation.

"Just a saying?" I repeated for Mateo's benefit. "Whose?"

Mine, okay? I made it up. She danced in place. *Let's go.*

"Hold your horses, you chiweenie worshiper," I said on a laugh. "Let me text Amber first." I did so, answering her questions and letting her know that we could be there within the hour.

> Amber: The customer is happy with that.
> See you soon.

Half an hour later, we walked into Crystal Mystique, and my stones were so quiet, I didn't even have to wear my hoodie. Besides, I knew the stones in Amber's store would be as chill as she was.

As Mateo made himself unobtrusive, I joined Amber at the counter where she gave me the garnet necklace. "The customer said you can just bring it back here when you've fixed it."

"Okay, I—"

Ivy. Ruby pawed my calf, trembling with urgency. *I just smelled that scent.*

What scent? I asked in confusion.

The one that was on the note stabbed in our door.

What the heck? I felt the blood rush from my face.

"Is everything all right?" Amber asked.

Mateo glanced up at that, obviously noting my paleness and Ruby's quivering nose. "Are you okay?"

I took a deep breath, trying to figure out what to say so Mateo knew what was going on without revealing anything supernatural to the human...yet still learning who the scent belonged to. "I—I think so." Turning to Amber, I said, "This may sound odd, but I'm sensitive to...bad auras. Was there someone in the shop recently who seemed...off to you?"

Amber didn't even give me an odd look. Thank goodness, she thought woo-woo stuff was normal. "As a matter of fact, there was. A man came by earlier to sell me some loose stones. He seemed a little strange, but I sensed something...bad from the stones. I bought them since I figured I could take better care of them."

Mateo started to break in, but I stopped him with a hand on his sleeve. This would sound better coming from me. "That may be where the uneasiness is coming from. Can I possibly see the stones?"

Puzzled, Amber said, "I don't see why not, I haven't had a chance to cleanse them yet, so they're in the back. Hold on."

When she left the room, I lowered my voice so only Mateo could hear. "Ruby caught the scent left on the note and knife in my apartment here."

His eyes widened, and he gave Ruby's ears a scritch. "Good catch, girl." Looking back at me, he asked, "Do you think the gemstones he sold her are—"

He had to break off when Amber returned, but I gave him a firm nod of agreement.

Amber laid them out in a tray. "Do you sense something wrong with them?"

I concentrated on the stones, and even with my reduced abilities, I could feel their anguish at being separated from their mountings and the other gemstones they'd shared the settings with.

"Yes, I'm afraid I do sense something wrong." Taking a deep breath, I said, "I'm sorry to tell you this, but I think these were stolen from the Stratton Art Museum's Edwardian jewelry exhibit."

"How would you know that?" she asked in disbelief.

At a loss, I wondered how I could possibly explain this.

Mateo stepped in. "We're from Relentless Protection Services, which was tasked with guarding the exhibit. The gems were stolen a few days ago, and we called Ms. Weiss in as an expert consultant on gemstones." He pulled out his phone. "I have photos of the jewelry pieces that were stolen." He showed them to her. "I believe the person who sold these to you removed those stones from these pieces."

Amber looked back and forth between his phone and the stones, then sighed. "He said they belonged to his mother, but I should have known there was something off about the whole thing. I just wanted to give the stones a good home."

"I'm so sorry," I said. Though these weren't all of the missing gemstones, at least some of them had been found.

"Not your fault," Amber said with a shake of her head. "What do we do now?"

Mateo took over. "Ivy, can you text Detective Thompson?" As I bent to do as he asked, he told Amber, "He's working this case. Did the man who sold you those leave his contact information?"

Amber smiled wryly. "I'm afraid not—he asked for cash."

Mateo nodded. "Was it one of these men?" He showed her pictures on his phone of several museum personnel.

She shook her head. "I haven't seen any of them before."

How disappointing. Though I guess her seller could be working with one of them.

Amber perked up. "But I can describe him for you. He's white, about five seven or eight, thin, with a pasty complexion and medium-length stringy brown hair. Maybe in his mid-thirties?"

That didn't sound like anyone we'd met so far. My phone pinged and I glanced up. "Derek is on his way."

He gave her a smile. "Thank you. Detective Thompson may want you to look at some mugshots or have you describe him for a sketch artist."

I could tell them what he smells like, Ruby offered.

I know you could, but that wouldn't help the police. When Ruby seemed to sulk, I added, *but you've been incredibly helpful already. We wouldn't have known about the stones if you hadn't scented the thief.*

That seemed to appease her. We spent the next twenty minutes chatting about various things until Derek arrived and took over.

After we explained what happened, Derek looked apologetically at Amber. "I'm afraid we'll have to take these into evidence."

She sighed. "I know. That's not a problem—I have insurance, and I want to help."

"Would you be willing to come to the station to see if you can identify the man who sold you these?"

"Of course."

Amber closed the shop and followed Derek. As Mateo, Ruby and I headed to the SUV, I asked, "You think he's a phase demon?"

"Maybe," Mateo said. "But we wouldn't be able to tell by just his scent."

But I can if I get near him, Ruby said eagerly.

He glanced down at Ruby. "But she can if she meets him."

I grinned. "Ruby just said the same thing."

We all got into the SUV, and Mateo checked his phone. "And that's why I texted Derek to ask if we can be present if he questions the seller. He agreed."

Smart, Ruby said in approval.

Mateo pursed his lips. "There's also a text from Ren. They've found Horvath."

"Really? Where?" I asked.

"In the hospital. He had acute appendicitis and needed

immediate surgery." He glanced up at me. "He was in surgery when Hank died."

I slumped. If Horvath didn't kill Hank, he probably didn't steal the gemstones either. "And there went our primary suspect."

"Yes, unless he had a partner."

"You think he did?"

He shrugged. "I don't know. Maybe we'll know more if Derek can find the man who sold Amber the gemstones."

We went back to the safe house where I went to work on repairing the garnet necklace and Mateo and Ren continued doing their thing online.

A few hours later, Derek called and talked to Mateo. When he hung up, Mateo said, "He has a suspect in custody —a small-time crook named Freddy Maul." He glanced at me. "You sure you still want to do this?"

"Heck, yeah." I'd be safe enough in the police station with Mateo and Ruby to protect me, and I really wanted to see the creep who thought it was a good idea to stick a knife in my door and threaten me.

"Okay. Ren, can you see what you can find out about Freddy Maul and if he has connections to anyone who works in the museum?"

Ren gave a heavy sigh. "I'm not sure how to do that, but I'll figure it out."

"I'm sure you will." Ren was awesome with ferreting out obscure digital information. I grabbed Ruby's gear. "Let's go."

When we entered the Special Crime Unit's building, Derek settled us on one side of a two-way mirror in an interrogation room. "Maul hasn't lawyered up, so I'll bring him in here. Have Ruby let me know what she senses about this guy."

Ruby wriggled with glee. *This is so cool.*

Derek brought in the suspect and handcuffed him to the table. Freddy looked vaguely familiar, but I couldn't place him. Had he been following me?

Freddy jiggled the cuffs. "Ain't this a bit over the top, dude?"

"Not if you're a murderer," Mateo muttered. He let Ruby out so she could sniff the door Freddy just went through.

That's the guy, Ruby confirmed. *But he's not a demon, so I can't read his mind.*

Derek's shoulders eased at Ruby's confirmation he wasn't the phase demon, but he ignored Freddy's question. "We have a witness who states that you sold her some stolen jewels."

Freddy slouched in the chair, looking sullen "I never did nothing."

Yes, he did, Ruby said in indignant tones. *He stabbed our door with that nasty note. My nose doesn't lie.*

Derek continued, "You're a thief, so I get why you stole the gems, but why did you murder the security guard?"

Freddy jolted upright, shock written all over his face. "I—I didn't. I ain't no killer. I swear."

His scent wasn't in the guard room, Ruby admitted reluctantly.

I don't think Derek really believes he killed Hank. I doubted the guy was smart enough. *He's just trying to scare him.*

Freddy gulped visibly. "No, it wasn't me. When did he die? I'm sure I gotta alibi."

Derek regarded him thoughtfully. "Tuesday afternoon, between four and six."

Looking triumphant, Freddy said, "I was outta town then, pickin' someone up at the Denver airport. You can check the toll road cameras."

"You could have had someone else take your car to Denver."

"No, I—"

Derek interrupted him. "Why would I believe anything you say? You threatened Ivy Weiss with a knife, and the security guard was killed with a knife. A coincidence? I think not."

"You gotta believe me," Freddy said, looking panicked. "I was just trying to scare her a little, get her to stop looking for—" He broke off as if he thought better of what he'd been about to say. "'Sides, it was just a cheap little knife that wouldn't hurt no one."

That rang true. Relief filled me—he didn't want to kill me. He just wanted to frighten me. And now that he was in police custody, he didn't even do that.

Derek agrees with you, Ruby told me.

"Get her to stop looking for what?" Derek asked implacably.

"I heard her at the pawnshop—she was looking for loose stones."

So that's where I'd seen him before. "He was that squirrely guy I saw checking out the electronics at the first shop we went to," I told Mateo.

Mateo nodded. "He must have picked up your card after the owner threw it away."

Derek leaned in, looking intent. "Loose stones? Like the ones you took from the jewels you stole?"

"No, I—"

Derek slammed his hand down on the table. "If you didn't steal them, why were they in your possession?"

Freddy's expression turned sulky. "Look, I don't know nothin' 'bout stealing from no museum. Some guy asked me to sell them for him, okay? *He* musta stole them."

Ha! Derek never mentioned the stones were from the museum.

"How? How did he steal them?" Derek demanded.

"I dunno. I don't ask questions."

"Who was he?"

Freddy's gaze skittered away. "I don't know—just some guy."

"What did he look like?" Derek persisted.

"I—I don't remember."

Even I can tell he's lying, Ruby said in derision.

Yeah, I didn't need the emerald to tell me that.

Derek scowled at him. "Well, you'd better remember right quick. Or you could go down as an accomplice for aiding and abetting a murderer."

Freddy slumped back in his chair and crossed his arms. "I ain't saying no more without a lawyer," he said belligerently.

Mateo turned away from the mirror and sighed heavily. "We won't get anything more out of him today."

"Yeah, too bad. Though, on the bright side, at least I'm not in danger anymore."

"Maybe, maybe not," Mateo said with a shrug. "Until we find his accomplice, I wouldn't take any chances with your safety. The man who killed Hank is still out there."

Well, crap. Suddenly, I didn't feel so safe anymore.

CHAPTER
NINE

THE NEXT MORNING, Derek met us at the safe house to discuss what Ren and Shade had learned. After we ate the pastries he brought, Derek said, "You three," he glanced at Ruby, "uh, four, have the most knowledge of what's going on, so I thought we could put our heads together to see what we know and what we still need to find out."

Are we going to do a murder board like they do on TV? Ruby asked, her eyes wide.

"We can do that," Derek said.

We found a blank wall and Derek taped up pictures of the stolen jewelry. "Let's start with what we know. Ren, did you get anything from Hank's laptop or phone?"

Ren scratched her head. "Not really. His texts show he was ticked off that the museum considered him a suspect, so he was looking into the backgrounds of everyone who worked there."

"Did he find anything?" Mateo asked.

"I'm not sure." She shrugged. "If he did, I haven't figured out what yet. He was concentrating primarily on management."

Derek looked thoughtful. "Keep digging, see what else you can find." When Ren nodded, he added, "So, we're fairly sure a phase demon actually stole the jewels, then gave the jewels to Freddy Maul to fence." He put up a picture of Freddy then glanced at us. "Any luck on finding a phase demon?"

Ren shook her head. "There aren't any in the Colorado demon databases I have access to."

I nodded. "Shade, my contact in San Antonio, knows a phase demon who lives there, but he has an unbreakable alibi. Ditto for his relatives. And Shade wasn't able to find info on any others."

Derek put up a sticky note that said PHASE DEMON THIEF?

Mateo frowned. "Based on the fact that Hank was surprised and didn't fight back, I'm thinking the phase demon is also the one who killed Hank."

Yikes. "You mean he..."

"I assume the coward stabbed Hank when he was out of phase," Mateo said grimly, "then when he phased back in, the knife was already in his neck."

I shuddered. Coward was right. "The mice!" I exclaimed in sudden realization. "He must have used the mice as practice, phasing in and out of their skulls without actually having to stab them."

Derek nodded and added a picture of Hank's body and the "suicide" note to the board. "I'm fairly certain it wasn't Maul. He has a rap sheet, but not for violent crimes. He's just a petty criminal."

A sudden thought struck me. "But if it is a phase demon, how on earth can we stop someone who can disappear at will?" Especially one who had no compunction about killing people.

Everyone frowned, except for Ruby, who said casually, *You could exorcise the demon out of him. That oughta stop him.*

I gaped at her, and, seeing Mateo's questioning expression, I explained, "Ruby just reminded me I can exorcise demons."

Derek's eyebrows rose. "You can?"

"Yeah—it's a spell I learned from..." I hesitated I trusted Derek, so I explained about the encyclopedia and asked Derek to keep it to himself—the knowledge and the books would be too dangerous in the wrong hands.

Seeing Derek's concerned look, I added, "I used the exorcism spell to remove the demon from the cursed stone. But don't worry, it's not something I'd use casually. It takes too much out of me. I'm at reduced power as it is."

Mateo got my attention. "Did Shade get back to you on whether or not Ruby could scent a phase demon when they are out of phase?"

"Yes—he experimented with his phase demon friend Josh and his own hellhound, Princess. She could hear Josh mentally when he was out of phase, but couldn't detect him with her nose. When he was in phase, even for only a moment or so, she was able to smell him." I sighed heavily. "But the only people you guys smelled in the guard room were museum and security personnel. And we've pretty much eliminated them."

"Maybe he wouldn't have left a scent if he was really fast," Mateo suggested. "Or maybe there's a spell that would do the same thing as a phase demon."

Well, crap. That opened up a whole other can of worms. "Any demon could use a spell," I muttered. "And probably a vampire. Maybe even a human?"

"Okay," Derek said. "Forget about the phase demon since that's getting us nowhere, and assume it's a spell even a human could use. Let's look at the museum personnel again, starting with Horvath. He doesn't have a good alibi for the theft, but he was in the hospital when Hank was killed." Derek added the information to the board.

"Did you find anything on his background check?" Mateo asked Ren.

She shook her head. "Nothing criminal. He doesn't appear to need the money. But he wasn't popular at the museum, and since Chad told us he was about to be fired, Horvath might have stolen from the museum as payback. But I didn't find anything connecting him to Freddy."

Mateo grimaced. "He didn't necessarily need to have a connection to Freddy to use him as a fence."

"True," Derek added. "But the way Freddy refused to tell us who the thief is means there's probably a personal connection there."

"How about Mrs. Honeycutt?" I asked. "Have we eliminated her as a suspect?"

"Pretty much," Mateo said. "With her alibi for the night of the theft and her lack of motive, I don't see her doing this."

Ruby snorted. *Yeah, I can't see her hanging out with Freddy either.*

Ditto. Not for any reason.

Ren spoke up. "Though Chad had an alibi for the night of the theft, I did find a tentative connection between him and Freddy. They both attended high school in one of the most crime-ridden areas in town."

Ruby perked up. *Were they delinquents together?*

Ren shrugged. "There's no proof they even knew each other, though they're around the same age."

Derek added the info to the board. "Nowicki doesn't have a rap sheet, but I only did a basic background check—I didn't check to see if he has a sealed juvenile record." He frowned. "I'll check."

"Does he have a motive?" Mateo asked.

"Not that I could determine." Derek tapped his chin thoughtfully. "He's not in financial straits, though everyone at the museum agrees he's very ambitious—he wants Horvath's job."

"How is that motive?" I asked. "You think he set Horvath up?"

Derek shook his head. "I don't know. I just have a feeling."

"In that case, you might want to double-check Chad's alibi, too," Mateo said.

"I will," Derek promised. "And I'll reinterview Horvath as well. But we're offering Maul a deal—if he tells us who gave him the jewels, we'll drop the accessory to murder charges. Hopefully, that'll shake something loose."

Mateo nodded. "That *would* be helpful."

Derek took off to do his police thing as Ren and Mateo went back to work on digging up any information they could find on our major suspects. I stared at the murder board. There was something there, niggling at the back of my mind, but it wouldn't come forward.

Giving up on figuring out what it was, I decided to interrogate the encyclopedia since Sybil had left the books here at the safe house. I sat down on my bed, the books spread out around me, and Ruby lying next to me. She rolled over to show her belly invitingly, but I ignored her. This need trumped belly rubs.

I murmured the spell to communicate with the encyclopedia and one of the books opened, the pages flipping to a blank one. "Can anyone use the spells inside you?" I asked.

The answer scrolled across the page in fiery letters: *Not*

anyone. Only those who have innate supernatural abilities to pay the price.

Price? Ruby asked, rolling back over to stare at me.

Pay the price in power, I assumed. "You mean a shifter or a vampire could use one of your spells?"

Yes, though I doubt other supernaturals are aware of the possibility, or that they would agree to lose their innate powers if they did.

Good to know. And I certainly wasn't going to tell them. "And can humans use your spells?"

No, they cannot pay the necessary price.

Ruby nudged me. *What about spells not in the book?*

I rubbed her ears in appreciation. Good point. "Can humans use other spells, not in you?"

Possibly. It depends on the parameters of the spell.

Well, crap. I'd hoped I'd eliminated humans altogether. What else could I ask? "Is there a spell that would mimic a phase demon's abilities?"

I host a spell that allows the caster to disappear, which might look like a phase demon.

"And if the person using it picks something up like, say, a bracelet, would it make them visible?"

There was no answer at first, then the book said, *I do not know.*

So there could be a spell out there that would simulate a phase demon, and a human might be able to use it, depending on the parameters the spell maker put on it. I sighed. Maybes weren't going to cut it. We needed more definite answers.

A cry of triumph came from the living room, and I rushed out to see Ren with her arms raised in victory.

"What did you find?" I asked. "Something concrete?"

She chuckled. "I don't know if it's concrete, but it's

certainly suspicious. We were digging around in Chad's background, and it looks like his credentials don't add up." She pushed the laptop toward me. "See here? His resume says he has bachelor's and master's degrees in Gallery and Museum Management from Western Colorado University, but when I checked, it looks like he started there but failed out of the program. He doesn't even have a bachelor's."

"He lied about his credentials?" What a jerk.

"Evidently," Mateo said. "I'm guessing he bribed someone to lie for him or forged recommendation letters from his teachers."

Ruby snorted. *Chad has been a very bad boy.*

I didn't understand. "How is that motive to steal?"

Mateo grinned. "It isn't, in and of itself, but if his high school buddy, Freddy, knew he didn't graduate and blackmailed him..."

Oh, I got it! "And he had to steal the jewelry to pay his blackmailer..."

Ren picked up the narrative. "Then he panicked when Hank looked into his background..."

Then he could be our murderer, Ruby finished in triumph.

Mateo frowned. "You think he killed Hank? He seems like such a wimp."

Ren snorted. "Even wimps would be brave enough to stab someone if they're invisible and they know the other guy won't fight back."

True. "And you did recognize his scent in the guard room," I reminded Mateo. Plus, someone had to leave that bogus suicide note. My gaze drifted toward it. "Oh!" I snapped my fingers, finally realizing what had been bugging me. "Look at the pictures Chad printed out for me of the stolen jewels." I tapped the pictures in question. "Now look at the picture of the note left next to Hank's body. His printer must have been running out of ink—it's faded out in the same place on all of them. Chad printed out the suicide note."

"Well, I'll be," Mateo drawled. "You're right. I've got to call Derek."

Mateo got Derek on the phone and put it on speaker, then explained what we'd found.

"That tracks with what Horvath just told me," Derek said. "He said he did call in to work to tell them about his emergency surgery, but he only talked to Chad."

Mateo snorted. "And Chad, wanting Horvath's job, didn't pass on the information. I bet if you ask him, he'll deny it."

"Horvath also said Chad has been trying to get him fired and making everyone believe he's a screw-up," Derek added. "Mrs. Honeycutt confirms Horvath's job isn't in jeopardy."

It figured. "And I bet Chad somehow bribed or black-mailed his roommate into giving him an alibi."

"My thoughts exactly," Derek said. "I don't want to alert Nowicki that we're on to him, so I'll bring the roommate in for an interview after he goes to work tomorrow. If this pans out the way we think, it appears Nowicki is our thief...and probably our murderer. But don't do anything to let him know we suspect him. We have to figure out *how* he did it first, in order for an arrest to stick." He sighed. "But...phase demon powers. That just makes things more difficult. Ivy, we may need your exorcism spell after all."

"It's more likely he found some kind of spell to imitate those abilities," I reminded Derek. "Ruby says he's not a demon."

Mateo interjected, "Is it possible for a part-demon to hide their abilities from a hellhound?"

Ruby's brow wrinkled. *I don't think so.*

I shrugged. "We're not sure, but I can ask the books."

"Okay," Derek said. "Do that. We need to find a way to stop him, one way or another."

I just hoped he wasn't part phase demon. I *really* didn't want to use that spell again.

CHAPTER
TEN

THE FOUR OF us were too brain dead to think straight on this anymore, so we took the rest of the night off, but got right back to it the next morning. While we waited for Derek's call, I pulled out the encyclopedia again and activated the communication spell while Ruby and Mateo watched.

"Can a demon or shapeshifter hide their abilities from a hellhound like Ruby?" I asked.

The word burned across the page. *No.*

I blew out a sigh of relief. "We aren't dealing with a phase demon then, just a human who must have found some kind of invisibility spell. But how?"

"It doesn't matter," Mateo said impatiently. "Can I ask the questions?"

"Sure," I said. "You're a supe, so you just have to be willing to pay the price in power to use the spells in the book. For the communication spell, it's negligible."

Mateo used the spell, then said, "We really need to get rid of his advantage. Is there a way to counter a spell?"

Most counterspells are protective in nature, intended to safe-

guard a person being attacked, not to counter a spell the insti-gator cast upon themselves.

Mateo made a frustrated noise. "How can we remove a spell the thief cast on himself?"

Another one of the books opened by itself and flipped through pages until it stopped...on the invisibility spell.

"How does that help?" I asked in exasperation. "We don't want to use it, we want to stop it."

Mateo pointed to the bottom of the page. "It also shows how to see through the invisibility spell. Place an amethyst over your third eye and say the incantation, and you'll be able to see what's hidden."

An amethyst I had, but... "I don't know if I have enough juice left to power this spell." It would take another chunk of power, power I couldn't spare.

Mateo grinned. "Maybe you don't, but I do."

"Is that wise? Your ability to transform into a wolf would be impaired. What if you need to shift?"

Mateo waved away my objection. "I won't shift in front of a human, anyway, so this is how I can best help. Do you have an amethyst I can use?"

It's a good plan, Ruby said. *Do it.*

"I suppose," I said in answer to both of them. At least I wouldn't have to lose any more power. I took a loose amethyst from my stash and gave it to him.

Holding the amethyst to his forehead, Mateo solemnly read the spell. "I call upon the power of the stone, percep-tive and wise, to pierce through all deception, all disguise. Reveal thyself to my discerning eyes."

A chill wind blew through the room, ruffling Mateo's curls. His eyes widened as he grimaced and rubbed his stomach. "It feels like I have magical indigestion."

"And it will until you activate the spell," I told him. In

this case, the trigger words were "Reveal thyself," said three times.

"Good to know. I'll let Derek know so we can hatch a plan to use this."

He put his phone on speaker, and I heard Derek say, "Is this important? I have the roommate—Russell—here, and he admits he lied about the alibi. It seems Nowicki has an impressive blade collection and threatened him. We've promised to protect Russell in exchange for his testimony."

"Good," Mateo said. "I think I know a way to capture Chad." He explained what we'd learned, then asked, "Where are you? At the station?" When Derek confirmed that, Mateo said, "I'll head that way now. Wait a few minutes, and use Russell's phone to text Chad, pretending to be Russell. Tell Chad that Russell is being questioned in an interview room, and hasn't said anything yet, but he's afraid he'll be arrested. Given the way Chad murdered Hank without remorse, I bet he'll show up at the station to get rid of any more loose ends."

Derek made a sound of agreement. "That should draw him out. But how will you know when to activate the spell?"

"You're having Chad watched, right?"

"Yeah, he's at work right now."

"Have your guys follow him, then text when he arrives. I'll activate the spell then so I can see him and stop him."

"Okay," Derek agreed. "It's a plan," and hung up.

Mateo jumped up and I did so as well, going to grab my bag. Ruby leapt up with me.

"What are you doing?" he asked sternly.

"Going with you."

"Oh, no, you're not. You're staying here. You should be

safe here since Chad is going to the station, but I'll send someone to guard you anyway."

"But—"

"No buts," Mateo said sternly. "I don't want to have to worry about you while we're dealing with Chad."

"But—"

He grabbed his keys and ran to the SUV, taking off before we could catch up with him.

Ruby barked furiously at the retreating SUV. *I can't believe he did that, after everything we did to help.* She whirled to glare at me. *You're not going to let him get away with that, are you?*

No! I had a really bad feeling about this, and just knew I had to be there to... Well, I didn't know why, but I had to be there.

Your car is still at the apartment, Ruby reminded me.

Yeah, but I didn't need it. Quickly, I brought up a rideshare app and booked a driver, making sure they allowed dogs. "She's only five minutes out. C'mon, Ruby. Let's go."

You betcha.

Luckily, the driver must've fancied herself another Danica Patrick, because she drove like speed limits were just a suggestion. I didn't think Mateo or Derek would appreciate us showing up without their approval, so we hid in the ladies' room in the lobby. *Can you tell what's going on?* I asked Ruby. She could read Derek, at least.

Yeah. Mateo and Derek have Russell in an interview room, waiting for Chad to show up. Oh, he just arrived, Ruby told me. *Aaaaand...Mateo said the trigger words to make him visible. The demons following Chad are thinking he's looking desperate, disheveled, and deranged.*

Desperate? Why did that ring a bell?

All of a sudden, I became aware of a new gemstone

entering my field of awareness. My abilities were still muffled, but I could vaguely sense a diamond seething with anger and desperation. It must be really strong for me to feel it now.

Oh, crap. Everything fell together all at once. Chad wasn't invisible—he had a cursed artifact with a diamond housing a phase demon activated by desperation. I'd bet anything it was in some kind of knife.

Why didn't you sense it before? Ruby asked.

Because it was never in range before.

And now, he was headed toward Mateo and Derek, who thought they were safe because of the visibility spell...which wouldn't work on the phase demon. *We have to stop him!*

But what can you do? Your powers are very weak.

I don't know, but I'll think of something.

We ran out the door and the guy at the counter tried to stop us, but Ruby growled at him, so he let us by.

"That worked?" I said in disbelief.

He's a demon. I explained what's going on. Hurry.

I bolted down the hallway, and opened the door Ruby pawed at. We rushed in, and Derek said, "What—"

No time to explain. I could sense the diamond in this room, somewhere.

Ruby whirled around. *The demon in the diamond...it's right in front of Mateo!*

Mateo...who was shielding Russell. What could I do? My voice! It worked on humans, and Mom said if I was emotional enough, the powers should amplify.

I grabbed my cuff bracelet and shoved as much power as I could through the opal toward the amethyst and citrine. "Chad Nowicki, drop that artifact!" I bellowed, pouring my vast fear and desperation into the command.

A dagger, with the cursed diamond on the pommel, clattered to the floor, and Chad appeared immediately in front of Mateo, his arm raised. Crap. My command didn't hold for long, and Chad lunged for the dagger, but Mateo kicked it toward me and grabbed Chad.

I couldn't chance Chad or anyone else using this cursed stone ever again. I had to exorcise it.

No! Ruby said. *You can't. It'll wipe you out. You don't know how—*

Dropping to my knees and slapping my hand on the ornate hilt of the dagger, I muttered the spell as fast as I could. "Demon thou art, demon thou shalt not be. Say it times three, I exorcise thee." I repeated the trigger words three more times, feeling power empty out of me and surge into the stone. The phase demon in the stone screamed, and evaporated in a puff of smoke.

Ivy, no, Ruby screamed as I fell into blackness.

I WOKE SLOWLY, feeling crappy—thirsty, groggy, and as empty of power as a squeezed-out tube of toothpaste. I tried to open my eyes, but it was too much effort. A bed—I was lying in a bed, and there were beeping noises all around me. A couple of warm, furry bodies lay cuddled against me.

Mateo, she's awake, Ruby said.

I felt something leave the bed then saw a bright light flash, even behind my closed eyelids. "Ivy?" Mateo said. "Ivy, are you awake?"

In answer, all I could do was groan.

"She *is* awake," he said on a sigh. He patted my hand. "You're going to be all right."

Huh? "Wha—"

"Wait," he said, "let me get you some water."

I felt a straw bump up against my lips and I sat up and sipped greedily. The cool liquid made my mouth and throat feel a thousand times better. I sat back in relief and forced my eyes open. Gradually, Mateo's dark curls and Ruby's fuzzy face came into focus as Mateo raised my bed to a sitting position. They both looked so concerned.

You scared me, Ruby said accusingly.

"Where— Where am I?" I glanced around, seeing flowers and balloons covering every available surface. "Florist?" My voice sounded weak, even to me.

Mateo squeezed my hand and chuckled. "It looks like that, but those are get-well wishes from, well, everyone. We all appreciate how you sacrificed your powers to eliminate the cursed artifact and save lives. It's the least we could do to thank you."

I just did what I had to do. "Even though I'd stupidly assumed a human couldn't use a cursed stone?"

"We all did. But, apparently, anyone with enough desperation can hear and use the demon inside it."

But if this wasn't a florist, then... "Hospital?"

"Sort of. You're in the underground's emergency room, in the care of their healer, Dr. Oliver."

I didn't know there was such a thing. "And Chad?" I asked.

Mateo settled on the bed next to me and twined my fingers with his. "Arrested and in jail," he assured me. "Thanks to you. With Freddy and Russell's help, we worked out that Chad bought the dagger for his collection, and when Freddy blackmailed him, his desperation to keep his secret activated the phase demon in the diamond. The more he used it, the more it fed his desperation, making him willing to do just about anything."

Like murder. I nodded weakly.

"Freddy will stay in jail, too. He's been charged with blackmail and 'theft by receiving'—receiving stolen property with the intent to sell it. But Derek dropped the accessory to murder charges, especially since he told us where he sold the rest of the stones."

"But Chad..." I croaked out, and took another sip of water. "He knows about demons now." Would they have to kill him?

Naw, Ruby drawled. *Worse luck.*

"Ah, and that's where our vampire allies came in. They selectively planted new memories to explain away any...irregularities. For Russell, too."

My eyes widened. "They can do that?" The possibilities were horrifying.

"It's okay," Mateo said. "Not many can do it well, but it seems your pal Maurice has quite a knack for it."

That made me feel better—I trusted Maurice. But so much had happened... "How long have I been here?"

"Five days," he informed me gravely.

I was out that long? Holy crap,

Ruby cuddled closer. *We were worried about you!*

A woman in a white coat bustled in then. Her hair was scraped into a no-nonsense bun, but her eyes were kind and focused on me. "Hello, Ivy," she said. "I'm Dr. Oliver. I'm so glad you're finally awake. You gave us quite a scare, draining your powers like that."

She's part healing demon, Ruby told me. *I didn't know there were such things.*

Dr. Oliver gave her a stern look. *We keep my abilities secret for a reason.*

Ruby cringed. *I know, I know. But not from my bestie. She needs to know.*

I didn't seem to be wearing any gemstones. "My powers...are they gone?" I asked.

"They're coming back slowly," Dr. Oliver assured me. "But you should never attempt two such power-draining spells so closely together again."

"I won't," I said. Not unless it was absolutely necessary.

Ruby growled. *It better not be necessary.*

Dr. Oliver pulled a small box from her pocket. "Mateo said you'd want this right away."

I opened the box and sighed in relief. Mr. Opal!

I put the pendant on. "Thank you!" Silently, I asked, *Mr. Opal, can you hear me?*

I can indeed.

His voice still sounded a bit weak and far away.

It will get stronger, he assured me. *You will get stronger.*

I glanced up at Dr. Oliver. "How long do I have to stay here?"

"Until I'm convinced you're not going to damage yourself any more." At my glare, the doctor smiled. "Another day or two, at the most, until you're stronger." She gave me a stern look. "So long as you don't over-exert yourself." With that admonition, she left.

Good. "I can go home then?" I asked Mateo. I didn't think there was any more need for the safe house.

He squeezed my hand. "Yes, of course. Ren gathered up all your things and took them home, gave the necklace you repaired to Amber, and even put that cursed diamond in one of your cleansing solutions."

"Glad to hear it." The diamond didn't need to suffer any more than it already had. "Thank her for me?"

"Of course. And there's another thing..." Mateo said

slowly. "After this near disaster, the shifters, vamps, and demons formed a supernatural council. They decided that the Special Crimes Unit is too understaffed to handle events of this magnitude, especially here on the west side, so they are each providing two civilian personnel to the SCU. They wanted people they knew would respect and work well with the other species, so the shifters are providing Kai and me, the vampires volunteered Maurice and Billy, and the demons are providing Ren and..." He paused, giving me an odd look.

"Who? Is it someone I know?"

"Well, yeah. It's you—if you agree to it."

"Me? How can I do a job like that?"

Mateo burst out laughing. "You've *been* doing it, sweetheart. Sybil just figured she'd make it official."

"Oh." I guess maybe I had. But he'd called me... "Uh...sweetheart?"

He leaned over and kissed my forehead, our hands still linked together. "When you passed out and I thought I'd lost you, I realized how important you are. How much the supernatural community needs you. How much *I* need you. I don't care what anyone says. If we want to...date or whatever, and see where this goes, then that's our business. Especially since I won't be your boss anymore." He paused, and cleared his throat. "That is, if you want that."

My heart leapt in my chest. "Yes, I want that," I assured him shyly. "Very much."

Wahoo! Ruby caroled. *Mateo and Ivy sittin' in a tree. K-I-S-S-I—*

Oh, shut up, I told her, feeling my face heat. *He hasn't kissed me yet.*

No, but he will!

Maybe. If I was very, very lucky....

MOONSTONES &
MALICE

CHAPTER
ONE

I STARED down at the ornate gold peridot ring and repressed the urge to cheer. This was a cursed artifact, for sure. The owner of said ring, a young woman who'd legitimately purchased the ring at a pawn shop, didn't have a clue why we were really looking for it. It was so worth it to come in before our shift to check this out.

She peered down at it. "Is that it? Is that the one that was stolen?"

Mateo Duran, my new shifter partner in the Special Crimes Unit which investigated cases involving supernaturals, glanced at me with a questioning look.

If I, the stone whisperer, could only sense a void where the stone should be nattering away at me, it was definitely a cursed gemstone. "I'm afraid it is," I told her.

As Mateo did his thing to take custody of the "stolen property," Ruby, my telepathic hellhound, said, *Whoo-hoo! The council will be sooooo happy.*

Yes, they would, and we were finding more cursed stones now that my roommate, electro demon and tech guru Ren, was also working for the SCU and had *carte blanche* to look into the pawnshop databases. It appeared Dahlia, the demon/shifter who'd sold her mother's cursed gemstones, had used false identification to sell some of the artifacts, but Ren was slowly rooting them out. I finally had hope we'd find most, if not all, of those Dahlia had sold.

I wore my gemstones in jewelry and piercings all over my body so I'd have easy access to my powers, and they cheered since I couldn't. Luckily, that's all they did. The wise opal my parents had sent me had them pretty much whipped into shape, so I no longer had to pull my silk hoodie over my head to block their incessant chattering.

Naw, my garnet said, *it's just that Ruby already said it for us.*

Okay, so I didn't get a total reprieve, but it was a vast improvement over their former babbling.

As we left the buyer's apartment, Mateo said, "I assume the peridot hasn't been activated?"

"No, thank heavens."

He bumped my shoulder with his and grinned at me. "Good. I'd hate to see you have to use that exorcism spell again so soon."

Me too. I'd just gotten out of the hospital two weeks ago after I damned near killed myself by using the spell twice in the same week. Talk about complete magical depletion—I never wanted to do that again. I sighed. "I'm just glad the council agreed I didn't need to exorcise the demons unless they're activated."

Mateo nodded. "Me, too. Let's see, that's four unactivated artifacts we found so far, right? The tanzanite pendant, the moonstone bracelet, the small turtle carved from tiger's eye, and this one." At my nod, he asked, "Any way of knowing what type of demons are trapped inside?"

"Unfortunately, no."

He nodded and opened the SUV door for me. "Okay, let's get this one back to the station before some desperate person senses it and tries to grab it."

Amen. When someone's desperation activated a cursed stone, they acquired the powers of the demon trapped inside it...to devastating effect. And we'd learned they didn't even need to be supernatural or touch the stone to hear it calling. That made the gemstones even more dangerous, and keeping them locked up was a necessity. "Works for me."

When we arrived back at the SCU, it was our normal afternoon shift change time, when Mateo and I took over from the other demon/shifter team, Derek and Kai. We'd be on the clock until eight, when vamps Maurice and Billy took over for the third shift, nighttime.

I nodded at Taylor Atwater, the twenty-something desk clerk and dispatcher, and Ruby caroled, *Hi, Taylor!*

Taylor's eyes widened and she clutched the leather medicine bag she wore on a cord half-hidden under her long dark hair. It must have some protective mojo or something, though it obviously wouldn't deter a smart-aleck hellhound, no matter how much she willed it.

Stop that, I told Ruby. *You know it freaks her out when you talk to her.*

Hey, she's part water demon, even if she's so weak she can barely squirt. She should get used to talking to other supes, Ruby said smugly.

I rolled my eyes. Why couldn't Ruby's dad have trained his pups to be mellow and laid-back? *Fang has a lot to answer for.*

Ruby harrumphed. *What good would I do you then?*

I sighed. *Most people want a dog friend for companionship.*

Yeah, but with me you get so much more!

Mateo grinned at me. His wide smile turned him from nice-looking to absolutely gorgeous. "Ruby freaking out Taylor again?" he asked.

I scowled. "Yeah, I told her to stop, but since she didn't, she'll lose TV privileges for a week." Though she'd learned how to use the remote, if I put it where she couldn't reach it, she had no choice but to ask Ren or me for help. And Ren would enforce the ban if I asked her to.

Hey, no fair, Ruby protested.

"You heard me," I said sternly then turned to Mateo as Ruby muttered something unintelligible...something I probably didn't want to hear. "Shall we secure the peridot?"

"Of course."

The evidence room held a locked cage guarded by Caleb Shaw, a thirty-something shifter with a military haircut and stern expression. He helped us log in the cursed artifact, then Mateo checked his watch. "Time for the shift change briefing."

Derek, Kai, and Ren were already waiting in the conference room, and we were joined quickly by Lieutenant "call me Leo" Jacobs. A shifter in his fifties with salt-and-pepper hair and a beard, he led the SCU and preferred to keep things informal. He sat at the head of the conference table, clasped his hands together, and said, "Derek and Kai, please brief Mateo and Ivy on what happened during your shift."

Derek nodded his acknowledgment. "We had an incident very early this morning with an assault by a wolf shifter on a human."

"What?" Mateo leaned forward. "Who? Which shifter?"

"Harley Ritter," Derek supplied.

At Mateo's questioning look, Kai grimaced and nodded. "Harley really tore the guy up, though he didn't kill him."

"I know Harley pretty well, and I don't believe it," Mateo said. "Unless he was provoked."

"That's possible," Derek admitted. "The victim is Aldo Becker, who has been charged in the past for aggravated assault and sexual assault, but never convicted."

What does that mean? Ruby asked.

I repeated her question, and Mateo frowned. "It means he got away with it. I'll bet he provoked Harley somehow."

Lt. Jacobs—I had a hard time thinking of him as Leo no matter how much he wanted us to—raised an eyebrow. "We do not take sides or blame the victim here. We investigate and find the truth."

Mateo winced. "I'm sorry. You're right." He glanced at Derek and Kai. "What did Harley say?"

Kai rubbed the back of his neck and grimaced. "Harley admits he attacked the human, but he doesn't have a reason."

"No reason?" Mateo said in disbelief.

"No," Derek said. "He says he felt compelled to do so...but doesn't know why."

"Like a vampire compelled him?" I asked.

Derek shrugged. "Perhaps. Or maybe some kind of demon."

Well, crap. That wasn't good.

"Do you want us to check it out?" Mateo asked the lieutenant.

Jacobs shook his head. "No, this is for your awareness only. There was another apparent shifter-on-human attack yesterday, but the human was able to get away and report it. We weren't able to identify the shifter. I'll have Maurice and Billy check these incidents out tonight, then Derek and Kai can follow up in the morning if necessary." He glanced at me. "The supernatural council is still concerned about the possibility of cursed stones, so I'd like you to continue to search for those."

Thank goodness. I was still a wee bit uncomfortable around violence. I'd been getting pretty good at using my stones to shield, especially since Ruby and Mateo had started randomly "attacking" me by poking me or biting me. Sometimes they even yelled "shield" before they did it, or Mr. Opal did if he sensed danger. But I sure didn't go looking for it.

Ruby pouted. *Why do the shifters and vamps get the fun stuff?*

Right, 'cause it's sooooo fun to put our lives on the line. Ignoring her, I leaned forward to address the lieutenant. "Ren found us another one today. We secured it in the evidence room."

"Excellent," he said, rubbing his hands. "With our newly beefed-up workforce, we might actually be able to accomplish some things."

Ren slid a piece of paper across the table to me. "Here are a few more possibilities you might want to check out." As before, she'd given us the buyers' names, addresses, and telephone numbers. "I'm not sure if these came from Dahlia, but they are all jewelry pieces with stones in them."

I glanced at the list, then passed it to Mateo. "You can take the second one off the list," I told her. At her questioning look, I added, "Gemstones, having been created by pressures in the earth, only achieve awareness once they are faceted and polished. 'Stones' such as pearls, coral, and amber which are organic in nature never achieve awareness."

"Huh," Ren said. "Good to know. I'll remove them from my searches."

"So, we have our marching orders then," Mateo said. "Shall we go?"

I nodded. I preferred to drive by the locations first, to see if I could sense the stones or the void left by an unactivated one. If necessary, we'd call to make appointments later to check out the stones.

Once we were out the door, Mateo said, "I'd like to make a little detour first." He headed toward the back of the building.

I followed him. "Where are you going?"

"I just want to talk to Harley for a few minutes. One of the old guard might not talk to me, but Harley will."

The old guard wouldn't talk to him? What did that mean? "But the lieutenant said not—"

Mateo patted the air as if to calm me. "I know it's not our case, but he is my friend, and I want to know what happened."

I shook my head and followed him.

Are you going to revoke Mateo's *TV privileges for that?* Ruby snarked.

I scowled at her. *Watch it, or I'll extend yours to two weeks.*

There was unaccustomed silence from my talkative hellhound, then she said in an uncharacteristically subdued tone, *I'm gonna talk to Ren,* then trotted off.

"Don't bug Ren too much," I called after her. Mateo raised an eyebrow at me. I shrugged. "She's like a sullen teenager, what can I say?"

He grinned and turned into the room with the cells. I couldn't tell if there was anyone in the vampire cell, since it was light-tight and closed up during daylight hours, but there was definitely someone in the shifter/demon holding cell—a guy maybe a little older than Mateo who was slumped over on the cot, his hands speared into a messy mop of brown hair, his clothes torn and bloody.

"Harley?" Mateo said in a subdued tone.

The guy raised his head, and I'd never seen such an expression of devastation on anyone's face before.

"I didn't do it, Mateo," he said brokenly. "Well, I did, but it wasn't me."

Huh?

I leaned against the wall as Mateo pulled a chair up next to the bars of Harley's cell. "Tell me what happened," Mateo urged.

Harley glanced at me with a dubious frown, and Mateo said, "This is my partner, Ivy Weiss. You've heard of the stone whisperer, right?" At Harley's nod, he added, "You can talk in front of her—she's the one who got my soul back. So...what happened?"

Harley ran a hand down his face. "I—I'm not sure. A lot of it is just...blank. The last thing I remember, I was at the bar, playing pool, then, suddenly, it's hours later and I've wolfed out, I'm covered in blood, and my teeth are in the shoulder of a guy I've never seen before." He shook his head. "Next thing I know, Kai is pulling me off him and yelling at me to shift back." He gave Mateo a pleading look. "You gotta believe me. I have no memory of why I did that, and I don't even know that guy." He closed his eyes and added, "At least he's not dead."

That *did* sound like he'd been compelled. Maybe Mateo was right.

Mateo nodded. "Which bar was it?"

"Crescent Taproom."

"It's a shifter bar," Mateo told me, then asked Harley, "Do you remember anyone at the bar talking to you? Someone who might have forced you to do that?"

"I—I don't remember anything like that, but I wouldn't just go off on a complete stranger—you know that."

"I know," Mateo said softly and patted his hand through the bars. "There was another possible shifter-on-human attack last night, but the shifter was scared off. Do you think you might be responsible for that one as well?"

"What?" Harley asked, his eyes wild. "I don't think so. I would have remembered, right?"

Very likely. If he remembered one, he probably would remember the other...if he was responsible. And I was with Mateo on this—I didn't think he did it. At least, not intentionally.

"Okay, okay," Mateo said. "That doesn't matter right now. Can you tell me who you talked to?"

Harley gave him as many details as he could remember, and Mateo wrote them all down. When Harley finished, Mateo asked, "Has Duncan been here yet?"

"No," Harley admitted. "I wouldn't blame the alpha if he wanted to let me rot for a while."

"Don't worry," Mateo said. "I'll let him know what you told me, and we'll see if we can find out who's responsible for this."

Harley glanced up, hope in his eyes. "You believe me?"

"Of course. Everyone here will do their best to bring the real perpetrator to justice."

I stepped forward. "He's right," I said softly. "We'll all help."

Harley's eyes filled with tears and his face crumpled. "Thanks, guys. You have no idea—" But he became too choked up to go any further.

"No worries," Mateo said with a smile. "I know you'd do the same for me."

Harley just nodded, unable to speak past his emotion.

"Well," Mateo said, "we'd better get to it." He rose and gestured for me to precede him through the door.

I called Ruby to let her know we were leaving, and she joined us in the hallway to head to the SUV. Partway down the hallway, she yelled, *Shield!*

I slammed it on just as she leapt up to bite me. Thankfully, the shield kept her teeth from piercing my skin. "Is that really necessary?" I asked.

Yep, she said smugly. *You're getting faster, too. Good job.*

I just wish she didn't enjoy it quite so much.

"Yes," Mateo added. "It might save your life someday. And, speaking of saving your life, don't forget your gear."

Our "gear" was a belt that carried shifter sedation spray —Triple S—to subdue shifters, pepper spray to deter humans, and wooden stakes and silver cuffs for vamps, though we only needed those after sundown. The belt was kinda awkward, but I assumed I'd get used to it.

When we got inside the SUV, I couldn't hold back any longer. "You're going to investigate, aren't you?" I accused Mateo. "Even though the lieutenant told us to look for more stones."

"Yeah," Mateo said. "I remember what it's like to be convicted of something I didn't do, with no hope of proving my innocence...until a certain stone whisperer decided I was worthy of being helped."

Boy, he's good at hitting the feels, Ruby said in admiration.

I just rolled my eyes. "All right. I admit it, I want to help him too. Can we do both?"

Mateo gave me that wide, ear-to-ear grin that I couldn't resist. "Of course. We're just that good."

You betcha, Ruby said. *Let's go!*

But we'd only gotten about three blocks away when the radio blared into life. "Team Bravo, respond to shifter assault in progress." Taylor went on to give the location—a field on the west side of the city, not far from us.

"Copy that," Mateo said. "We're on it."

Oh, crap. An assault in progress.

Oh, yay, Ruby countered. *An assault in progress!*

CHAPTER
TWO

Suck it up, Ivy, I told myself. I had two ways to defend myself now—I could compel both humans and wolves in human form, plus I had the shield...if I could make it work under real-life adverse conditions.

You've also got the Triple-S and Mateo, Ruby reminded me, *and, best of all, me.*

Yeah. It would be enough. If I said that to myself with enough conviction, that would make it true, right?

Riiiiight, Ruby said with a snort.

Mateo hit the lights and siren, and we were at the scene within minutes. There, a wolf shifter snarled and lunged at a parked car near a vacant field. Luckily, there was no one else around.

There's a human inside the car, Ruby said. *He's bleeding but still alive.*

I passed on her information, and Mateo nodded as he jumped out of the SUV. "I'll take the shifter. You call an ambulance."

Between one breath and the next, Mateo shifted into his wolf form with a flash of light and took off after the shifter.

262

Ruby ran after him, and I called dispatch who told me an ambulance was already on its way. I glanced up and saw both Mateo and Ruby growling, darting in and out with sharp nips to get the aggressive wolf's attention, but he completely ignored them.

"What are they saying?" I asked Ruby. She could hear the shifters when they were in wolf form.

Sorry. Forgot to echo it to you.

With Ruby relaying their thoughts, I heard Mateo yelling, *Back off. Now! Stand down!*

The other wolf just kept repeating, *Attack Lars Burton. Teach him a lesson.* He said it over and over like a mantra, intent on tearing his way into the car where his prey was cowering.

Crap. I scrambled out of the vehicle, pulling out the Triple-S as I did so. "Mateo and Ruby," I yelled, "move away. I don't want to hit you with this stuff."

They saw the canister in my hand and backed off. The attacking wolf was so intent on what he was doing that he didn't even notice me coming up behind him. Remembering the instructions, I depressed the nozzle and sprayed it so it enveloped his head.

The wolf turned his head with a snarl and Mateo shoved me away to stand protectively between us. But it wasn't necessary. Not only had I activated my shield, but the wolf shook his head briefly, then his eyes rolled back in his head and he passed out, shifting back to human as he did so.

Mateo whirled on me. *Are you okay?* His gaze roamed my body rapidly, as if to assure himself I was all in one piece.

"Yeah, sure." I glanced at the canister. "This is strong stuff. What's in it?"

I'm not sure—wolfsbane and other ingredients, Mateo said.

"Well, it sure works."

With a flash of light, Mateo changed back, fully clothed. Gotta love that shifter magic. "I hear sirens. Come on, let's get him in the back of the SUV before the ambulance gets here."

Luckily, Mateo didn't mean for me to help lift the heavy shifter. He did that while I opened the door, then closed it after him. Once the guy was in, we ran back over to the human inside the car. The doors were locked, but we could see someone huddled over the steering wheel. Was he unconscious?

Mateo banged on the window as the ambulance drove up. "Open up, sir. We're here to help."

The twenty-something guy with lank, dishwater blond hair, looked up with terror clear on his face.

"You're safe now," I assured him, "and the ambulance is coming to take you to the hospital."

"What about the—the wolf?" the guy said in trepidation.

"The *dog* is gone," Mateo said shortly.

The medics reached us then, and when the guy in the car saw their uniforms, he unlocked the door and allowed them to help him out. His arm was bloody and maybe a bit chewed, but I didn't see any other injuries.

They took him away, and Mateo said, "We'll question him at the hospital later. Right now, we need to get Devon to the station."

"Is that the same Devon I met?" I asked. The one who had helped rescue me from the vampires at Dahlia's farm?

"Yep. Now I know there's something wrong—this is not like Devon at all." He glanced at me as he opened the front passenger door. "Can you drive to the station?"

"Sure. Why do—"

"I need to talk to Ruby," he explained, then got in, shut the door, and shifted so he could.

"Okay, but first, how long will Devon be out?" I asked. "Will we need help subduing him to get him inside the station?" That part of the briefing was a bit vague in my mind.

Ruby echoed Mateo's thoughts to me. *No, the sedation should last at least a couple of hours or so. You'll be fine.*

"Okay." I drove while Mateo questioned Ruby about what she'd heard in Devon's mind.

He wasn't thinking much, she told us. *Mainly, he was focused on doing as much damage to that guy as possible, to teach him a lesson.*

Teach him what lesson? Mateo asked.

I don't know. He was all "Attack Lars Burton. Teach him a lesson." That just kept repeating in his head over and over again.

"You didn't hear that through the pack bonds?" I asked Mateo.

No, but I wouldn't unless he was talking directly to me. He wasn't. He wouldn't respond at all.

It was weird, though, Ruby added hesitantly. *It wasn't like it was his own thoughts.*

"What do you mean?" I asked.

It was more like it was someone outside him, telling him what to do, and he just kept repeating it like a command.

I thought so, Mateo said in satisfaction. *He was being controlled. Did he give any idea who was doing it? Picture someone in his head? Hear a voice?*

No, sorry, Ruby said. *Nothing like that.*

Okay, thanks, you've been a big help.

When we arrived back at the station and I let Mateo know the coast was clear, he shifted back into his human form and carried Devon inside. The lieutenant met us there to lock him into the same cell with Harley.

"This is becoming a real problem," Lt. Jacobs said after he followed us outside. "That's three shifter attacks on humans now."

"Yeah," Mateo said. "But I don't think they're fully responsible. I think they've been controlled." He passed on what Ruby told us.

The lieutenant nodded grimly. "If so, it must be a demon or vamp controlling them. We need to brief the council." He rubbed his hand over his face tiredly. "I'll set something up for tonight and let you know what time."

"Okay," I said. "But we may need Maurice's help to convince this latest victim that he was attacked by a dog, not a wolf." Apparently, my vampire friend was some kind of prodigy when it came to getting into people's minds and convincing them black was white...or orange, or even an apple.

"Noted," Lt. Jacobs said shortly. "I'll have him do that on his shift. What else did the victim say?"

Mateo shrugged. "Not much. An ambulance took him to the hospital, and we're on our way to interview him now."

"Good," the lieutenant said, turning to go back inside. "Keep me posted."

"We will," Mateo assured him. "And we'll be back later to talk to Devon. I think this takes priority over finding cursed stones that haven't even been activated."

The lieutenant waved a hand in acknowledgment and closed the door behind him.

"You ready for this?" Mateo asked me.

Born ready! Ruby exclaimed.

My response was a bit more subdued. "Of course."

He grinned and slung an arm around my shoulders,

snugging me to him. "You sure are. Great job with the Triple-S there. You didn't even hesitate."

I cursed my fair complexion as I felt my cheeks heat. I loved his warm hugs, his affectionate personality. But snuggling wasn't the best idea when we were work partners and prejudice existed in the entire supe community for inter-species relationships.

I don't think Mateo cares, Ruby said frankly.

That's what I'd thought before, but, at the hospital, he'd said he wanted to date me...then never mentioned it again. I didn't know why, but I certainly wasn't going to bring it up. I mumbled something incoherent and pulled away to open the door of our vehicle.

Mateo seemed to sense my reticence, and we remained silent until we got to the hospital. As he questioned Lars, I texted Ren to see what information she could find on him.

Once Mateo finished, not having found out anything other than the fact that Devon had attacked Lars without provocation, we left and got in the SUV.

"I asked Ren to check him out," I told Mateo.

"And?"

"Lars Burton is on the sex offender registry, convicted of unlawful sexual contact."

Mateo nodded. "The guy Harley attacked—he was also arrested for sexual assault."

"But not convicted."

"True, but that could be the connection between the two victims. They're sexual predators."

"Probably," I said, though we certainly didn't have any proof. "I wonder if the third guy who reported an attack—the one where the shifter got away—has a similar past."

Mateo nodded toward my phone. "Check with Ren."

I did, and sure enough, the third victim—if you could

call him that—was also on the sex offender registry. "You may have a good working theory there," I confirmed.

He nodded. "Let's see if Devon is awake and coherent yet, then later, we can question the patrons at the Crescent Taproom."

Devon was indeed awake, and, much like Harley, was stunned and horrified by what he'd done. "I would never—"

"We know," Mateo assured him. "But how do you know Lars Burton?"

"Who?" Devon looked puzzled.

"The guy you attacked," I told him. "Ruby heard you say his name in your mind, that you had to teach him a lesson."

"I did?" Devon grimaced. "I don't remember that. The last thing I remember, I was changing out a carburetor at the garage, then I was attacking that guy and you all stopped me. Thanks for that, by the way."

"So you remember doing it?" Mateo persisted.

"Yeah, but I don't know why."

Harley bumped Devon's shoulder with his. "Same thing happened to me."

Devon ran a hand down his face. "Really? What's going on here? Who's doing this to us?"

"That's what we want to find out," Mateo said. "We figure it has to be a vampire or a part-demon who has the ability to control others. Have you run across anyone like that?"

Both shifters shook their heads. "Not that I recall," Harley said. "Not lately."

"If they were told to forget, they wouldn't remember," I reminded him.

"Yeah," Mateo said reluctantly. "But a bystander may

have spotted someone talking to them who could have planted a command. We need to interview people who were present when they were last...in control of their own minds."

I shrugged. "That works if the controller did it with other people present. If it were me, I'd catch them alone."

Mateo regarded me thoughtfully. "Well, let's hope they're not as smart as you."

I glanced at Harley. "Kai said he was able to stop you from attacking, but Mateo wasn't able to stop Devon. Why is that?"

Harley looked puzzled. "I don't know."

"What do you remember?" Mateo asked him.

"I was pretty much focused on doing damage to the guy until Kai called my name and told me to stop."

"He called your name?" I turned to Mateo. "I don't think you called Devon's name. I don't remember hearing it until after he was sedated."

"Huh," Mateo said. "I think you're right—that may be the key to stopping them. We'll have to let the others know. Of course, that will only work if we know the shifter in question."

I grimaced. "And the vamps probably don't know many shifters, though they have other abilities that will come in handy, not to mention the Triple-S."

"Very true." Mateo checked his watch. "We still have time to visit the garage before they close, then the bar should be open and we can head there."

My phone dinged with an incoming text. I glanced down at it. "The supernatural council is scheduled to meet here at the shift change briefing, and Lt. Jacobs wants us present."

Devon grabbed hold of the bars. "You guys know we

didn't do this on purpose. Do you think Duncan will convince them to let us go?"

Mateo shook his head. "I don't know. I'm sure someone will let you know when the meeting is done."

Devon sighed heavily. "Yeah, okay. I hope you're able to find something to prove we were being controlled."

"Me, too," Mateo and I said in unison.

Me three, Ruby piped up. *I like these guys.*

CHAPTER

THREE

Unfortunately, the interviews at the garage and bar didn't elicit much additional information. The garage employees remembered Devon working on the carburetor, then heading to "take a leak," but never came back.

The bar was of even less use. None of the patrons we interviewed this afternoon were present when Harley was there, and the bartenders were so busy, they hadn't noticed anything. We planned on tracking down the guys Harley remembered drinking with, but called in a report to Lt. Jacobs first, then headed to the council meeting.

As we entered the station, Ruby called out a greeting to the dispatcher now on duty—a fiftyish balding guy named Joe Berry who was part weather demon. He was a lot friendlier than Taylor, and he treated Ruby like a grand-child...granddog? Whatever—he was definitely grandfatherly. Ruby stayed to chat with him while Mateo and I headed to the conference room.

Everyone was already there. The three council members —eco demon Sybil, representing the Demon Underground; Duncan, the alpha shifter representing the Pikes Peak Pack;

and Bartholomew, Protector of the West, representing the vampires—were seated on one side of the table. We sat on the other side with Derek, Kai, Maurice, and Billy, while Lt. Jacobs sat at the end.

Duncan curled his lip at us, and I gave Mateo a questioning glance. What was his problem? We weren't late.

Mateo just shook his head.

Once we sat down, they wasted no time getting down to business. Bartholomew scowled at Duncan. "What are you doing about your shifter problem?"

Duncan's eyebrows rose, but he kept his voice even. "I don't have a shifter problem—we have problem with someone *controlling* shifters." He turned to Lt. Jacobs. "What have you learned?"

"You are correct—it appears the shifters were being controlled by some unknown party who incited them to assault humans."

"You're a shifter," Bartholomew said with a snort. "Of course you'd say that."

As one of the non-shifters present, I spoke up. "It's true. I witnessed one attack myself, and it was clear the shifter was not in control of his own actions. Someone else was controlling him."

Bartholomew glared at me. "Are you accusing one of my people?"

Taken aback, I said, "I'm not accusing anyone. But the controller pretty much has to be a vampire or a part-demon."

"Hold on," Lt. Jacobs said. "What's important here is that shifters are being weaponized to attack humans, which threatens to reveal the existence of all supernaturals. We must find who is doing this and stop them immediately."

"Agreed," Sybil said.

"Well, it's not a vampire," Bartholomew said. "We have no reason to control shifters. Plus the attacks happened during the day."

Sybil raised an eyebrow. "Vamps could have told shifters at night to attack during the day. And, can you really speak for all vampires?" Before Bartholomew could answer, she said, "I think not. And, it's possible it's a part-demon—a Dolittle maybe, or a siren or a succubus."

"Or even a demon in a cursed stone," Duncan said with a sideways glance at me.

"That could be," I admitted. "Though I haven't sensed one in use. But, uh, what's a Dolittle?"

Sybil shook her head, seeming annoyed at herself. "Sorry, that's slang for an animal communicator who can not only talk to animals, but force them to do things."

"Can a Dolittle control a shifter?" Duncan asked, appearing taken aback by the thought.

"If they are in wolf form, maybe," Sybil said with a grimace.

"Do you have any in your underground?" Duncan demanded.

"I'm not sure—I haven't memorized the abilities of all demons in the underground, but I can check."

"Do that," Lt. Jacobs said. "And look for sirens and succubi as well, and any other part-demons who might be able to do this. Ivy will, of course, let us know if she senses a cursed stone in use." When Sybil and I nodded, he turned to Bartholomew. "And you should question your people to see if there is anyone who has a grudge against humans...or shifters."

Bartholomew started to speak, but Maurice held up his hand. "Billy and I can do that, sir. We'll be discreet."

The vampire leader frowned, but nodded in agreement.

Billy continued, "We haven't had an incident on our shift yet, and haven't been read in on what's happened. What can you tell us?"

After Lt. Jacobs told them everything we'd learned, Duncan said, "What about the pack members you have behind bars? As their alpha, I can compel them to tell you the truth, which is obviously that they are not responsible for their actions. Are you going to release them soon?"

Whoa. His tone was definitely belligerent, and he seemed to have a bug up his butt for some reason. Weird— he hadn't been like that before. Maybe he just didn't handle stress well.

Lt. Jacobs grimaced. "We already know they aren't responsible for their actions, but I don't think releasing them is a good idea. We have no idea who forced them against their will, or how. If they were controlled once, it might be easier to use them again."

Before Duncan could object, Sybil interjected, "He's right. They would be safer staying here, so they can't be manipulated again. Since they both work for Relentless Protection Services, we can make sure they don't lose any pay." When Duncan ran a hand over his face, she added, "And you might want to find out who the third shifter is who got away."

Mateo shook his head. "How can we do that if they don't want to come forward?"

Duncan turned on him. "You'll have to find some way to figure that out, won't you?" Speaking to the room as a whole, he added, "This is extremely important—the revelation of our existence is at stake, and I don't need to remind you how humans react to perceived threats."

I shuddered at the thought—if they learned of our existence, it would make the Inquisition look like child's play.

Duncan rose to his feet and glared at all of us equally. "I insist you focus on this exclusively, even if you have to work overtime to do it."

Lt. Jacobs raised an eyebrow. "You are not *my* alpha," he reminded Duncan.

Really? I hadn't known that.

Before Duncan could go ballistic, the lieutenant added, "But as it happens, I agree. We can't force anyone to work overtime, but we'll encourage it."

The alpha whirled on Mateo. "That won't be a problem, will it, Mr. Duran?"

Sheesh—why was he attacking Mateo and not the other two shifters in the room?

"No, sir. Not a problem at all," Mateo said. He somehow managed to sound respectful but not subservient.

The rest of us made noises to show we were all cool with it.

"That's settled then," Bartholomew said. "Let Maurice know if you need assistance in...adjusting memories, or if you need additional manpower."

"Same here," Sybil said. "Stopping this before it gets out of hand is imperative. We've already seen news reports of wolf attacks. We can't let it get any further." She glanced at Lt. Jacobs. "You'll keep us informed?"

"I will," he said solemnly. "And let us know what you find out about possible suspects." The lieutenant rose. "Maurice, Billy, I think you'll need to visit the victims to...persuade them they saw wild dogs, not wolves."

The vampires nodded, and, as the others left, Mateo stood and beckoned for me to follow him as he headed out to the lobby.

"Aren't you going to let Harley and Devon know what's going on?" I asked him.

He shook his head. "No, Duncan will do that."

"About Duncan—" I began, but he interrupted me.

"Not here. Do you have plans for after work, or would you like to go back to the bar, see if we can find the people Harley was drinking with?"

"My only plans were to eat dinner," I told him.

"They serve food there, too, so we can get something to eat if you're willing. A work dinner," he added hastily.

And why was that clarification necessary? "Okay, but we should probably drop Ruby off at home first."

Why? she whined. *Why can't I go with you?*

"Because they weren't too happy when you came with us earlier," I told her. "Your hair in their food is not exactly appetizing, even though we're allowed to bring you in as a service dog."

She pouted. *I can't help it if I shed.*

"I'm sure there won't be any more action tonight," Mateo assured her. "And we'll bring something back for you to eat. Pizza?"

Yeah! Ruby exclaimed and leaped up to lick his hand. *He's my favorite.*

I chuckled. "You do know her well. And now you're her favorite."

He smiled, though there was some strain around his eyes. "When am I not?" He held up his keys. "I'll head out and meet you there."

After I dropped Ruby off with Ren, giving her instructions not to let Ruby have control of the TV remote for a week, I drove to the bar and went in search of Mateo. I wouldn't have known it was a shifter bar if he hadn't told me—it looked pretty much like any country bar, with neon beer signs, dark wood and leather, and pool tables and dart boards in the back.

Mateo was talking to a guy at one of the tall pub tables, so I waited until he finished to join him. "Any luck?" I asked.

He sighed. "Not yet. I talked to a couple of the guys Harley was with, but they don't really remember when or why he left."

"That's the problem with interviewing people who were drinking..."

"Yeah." He rubbed his stomach. "Now I'm hungry. Let's get a booth and order some food."

We went to a corner booth out of the way and both ordered burgers, though Mateo got the humongous specialty platter no doubt designed with shifters in mind while I got the small plate. And, of course, we ordered Ruby's pizza to go.

We talked about insignificant things, then I decided to ease into what I really wanted to know. "So, Lt. Jacobs isn't a part of your pack?"

"No. It would be a conflict of interest to have him working law enforcement in the same area with his own pack."

I nodded slowly. "Yeah, I can see that. If Duncan was his alpha and ordered him to let Harley and Devon go..."

"He'd have no choice but to do it."

"So how does it work?"

They delivered our food then, and, as we ate, Mateo explained the pack hierarchy. There were a number of packs around the state, and they were overseen by a state shifter council. The state councils were, in turn, governed by regional councils. They didn't rule over the packs, but set policies they all followed and helped solve any inter-pack disputes and the like. Our lieutenant belonged to a pack in the Denver area, and the state council had assigned him here. Seemed like a good system—the DU ought to have something like that as well—it would make it easier to search for demons with certain abilities.

Mateo seemed a little down, not his usual joking self, so I asked, "What's up with you and Duncan?"

"I don't— He's—" He paused, obviously frustrated.

I covered his hand with mine. "It's okay. Just take your time and talk to me, partner."

He slid his hand out from under mine, but wouldn't look me in the eye. Gee, I thought we'd gotten over the whole no-touching-the-demon-in-public thing.

He winced. "I thought once I got my soul back and they realized Endymion was lying about me, everything would go back to normal."

"And it hasn't?"

He shook his head. "My friends, sure, they're the same. But the old guard..."

"They're different?"

"Yeah. It's like they still don't trust me. Endymion's cronies, mostly, but they're convincing others that I can't be trusted, that I'm a slacker."

"You?" I asked in disbelief. "You work harder than anyone I know. Are they...are they trying to get rid of you?"

Mateo shrugged around a bite of burger. "I don't know. I think they may be trying to convince Duncan to let Endymion come back to the pack, and badmouthing me to do it."

"After he lied?" I asked in disbelief. "After he had Dahlia rip out your soul?"

"Yeah. I don't know what they're thinking."

"You think it'll work?"

"I hope not, but Duncan hasn't seemed happy with me lately."

"Yeah, I noticed that."

He darted a glance at me, then, just as quickly, gave his attention back to his meal. "That's why, uh, I haven't asked you out."

My stomach rebelled at the food I'd already put in it, and I set my burger down, no longer hungry. "I see." It was my turn to avoid his gaze, unwilling to let him see the hurt there.

"It's not you," he assured me quickly. "It's them. I mean, you know how he feels about inter-species relationships. I don't want to rock the boat."

Guess that "friend of the pack" status didn't mean anything to Duncan. "Okay." I took a sip of my soda to keep from looking at him. That was a switch from what he'd said before.

"Really, I want to take you out, but until the pack and the alpha accepts me wholly, I think this is best."

Best for who? But I didn't say that out loud. Instead, I picked at my fries. "Your pack comes first. I get it." I really did, but I couldn't help the hollow feeling in my core.

Story of my life. My parents loved me, but always put each other first. And the one real relationship I had in Arizona had failed when he put his daughter first and had little time for me. Not that I blamed any of them for their priorities, but for once, I wanted to be the most important person in someone's life, to really matter. I thought that person might be Mateo, but I guess that was a big nope.

"It won't always be like this," Mateo said, looking at me pleadingly.

"Uh huh." But I certainly wasn't counting on it. His pack would always come first. I just wish it didn't hurt so much.

"Ivy—" he began.

But he was interrupted by a curvy shifter who stomped

up to our table. Luana, damn it—Endymion's sister, Mateo's stalker, and my nemesis. "What are you two doing here?" she demanded, hands on hips.

"Working," Mateo said.

I barely stopped myself from rolling my eyes. Of course, we couldn't let anyone in the pack think we could possibly be on a date.

"Doesn't look like it," she countered.

"We were questioning witnesses," Mateo added, "and when we finished, we decided to get something to eat."

Luana gave Mateo a lascivious smile and ran a hand up his arm. "So, since you're free, maybe you'd like to..."

What was that on her wrist? "Where'd you get that?" I demanded, pointing at the bracelet that looked a lot like the one we'd bagged and tagged and put into evidence.

She jerked her hand away. "None of your business."

I gave Mateo a significant glance. "Well, it looks a lot like a cursed artifact we found earlier this week."

Mateo laser-focused on the bracelet. "It does. Can I see...?"

Reluctantly, Luana held out her wrist to him. Mateo turned it around, and sure enough, wolf heads circled the piece with a moonstone in the center, but... "I don't understand," I said, frowning. "It looks just like the one we have in evidence, only this one isn't cursed."

Luana rolled her eyes. "Like there couldn't be a dozen more bracelets just like it?"

Yeah, but what were the odds? Then again, wolves and moonstones would be attractive to wolf shifters....

"Where'd you get it?" Mateo asked.

Luana removed her wrist from Mateo's hold and gave him a coy smile. "Wouldn't you like to know? I have admirers, you know."

This was pointless—she wasn't going to tell us anything. I pulled out my purse, dropped some cash on the table, and grabbed Ruby's pizza.

"Where are you going?" Mateo asked.

"Back to the station." I had to see if that moonstone bracelet we'd found was still in evidence.

"I'm coming with you," Mateo said, also throwing some cash on the table.

"Wait," Luana said, clutching at his arm.

Mateo tugged himself free. "Sorry," he said. "Police business."

Annoyed, I stomped off to my Mini. He just had to clarify that, didn't he?

CHAPTER

FOUR

I WENT HOME and grabbed Ruby first, letting her eat her pizza in the car on the way to the station.

What's the matter? she asked as she chowed down. *You seem upset.* Her chewing didn't impede her mental speech one bit.

I hurrumphed. "Mateo's pack is obviously the most important thing in his life, but that's just fine. I don't need him, and I don't need to have a man in my life to be complete."

That's right, Ruby said. *You don't need no stinkin' man. You have me! I'm your pack.* She lifted her head and changed the subject. *Where are we going?*

I told her about seeing the wolf head bracelet on Luana. "We need to see if it is still in the evidence room."

You think Luana stole it?

"I don't know what to think. The moonstone she was wearing wasn't cursed." And never had been—it would have definitely shown signs of stress in that case. All I got from Luana's moonstone was irritation. I wasn't sure if it was because it was reflecting Luana's annoyance, or if it was annoyed *by* her.

Both, Mr. Opal told me.

Ruby snorted. *Do you really think it's pure chance that she has the same bracelet as the cursed artifact you found?*

"Not really. Now I'm even more puzzled. Let's see if the one we found is there or not."

We pulled up to the station, and Mateo was already there since I'd stopped to pick up Ruby. As I entered the station, Mateo headed me off. "Hold on," he said. "There's no one manning the evidence room right now. I called the lieutenant, and he's going to let us in. He said he was nearby."

"I'm here," Lt. Jacobs said behind us. "You said you need to see if a piece of evidence is missing?"

"Yes," I answered. "It's a long shot, but I just saw a wolf shifter wearing a bracelet identical to the cursed artifact we turned in a couple of weeks ago...but the one she wore wasn't cursed."

The lieutenant gave me a perplexed look. "That's probably a coincidence."

"Maybe," I agreed. "But it's odd enough that I think we need to check it out."

"Okay." Lt. Jacobs led us to the room, unlocked the outside door, and fired up the computer. "I'll check the log to see where Caleb put it."

No need. "I saw him put it on the bottom shelf in the first box on the left, along with the other cursed stones." And I could feel their unique void sensations, but they all kind of blended together so I couldn't distinguish one from another, much less count how many there were.

The lieutenant unlocked the cage door, pulled out the box, and we all peered inside. The other artifacts were there, but not the bracelet. "It's missing," I said with a frown.

"That's odd," Lt. Jacobs said, and went back to check the computer. "The log says it's still here."

"Maybe it was moved to another box...?" Mateo suggested.

"I don't think so," I told him. "I'd be able to sense it if it was."

"Unless it was covered in silk," Mateo reminded me.

"Of course." And duh, that's exactly what we *should* have done with all of them. "Should we check the other boxes just in case?"

"You two do that," Lt. Jacobs told us, "and I'll call Caleb to see if he remembers what happened to it."

Luckily, it was a small station, so there weren't that many boxes. We checked them, but I didn't find anything, and neither did Mateo.

The lieutenant lowered his phone. "Caleb says he didn't check it out to anyone, and doesn't remember seeing it after you two checked it in. Then again, he had no reason to look for it."

"This is very weird," Mateo muttered.

You got that right, Ruby quipped.

And very suspicious. "Yes, it is. What are the odds the artifact would go missing and Luana would show up with the exact same bracelet...only it's not cursed?"

"Doesn't sound like a coincidence to me," Mateo said, frowning.

"Ditto," our boss agreed. "Did you ask her where it came from?"

I nodded. "Yes, but she wouldn't say—just played coy." Before he could ask me to try again with the emerald, I said,

"I doubt she'll answer my questions anyway. But she'd probably talk to Mateo."

Of course she would, Ruby snarked. *She wants to get in his pants.*

My eyebrows rose, but I wasn't passing on *that* observation.

Mateo grimaced. "Maybe, but she probably already thinks we're accusing her of stealing it. It might be a good idea to have Duncan involved."

"Good point," the boss said. "As her alpha, he can compel her to tell the truth." He checked his watch. "It's getting a bit late, so let me make arrangements with Duncan to have her interviewed tomorrow during Kai and Derek's shift. And I'll follow up with Caleb to see if he remembers anything else."

I grimaced. "In the meantime, I can fix my mistake in not covering the artifacts in silk. There's liable to be more than one desperate person coming through here, and we don't need to tempt them." I took off my silk hoodie and said, "Here, wrap them in this. That will keep the cursed stones from calling out to anyone susceptible."

"We should have thought of that earlier," the lieutenant confirmed as Mateo bundled the stones in my hoodie. "I'll let Caleb know that any future stones should be covered as well."

"Thank you both for believing my paranoia and coming to check," I told the guys.

Mateo shrugged. "It's not paranoia if there really is an issue. I'm glad we did."

"Me too." But it didn't get us any further than we had been before.

The lieutenant ushered us out of the evidence room and

locked it back up. "I'll keep you posted about what we learn tomorrow."

"Thanks," I said in appreciation.

As Lt. Jacobs headed in one direction, I headed back out to my car, Ruby right beside me.

Mateo hurried to catch up. "Ivy, I just wanted—"

"Save it for tomorrow," I said waving my hand to stop him, not willing to hear again how all-important the pack was to him. "I'm beat and need to get home."

His step faltered, and his face fell. "Okay. I—I'll see you tomorrow."

"Have a nice night," I chirped, hurrying faster.

Huh, Ruby protested. *You didn't mean a bit of that, did you?*

Liar, liar, pants on fire, my emerald taunted.

I grimaced. "Well, I am tired. Let's go home."

THE NEXT MORNING, I waited until Crystal Mystique opened at nine and went to visit the new age store.

Why are we going there? Ruby asked in the car. *You have some more jewelry to consign?*

"No, I'm thinking that if Luana has the original wolf bracelet with the cursed stone, she might have traded the cursed moonstone for a clean one. And I heard the shifters frequent Amber's store."

Why would Luana change the stone?

"With the wolf heads, the bracelet would be irresistible to a shifter, plus it has the stone representing the moon, their goddess. If Luana replaced the moonstone, she could wear the bracelet without worrying about me sensing the cursed stone."

You think she's that smart? Ruby asked doubtfully.

I choked on a laugh. "Well, if she thought it was smart, it's not working, is it?"

True. But maybe someone replaced it before they gave it to her.

I grimaced. I should have thought of that, but I was obviously too fixated on Luana being the guilty party. "In any case, we need to see if Amber has sold a loose moonstone."

Okay. Shouldn't Mateo be with us?

"Nope," I said, popping the p. "We're not actually on duty yet, and there shouldn't be any danger in going there alone."

I know that, but you're going to have to see him eventually. You're a team, remember?

I snorted. "At work, yeah, but otherwise, nope. And that's the way he wants it."

Ooooookay. I get it—you have a bug up your butt. Must be really uncomfortable there.

Smart aleck. Though I was determined not to let Mateo's attitude affect my job, that didn't mean I had to be around him any longer than necessary. Ignoring her, I pulled into the parking lot for Crystal Mystique and went in to see Amber.

Once again, the store pulled me in, making me feel welcome. The gemstones in the display cases were all calm, peaceful, like the owner of the store. She must be bathing her new stones in the cleansing bath I'd recommended.

Amber greeted me with her usual serenity. "Ivy, so glad to see you. Your pieces are selling well." She paused. "Or are you here looking for stolen gemstones again?"

"No, not this time," I assured her. "But I am wondering if you sold a loose moonstone to someone within the past few weeks. A round cabochon in white, maybe half an inch in diameter?"

She frowned. "I sell a lot of loose stones. I'm sorry, but I don't actually recall selling one, though my clerk might have. I could check with him and my inventory later, if you like."

I texted Mateo and asked if he had a picture of Luana. Of course he did, so I had him send it to me. I showed it to Amber. "It might have been this woman. Do you remember seeing her?"

"Not lately," Amber said with a frown. "But she has been in here before."

"Thanks," I said with a sigh. "It was a longshot, but I had to try. If you do find out anything about a moonstone, can you give me a call?"

"Sure," she said. "I still have your card."

As we headed back out to the car, Ruby said, *Too bad. You might've caught Luana red-handed. Red-pawed?*

I snorted. "Yeah, that would've been too easy," I said with a grimace. We could check other shops in the area, but I might have to do it on my own time.

As I put on my seatbelt, I got a group text from Lt. Jacobs, telling Mateo and me that the alpha had interviewed Luana, and Kai and Derek were on their way back to the station to report.

The lieutenant didn't actually say we should come in while we were off-duty, but Mateo texted that he was on his way to the station, so I sighed and let them know I was coming as well.

When we got to the conference room, Kai, Derek, Caleb, Mateo, and Lt. Jacobs were already waiting. The lieutenant nodded at Kai. "Can you tell us what you learned?"

"Sure, boss. Derek and I went with Duncan to interview

Luana about the bracelet. He used his alpha voice on her, and made her tell the truth. She didn't steal the bracelet."

Surprised, I asked, "Then where did she get it?"

Derek shrugged and glanced at the evidence room clerk. "She said Caleb gave it to her as a gift on their date."

Caleb's mouth dropped open. "I did no such thing."

Lt. Jacobs' eyebrows rose. "Are you dating Luana?"

"We've gone out a few times, but I never gave her anything like that," he insisted. "I wouldn't compromise my job or the evidence for a...a..." He shot a wary glance at me.

For a woman? Ruby snarked.

"For a date?" I suggested.

He nodded vehemently. "For anyone."

Surreptitiously, I checked with my emerald. *Is he telling the truth?*

Yep.

Cutting through the noise of surprised exclamations and demands to know what happened, I said, "My emerald confirms he's telling the truth. At least, so far as he knows."

Caleb seemed conflicted about whether to feel relief or irritation. The latter won out. "What's that supposed to mean?"

I shrugged. "Well, it's possible you did give it to her, but were compelled to do so, then told to forget."

He sat back in disbelief. "You've got to be kidding me. Who would do that to me?"

Wow, Ruby muttered. *Everything's about him, isn't it?*

It seemed so. Maybe he and Luana were a good match.

Mateo frowned. "Someone who wanted to cover up the theft of the stone, and make it look like Luana was at fault."

"Right," I bit out. "Because it couldn't possibly be sweet little Luana."

Oops, did I say that out loud? Apparently, I had, because there were a lot of odd looks thrown my way.

Jealous much? Ruby asked me.

Oh, shut up.

"Duncan has cleared Luana," the lieutenant said firmly.

"Then we're back at square one," I said in an attempt to redeem myself.

Mateo nodded. "Right. The only thing we know for sure is that someone is controlling shifters. It could be a vampire, siren, succubus, Dolittle, or any of those demons trapped in a stone. We don't know which. We need to start there."

Lt. Jacobs looked thoughtful. "Well, with the bracelet no longer in evidence, it strongly suggests someone had Caleb steal it, then replaced the moonstone before he gave it to Luana. The person who has the original moonstone is probably the controller."

Derek glanced at me. "Does someone have to be touching the stone to use it?"

"Yes," I confirmed.

His brow furrowed. "So, the stone was locked up, right? If they couldn't touch it, how could they use it to convince Caleb to steal it?"

This was making my head hurt. "They couldn't."

Derek nodded. "So it's possible the controller stole the bracelet and moonstone somehow, replaced the stone, and had Caleb give the bracelet to Luana to throw us off the scent."

"How would they even know to do that?" Kai asked.

Derek shrugged. "It's not like it's a secret in the supernatural community that Ivy is confiscating cursed artifacts and that she doesn't know what they can do until they're activated. They could have taken any one of the artifacts, and we'd assume that stone was the target."

"Yeah," Mateo said slowly. "So, once again, we don't know exactly what kind of supe is doing this."

"We don't know *why* they're doing this, either," I reminded them. "But we do know all of the attack 'victims' were sex offenders. Maybe we could start there instead."

"True," the lieutenant said. "We need to cover all the bases, just in case. I'll have Maurice and Billy continue to investigate a possible vampire connection. Mateo and Ivy, you check with Sybil and Ren and their databases for potential part-demons in the area, and Derek and Kai will look at connections between the victims. Any questions?" When we all shook our heads, he said, "Thank you. Dismissed."

As I was leaving, I noticed a tall, lean blond guy waiting outside the lieutenant's office, facing away from us. When he turned toward us and I saw his refined features and turquoise-blue eyes, my mouth dropped open. "Liam? Liam Seacrest?"

He didn't look as surprised as I felt. "Hello, Ivy. I'm so glad to see you again."

"You knew I worked here? Why didn't you contact me?"

Liam smiled. "I wasn't sure you'd remember me."

I moved closer to him. "Not remember you? We—"

"You know this guy?" Mateo asked, frowning.

"Yeah, we went to high school together. We were best friends for a long time, bonding over our shared love of woo-woo mysteries—until his family moved away in eleventh grade and I never saw him again."

"Woo-woo mysteries?" Mateo repeated, looking puzzled.

"You know—fantasy, paranormal, science fiction." I turned to Liam. "What are you doing here?"

"This is where we moved to—Colorado Springs."

I didn't remember ever knowing that. "That's not what I meant. What are you doing here in the SCU?" If he was in the Special Crimes Unit, did that mean he was...special? I didn't remember him being a supe. I thought he was fully human.

Hi, Liam, I'm Ruby, my hellhound said, proving he must be part demon. *Wow, he's a—*

Liam shot her a sharp glance and she cut off what she was about to say.

"He's a what, Ruby?" I asked.

I can't tell you. It's a secret.

"It's a secret?" I said in disbelief. *Even from me?*

She squirmed, but didn't answer.

"Well, that's not suspicious," Mateo muttered.

Lt. Jacobs shot him a glance. "Never mind," he told both of us. "You don't have the need to know."

Oooookay.

"I just dropped a report off for Lt. Jacobs," Liam told me. "Would you be free for lunch to talk over old times, Ivy?"

"My shift doesn't start until one, so it sounds great," I said.

Mateo started, "Are you sure—"

"Is there some reason I'm not free?" I asked him as politely as I could, giving him a chance to redeem himself.

"Uh, no," he admitted.

That's what I thought. "Okay, see you during our shift."

He scowled, but didn't say anything more.

Turning to Liam, I said, "I drive a Mini, which might be a little tight for your height."

"No problem," Liam assured me. "I'll drive, and I'll

make sure to have you back in time for your shift." He offered me his arm. "Shall we?"

Delighted, I said, "We shall." And if I felt a little smug at Mateo's pinched expression, I wasn't going to let it show.

A little? Ruby said. *Yeah, right, Miss Smug-a-lot. Or should I call you Poison Ivy? You're being mean to Mateo.*

Maybe a little, but he'd hurt me. It might be petty, but I wanted him to hurt too.

Liam tucked my hand in his arm, and, strangely enough, little explosions went off all over my body—everywhere I wore a stone. Whoa. What was that all about?

Little explosions of happiness, my amethyst assured me. *We like Liam.*

Puzzled, I said, *I thought you liked Mateo.*

We do, but Liam makes us feel all sparkly.

Huh, Ruby said. *Weird.*

But Liam didn't seem to notice anything different. Or, if he did, he didn't say anything.

Liam led me to his car—an older model Toyota. "Have any food preferences? Allergies?"

"Uh, maybe somewhere that Ruby can join us easily? And where we can be a little private? I'm still pretty new here, so I don't know too many places."

"Sure. How about Poor Richard's? They primarily have pizza, but there's outdoor seating, and the weather is pretty nice right now."

Pizza! Ruby exclaimed in excitement.

"I guess that's a yes." I squeezed his arm.

He drove to Poor Richard's, not too far, and led us into the rustic restaurant which also had a bookstore and wine bar attached. We were seated fairly quickly outside and ordered.

We chatted for a while about inconsequential things,

sharing stories about our high school past and what we'd been doing since then, until we were finished eating. Then, Liam leaned close and said, "So, I hear you're a stone whisperer."

Though no one was near enough to hear us, I nevertheless spoke softly. "That's what they call me. I'm just a plain old rock demon. Did you know that...before?"

"Yeah, but I kept it to myself." At my appreciative nod, he added, "And my family pretty much tries to stay out of politics and joining things like the DU. "

"Really? Why?"

"Because of what we are." He cast a wary glance at Ruby.

I ain't sayin' nothin', she told him. *My lips are sealed.*

Hmm. "I understand you can't tell me exactly what you are, but can you tell me *why* you can't tell me?" I probed.

"Not really. But Lt. Jacobs and Sybil Warburton are both aware of my...abilities and use me from time to time as a...consultant."

I was too curious to drop it. "Is it deadly...what you do?"

He laughed. "No, it's just that, in the past, when people find out what my family can do, we become in great demand. Some have gone to great lengths to...obtain our services, even resorting to kidnapping."

Yikes. "Oh, I see. Does it have anything to do with those strange explosive sparks I felt when you took my arm?"

He blinked. "Explosive sparks? Not that I know of...."

I guess it was best to just drop it. "Okay, sorry. I'm just nosy. So, how did you end up working with the SCU?"

"I wanted to do some good with my abilities, not just let them stagnate." I could understand that. When I took a sip of my soda, he changed the subject. "So, are you and Mateo a thing?"

She wishes, Ruby snarked.

I shot her a sharp glance, but luckily, she only said that to me. "No. I just moved here, and I don't know many people. He's my work partner, so..." I shrugged. "You know Ren?" At his nod, I added, "She's my roommate. They're pretty much my only friends here."

He smiled shyly. "I'd like to be your friend."

I returned the smile in kind. "You already are. Maybe we can see more of each other. Unless you can't for some reason?" Yeah, I was fishing. So sue me.

"I'm not seeing anyone at the moment, and I'd love to get to know you again."

"That sounds great." I beamed at him and checked the time on my phone. "But for now, I need to get to work."

We exchanged phone numbers and I went to work feeling a whole heck of a lot better about myself. *He was nice,* I told Ruby as we walked into the building. *Wasn't he?*

Yeah, he was.

I glanced down at her, one eyebrow raised. *Any reason I shouldn't like him?*

Ha! You tryin' to get me to tell you his secret?

No, I just need to know if there's any reason I need to be wary.

Not that I know of, she assured me. *But if that ever changes, I'll let you know.*

Okay. But it was bugging the heck out of me. What kind of demon could he be? Probably not something common.

I know something you don't know, Ruby taunted in a sing-song voice.

Oh, shut up.

She just laughed at me as I met Mateo near the lockers. As soon I saw his face, I knew he was just as eaten up with curiosity and jealousy as I was. Served him right.

"How was your lunch with Pretty Boy?" Mateo asked.

I raised my eyebrows, but didn't comment on his description. "Good. We had a lot of catching up to do."

"So he was your best friend, huh?"

"Yep." Keep my answers short and I'd keep him guessing.

"Not boyfriend?"

"Not then," I said, and changed the subject. "Let's go visit Sybil to search for possible demon suspects." I headed toward the SUV, forcing Mateo to hurry to catch up.

CHAPTER
FIVE

MATEO DROVE us to Relentless Protection Services where Sybil met us in her office. "Lt. Jacobs asked us to check your database for local sirens, succubi, and Dolittles," Mateo told her.

"Yes, I thought he might, so I looked already." She opened a drawer and pulled out a piece of paper. "Actually, I found one of each. There's a succubus up in north Denver..."

"That's so far away," I said. "At least an hour and a half. Why would she want to come down to Colorado Springs to control shifters?"

Mateo shrugged. "Because you don't poop where you eat?"

I made a face. *Eww. Gross.*

Ruby had a different opinion. *Oooh, kewl.*

I rolled my eyes. "Very colorful. But let's assume sex offenders are the target. If that's so, it stands to reason that our perpetrator is targeting people who have assaulted them, their family, or close friends."

"That makes sense," Sybil said.

"So," I continued, "I would assume the person we're looking for is in the local area."

"Good point," Mateo said. "But we shouldn't exclude anyone until we're sure."

I nodded. "Who is the siren?"

Sybil checked her notes. "Another person who doesn't live in the Springs—she's west of Denver, out near Silverthorne."

"Again, too far away," I said.

"Again, we have to check her out as well," Mateo said.

"I wasn't disagreeing," I snapped. Though I was a little annoyed by his attitude. I glanced at Sybil. "And the Dolittle?"

"He lives in the Northeast part of the Springs, so he's definitely local."

Mateo frowned. "I assumed the controller would be female."

"Why?" I asked.

"Because women have the most to lose when it comes to sexual assault. If this is personal..."

"A man could want to get revenge for something that happened to a woman in his life," I protested.

"True, but controlling other men...shifters...it doesn't seem sporting for a guy. Unless he's very weak."

That was a very male-centric way of looking at things. "Well," I said, grabbing the piece of paper. "We won't know until we check it out, will we?"

"True."

Sybil glanced at us. "Be careful. Especially you, Mateo. If this controller is targeting shifters, you could be next."

He seemed surprised to hear that. Huh, for once, I wasn't the one who seemed most in danger.

Sybil rose. "But please, find the controller soon." She

slapped a copy of *The Gazette* newspaper down on the table. "This wasn't page one, but it wasn't buried either."

I glanced down at the headline she pointed to. Wild Wolf Attacks Springs Citizens.

Oh, crap. "I thought Maurice was going to kill this story."

"Apparently, he wasn't able to get to the reporter in time," Sybil said. She squinted at the byline. "One Harry Fowler."

"Have we seen any backlash from this?" Mateo asked.

"There has been some excitement on social media, and one or two news reports. They're asking everyone to be careful and to report any wolf sightings."

"Great," Mateo muttered. "Just what we need—hysteria. Don't they know it's extremely rare for wild wolves to attack humans?"

I grimaced. "Would you rather they figure out shifters exist instead?"

"Of course not," he said, looking annoyed. "I'd rather they just drop it entirely."

"We can probably make that happen," Sybil said, "if we find the controller." She raised an eyebrow at both of us.

"That's our cue to get going," I said with a smile.

Mateo drove the SUV as we headed toward the Dolittle's residence. After a tense silence, Mateo finally burst out with, "So what do you really know about this Liam guy?"

"I know that Lt. Jacobs and Sybil trust him, and that's good enough for me." I made a show of studying him. "What's that on your face, Mateo?"

He glanced in the rearview mirror and rubbed at his cheeks. "I don't see anything."

"Huh. Looks like sour grapes to me."

Good one, Ruby said with a chuckle.

He snorted. "Yeah, right."

Not wanting to encourage this discussion, I watched the scenery outside the window. I really enjoyed the beautiful views in Colorado Springs, especially with Pikes Peak visible from just about anywhere in the city. Snow covered the peak pretty much ten to eleven months out of the year and, seeing the city against the backdrop of the Front Range made it appear almost like a postcard or a snow globe.

What's a snow globe? Ruby asked.

I tried to describe it to her, but wasn't sure she got it. I looked one up on my phone and showed it to her.

"What are you doing?" Mateo asked.

"Just showing Ruby something. A teaching moment."

"Uh huh. Hey, did Ren find out anything else about our so-called victims?"

I raised my eyebrows as I glanced askance at him. "Don't let the boss hear you call them that," I warned.

He snorted. "I have no sympathy for them. They probably deserved exactly what they got. If it wasn't for the fact that this controller chose shifters to do her dirty work, I'd say let 'em go."

"But she or *he* did choose shifters. Why is everyone so concerned about that specifically? Is it because the reporter might reveal your existence?"

"Yeah. Our history is full of stories where shifters were persecuted, hunted, and vilified just for existing until we found a way to go underground." He scowled. "In this day and age, we'd also have to worry about scientists and the government wanting to cage us to study our abilities. I doubt they'd worry much about personal rights, either." He glanced at me. "Same holds true for part-demons, you know."

He had a point. And though Alejandro, the leader of the

vamps in San Antonio, wanted to come out to the world, I didn't think they were ready to know about us yet. We needed to do everything we could to make sure our existence stayed a secret. For as long as possible. "I'm with you," I assured him.

We pulled up to a nice little two-story house in a decent neighborhood with kids' toys scattered over the lawns. "Doesn't look very menacing, does it?" I said.

"No, but appearances can be deceiving," he muttered as he brought the SUV to a stop and killed the engine.

Yeah, Ruby said. *Like we thought you were one of the cool ones, Mateo.*

I snorted in amusement, and when Mateo looked at me questioningly, I shrugged. "Sorry, Ruby said something funny." But I really didn't want to repeat it, so I quickly opened the door and got out. When Mateo joined me, I said, "What was his name again?"

Nice avoidance, Ruby said in admiration.

He checked his notes. "Richard Gatti. He should be home. Sybil told him we were coming."

We knocked on the front door, and a slight, nerdy-looking guy in his thirties answered. He looked stressed as he held a crying child in his arms—a boy, maybe three years old or so.

"Mr. Gatti?" Mateo said. "We're from the DU."

"Yes, yes, come on in." He jiggled the boy in his arms. "Let me just—"

But the boy suddenly stopped crying when he saw Ruby. "Doggie?" He squirmed. "Daddy, down. I wanna see the doggie."

"I don't know..." the man hedged and looked at us in question.

I glanced at Ruby with my eyebrows raised.

I like kids, Ruby said. *Sometimes. Depends on the kid.*

"Doggie talk?" the kid said in surprise.

Oops—part demon kid equals ability to hear Ruby.

Don't let children hear you, I warned her. *They don't know how to keep their mouths shut.* Out loud, I said, "No, no. That was me being silly, throwing my voice."

"Do it again," the little tyke said.

Don't, I warned my talkative hellhound. *You can explain to his father if you want.*

From the sudden alertness on the man's face, Ruby was doing just that.

He wrestled with his kid. "No, Georgie, these people are here to talk to me, not to play with you. But you can pet the...dog if you're nice about it. Remember how I showed you?"

"Yes, Daddy. Down." Georgie squirmed even harder.

Please tell me I'm not going to regret this, Ruby said with a whine.

I repressed a smile. *Just tell his father if he gets too...rambunctious.*

Richard let his son down and little Georgie squatted next to Ruby and gently rubbed her head.

Hoping the petting would stay that nice and easy, I sat on the couch the man indicated, with Mateo next to me, Richard in a chair across from us, and the boy and Ruby on the floor between us where we could keep an eye on him.

Mateo began. "Mr. Gatti—"

"Call me Richard, please."

Mateo nodded. "Richard, we understand you're a Do—"

"An animal communicator," I interrupted. I wasn't sure if Richard would consider Dolittle an insult or not.

"Yes, that's correct," he said. "And I'm not offended by the term Dolittle. I do talk to animals, after all."

"Can your son do that as well?" I asked, curious.

"Not yet. That ability usually comes into play around puberty." He sighed and glanced at his son who was still playing nice with Ruby. "Lots to look forward to."

No sarcasm there....

"Can you let us know how your ability works?" Mateo asked.

Richard frowned. "What's this about?"

Mateo hesitated, then said, "We're trying to eliminate you as a suspect for a series of crimes."

His mouth dropped open. "Crimes? Me? That's ridiculous."

He's telling the truth, Ruby said. *He has no clue what crimes you're talking about.*

In a prearranged signal, I nodded at Mateo to tell him the guy was being truthful.

Mateo relaxed a little. "There have been a number of situations where someone has controlled a...an animal to attack people."

Why doesn't he just tell him they're shifters? Ruby asked me privately.

Maybe because he's not sure if Richard is aware of them, I suggested.

"I see," Richard said. "Well, animal communicators can, as the name suggests, speak with animals and, to some extent, control them."

"To what extent?" Mateo probed.

"It depends on the communicator's strength, and the intelligence of the animal. The more intelligent the animal, the harder they are to control."

"Could you control Ruby?" Mateo asked.

No way, Ruby protested.

"She seems very intelligent," the man demurred. "Maybe not."

Good answer, Ruby said, then added, *Oh, and he knows about shifters.*

Looked like we were going to have to address the elephant in the room. "And what about people who can shift into animal form? Would you be able to control them?"

Mateo cast me a dirty look. "Ruby said he already knows," I murmured.

Mateo scowled but didn't say anything.

Richard shook his head. "Me, no. They're too strong-willed."

Truth, Ruby confirmed.

I nodded at Mateo again. "Does that mean there are those who can?" he asked.

The man thought a moment. "My grandfather could, but he married a human, which reduced my mother's power. She and each successive descendant who doesn't marry another animal communicator would have less power." He glanced at his son. "My wife is human as well. It will be rather weak in my son, I'm afraid."

"Do you know of any other...Dolittles who would have the power to control shifters?" Mateo pushed.

"I'm sorry, I don't. Not locally, anyway. Some in upper New York, maybe. That's where we came from."

And Ruby confirmed that, so I rose. "Well, thank you for your time. We really appreciate it."

"No problem."

As Ruby extricated herself from Georgie's grabby hands, we headed toward the door.

Once we were outside, Mateo said, "Well, at least we eliminated one type of demon. I—"

Ivy, shield! Ruby boomed in my head.

I slammed up the shield, expecting it to be another one of her tests. Instead, a streak of dark gray dashed across the lawn and smacked into me, flattening me to the ground. My head hit the ground, hard. *What the—*

CHAPTER
SIX

ADRENALINE PUNCHED through me and I threw up my arms to shield my face as a huge wolf, heavy as all get-out, crushed my chest, his teeth snapping at my arms. Shaking, I pushed even more power into my shield. Though I felt some pressure from the jaws clamped on my arm, the shield kept his teeth from piercing my skin.

"Stop, Reggie," Mateo shouted, grabbing at the wolf's scruff as Ruby snapped at the wolf's back leg.

Once Mateo called his name, the wolf stopped immediately. And if a wolf could look sheepish, this one did as he clambered off me.

Better he look sheepish than wolfish, Ruby said. *Are you okay?*

I think so.

"Bad dog. Into the car," Mateo ordered, and used his grip on Reggie's ruff to shove him into the SUV.

Bad dog? Oh—there was a human present.

An older woman came running over to help me up. "Are you okay?" she asked. "Was that a wolf?"

"No," Mateo said. "Just our overly enthusiastic German

shepherd greeting his mom. He forgets how big he is and how small Ivy is sometimes."

"I'm fine," I assured her, standing up. Well, my head hurt from hitting the ground, and the comedown from the adrenaline rush made me a little dizzy, but no bite marks. Yay, me.

The woman glared at Mateo. "That didn't look like a friendly greeting."

I forced a chuckle. "That's Reggie for you. Looks like he needs more training. Look, no damage." I showed her my arms, free of scratches and bites. And Reggie played along, looking calmly out the window with his tongue hanging out.

"Hmpf," she said in disbelief. "Well, I—"

Remembering my stones could help me control humans, I let my power surge through the ones on my cuff bracelet and told her firmly, "You can see I'm fine. Nothing is wrong. The dog was just overly friendly. We appreciate your concern."

She nodded. "I see you're fine. Nothing is wrong," she parroted.

Whew—that worked, but I didn't know for how long, so I sent Mateo a pleading glance. I hated to admit it, but I was still feeling a bit shaky. He put his arm around me and supported me to the SUV.

As we drove off, Mateo told Reggie, "Get down, but don't shift yet." Glancing at me, he asked, "Are you really okay?"

"My head hurts a bit where I hit the ground." And my ribs were complaining about the weight of that wolf. "But my shield protected the rest of me." Maybe I needed to look into the properties of healing stones next....

"Good. Your diligent practice probably saved you from

being severely savaged. But we'll have the doc check you out just in case." He called Sybil and asked her to have Dr. Oliver meet us at the station. Once we were out of the neighborhood, Mateo said, "Okay, Reggie. Shift."

I saw a bright light out of the corner of my eye and I turned to look as Reggie sat up in the back seat. Balding and in his forties, he was a bit older than the other shifters who had been controlled, but still built like a linebacker, like many shifters at the security company.

"I'm so sorry," Reggie said. "I have no idea why—"

"Yeah, yeah," Mateo said dismissively. "You were being controlled. We know all about it."

Reggie drew back in surprise. "You do?"

"We do," I confirmed. "You're not the first shifter who this has happened to."

Just the first to attack you, Ruby protested. *And from what I heard in his mind, you were definitely the target.*

Not his fault. "What's the last thing you remember?" I asked him.

He thought for a moment. "I was driving to RPS, then next thing I know, Mateo was pulling me off you." He grimaced. "Now I'm late for work."

"You're more than that, I'm afraid," Mateo said. "We'll have to detain you in the holding cell in case the controller tries to get their hooks into you again. Don't worry, we'll let Duncan and Sybil know. You won't lose any money over this."

He sighed heavily. "Okay, thanks. And, uh, I guess I should tell you—I think this happened once before. A few days ago, I woke up in wolf form with blood on my teeth and vaguely remember attacking some guy."

"Reggie must be the missing shifter who got away," I

said to Mateo. "Can you give us details, Reggie? The ones you remember, anyway."

He did, and Mateo nodded. "That checks out. Well, one mystery solved anyway. Duncan will be happy." But the grimace on his face seemed to say the opposite.

Mateo took Reggie into the station to process him while I went into a separate room with Dr. Oliver. "I didn't expect to see you again so soon," she said with an admonishing look.

"Hey, it wasn't my fault this time." I told her what happened.

"Did you lose consciousness?" she asked as she examined me.

"No, just bumped my head."

Lt. Jacobs stuck his head in the door. "How's she doing, doc?"

"Okay. She doesn't show any signs of a concussion, so that's good."

"I'm just a little stiff and sore," I assured him. Plus I had a slight headache where I'd hit my head. "I can return to work then?"

"Medically, yes," Dr. Oliver said. "Though you should probably take it easy for the rest of day and take acetaminophen as needed for pain."

The lieutenant nodded at the doctor. "Thank you for your help."

"My pleasure," Dr. Oliver said, "though I hope I won't see *you* again anytime soon," she told me pointedly.

I smiled at her. "Me either."

The lieutenant gave me a stern look. "I'll take you home so you can rest."

"I can drive," I protested.

"I have no doubt, but you were targeted specifically, even though you don't fit the profile of the other victims. I want to make sure you have someone with you at all times."

Like I don't count? Ruby said in indignation.

It's a shifter thing, I told her. *They have some kind of protection gene, I think.* I turned to my boss. "Okay, but—"

"I'll have Mateo pick you up for the shift changeover briefing later this afternoon if you're feeling better."

I sighed. Looked like I wasn't going to win this one. And, actually, a hot bath to soak out my aches and pains sounded like a good idea. "Okay, let's go."

Ruby pouted the whole way home, but felt better when the lieutenant told her to keep me safe since we were home alone.

Well, sheesh. I might be benched for the moment, but that didn't mean I couldn't do a little research. I called my succubus friend Val in the San Antonio DU.

"Ivy," Val exclaimed. "How are you?"

We caught each other up on what had been going on in our lives since we saw each other last and exchanged messages between Ruby and Val's hellhound, Fang. It seemed hellhound telepathy didn't work over the phone.

Once they were happy, I said, "I called you for a reason." I explained what we were up against, and asked, "Is it possible we're dealing with a succubus?"

"Probably not," Val said. "I can only control men who are near me, within a limited range. Once they're out of my range, they're no longer in my thrall."

"So if you gave them a command while they're in your control, it wouldn't last once they leave your range?"

"Right."

I sighed. "It's not a succubus then. Thanks so much for explaining."

"Any time," Val said. "And don't be a stranger."

"I won't." Val was one of the few people I still counted as a good friend.

After I hung up, I started really noticing those aches and pains, so I took a hot bath then a nap. I felt a lot better after that, so I asked Mateo to pick me up for the briefing.

All three teams were there, and Lt. Jacobs explained what had happened to me. "We have Reggie in the holding cell, but it's getting crowded with all the shifters in there. Unfortunately, we can't release them for fear the controller will use them again."

"I might be able to help with that," Maurice said.

There was no vampire dress code that I knew of, but Maurice always looked so put together, like he had just come off a runway. Today, he wore tailored navy pants and a sky-blue shirt that looked awesome against his dark skin. His trendy glasses and subtle jewelry completed the look.

Maurice continued, "You are aware that I can help influence people to do things?"

Billy, his ex-Marine boyfriend and partner, snorted. "You're the master of it, you mean."

"Yes," the boss said. "Go on."

"Well, I can place a command in their minds to ignore any past or future commands from anyone, including any future ones from me."

The lieutenant looked dubious. "I'm not sure the shifters will let you—"

"Let's try it," Mateo said. "I trust him—he helped me out when my pack ostracized me."

"Okay. But how will we know it will work?" the boss asked.

"We test it," Maurice said, and looked at me. "You can

force humans and shifters in human form to do your bidding, right?"

"For a short period of time," I conceded.

"How about we use that as a test case?"

He explained his idea, and I glanced at Mateo. "You sure about this?"

"Sure. Go for it."

"Okay." Focusing my powers through the stones on my bracelet, I said, "Mateo, bark like a dog."

"Woof, woof," came the immediate answer, though he was not at all happy about what I'd told him to do.

Whoa, Ruby said. *I think you pissed him off.*

I bit back a grin. "Sorry about that, but I wanted to make it clear that this is something you wouldn't normally do. I don't think anyone here thought you were pretending."

He scowled at me, but couldn't argue with my methods.

Maurice pulled him aside and, peering straight into his eyes, he murmured a few words, then backed away.

"That's it?" Kai asked.

"If it worked," Maurice said. "Ivy, can you try again?"

"Sure." I concentrated on shoving my powers through my stones again. "Speak, Mateo," I commanded. "Bark like a dog."

His lips thinned, but he kept them closed.

"Excellent," the lieutenant said. "It worked. Now, we just have to convince the shifters we have in lockup to let him do the same to them."

Kai shrugged. "If it's that or stay in jail, I know which I'd choose. And I'll let him protect me first, so they know it's okay."

The lieutenant nodded. "It's probably a good idea to let him safeguard all of us in this way. After the meeting, that is. For now, let's talk about what we know." He nodded at Derek. "Did you find any connections between the victims?"

"Nothing beyond their appearance on the sex offender registry," Derek said, "but we thought it was important to look at some of the people who might have been victimized by a sex offender, to see if we could narrow it down to who the controller might be. Since the controlled shifters were told to 'teach them a lesson,' it feels like the motivation is revenge. And, since the controller is using male shifters as the instrument of their revenge, we're thinking the controller is a woman."

"Or a man who has a woman in his life who was victimized," I reminded them.

"That could be," Derek conceded, and glanced at the vamps. "We're fairly certain it isn't a vampire. It just doesn't feel like their MO."

Billy nodded. "Most vampires wouldn't work through an intermediary to control someone—they'd do it directly. And we haven't found any indication of anyone we know who fits the profile."

"Exactly," Kai said.

"It's not a succubus either," I said. "I talked to my succubus friend Val, and she said she can't control men beyond her immediate area." I glanced at Mateo. "And we know it's not a Dolittle. At least, not the one in the Springs."

Kai nodded. "For part demons, that leaves the siren. From what we know, sirens can use their voice to control members of the opposite sex. We need to find out if their commands can extend beyond their immediate area." He checked his notes. "Though the siren lives about three hours away, near Silverthorne, she does have a cousin here. And that cousin is a victim of attempted sexual assault."

Aha! There was motive anyway.

"Looks like we need to check out the siren then," the lieutenant said.

Derek nodded. "And, of course, it could be that the controller has a cursed gemstone with a siren's abilities."

"Which means it could be anyone," the lieutenant said.

"Exactly," Derek said. "Since the moonstone was stolen from the evidence room, we thought it important to look at anyone who might have access to shifters or this station." He glanced at me. "And it's fairly well known now in the supe community that you can't hear stones covered in silk, so the controller would know how to keep it hidden."

Lt. Jacobs leaned forward. "And, what did you find?"

"We found a few people in the community who had either been personally assaulted, or who had family members or friends who were." Derek glanced down at the list, and said somewhat reluctantly, "That includes our own Taylor, Luana, and two other shifters—Luana's female cousins Mina and Phoebe, along with their male relatives."

"Including Endymion?" I asked. He certainly had a reason to attack me.

"Yes," Mateo said. "But the last we heard, he'd moved to Wyoming." He turned to Kai. "Mina and Phoebe were assaulted, really?"

I understood his disbelief—couldn't a shifter defend herself?

Kai grimaced. "Mina was. You know how meek she is. When she was assaulted, she froze at first. She was able to eventually fight her way free without revealing what she was, but it traumatized her."

Mateo nodded. "That makes sense. But I can't see Mina or Phoebe formulating a revenge plot."

"The cursed stones seek out desperate people," I

reminded him. "And they feed on that desperation so people do things they ordinarily wouldn't."

"True," Mateo said, though he still looked dubious.

"Good work," the lieutenant said. "Luana has already been cleared, but we need to check out the others, plus their relatives and close friends. This can be rather delicate, so I'll talk to Taylor, Kai and Derek can interview Mina and Phoebe with Duncan's help if necessary, and Mateo will take the siren."

What are we? Chopped liver? Ruby said in disbelief.

As if he'd heard her, the lieutenant glanced at me. "You've already been attacked once, probably because the controller fears you. So, I'd like you to stay here for now."

I grimaced. I didn't like it, but I did understand his reasoning. "Okay, boss."

He rapped his knuckles on the table. "Let's do this. But first, Maurice, if you could command-proof the folks in here, then do the same to the shifters in lockup, we'll be able to release them."

Kai sighed. "Duncan will be glad to hear that."

Once Maurice command-proofed the shifters present, the lieutenant pulled me aside. "Come with me to talk to Taylor."

"You're going to ask her about her assault?" I wasn't sure that was such a good idea....

"No," he assured me. "Just check to see if she took the moonstone. And if she did..."

I nodded. "You'll need me to exorcise the stone. And, uh, she wears that medicine bag around her neck. If she lined it in silk, the moonstone could fit there easily."

He nodded. "My thinking exactly."

I went with him to the front desk, and Taylor glanced

up, saying, "Some reporter was looking for you, Ivy. He said something about a wolf attack."

Well, crap. I bet Richard's neighbor learned my name from him and called the journalist. "What did you tell him?"

She shrugged. "That you weren't attacked and you weren't here."

I sighed in relief. "Thanks for that."

The lieutenant took over and gave Taylor some spiel about needing to search everyone in the station.

Bemused, she let me pat her down and search her pockets. Nothing. "Can you show us the contents of your bag?" I asked, nodding to the one strung around her neck.

She clutched at it. "This? But..."

"Please," the lieutenant said firmly. "It's necessary."

She handed the bag to me reluctantly, and I tensed as I opened it, expecting the moonstone to scream its feelings at me. But nothing happened. The only things in there were a few fragrant herbs and plants. Frustrated, I gave Taylor a stern look. "Did you have anything to do with the theft in the evidence room or controlling shifters?" Privately, I added to Ruby, *Okay, this time, you can read her mind. Just don't let her know.*

"M-me?" Taylor stammered. "No. I don't know anything."

Huh, Ruby said. *She's telling the truth.*

My emerald confirmed it.

Ruby suddenly whirled and stared toward the back of the station. *Oh, no.*

"What's wrong?" I asked her.

The shifters in the holding cell... Derek said they've disappeared.

CHAPTER
SEVEN

"The shifters have escaped from the jail cell," I told Lt. Jacobs urgently.

"What? That doesn't even make sense," he said as the other team members rushed into the lobby and confirmed it. He turned to Taylor. "Bring up the camera footage in the jail cells for the last hour."

Taylor did her thing on the screen, fast-forwarding through everything.

"Stop there," the lieutenant said, then let out a sigh of exasperation. "I don't believe it. Caleb let them go." He pulled out his cell and must have called the evidence room clerk, for he said, "Meet me in the conference room. Immediately."

Naturally, we all followed him, wanting to know why the heck Caleb would do such a thing—and ready to apprehend him if needed.

Turned out, he didn't remember doing it, which my emerald confirmed. The controller had struck again.

The lieutenant said, "The guys in the cell probably thought this was legitimate, that we were releasing them intentionally. Mateo, can you contact them, see where they are? Kai, help him, after Maurice protects you. We'll need to get the pack members back here so Maurice can stop the controller from using them again."

"Hold on a minute," Billy protested. "Maybe you haven't noticed, but this takes a lot out of Maurice."

"I'm fine," Maurice assured us, though he did look a little gray—not a good color on him. "I can do a couple more, but then I need to rest for a while."

"Not a problem," the lieutenant assured us. "Don't let us deplete you. Will you be able to do Kai before they leave?"

"Yes, of course."

He did, and Kai and Mateo headed off to track down the missing shifters.

The lieutenant did some texting and said, "The only non-employee who has been in the building today was that reporter, Harry Fowler." He frowned. "Could a man use a female siren's abilities through the stone?"

"No," I told him. "Only if it was a male siren trapped in the stone, and then he'd only be able to control women. I don't think he's responsible."

"We cleared Taylor," Lt. Jacobs mused.

"There is another woman working here," Derek reminded us. "Ren."

"It wasn't her," I told him. Not my roommate. "She talks to Ruby all the time. Ruby would know if Ren was doing something hinky."

Dang right, my hellhound agreed. *She's clean.*

But how—? And suddenly, realization hit me. "A siren controls by the use of her voice, right?"

"That's right," Derek said.

"So maybe the controller is using phone calls to direct them." It made total sense to me.

Derek nodded slowly. "From what we've learned, it's easier for a siren to control someone in person, but once they've done it that one time..."

I filled in the rest. "Then, hearing their voice on the phone would just reinforce the connection already made."

"Exactly," Derek confirmed.

"Hold on," the lieutenant said. "Get me the phone numbers of the shifters we were holding. We need to tell them—the whole pack, really—not to answer their phones, but to use text only. Caleb, you start on that, but let Kai and Mateo know first. Duncan next, so he understands why we're doing this." He glanced at Caleb. "Before you do that, check your phone. Who called you last?"

Caleb checked his cell. "You did. When you told me to come here."

"And before that?"

Caleb grimaced. "All my other recent calls were deleted." He glanced up. "I don't remember doing that—it must have been another command."

Well, shoot. A *69 wouldn't work either, since the last person who called him was the lieutenant. And the siren probably had the other shifters she controlled delete their call history too. Yeah, I had to concede the controller was probably a female siren.

"Look up your call history online," Lt. Jacobs said.

Caleb frowned. "I can't. I have a pre-paid phone—no network carrier." Seeing the confusion in my expression, he added, "Hey, it's cheaper and more secure." He turned to the lieutenant. "Why would the controller make me do that? Why make me release the shifters?"

Lt. Jacobs grimaced. "To give her puppets the freedom

to do her bidding, to sow confusion, to pull our tails...pick one."

Probably all of the above, Ruby said.

"I'm getting tired of her pulling my strings," Caleb complained.

"We have a fix," Lt. Jacobs told him, and explained about Maurice. Caleb seemed reluctant to have a vampire in his mind, but since the controller had used him more than once, Lt. Jacobs insisted. Once Maurice did his thing, Billy pulled him away to rest, and Caleb left to make his texts to the shifters.

"What do you want us to do?" Derek asked the boss.

"Maurice should stay here—Billy, too. Once he's rested sufficiently, he can protect others from the siren's commands,. That includes you and me, Derek. For now, help Caleb contact all the shifters and stay on call. And, Ivy? I don't want you to leave the station."

"What about the siren in Silverthorne? Are you sending someone to interview her? Since I can't be affected..."

"Not you." The lieutenant ran his hand down over his face. "Mateo is protected. I'll text him and have him go to her once he's done warning the shifters." He shook his head. "One thing at a time."

"If you don't want me leaving, how can I help?" I asked him.

"All of the controlled shifters were probably told to delete their call history, but the cell phone companies should still have that information. Once the shifters are back here, we'll ask them to look up their call history online. Or we'll get warrants for them if we have to. Ren knows how to do that. See if she needs any help."

Busywork. I sighed and headed off to find Ren.

Benched again, Ruby complained.

"He just wants to keep us safe," I told her.

But I can take care of myself. And take care of you, too.

"I know, I know." But that shifter attack had been really scary. If I could avoid playing chew toy again, I was all for it.

I found Ren in her office. She took one look at me and asked, "What's wrong?"

I explained what was going on and she came around the desk to give me a hug. "I'm so sorry this is happening to you," she said. "I—"

"Excuse me," someone said from the doorway.

I looked up to see a young man standing just inside—kinda short, thin, pretty, and very pale.

Vampire, Ruby told me.

"Can I help you?" Ren asked.

He stared at her. "Which one of you is Ivy Weiss?"

I raised my hand. "I—"

Shield! Ruby and Mr. Opal blasted in unison.

He lunged for me, and I barely slapped up the shield before he grabbed my arms and aimed his fangs for my neck.

I screamed and Ruby went for his ankles as Ren stabbed two fingers into his neck. Electricity arced between her fingers like the prongs of a stun gun. He convulsed and fell to the ground.

My hand flew to my undamaged neck as I stared at the downed vampire. After I shut my gaping mouth, I asked Ren, "How'd you do that?"

As Billy, Caleb, and Lt. Jacobs came running in reaction to my scream, Ren just smiled and blew pretend smoke off her two fingers. "Electro demon, remember? I just gave him a taste of my own personal stun gun."

Awesome! Ruby declared.

It was indeed. "Oh, wow. I didn't know you could do that."

Ren grinned. "Did you think my abilities were confined to coding and hacking?"

Not really, but some part demons were touchy about discussing their powers, so I'd never asked.. "Uh, no, but you never said—"

"What happened here?" Lt. Jacobs demanded as Billy, the former Marine, subdued my groggy attacker.

"The vamp attacked me, and Ren stunned him," I said, keeping it brief. "Better get Maurice to see if he was being controlled."

Maurice shoved his way through as the lieutenant asked, "Are you hurt?"

"No, my shield protected me from becoming a chew toy again." And luckily, this vamp was a lightweight, so my ribs weren't hurt.

Maurice frowned at the vamp. "Terrence, snap out of it."

Terrence blinked then stared at me in horror, looking all of fifteen years old and very apologetic. "I'm so sorry. I don't know why I did that. I *wouldn't* do that—it's forbidden to feed on demons."

Yeah, 'cause drinking demon blood would make vamps lose their minds.

"It's okay," I told him. "We know why. Maurice will help you."

"Omigod," he said, looking horrified. His hand flew to his mouth. "Did I hurt you?"

"She's fine," Billy told him. "Come on, now, and we'll explain it to you."

Billy and Maurice led Terrence away and I sighed. "This is getting old."

"It's getting dangerous," the lieutenant corrected me. "Whoever this controller is, she wants you out of the picture."

I nodded. "Which indicates it's probably a cursed stone with a siren trapped inside."

"Right. And obviously, the controller knows how to find you at work, and probably at home. And she's no longer using only shifters to get to you. We need to get you somewhere safe and provide 'round-the-clock protection until this is over."

"Like where?" I asked in trepidation. "Another safe house?"

"They seem to know a lot," Ren said. "They might know about the safe houses."

The boss sighed. "I don't know... Wait. Liam is a friend of yours, right?"

"Yes...?"

"He's not on the station roster, so they won't know about him. Let's see if he'll let you stay with him for a while. He can protect you, too."

"It might be a little awkward since we don't really know each other all that well anymore..."

"I'm sure it'll be fine," the lieutenant said as he stepped into the hallway to call Liam.

Ren held out her hand. "Let me see your phone for a minute."

I unlocked it and handed it to her. "Why?"

She tapped rapidly on it as she said, "I'm going to install a tracking program so we can find you in case something happens. I'll also put in a panic button you can use to call us for help." Once she finished and I told the phone to accept the apps, she showed me how to use them.

The boss came back in. "Liam has agreed to host you for

a few days until this is all over. Let Ren know what you'll need, and we'll have her pack a bag for you. I don't want you going home, and you shouldn't take your car in case someone is tracking it."

"I can check on her car when I get back," Ren said.

Lt. Jacobs nodded. "Good. I told Liam to park by the rear door. We'll sneak Ivy out to Liam's car when he gets here."

"Okay," Ren said. "Oh, and I put a tracking app on her phone." When he nodded in approval, she turned to me. "Pack the same as when we went to the safe house?"

I nodded. "Sounds good." At this rate, I probably needed to keep a go-bag handy.

She grabbed her keys. "I'll be right back."

As she headed off to get my stuff, Billy stuck his head in the door. "Hey, boss, we checked Terrence's calls and it looks like she caught him in person, not on the phone. We put him in the vamp cell until Maurice is able to command-proof him. Should we let him go after that? No sense keeping him around when he can't be used against us again."

"That's fine," the lieutenant said. "Ivy, you—"

But both he and Billy froze as they turned their heads and appeared to be listening to something.

What the heck?

Taylor just got a call, Ruby told me. *There was another shifter-on-human attack, but this time, the shifter was shot!*

Oh, crap. "Who was shot?" I demanded. Please, not Mateo....

EIGHT

It wasn't Mateo, Ruby assured me. *It was Reggie. Derek is on the scene already.*

I winced in sympathy. Though Reggie had been forced to attack me, he didn't deserve to get shot.

The lieutenant rushed out to the desk to talk to Taylor and I followed him. "Tell Derek to make sure Reggie gets to the *pack* doctor and have him bring that shooter in here before he can talk to a reporter. If he's another ex-con, possession of a weapon would violate his parole and we can hold him for that until Maurice can alter his memory." He ran a hand down over his face. "What else is going to go wrong?" he muttered.

Then his gaze fell on me. "Billy, guard Ivy until Liam can pick her up. We'll have you and Maurice stay here so we can send shifters to get command-proofed once Maurice is up to it. Make sure you keep a list of who's been protected and who hasn't."

"Already doing that, boss," Billy assured him. "I've got it on my phone. Want me to share it with everyone?"

"Yes, please, and update us as you add each person." He

gave Billy a harassed smile. "Thanks. You and Maurice are lifesavers. I'm going to call Duncan to let him know what's going on."

"Uh, better make that a text," I reminded him. "You had Kai tell him not to answer his phone."

"Right, right." He wandered away, intent on his phone.

Billy grinned at me. "Let's wait in the break room." He gestured for me to follow him. "So, what did you do to make yourself a target?"

I rolled my eyes. "Sense cursed stones, I guess. Seems the controller doesn't want me interfering with her. So, how's the undead life treating you?" It wasn't that long ago that he'd been on the verge of dying, so Maurice had turned him.

"It's treating me well," he said. "It didn't quite happen the way Maurice and I expected, but we were grateful Bartholomew gave Maurice dispensation to bring me to my second life. Our only problem has been finding someone else to take on the duties I used to do during the day."

"You're irreplaceable," I said with a grin.

He shrugged. "Naw, but we're picky. Don't worry—we'll find someone." He went on to amuse me with their trials in finding the right candidate until Ren stuck her head in the door.

"Liam's here," she said. "I put your suitcase in his car already, and all the lights back there just happened to go out. If Billy can let us know when it's clear..." Billy nodded. "Then you and Ruby can sneak into his back seat."

I nodded. It seemed silly to go to all this trouble, but they seemed so earnest about it.... I followed Billy and Ren to the side entrance.

As Billy slipped out, Ren said, "Oh, and one more thing." She reached into her pocket and pulled out a coin. "My lucky quarter." She placed it in my hand. "Keep it with you at all times. Can't be too careful, y'know?"

I grinned at her. Who was I to discount someone's lucky coin? "Sure will," I said and stuck it into my jeans pocket. "Thanks."

Billy came back in. "All clear, and the back door is open, along with his car door. Just slip in, and keep your head down until you get to his place and the garage door is closed. Ruby too."

"Will do. Thanks." On impulse, I hugged both of them. I couldn't believe how much people cared about what happened to us.

Face it, Ruby said. *We're special.*

At least some people thought so. I went out the door and Ruby leapt up into the back seat. I ducked down and followed, then closed the door softly. "We're in," I told Liam.

He took off, and we stayed hunkered down out of view for about twenty minutes. Finally, we came to a stop and I heard a garage door closing.

Liam got out and opened the back door. "You can come out now," he said.

Feeling a little foolish, I rose from my position in the back.

Ruby leapt out. *Thanks, Liam!*

I followed her a little more slowly and he grabbed my suitcase from the trunk then gestured to the door between his garage and the house. "Welcome to my house," he said. "Well, townhouse, I should say. It's not much, but it's mine."

I followed him in, and it was nicer than I expected. A little small, but nicely furnished in early bachelor. The best part were the floor-to-ceiling bookshelves in his living room, showcasing his book collection.

I ran a finger over a few of the spines. "I see you kept up with our mutual hobby. And you have quite a few here I haven't read."

"You're welcome to borrow whatever you like," he said generously. "Want to see your room?" At my nod, he added, "It's upstairs next to mine. Follow me."

The guest room was a little sparse, but had everything I needed, including a bathroom across the hall. "Looks great," I told him honestly.

"It's no hotel," he said apologetically.

"No, but it comes equipped with a friend, so it's even better," I assured him.

"Good." He placed the suitcase on the bed and we went downstairs. Though it was late, we were both hungry, so we ordered Chinese food to be delivered. He turned on the television for Ruby—some movie with a lot of explosions—and the two of us went into his small dining room.

"So, while we're waiting," he said. "Tell me more about being a stone whisperer. From the stories I've heard, you do far more than just talk to rocks."

I shrugged. "A little." I fingered my pendant. "My parents gave me this opal. It's very wise and it's helped me find ways to amplify my power."

He cocked his head to the side. "Really? How?"

"Well, most of them are on my cuff bracelet." I showed it to him. "The combination of the cinnabar and quartz gives me the ability to control humans...a little. Enough to command them to stop or freeze for a few moments."

"Huh." He leaned forward. "Does it work on supes?"

"Not on demons or vamps, and on shifters only when in human form."

"What about the other two stones? Are they special as well?" He skimmed a fingertip over the amethyst and citrine combo.

"Those allow me to construct a shield around my body, especially when I amplify it with the opal. Wanna see how it works?"

"Sure."

"Poke me." At his raised eyebrow, I said, "Go ahead, poke me, and you'll be able to see what I'm talking about."

I put up my shield and he jabbed his finger at my arm, but was stopped an inch from my skin. "Fascinating," he said. "And that keeps you safe?"

"Mostly." I grimaced. "When Reggie and the vamp attacked me, I was able to keep their teeth from piercing my skin, but they were still able to throw me around. Not sure I'll be able to figure out a way to fix that."

"Nevertheless, it's an excellent defense," he said admiringly. "Which stone allows you to, er, uncurse another stone?"

"It's not really a stone. It's a demon exorcism spell." I didn't want to explain the whole keeper of the *Encyclopedia Magicka* thing, so I said merely, "I just say 'Demon thou art, demon thou shalt not be. Say it times three, I exorcise thee.'" At his alarmed look, I said, "Don't worry, I have to say the trigger words three times before it works...plus sort of aim it mentally at my intended target. You won't be hit by a random spell, I promise."

Though now that I'd said the words, the spell was laying there in my gut like a rock, just jonesing to be invoked. Stupid spells—this was why I didn't like using them.

"That's good to know."

The doorbell rang then with our food order. After we

ate, I chose a book in a series I'd been dying to read and we went to our separate bedrooms to sleep. Maybe tomorrow would be a better day.

Ruby snorted. *Couldn't get much worse.*

THE NEXT MORNING, I woke to a gloomy day and rain pelting against my bedroom window. It was a good thing we didn't need to go anywhere today. Ruby didn't like to get wet.

Liam made us French toast for breakfast, and we were trying to figure out what to do with ourselves for the day when my phone rang. It was the lieutenant. I hesitated for a moment, then remembered the siren couldn't control me so I answered.

"Did you catch the controller?" I asked eagerly. Okay, sure, I probably should have started with the niceties, but I didn't think he cared about that when so much was at stake.

"Not yet."

Liam looked at me questioningly, so I said, "Hold on. Liam and Ruby are here, so I'm going to put the phone on speaker so they can hear as well."

I did so, and Lt. Jacobs' voice came over the tinny speaker. "We haven't found the controller yet—we haven't even been able to find the shifters we had locked up. They've all disappeared and aren't answering our texts, so we couldn't get them to Maurice to protect them."

I nodded. And now they'd have to wait until after sunset. "The controller must have told them to hide."

"But why?" Liam asked.

The lieutenant answered him. "Probably because she wants to be able to send them after someone else. Unfortunately, it also means we can't get easy access to their phone records. Ren is working on getting warrants to check them, but it'll take a while."

"What about Reggie?" I asked. "You have his phone, right?"

"Yes, but with him unconscious and unable to provide consent, I have the same issue. It'll be a little easier because we know what cell company he uses, but not a lot."

"I see. I know we're thinking the controller is using a cursed stone, but did Mateo check on the siren in Silverthorne?"

"She's cleared. Ren did some research and learned she's older and had a severe stroke a few weeks ago, leaving her speech impaired to the point where we are positive she's not our controller." He sighed. "We're watching the men who were attacked before in hopes of preventing the shifters from targeting them again, but we're pinning our hopes now on the phone companies identifying who called the shifters."

Liam leaned in. "Ivy was also assaulted—twice. Maybe it would be a good idea to send her partner here for additional protection."

"I would, but Duncan refuses to let Mateo leave the pack while this is going on," the lieutenant bit out.

I got why he was annoyed. You didn't offer up a resource then take it away when it was no longer convenient.

"You should be able to help her, right?" the lieutenant asked Liam.

"Yes, of course," Liam said. "I'd just feel more comfortable with backup. Offense is not my strongest suit."

"I know that," Lt Jacobs said, sounding frustrated, "but

it'll have to do. Your defense is as good as other people's offense."

"Got it," Liam said.

Really? I wondered what that meant...not that they'd tell me.

Liam's phone rang, and he raised it in apology as he went to another room to take the call.

"Thanks," I told the lieutenant. "You'll keep us posted?"

"Of course. Stay safe," he said, making it sound more like an order than a wish for my safety.

I hung up, and noticed I had a missed call from Amber. I called her back. "Hi, this is Ivy. You have something for me?"

"I think so," she said, sounding hesitant. "I did an inventory and there does seem to be a moonstone missing. Neither my clerk nor I remember selling it, so I checked my video footage."

"You have video?"

Awesome! Ruby declared.

"Yes, and I think you need to come look at it."

"Can you email it?"

"Sorry, I don't know how to do that."

"Okay. I'll see if I can come. If I need to send someone else, I'll let you know. And thank you so much!" This might be just what we needed to crack the case.

Liam came back in the room just as I said goodbye to Amber and hung up. "We might have a lead on who replaced the moonstone in Luana's bracelet," I exclaimed. "But should we let someone else handle it?"

Why? Ruby demanded to know. *The boss said Liam's defense was as good as offense, and you have your shield and your gear. We got this.*

I glanced at Liam, wanting to do the right thing. "What do you think?"

"Where is this lead?" he asked.

"Crystal Mystique. It's a new age store that sells gemstones as well as...other new age stuff. She might know who replaced the moonstone."

He thought for a moment. "It should be okay."

Yay! Ruby declared, and bounced around the room, full of enthusiasm.

Liam wiggled his phone. "I just need to make a couple of texts, then I'll meet you in the car."

I nodded and put on my gear, just in case I needed more than my shield, then headed toward the garage, with Ruby practically vibrating with excitement as she burbled about how we were going to find the controller all by ourselves and she'd be the hero of the day—even better than Fang.

I stayed out of sight with Ruby as she continued to spin her story—starring herself as the conquering hellhound—all the way to the store.

"Is she always like this?" Liam asked as we got out of his car and dashed through the rain to enter the store.

"No, this is new," I said in amusement. "I think she's just bored."

"Ivy," Amber called out. "That was fast. Come on over here, behind the counter, and I'll show you the video."

Liam came with me as Ruby wandered through the store. Amber might think it weird if Ruby tried to watch the video, and she didn't need to anyway, since she'd see it through me. Thunder boomed as we went behind the counter and I glanced outside. It was really pouring now.

"This recording is from a week ago," Amber said. "My clerk was here, but I wasn't."

She started the video, and on it, a woman approached

the male clerk at the counter. Since we could only see the back of her head, all I could tell was that she had long, dark wavy hair. Might be one of Luana's relatives. The woman spoke to the clerk and showed him something—something that looked like the wolf head bracelet. He nodded and reached into the display case and pulled something out.

"Can you freeze that?" I asked.

She did, but I wasn't able to tell what he had in his hand. "Is that a moonstone?" I asked.

"I believe so," Amber said, "but what's strange is, after he replaced it for her, she didn't pay for it, and he just let her go. Even weirder, he doesn't remember anything about this whole transaction."

"He could be lying," Liam said.

"I don't think so. I trust him completely," Amber said.

"Does the video show anything else?" I asked.

"There's a brief showing of her face..." Amber said and restarted the video. The woman on the screen finished talking to the clerk, then turned to leave. Amber froze the frame when three-quarters of her face came into view.

I gasped. *Luana!* I'd recognize that smug smile anywhere.

Luana? Ruby bounded over. *But wasn't she cleared?*

"You know who that is?" Amber asked.

"Yes," I told her and pulled out my phone to call the lieutenant. He needed to know this right away.

Liam covered my phone with his hand. "Not here. Outside would be better." He nodded toward Amber.

Okay, doing this away from the non-supe made sense. "Sure. Thanks so much for your help, Amber. Can I send someone to get a copy of that video?" Ren would be able to copy it, no problem.

"Of course."

"Great. I'll see what I can do about getting your moonstone back to you, but since it's evidence, I might not be able to."

"No problem," she said. "I'm just glad I was able to help. But can you explain how—"

"Sorry, no time," Liam said as he took hold of my elbow and steered me out the door.

I paused in the doorway, wishing I'd brought an umbrella. Ruby bounced around me, looking frantic. She jumped up on my legs then grabbed a mouthful of my jeans and tried to pull me back inside the store. When that didn't work, she growled and barked.

Ignoring her, I hurried toward Liam's car, trying not to get too wet. "What's wrong with you?" I asked her irritably. "Use your words."

"I'm afraid she can't right now," Liam said in a strange tone.

I glanced at him in confusion. His eyes were blank, unemotional, all semblance of feeling totally gone. What the heck?

He opened the back door of his car and pushed me inside. A man was already seated there, and another one got in on the other side of me. No, not a man—they were both shifters, Harley and Devon—and they each grabbed one of my arms, immobilizing me.

Something was off. I slammed up my shields, just in case. "Hey, guys," I said tentatively. "Is something wrong? I—"

I tried to surreptitiously press the panic button on my phone, but Liam pulled it away before I could see if it worked. "Quiet," he said and Harley clamped a hand over my mouth. Ruby leapt at Liam, snarling. He caught her, and she immediately went limp. What did he do to her?

Ruby!

My screams were too muffled for anyone to hear, and with the rain keeping everyone inside, no one was around to see what they were doing to me, no matter how much I squirmed. Worse, my shields did nothing to keep them from keeping me pinned in the seat and putting a gag on me.

Liam tossed Ruby in the front seat and the last thing he did as he drove away was to throw my phone out the window.

Crap—Ruby was out for the count, my shields weren't helping, I couldn't command the shifters with the gag in my mouth, and Liam had just thrown away my only means of anyone finding me.

I closed my eyes in despair. He'd effectively rendered me helpless...and, stupidly, I'd told him exactly how to do it last night.

As Liam drove, he gave the shifters orders. "One of you keep hold of her while the other strip her of her weapons and every single gemstone she has on her body. Make sure there are none left, then wrap them all in her silk hoodie."

They tried, but my shield kept them from getting too close. I felt a little smug about that until Liam said, "Okay, use the chloroform."

The what? Devon clamped a cloth soaked in some sweet-smelling substance over my nose. Frantically, I tried to fight it, but the chemical made it past the physical barrier of my shield with no problem. Soon, I stopped fighting and lost consciousness.

CHAPTER

NINE

Ivy. Ivy, wake up, Ruby urged, poking her cold nose in my neck.

Wha—? I woke slowly, feeling groggy, headachy, and like something was totally off. What was going on?

Then it all came slamming back and I jerked upright on the dusty bedcovers. Where were we? I glanced frantically around the room and realized I recognized this place—it was a bedroom in Dahlia's house, on the ranch Luana had inherited.

My gag was gone, and I wasn't restrained, so I looked Ruby over frantically. "Are you okay? What did Liam do to you?"

I'm okay, she assured me. *He just used his powers on me.*

"What powers?" Surely she'd tell me now.

He's a regulator.

I assumed she wasn't talking about a government official.

She snorted. *Nope. He can identify any supe's powers and regulate them—dial them up to maximum or drain them down to zero. He drained me,* she said petulantly.

"But you're okay now?"

Yeah. Are you?

"I'm fine. Feeling a little naked with all my gemstones missing, though. I wonder why he didn't use his powers on me."

He did by mistake, the first time he touched you. He didn't know how strong you'd gotten, so he accidentally ramped you up a little, which is why your stones felt all sparkly. But I guess he didn't need to this time—he had those two shifters to help him keep you subdued.

And way too easily, too. I hugged her. "I'm so sorry about this. I was so proud of my ability to take care of myself, and look what happened."

She nudged me and licked my hand. *Hey, you didn't know. But don't worry. We'll find a way to get out of this.*

I leapt off the bed and ran to the door. Locked. I looked out the window, but Devon stared back at me, implacable. Crap. I wasn't getting out that way. But at least it had stopped raining. I closed the curtains and lowered my voice. "Can you tell how many are here?"

Just the three who took us. The shifters are outside, waiting for Luana to arrive. Liam is in the living room, but he can't hear me since I'm talking to you privately. Besides, all he's thinking about right now is that he has to keep you imprisoned until Luana gets here.

I sent my senses out as far as they would go, looking for stones to talk to. Since the shifters might be able to hear me, mental speech was a better idea. *I can't find any gemstones nearby.*

What about rocks? You moved them before, remember? Ruby said eagerly.

Yes, but that was with the opal's help. Here, I can't feel anything larger than pea gravel. What was I going to do? Pelt them with pellets? Yeah, that would work. Not.

It might, Ruby said loyally.

I snorted. I wasn't holding my breath. At least they hadn't put any restraints on us. Probably because we were absolutely no threat to anyone.

Hey, Ruby protested. *Don't count me out.*

I'm not, I assured her. *But Liam subdued you so easily.... Does he have to be touching you to use his powers?*

They work better and faster when he's touching someone, but he can still use them to a reduced extent if we're within his range.

I slumped back down on the bed. *I can't believe Liam betrayed us like that. I thought he was my friend.*

He was. He is. Luana saw him take us to lunch and followed him home, then ensnared him with the siren moonstone.

I shook my head. *And we didn't even think to command-proof him...because we thought the controller didn't know about him.*

Yeah. Apparently, that was her calling him at his house right after you talked to the lieutenant. I wasn't checking in on his thoughts then, not until we got to Amber's. When I figured out he was her puppet, I tried to warn you, but you couldn't hear me. He must have blocked my voice. Ruby jerked up to a standing position. *I hear a car. Luana's here.*

Crap. I rose to my feet. I didn't want to face her while lounging on a bed. What the heck did she want with me? Since she'd already sent a shifter and a vamp after me, she obviously didn't care about my physical well-being. Frantically, I searched the closets and drawers for a weapon, but everything that could remotely be used as a weapon had been removed from the room. The only thing left was the bed. Maybe I could use the bedspread to throw over her and run past her. It was a dumb idea, but my only chance.

As I gathered the folds of the slippery material in my hands, Ruby said, *Wait. Didn't they use the shifters' names to stop them before? You know their names!*

I froze. Would that work? I ran to the door and yelled, "Liam, snap out of it. You're being controlled."

Well, crap, Ruby said. *I know he heard that, but it's like it didn't register. Aaaand the shifters are all now in the house.*

Are they coming this way?

Yep. I'm ready to fight.

Okay. They're being controlled, so try not to hurt them.

I backed away from the door and held the bedspread ready. The knob rattled, then turned, and as it opened, I threw the bedspread. It landed partially on Luana and I tried to rush past, but Harley caught me and Devon grabbed Ruby.

"Harley, Devon, let us go," I said urgently. "She's controlling you."

And that, too, did absolutely nothing.

Luana glared at me. "Oh, I figured out that loophole already. They don't know their own names anymore." She sneered down at the bedspread. "And what did you hope to accomplish with that smelly old thing?"

Embarrassed, I just shrugged. "What did you hope to accomplish by bringing me here?" I shot back.

She grinned. "Boys, bring her into the living room. Sit her down in the armchair and keep her there." The shifters manhandled me into the chair and Luana glared at Ruby. "And you, attack any of us again and we'll hurt your master."

Master? we both thought indignantly, but Ruby stopped fighting to get free. The two shifters stood behind me while

Liam just watched dispassionately. I guess he really was controlled. Devon dumped Ruby in Liam's lap where he absentmindedly petted her. Weird.

"You—" she ordered, pointing at Liam. "Keep Ivy's powers subdued."

He glanced at me and I felt something like a mental blanket settle over me. Well, there went my last hope of using my abilities.

"What do you want from me?" I asked, doing my best to sound defiant, and hoping it didn't come out sounding as scared as I felt.

"I want you to stop searching for this," Luana said. She pulled a small silk pouch out of her pocket and let the moonstone fall into her palm. "Just let it go."

Yep, that was the cursed stone all right. Even with my powers dimmed, I could feel the agony of the moonstone and hear the trapped siren yelling instructions and curses at Luana.

I concentrated hard, but I couldn't get the moonstone to listen to me—it was too busy suffering with the pain of the siren's takeover. Dang it, I hated how helpless I felt.

"It's my job," I said. "I was tasked with finding it. I can't let it go."

That seemed to infuriate her. She clenched the stone and intoned, "Boys—" Her enhanced voice contained the threads of irresistible command, but before she could tell them to do something that might actually hurt me, I interrupted. "Wait. Maybe if you tell me why you're doing this, I can help. You're after sex offenders, right?"

That shouldn't have worked, but she seized on it like a trout on a worm. "Do you have any idea how many sex offenders are in Colorado Springs?"

"No," I admitted.

"Over sixteen hundred. That means about one in every three hundred men in the city are out there, just waiting to attack and defile a defenseless woman."

"Did someone attack you?" I asked softly.

What are you doing? Ruby asked me. *You really think you can reason with this madwoman?*

I don't know, but I have to try.

"No one attacked *me*," she said, waving that away. "I would have torn him apart. But one creep attacked my little cousin, Mina. She's not as strong as me, and she barely got away. It traumatized her, and she still isn't back to normal. She's scared of her own shadow. He needs to pay. They all need to pay."

As she paced, I caught a glimpse of my gear and my pink silk hoodie in the far corner of the room. Crap. My stones were there, but could I use them even if I could get to them? Hmm, my gear wasn't dependent on my powers....

If I get a chance to get free, I'll try to grab the Triple-S and your stones, Ruby told me.

Okay, but don't do anything that will get you hurt, I told her. Aloud, I said, "I'm so sorry that happened to your cousin." I meant it—no one should be subjected to that, not even Luana.

"You see why they have to suffer like she did?" she demanded.

"It seems a bit like overkill—"

"I wasn't trying to kill them," she said impatiently. "Just damage them a little, make them afraid like they did Mina."

"Yes, but wouldn't it be better to work through the police—"

"I tried that," she said fuming. "They took the report, but said they couldn't do anything, that we had no evidence. It was so frustrating. I wanted to help Mina so bad, make the man who attacked her pay for his crime." She started pacing. "That's when you brought this little sweetheart into the station." She looked a little crazed as she petted the moonstone. "And you told me exactly what to do, didn't you?" she crooned at it.

Ah, so that's how her desperation and the stone had come into play. Realizing this was my chance to find out more about how the curses worked, I asked, "You could hear it even before you touched it?"

"Yes, it called out to me, begged me to help it. Said it would help me as well."

"So what did you do?"

She shrugged. "After you left, I...convinced Caleb to let me see it, just for a minute."

Convinced? Ruby snorted. *I'm guessing seduced.*

Luana continued, "And once I was able to touch it, it told me how it could make my voice irresistible, make every man obey my every whim."

"So why did you replace the moonstone?"

"To throw you off, but that didn't work. You're too smart for your own good." She frowned and took a step toward me.

To head her off, I said quickly, "That's when you hatched a plan to punish the sex offenders?"

"Of course. Wouldn't you?" she demanded. "I mean, what right-minded person wouldn't want them punished?"

Her desperation must make her foolish. "But don't you see how you're affecting others?" I asked gently. "The shifters you're controlling—they're being hurt. Reggie was shot last night, and the others were incarcerated, missing their jobs, their families, their freedom. You're ruining their lives."

She blew that off with a wave of her hand. "They'll get over it."

"And you've got a reporter focused on printing stories about rabid wolves. Isn't that dangerous for your pack?"

She snorted. "I can make him retract everything he said. Duncan won't blame me."

"Wait. Duncan questioned you with his alpha voice. He said you were innocent of stealing the bracelet. How did you fool him?"

She had the nerve to laugh. "He's a man, too, isn't he?" she gloated. "And so are Derek and Kai. They believed what I wanted them to believe. He only *thought* he questioned me."

Duh. Of course. I guess I should have questioned her myself. But if she'd been controlling Duncan too... "Are you responsible for making him turn on Mateo?" I asked in sudden suspicion.

She shrugged. "Maybe. Mateo doesn't need to hang around with demons and vamps—he's a *shifter*. He belongs in the pack, with *us*, not *you*."

That's a yes, Ruby said.

"And did you have control of Mateo as well?"

"No—I could never get him alone," she said scowling. "But Duncan is keeping him on pack lands for me, so I'll fix that very shortly." She cast a sharp glance at me. "You're nothing but a filthy demon—you need to stay out of shifter business."

"You're right," I said, trying to placate her. "And I do see where you're coming from. Maybe together, we can—"

But I broke off as the three shifters suddenly turned their heads toward the door, looking alert. Luana inhaled, her nostrils flaring with her enhanced shifter senses. "It's

Mateo," she said with satisfaction. "And he came alone. Finally."

Oh, crap. He didn't know what he was walking into.

Maurice command-proofed him, Ruby said. *She won't be able to control him.*

No, but if he's the only one out there, then it'll be four against one.... Crap, crap, crap. What could I do? With my powers, stones, and gear gone? Nothing.

Rubbing her cursed moonstone, Luana called out in her spooky siren voice, "Come on in and join us, Mateo."

That didn't work, of course, since Maurice had command-proofed him.

Luana waved at the three men in the room. "Go get him, boys. Bring him inside."

Cold despair lodged in my gut like a stone as I desperately tried to figure out how to help Mateo.

Wait. That stone in my gut? I wasn't helpless—I still had the spell! The book didn't say I had to use my power to activate it, only that I had to have powers to use it. Would it work with my powers damped? Only one way to find out.

As the shifters burst through the door, I concentrated on the moonstone in Luana's hand and uttered the words to activate the spell. "I exorcise thee..."

Liam whirled. "Shut her up," he said, pointing at me.

But before they could reach me, I said the final words as quickly as I could. "I exorcise thee, I exorcise thee!"

The trapped siren screamed and left the moonstone in a wisp of smoke. My powers surged back for a moment as Liam was released, but then they fell again immediately in response to using the spell. Whoa—talk about magical whiplash.

The three men faltered in their rush out the door and paused, shaking their heads. They all turned to glare at

Luana. Thank goodness releasing the siren had broken her control. I wasn't sure how much use I'd have been, even if Ruby had been able to get my stones to me.

"No," Luana screamed, shaking the stone at them. "You have to do as I say. Right now. Grab Mateo!"

"I don't think so," Liam said grimly and strode over to grab her wrist.

Whoa, Ruby said. *He's pissed.*

He must be, because Luana's eyes turned up in her head and she fell limply to the floor.

Mateo rushed past Luana's former puppets and grabbed me up in a big hug. "Are you all right?" he demanded. "They didn't hurt you, did they?"

"No, just my pride," I said. "But how did you know I was taken?"

"Your panic button worked—Ren got the notice and notified us immediately."

"But...tracking? They got rid of my phone right away."

He grinned. "It seems Ren is a little devious and gave you another tracker you weren't aware of."

"Another one? What—?" Then realization hit. "Her lucky coin."

"Yeah, lucky for you. It told us exactly where you were. The other guys should be right behind me."

I so owed her—big time. "I thought Duncan ordered you to stay with the pack."

"He did," Mateo said solemnly. "But when I heard you were in trouble, I couldn't stay."

He put you first, before the pack, Ruby said gleefully. *Good boy.*

Wow, he really did. And even after I'd been so mean to him. I squeezed him back. "So you realized Luana was controlling him as well?"

He looked surprised. "No, I didn't. But that explains a lot."

And that made his choice all the better for not knowing Duncan was Luana's puppet. "Maybe you won't be in trouble for it."

He grinned down at me. "It doesn't matter either way. I wouldn't change a thing."

"Hey, guys," Liam said. "What shall we do with Luana?"

Mateo released me and frowned down at the unconscious shifter. "We'll take her to the holding cell, but her punishment is for the pack council to decide."

A bunch of people arrived then and rushed around to figure out what had happened. Though exhausted, I filled them in, assuring them many times that I was okay and that the three who had kidnapped me had been under Luana's control. I also managed to retrieve my gear and, most importantly, my stones I felt much better for having them all around me, even if the gemstones wouldn't stop whining about being cut off from me. I slipped the moonstone in my hoodie pocket so the silk would mask its agony, resolving to cleanse and purify it as soon as I could.

This time, Liam pulled me into a hug. "Ivy, I'm so sorry—"

Devon and Harley looked like they were about to drown me in apologies as well, but I stopped them as I hugged Liam back. "It's okay. I know you guys were only doing what Luana told you to do."

Wow, look at you with all the hugs today, Ruby said.

Hey, back off. They feel really good and I deserve aaaaall the hugs for what I've been through.

And Ruby couldn't argue with that.

A WEEK LATER, the three teams plus Ren, Liam, Sybil, and Duncan all gathered in the station's conference room for a debriefing. Bartholomew had elected to let Maurice brief him afterward.

I explained what had happened to me, and with the exorcism of the demon siren, everyone's memories had come back so we knew exactly how she'd accomplished everything. "She was able to use the siren's abilities to fool us all," I concluded.

"Well, not all of us," Mateo said. "You weren't fooled. We should have listened to you."

That was gratifying, but I shook my head. "Only because I'm female."

Yay, girl power! Ruby exclaimed.

Sybil and Ren snorted in amusement, but I added, "There wasn't much you could do with a siren controlling your thoughts and actions. Did the shifter council decide what to do with Luana?"

Duncan nodded. "Once she was no longer under the influence of the cursed artifact, she was contrite and apologetic."

Yeah, right, Ruby said and rolled her eyes.

The alpha continued, "And since she didn't hurt anyone except for human sex offenders—"

"Not hurt anyone?" Liam said in disbelief. "She had Ivy attacked three times. She could have died or been seriously injured."

"But Ivy wasn't hurt," Duncan said. "And Luana said she was just trying to discourage her, not kill her. She knew about Ivy's shield."

So she said. I guess that was possible, but I wasn't buying it. "But what about Reggie?" I asked. "He was shot because of her."

"He's okay now," Duncan assured me. "Fully healed."

That rapid shifter healing came in handy. "She was also the one responsible for the wolf sightings...and the newspaper articles," I reminded him.

"Maurice took care of the reporter, who retracted his articles and reported that there were no wolves, just a violent German shepherd who had since been caught," the lieutenant told us. "Maurice convinced the men who were attacked of the same. Shifters are safe from discovery...for now."

Duncan nodded at Maurice. "We appreciate your assistance in that, and with finding Mina's attacker." Turning to the rest of us, he explained, "While he was in the shooter's mind, Maurice discovered he was the one who assaulted Mina, and 'convinced' him to confess. Between that, the parole violation, and weapons charge, he'll be in jail for a long time." He shrugged. "Once Luana learned that, and we ensured Mina was referred to a therapist, Luana was no longer so adamant about making all sex offenders suffer."

"So, what?" I asked. "They're just going to give her a slap on the wrist?" My fists clenched as I tried to keep my anger from showing.

Duncan grimaced. "No, but they did take that and everything else into account. They fined her—she'll turn over the ranch she inherited from Dahlia to Relentless Protection Services for use as a training center."

That was a good use of it, benefitting both shifters and demons. Maybe this way, people would stop imprisoning me there. "That's it?"

"Plus," Duncan added, "they banished her from the region for a period of three months. She can return after that, but trust me, I'll watch her closely to ensure she doesn't stray again."

It didn't seem long enough, but I had absolutely no say in the matter.

Sybil spoke up. "We need to ensure this sort of thing can't happen again. If Luana hadn't sensed the stone, she wouldn't have come under its influence."

Huh? Was she blaming me for this?

No, Ruby assured me. *Just wait.*

"So," Sybil continued, "we have purchased a safe for use in the evidence room. It is lined with silk, and only Ivy will have the combination to it. You can put any artifacts you find in there, Ivy, and no one else will be able to take anything from it."

I relaxed. "That's a good idea."

"It also became evident that tracking down demon abilities is more difficult than it should be, so I'm working with other Demon Undergrounds to form a regional council like the shifters have, so we can share information and databases. It might take a while, but I'm getting some positive responses, especially since they know we have the keeper of the *Encyclopedia Magicka* here and this might give them access to the books."

Yeah, bribery will work every time, Ruby snarked.

"We'd have to make it under strictly controlled circumstances," I warned Sybil. "Those books are dangerous."

"Of course," she agreed. "We'll implement whatever measures you feel are appropriate."

I nodded, though I still wasn't sure this was such a great idea.

"Good," the lieutenant said. "Now, if no one has anything else...?"

No one did, so we all rose to leave. Duncan stopped me

with a hand on my arm. "Ivy, I would like to apologize for anything I said or did while I was under Luana's influence. I know that Mateo is a valuable member of the pack, and..." He paused, his face becoming even more stoic than normal. "While I do not believe species should intermingle...date...I will not put any roadblocks in your way. You are, after all, a friend of the pack."

I'm glad he finally remembered that. "Thank you. I appreciate how difficult that must have been for you to say. But I don't really know if that's what I want."

After all, I had options now. I glanced at Liam and Mateo, who both hovered in the doorway, watching me with anticipation. On the one hand, Mateo had disobeyed his alpha's orders to rescue me, but it had taken him too long to come to that realization. On the other hand, no one would object to a relationship with Liam, and he hadn't made me play second place to anyone or anything. But he hadn't trusted me with his secrets either.

It would be difficult to choose between them.

So date them both, Ruby said, as if it were obvious. *See who you like best, who treats you best.*

I raised an eyebrow. *You think they'd go for that?*

Well, if they don't, then you might have your answer.

I grinned down at her. *Anyone ever tell you that you're incredibly smart?*

Not often enough, Ivy. Not often enough.

The Demon Underground Series
If you haven't read the original series yet starring Val Shapiro, part succubus, get started with *Bite Me!*

<u>Follow me</u>

Be the first to know when my next story is available. Follow me on Amazon or BookBub to get an alert whenever I have a new release, preorder, or discount!

Join my newsletter at ParkerBlue.net/newsletter and get updates on my upcoming stories, contests, and great deals on books! Or check out my website at ParkerBlue.net for more info on me!

Finally, thank you so much for taking the time to read my story. I really do appreciate it! And, if you have the time and inclination to leave a review where you purchased the book, Ruby will love you for life!

Also by Parker Blue

The Demon Underground Series

Bite Me

Try Me

Fang Me

Make Me

Dare Me

Catch Me

Forget You

The Stone Whisperer Chronicles

Sapphires & Souls

Diamonds & Deceit

Moonstones & Malice

Others

"Wolf Rising" in the *Magick Rising* anthology

Time Raiders: The Healer's Passion

About the Author

Parker Blue lives in Colorado Springs with her latest rescue dog, Honey. She has had a number of rescue dogs over the years, one of whom bore an uncanny resemblance to Val's part-hellhound mutt, Fang. Her current dog, Honey, is kind of a mini version of Mo/Fang and resembles part-hellhound Ruby, oddly enough.

She hates writing bios so that's all you're gonna get. Okay, okay. Instead of more boring bio stuff, how about some of her likes and dislikes?

Stuff she loves, in no particular order:

- The color red—a bright, orange-red just makes her happy.
- Shiny things. She must have been a magpie in a previous life.
- Making shiny things. She loves to bead!
- Dogs—they love you unconditionally and are great at stress relief.
- Numbers. So sue her—she loves math. It always makes sense.

- Chocolate. Come on, that's a no-brainer.
- The mountains of Colorado. Their awe-tastic beauty is good for the soul.
- Diet Coke and Zero Sugar A&W Root Beer. What can she say? She's addicted.
- Reading. Escaping into a cool new world someone created out of their imagination? It doesn't get much better than that.
- Oh, yeah. And writing. Making up her own world out of random bits of her twisted psyche is the best!

Things she's not so crazy about, besides the obvious things everyone hates (war, pestilence, famine, you know the drill):

- Blogs and trolls who dis other people online. What's up with that?
- Going to the dentist. Need she say more?
- Politics. Big yawn.
- Television shows that ask people do stupid things for money then make fun of them.
- Seafood. Ick. Just...ick.
- Yard work. And that's why she now lives in a condo.
- Writing bios. Enough already!

Find out more about Parker Blue and her books on her website at ParkerBlue.net or on Facebook at Facebook.-com/ParkerBlueWrite and make sure you follow her on Amazon or BookBub to get notices of new releases and discounts!